T5-CRD-404

Finders, Keepers, Losers, Weepers

OTHER FIVE STAR TITLES BY ROBERT S. LEVINSON

Phony Tinsel

A Rhumba in Waltz Time

In the Key of Death

Where the Lies Begin

Ask a Dead Man

Finders, Keepers, Losers, Weepers

Robert S. Levinson

FIVE STAR
A part of Gale, Cengage Learning

Detroit • New York • San Francisco • New Haven, Conn • Waterville, Maine • London

LIBRARY OF CONGRESS CATALOGING-IN-PUBLICATION DATA

Levinson, Robert S.
Finders, keepers, losers, weepers / Robert S. Levinson. — First Edition.
pages cm
ISBN-13: 978-1-4328-2781-6 (hardcover)
ISBN-10: 1-4328-2781-2 (hardcover)
1. Music trade—Fiction. 2. Ex-convicts—Fiction. 3. Women journalist—Fiction. 4. Revenge—Fiction. I. Title.
PS3562.E9218F56 2014
813'.54—dc23 2013031787

First Edition. First Printing: January 2014
Find us on Facebook– https://www.facebook.com/FiveStarCengage
Visit our website– http://www.gale.cengage.com/fivestar/
Contact Five Star™ Publishing at FiveStar@cengage.com

Printed in Mexico
1 2 3 4 5 6 7 18 17 16 15 14

FOR SANDRA
and
FOR DEBORAH AND DAVID
Three Keepers

★ ★ ★ ★ ★

1989

★ ★ ★ ★ ★

CHAPTER 1

The girl was beautiful, prettier than that.

Nat couldn't resist the way she smiled at him with her eyes, sending an incandescent stare that made them old friends even before they met, lovers before they could crawl between the sheets to share the kinds of innocent lies strangers tell so well.

She would tell stories tomorrow that none of her friends would believe. In a day or so, she would not believe them either, like Nat Axelrod was some dream too good to come true, except when she thought about the way he came up with the magic of a melody and lyrics too romantic to resist every time he came up for air.

These groupies.

How many went searching for paper and a pencil to write down the words he swore he had invented just for them, inspired by them, humming the melody to them in the off key of life before they tucked their tits back inside their bras, checked their panties for telltale signs of lust and clung to one last hug immortalizing their night together?

Before slipping through the hotel door and out of his life, how many left a love note under the stained pillow, hastily written and poorly spelled, a name and a telephone number, buzzwords of affection never to be shared with anyone else?

All of them.

All these scene queens.

The same way he always put one of his embossed guitar picks on a table.

Easy to steal.

A guilty souvenir to be hidden away inside some book and years from now rediscovered; fitting memorial to the eternity of rock and roll.

And youth.

And Nat Axelrod.

Somehow, this girl standing in the doorway of his makeshift dressing room behind the Indianapolis Speedway's Gasoline Alley bleachers was different. She did not retreat from his stare or make any of the usual groupie shows of anxious modesty or overt seduction. This one seemed suspended in eternity, accepting the inevitability of his gaze while her own cat's eyes appeared to coolly collect memories.

And there was the Weasel, twitching and hanging on to the girl's elbow while he signaled a pair of straw-headed Purdue linemen busting out of their "Nat the Axe" T-shirts it was okay for her to join the crush of backstage guests.

Gasoline Alley had been specially secured and scrubbed clean for his concert tonight, but still lingering was a putrid stink they said was blended from years of gas, motor oil, burnt rubber and whatever else was still plaguing his well lubricated, white-walled nose.

Nat looked indifferently over the heads of the fifty or sixty local VIPs cramped inside the connecting garages decorated hours ago by the hometown weenies with crepe and balloons and dozens of framed posters of Indy 500 champions borrowed from the Indianapolis Hall of Fame Museum next door, before they bowed and kicked dirt and backed away like he was a goddamn king, which he was, short of goddamn Elvis.

The *machers* were pressing tighter and tighter against each other, devouring the catered platters of meats and cheeses;

grabbing at the towering arches of fresh fruit and vegetables and shrimp set up on a makeshift buffet table, an unfinished wooden door slab resting on a pair of oil-stained, weather-beaten wooden horses; drinking red wine from cheap plastic cups.

They tried not to let him catch them staring, except one flaming redhead, maybe twenty, or a burned-out fifteen, who made certain he noticed the promise every time she pushed the hair off her sly face. He gave her the Nat The Axe Look that told her to forget it. She got the message fast, shrugged and sank into the floor without so much as a last, desperate flash of tit.

He recognized the hyped-up promoter, Hugo Waldorf, angling toward him.

He didn't like Hugo any better now than he did at the sound check three hours ago, when Hugo showed up full of nervous predictions about box-office history being made tonight, huffing and puffing how rock stars had been banned at Indy for more than seventy-five years, even Elvis, until Nat Axelrod came along.

"Hugo, my man!" Nat said, ahead of an artificial smile. Held his breath defending against Hugo Waldorf's death-dealing body odor and breath-defying tobacco stink, strong enough to cut through the wall of coke blocking his nasal passages, lung-powered his thanks for giving him the inspiration to go on tonight and give a great performance, and planted a wet kiss on Hugo's lips.

The promoter laughed like he didn't mind, answered Nat's hug with statistics about the box-office take and an attendance record, and ran off to share the numbers with a trio of local music reviewers banging back tall-necked beers at one of the service bars.

Nat got back to studying the girl in the doorway.

Earlier in the day, after the sound check, before splitting back to the motel for a couple joints and a catnap, he had ordered, "Weasel, you runt bastard. Be sure to find me someone for after the show."

"Anything special, Nat?"

"One with the kind of legs I like. The kind that start at the ground and reach all the way up to the pussy."

His roadie had twitched and covered his mouth with his hand. His stomach wobbled with the muffled sound of his laughter, like this was the first time they had traded the question and the answer, and he backed off into the errand.

Now, here was the Weasel with his best score ever, moving like a ferret, carrying on like he was trying to impress the groupie with the authority he wore like a religious medal whenever he thought nobody was looking, only it wasn't working.

He didn't have his tour badge on, having traded it away two days ago for a quickie blow job from a waitress at the Tiltin' Hilton in Kansas City, who said she didn't give free samples to anyone below the rank of personal manager.

The Purdue linemen didn't recognize the Weasel and were getting ready to treat him and the groupie like fourth and one until Nat shouted above the noise, "Let both of 'em through, you bozo milk shits." The linemen recognized his voice, answered with a power salute and stepped aside. Nat gave them one of his own and answered their smiles with a stupid grin that had them laughing down to lard-ass level.

The Weasel, looking as bleak as a bad enema, tried faking a smile back to Nat, making him wonder if the Weasel was mentally milking his own bologna over the girl, figuring himself in line for sloppy seconds when Nat was through with her.

Fat porking chance.

This child was a keeper.

Nat hurried across the room, his eyes intent on her, rudely

indifferent to anyone slow to clear out of his way. The Weasel grinned at him, squeezed the girl's shoulder and backed through the doorway, turned and fled.

Not her.

The girl stood her ground and locked Nat's eyes in combat, giving him a rush of stinging intensity like he had never experienced before. The pleasure hurt. He stopped half a foot in front of her and heard his breath make a noise somewhere between a sigh and surrender. She returned his smile, revealing two perfect rows of white teeth; a smile to inspire miracles.

Close up, she was younger than he had first guessed, nineteen or twenty tops. In open-toed sandals she stood barely a half foot shorter than his own six-two in boots. Her pale green eyes glowing with secrets dominated an oval face set off by a cascade of light brown hair. Her model's body, long and lean, leggy, sent hints of sensuality under a silk sheath dress that quit above her knees and sorely troubled his imagination.

Nat wanted her to say something first, but she only played with her lips, rubbing them nervously over one another while he studied her face, not quite answering his smile.

He couldn't find the right words to use on her.

His song lyrics came easier.

Finally, he said, "Wait for me."

She nodded.

"You'll wait?"

She nodded again.

"Tell me your name?"

"Mae Jean." She smiled that smile. "What's yours?"

He played the whole show for her, like he had never played before, a two-hour party fit for gods, a hundred thousand or more fans on their feet dancing in the aisles to the songs of Nat Axelrod. Clapping and chanting. Shouting out the lyrics they all knew by heart. Lips moving in perfect, effortless synchronization. Calling out the words in a wave of affection as he played and sang to the core of his heart and soul.

He sensed more than he saw, trying to stare down the blinding spots illuminating him on the massive flatbed stage built overnight on top of the historic asphalt surface, in front of steel and concrete grandstands that usually swayed with other thousands caught up in the real rock and roll of the raceway. He listened to the crowd and took the noise for love. It inspired him the way it always did.

He imagined he could hear her voice above the clamor.

It made him climb higher.

When he heard only her voice, he stretched again.

He had pressed after forever tonight, but knew there would come a point when another encore would be a mistake, that even forever must have an ending. He left the audience begging for more and ran from the stage, feeling his elation melting into the gloom that follows climax until he saw Mae Jean and her smile waiting for him in the shadow of the wings. She seemed to be taking his eyes for her own.

He felt better at once.

He passed off his Strat to the Weasel and held out his hands for her.

The noise startled Nat awake.

He bolted upright in the king-sized bed and surveyed the suite, trying to remember where he was.

Indianapolis.

Yeah, Indianapolis.

Airport Holiday Inn on South High Drive.

He glanced at the luminous hands of the clock on the nightstand. Noon coming up. The blackout curtains drawn, so you wouldn't know it otherwise.

The noise had sounded like it came from the parlor, not quite a crash, but too loud to be mattress athletes playing Hump Your Honey in the next suite.

What the hell was going on?

The Weasel playing one of his stupid wake-up games?

No, the little bugger had learned his lesson earlier in the tour, in Atlanta, when that kind of funny business almost cost him the gig.

The Weasel knew better than to get here a minute too soon with anything more than the coaxing nudges it took to get Nat up for a fast crap and a cold shower, maybe a gallon of black and a toasted bagel before the stretch headed for the airport and the four o'clock to Chicago, so what the—

The connecting door to the parlor kicked open.

The overhead snapped on, blinding Nat momentarily.

"Don't even cough, you son of a bitch," the cop said from across the room. Legs astride. Hands clamped on the service revolver he had aimed at Nat's chest. Using the gun to punctuate every word.

A panicky confusion closed in on Nat. He felt the sweat oozing from his pores. His mind raced to comprehend the situation.

Drug bust?

It wouldn't be the first time.

A hassle that wouldn't last long. He was clean—hadn't used any shit since before the show last night—and so was the suite.

Nat answered the cop with a smile. They were about the same age. Maybe an autograph in a few minutes to help him go away happy.

"Bastard," the cop said, spitting the word. He marched over and pressed the gun hard against Nat's forehead. "If these sheets were mine, I'd be happier than a flea on Fido to drain your brains all over them, Mr. Rock-and-Roll Star, you glass of jizz."

Someone commanded him, "Ease up a minute, Carl."

Carl hesitated, then got in another hard poke before he stepped aside.

The second cop was an older man with crooked teeth and a nicotine-stained mustache. Sergeant's stripes on his powder blue uniform. His revolver still holstered.

Carl took aim again, announced over his shoulder, "Be happy to kill this long-haired, furry-faced, fag bastard."

"Lots of time for that it comes necessary."

"I'd say it's already necessary, Sarge. Save the state effort and cash-money expense."

The sergeant grunted. "Well, first things first." Nat watched him anxiously as he turned and called into the parlor, "I would sincerely appreciate if you folks stepped in here for a look."

After one of those minutes that last forever, a middle-aged man limped through the door dragging one leg slightly behind the other.

He stopped alongside Carl and studied Nat with the ugly look of quiet anger, covering his mouth with one hand, elbow couched in the other, accentuating a bad eye poking out from under a wide swatch of pink scar tissue.

One side of his face was a bloated mass of freshly broken veins blistered a bright red.

A small bandage barely covered a deep cut.

He toyed with the bandage as he pondered Nat and seemed to be talking to himself.

Nat said, "Will somebody please tell me what the hell this is about?"

Carl took a step forward, using the gun like a pointer. "Watch it, you shit-turd. It's about your dying, you move another inch or fraction thereof."

The sergeant admonished him. "Your language, Carl. Remember we got a young lady here with us, too."

Nat turned from Carl to the sergeant.

And saw the girl.

It was her, Mae Jean.

Her pale green eyes ringed with circles of purple and black.

Other bruises on her face.

An open wound on her right cheek.

Her lips swollen closed.

"This him, miss?" the sergeant said, delicately. "You just nod your sweet little head if it's too hard to talk some, Mae Jean."

Mae Jean wrapped her arms around her body, clutched her shoulders trying to ward off a trembling that seemed to overcome her suddenly. Her knees buckled.

The sergeant moved in quickly and caught her.

The limping man called out, "You answer the question now, daughter. Tell these good officers what they gotta know."

"Jesus Christ!" Nat said, studying Mae Jean, beginning to understand.

"Not even Him gonna help you, we hear what we think we gonna hear," Carl said. "Any way you look, He's on our side."

"Go on and answer," Mae Jean's father ordered her. "Is this the man what beat you silly and then raped you?"

"This is crazy, this is nuts," Nat said. He heard the fright wobble in his voice and felt sweat greasing the hair in his armpits. He looked at all of them and then at Mae Jean. "Girl, you know this is crazy. Tell them this is crazy."

Her father said, "Mae Jean?"

Mae Jean screamed. She pulled herself loose from the sergeant, took a step forward, then another, then seemed to pirouette off the ground before falling onto the pile carpeting and into a bouncing seizure.

"I been trained," the sergeant called out. "Red Cross." He got a ballpoint from his pocket as he moved quickly to his knees and worked to jam the pen between her teeth.

Mae Jean's father seemed transfixed.

Nat started to move.

Carl looked at him and, without a word, pulled the trigger.

The weapon exploded.

Nat felt something cut into his chest. Its force pushed him backward onto the bed and crashing against the wall.

He watched his blood roll over his naked chest as the room became a merry-go-round and then a roller coaster.

He wondered where the thunder was coming from, tried to imagine his fingers painting magical licks on his Fender Strat while thousands of his idolizing fans thundered their approval in the brisk night air of the Indianapolis Speedway.

Carl challenged, "You survive that, you hotshot prick. You'll have a whole lot of years behind bars to think about what you done to this poor girl here."

Nat didn't hear him after that. He was listening to the adoring crowd pick up his beat with spirited clapping that contributed to the joyful rhapsody. He spied Mae Jean, a speedway full of Mae Jeans, all of them smiling for him, only him, and he began playing only for them.

He heard the sound of rain.

Mae Jean disappeared, leaving only her smile.

The sky turned black and the music went dead.

But not her smile.

CHAPTER 2

Danny Manings was on the clay court of his 4.5-million-dollar gated Colonial estate on Lexington Road above the Beverly Hills Hotel, about to connect on a killer shot back at Jimmy Caan, when he heard Dory shouting his name. The sound broke his concentration. Caan whooped delightedly as the ball hit the net, running him back into deuce.

Dory, wearing a string bikini that showed off too much of her budding sixteen years, was racing barefoot toward him from the pool area, down the terraced cobblestone path, carrying her portable Sony, gasping for breath.

She waved her free arm as she sucked in air and called to him: "It's Nat, Daddy. Just now on television. They said Nat's been shot! Some cops went and shot Nat!"

Danny froze in place. He traded looks with Caan while trying to comprehend what Dory was shouting. As her words sank in, he felt the color draining under his tan. Without thinking, he relaxed the grip on his racket. It hit the clay surface with an awkward bounce. Ten minutes later, Caan was gone and Danny was on the phone with Decade Records's rack jobber in Indy.

"Big headlines and stuff," Leo Parriott said, wonderment edging his cough-hoarse voice. "They're saying Nat got shot resisting arrest, Danny. Saying he raped some little girl. There's talk about drugs, too."

"Nat isn't like that, Leo."

"They never are until they get caught."

Danny was in no mood to argue. "I'm going to fly in. Can you have someone pick me up at the airport?"

"Have someone call me back with the particulars and I'll have my kid, Laddie, and a limo waiting for you at the baggage curb."

"Thanks, Leo."

A growl of dismissal. "Least I owe you back for all you've ever done for me, Danny, so, anyway, when you pack, you might want to include a dark suit."

"What's that mean?"

"Something suitable for a funeral, you know? It just come over the radio five, ten minutes ago. News bulletin. Nat's in critical condition and may not make it past tonight."

Laddie Parriott let Danny slip into the limo first, hopped in, pulled the door closed before the driver could get to it. He leaned forward and flipped on the radio in the communications bank of inlaid walnut that included a small television and CD and cassette decks.

Nat's new single, "Charcoal Diamonds," blasted out.

Laddie beamed. "How's that for a neat welcome-to-Indianapolis present, Mr. Manings?" Danny returned his smile, not meaning it. " 'Charcoal Diamonds' went and jumped fifteen places straight into heavy rotation after news about the shooting got out. KVC's PD told me personally it'll be every hour on the half hour until further notice." Danny flicked him another empty smile.

Laddie was a rangy six-footer with a beer gut and loose, blond-streaked black hair that fell past his shoulder blades. Danny'd put him to work as a local promotion man for Decade Records last year as a favor to Leo. The kid turned out to be a natural.

Laddie said, "I got on the phone to the trades right away. I caught *Billboard* in time for next week's charts."

"Good for you," Danny said, recognizing the kid needed some stroking, then tuned him out. He stared past the window at the open countryside and infrequent clusters of shopping malls, reflecting on the clear crystal blue of the sky and low banks of lingering cumulus clouds, white and bright in their pristine, deceptive elegance.

Danny knew how the weather could turn momentarily and without warning in Indiana. The locals had a saying: "If you don't like it, just you wait a minute." *Nat's life is like the weather now,* Danny thought. *If Nat survives, his career will survive. America loves notoriety more than it loves celebrity.*

He watched the old buildings pass by in mindless progression, all board and mortar, the settled sameness of immobile history. Stifled a yawn behind his hand and rotated his neck to ease the tension building there.

". . . want some more good news?" Laddie was saying. "Leo, my father, he says all of Nat's product is moving fast and furious, same as happened for Janis and Jimi. The new album, the old catalog also. Except, he says there could be a backlash because of the girl. That's the bad news, she is. Mae Jean Minter? Police say there don't seem to be much question about her being raped or Nat beating her up something fierce."

"Nat's innocent until proven guilty, Laddie." The kid appeared confused. "Until then it's *alleged* rape, an *alleged* beating." He nodded, and that made the kid nod, like they were playing a game of Simon Says.

"You didn't see it on the TV, Mr. Manings. Mae Jean Minter's old man? He said—alleges, anyway—how he was the one who caught Nat at it. Pumping his daughter like gas was going for a bargain. In the backseat of a stretch limo. Right outside her own house." And nodded without a prompt.

★ ★ ★ ★ ★

Dr. Wolf Heidemann gave Danny a hard stare.

"You cannot accuse me of urging you to come when you phoned me from Los Angeles, Manings," he said, adding an indifferent shrug. "That the police will not admit you to Axelrod's room is outside my jurisdiction."

The hospital administrator was in his mid to late forties; a thick mane of snow-white hair made him look older, professorial. He walked with an erect carriage, spoke with a heavy middle-European accent and, as if to emphasize his origin, held his filter-tipped cigarette underhanded, like Major Strasser in *Casablanca.* He worked it into a carved ivory holder before reaching for the pirate's pistol lighter on his uncluttered desk.

His pale appearance and overbearing manner reminded Danny of a rock promoter he had decked at the Rocky Mountain Pop Festival, after catching the scuzz bucket dispensing snow like candy kisses to girls Dory's age, some of them younger, looking to trade the blow for blow jobs, the son of a bitch.

Danny said, "The police officer guarding Nat's door said he'll make an exception if you authorize it, Doctor." He tapped his fingers nervously on the desk.

Heidemann shrugged, blew smoke from the side of his mouth. "I save lives, Manings. I am not a social director. He was wrong, the officer, to confuse me with his chief."

"You don't like me, Doctor, do you?"

"I do not know you well enough to have formed an opinion, Manings. On the other hand, your friend Nat Axelrod? Meeting him was no choice of mine. That kind comes with the oath I took."

"I understand Nat owes his life to you."

The doctor made a sweeping gesture of disinterest. "In an emergency hospital we first do the best we can, then we can ask questions afterward. The gunshot wound to his chest caused extensive internal bleeding. Life-threatening. He almost lost a lung, that bad for him, maybe not bad enough. You would understand better after seeing the beautiful girl he attacked like some savage."

"Did Nat say he did it?"

"Also outside my jurisdiction, Manings. A matter for the police. Or the confessional."

"I wish you'd understand Nat isn't a common criminal. Nat's an important musician."

The doctor laughed sarcastically. "Mozart, now he was a very important musician. Beethoven. Bach. Brahms. Leonard Bernstein, even. Some of them you may have heard of?"

Danny crossed his arms and turned away. He began tapping a foot.

Heidemann sifted through a neat pile of medical folders and pulled one. "Here, I show you something," he said, holding it up for him to see. Nat's name was printed in block letters on the index tab. The doctor placed the folder on the desk and flipped to the last of several pages, the emergency admittance, running his finger along the lines until he found the entry he wanted.

Turning around the folder, he said, "See where it says *Occupation*? When the ambulance arrived with your so-called important musician, he could not tell us this. He could not speak and he almost could not still breathe. We know only that he is dying from a gunshot wound and, so, we make some important medicine. Later, when the officers tell us why he is shot, we can fill in the occupation properly. See?"

The line read: SHPOS.

Danny repeated the letters aloud, thought about them. "I don't understand."

"I would not expect you to, Manings. It is our medical

shorthand, like the illegible Latin we all must learn for the writing of prescriptions." He smiled faintly, leaned back in the chair, concentrated for a moment on the cigarette holder. "It stands for *Sub-Human Piece of Shit,* and I believe that describes your friend perfectly."

Danny leaned forward and placed his elbows on the desk. He rubbed hard between his eyebrows, closed his eyes and took a deep breath, struggling to hold his temper. He pulled his checkbook from an inside pocket. Flipped open the cover. Snatched a ballpoint pen from the calendar set on Dr. Heidemann's desk.

He made out the check for ten thousand dollars, pushed it at the doctor and replaced the pen.

Heidemann stared back at him, puzzled.

"My personal check, Doctor. On account," Danny said, rising. "On account of wanting Mr. Axelrod to continue getting very important attention and very important treatment for the duration of his time with very important you."

"Herr Manings, I did not mean—"

Danny threw a finger under the doctor's nose.

"You have said enough about the quality of your service and the quality of your mercy, Dr. Heidemann. You keep Mr. Axelrod alive and when the ten grand runs out you let me know and I'll send you more."

The doctor rose abruptly. "You know you have just insulted me, Manings."

"I've just paid for the privilege and I do not give a flying fuck for your feelings, Doctor." He pointed at the phone. "Now, if that thing works, I'd like you to please make the call that gets me past the cop to Mr. Axelrod."

Three phone messages from Joe Wunsch, all marked "Urgent," were waiting for him when Danny checked into the patriarchal

Columbia Club on Monument Circle in the heart of downtown Indianapolis. He stuffed them inside a pocket and followed the club's hunchbacked bellman, ancient "Lightning Dickie" Porterfield, to the four-room, fourth-floor guest suite Leo Parriott always reserved for him. For all the historical elegance of its antique furnishings, the room felt slightly damp and musty.

Danny practiced patience while Lightning Dickie went through his usual routine in slow motion, with sagging shoulders and a Stepin Fetchit shuffle. The bellman struggled to get the overnighter onto the narrow bed, then fussed with switches, curtains, the heat control panel, television knobs and, always last in order, the nylon pull cord on the closet lightbulb before he accepted Danny's ten-dollar handshake as if it were a surprise.

The instant he was out the door, Danny grabbed the phone, signaled the switchboard operator, and gave her Joe's direct number at Decade Records in LA.

Momentarily, Joe came on in mid-sentence, shouting, "You can't believe how that rock-and-roll motherfucker is out to get you, Captain."

"Which rock-and-roll motherfucker this time?" Danny said. He adjusted his position on the side of the bed, one leg tucked under the other, and studied his reflection in the dresser mirror across the bedroom.

"Who do you think? Drummond, of course. The minute he heard you were on a plane to Indianapolis, Drummond got on the damn phone to the powers in New York. He sees what's happened as a chance to get the suits to dump you and promote his scrawny ass into your office, finally get even with you for denying him any glory when Nat signed with the label."

Danny knew better. The Nat signing was a thorn, but his real problem with Drummond came from an older wound that cut deeper. Along with everyone else in the business who knew about Manings versus Drummond, let the kid think what he would. The truth was their secret, his and Drummond's; nothing Danny cared to share, not even with Joe.

He said, "Another Clive Davis he ain't, Joey, so don't give me history. Give me now."

"Now? *Now* Drummond has spent the last six hours turning it all against you. He has some of the powers convinced that this rape business can hurt every other act on the label, as in goodbye profits, hello irate, tone-deaf shareholders." He paused to catch his breath, resumed before Danny could begin a thought. "Allowing as how Nat's new album is yet to spin the world on its dick or return its horrendously astronomical production costs you authorized, Drummond is close to convincing old Count Dracula himself."

"He got to Stoker?"

"Even as we talk. He's down the hall, following his tongue through Ma Bell and up-up Stoker's tunnel of fudge."

Danny put a confident spin on his voice. "I'll handle it when I get back."

"While he's talking long distance, I think you need to seriously consider putting a long distance between you and Nat Axelrod, Danny." The humor had drained from Joe's voice. "Right now, dig? I'll get you booked first plane out."

Danny said, finally, "No can do, Joey. So far, the worst criminal I've heard about here is the gun-happy cop who put a bullet in Nat and almost blew his heart into Illinois. Those are the facts. Everything else is hearsay and horseshit."

"Come home, or head for New York and tap-dance your way around all the evil hearts at Decade. Purify yourself on spec. Stroke Stoker, you know?"

"I owe this to Nat, being here for him. We grew up together, we—"

"You don't owe him *bopkehs*. You got Nat a deal anybody else would reserve for Elvis, he showed up again. Decade owes Nat a royalty statement every six months and even an honest accounting, maybe. But nothing in the deal says you have to babysit felons."

"I'd do it for you."

"Then save it for me. Danny, please? I know whereof Harry Ratfuck Drummond speaks. Remember, Drummond doesn't just have a forked tongue. Drummond is out to fork the whole world, beginning with you."

"I'll think about it and let you know."

"That tone is the one I hate the most."

"I gotta be me, Joe."

"That's Sammy Davis Jr. you're confusing yourself with, Captain. He hadda be him. The way you're coming on, it's closer to Richard Nixon. He hadda be him, too, and look where that got him."

Danny phoned home.

He knew from Vickie's voice, her muffled yawns, that he had awakened her, no matter how hard she tried convincing him otherwise, and what else? He was hearing something else in her voice.

He reported on the day, including the call from Joe, only the parts he wanted her to know, holding back on Harry Drummond.

"What are you going to do, honey?" she said.

"What do you think?"

"I think what you think."

"Nat's my best friend. If our positions were reversed, Nat would be here doing the best he could for me."

"Then there's your answer, isn't it?"

"If Joe's right, it could mean my job, and that's not being fair to you or Dory, the boys . . ."

"You've been unemployed before. We managed."

"We were younger then. There were no kids for us to protect from the real world. It'd be harder now."

"When you come home, you'll have to show me how hard it can be."

"Damn, I love you, Vickie."

"Same, honey."

He told her to kiss Dory and the boys for him, wished her sweet dreams, and hung up wondering if he had only imagined the slight slur in her voice.

Damn.

That's what he had heard.

The slur.

Vickie had sworn to him she was off the stuff and that looked the case since the last time she graduated from Betty Ford, four months ago.

His one hesitation about coming here had been for her, fearing she might use his absence to slide again. When he told her that, she'd laughed at his concern, then loved him for it, packed his suitcase, and almost pushed him out the door.

That should have been his clue.

She was too damned anxious for him to be gone.

She stayed on his mind throughout the day, and that night he slept fitfully, waking a few times to turn off a nightmare from the past—

Watching himself coax Vickie into sharing his habit and almost letting it kill him before he quit cold turkey, but unable to get her out as easily.

At all.

Vickie was still a victim and it was his fault, a realization that kept him a victim, too.

Chapter 3

The early-morning warmth had turned into an abrasive chill kicked swirling by frivolous winds that seemed to whip around every corner, and the clouds were turning a haunting black as Danny hurried from the Columbia Club and around Monument Circle to the old City Market four blocks away. He tugged protectively at the Dodgers cap he'd appropriated one night in the team locker room and this morning would identify him to Nat's lawyer, Benjamin Harrison Hubbard.

Studying the sky, Danny was glad he had taken the lawyer's advice and worn his heavy-duty military Woolly Pully under a Windbreaker that was more decorative than effective. "Come out prepared for rain," Hubbard had urged, an informed chuckle coating his dramatic baritone. "And I don't mean the piss bath that's ready to gush down upon my woebegone client, Mr. Nat Axelrod."

The City Market was a gigantic converted warehouse under an arched roof, modernized periodically over the past hundred years. It was filled with eccentric aisles of open counters and cubicles, where merchants sold an infinite variety of attractively displayed fresh meats, fruits, specialty foods and baked goods straight out of the oven.

Danny paused inside the entrance to survey the scene before wandering anxiously down the center aisle toward the rear, sucking in all the sweet, conflicting smells, trying not to appear too rude as he studied one strange face after another in the comfortable customer traffic.

"Manings, here!"

He followed the voice to the mezzanine landing, where a man stood like a victorious Caesar against the protective ornamental railing, thumbing at himself and pointing to a small table that butted from the railing. Danny headed past the last stalls and turned for the stairway.

Hubbard was sitting when he reached the table, working aggressively over the last of a jelly doughnut. A dozen other tables along the railing were occupied by people engaged in quiet conversation or entertaining themselves by studying the busy scene below.

The lawyer licked at his fingers, then used them to rub away some jelly residue before extending a hand. His grip was strong and firm. So was the look of inner merriment constant in his eyes. He greeted Danny like an old friend and gestured toward the empty seat and the tall container of steaming coffee waiting like a party favor.

Hubbard urged him to pick something from the heady pile of doughnuts, cookies and small cakes on the paper platter in the center of the glass-topped table, chose a huge chocolate chip cookie for himself while pointing to the disposable cream containers and low-cal packets.

"You sounded like a Sweet'n Low man over the phone, so I didn't bother with sugar," Hubbard said, toasting him with his paper cup.

"Black is fine, Mr. Hubbard."

"It's Hub, call me Hub. Short for Hubba-Hubba. Some people call me Mother, mostly my most worthy worthless courtroom opponents, as in, *Here comes that mother now.*" He chuckled again. When he didn't get so much as a smile back, his bother flashed momentarily.

Danny judged Hubbard to be in his mid-fifties. He was of

average height and appearance, except for an overgrown mustache desperate for a trim and showing traces of the jelly doughnut. He had a high, expansive forehead and disguised a receding hairline with a clipped, almost butch hairstyle; wore plain, steel-rimmed glasses that were resting on the table next to his cup.

Hubbard's manner matched his voice, both given over to a theatricality Danny invariably discovered in lawyers who live half their lives in courtrooms.

"Turns out how the Dodgers cap was unnecessary, Manings. I recognized you by instinct. You arrived looking lost, both thumbs up your bunghole like a self-serving fairy. That was my clue, that and the way your head was twisting in orbit, like some goddamned display mannequin at a chiropractic convention."

"Can we talk about Nat?" Danny said. He was too tired for banter and in no mood for games, although he had liked Hubbard at once. The lawyer came across as someone he could trust.

Hubbard studied him long and hard without losing the appearance of good humor.

Danny said, "After Leo Parriott gave me your name and I called, you said there were things I should know about Nat's situation. That's why I'm here, not to make a new friend."

Hubbard nodded and frowned. "I know what I said, Manings." He put his cup to his mouth and stared at Danny over the rim. Danny began tap-dancing his fingers. "And with that attitude, no never to worry about making the new friend." He put down the cup, reached for a cream cake. "You should try one," he said.

Danny shook his head.

The lawyer devoured the cake and a second one, then swiped at residue on his mustache. "I like to have a feeling for folks before I take them into my confidence, Manings."

"What you should be feeling now is my frustration, Mr. Hubbard. And no small amount of anger. From all I've seen and heard so far, I get a nauseous feeling there's a conspiracy to bury Nat Axelrod under a shit pile deep enough to make the *Guinness Book of World Records.*"

Hubbard reached out and put a hand on Danny's arm, almost tipping over his cup. "Now we are beginning to get somewhere, sir. I truly appreciate connoisseurs of deep shit." His noise was more than a chuckle and his look more candid and inviting than before.

Danny couldn't resist grinning.

Hubbard's eyes twinkled with victory. "Manings, do you know the expression *going to hell in a handbasket?* You don't, get to know it. It most certainly applies to the man whose interests we commonly share."

Hubbard reached for the Dodgers cap and put it on. He moved his eyebrows up and down Groucho fashion, to make the brim dance, and signaled it was time for Danny to say something.

"They're out to get Nat, aren't they?"

"Got him, Manings. Got him."

"I want to know the worst."

"Then I'm your man," the lawyer said. He leaned forward and pushed his face closer to Danny. "How much do you know so far?"

"I went to the library here yesterday, the newspaper office. I read everything about Nat's concert and what happened afterward, the arrest and how Nat was shot. I talked to the reporter who's covering the story, and—"

Hubbard threw a dismissive hand. "Forget about the public record, son. After the cops refused to tell you a lick and you headed on over to the DA, what did the DA have to say? Malcolm Benedictus?"

"How did you know that, about my going—"

Hubbard answered by tapping his temple. "It's what any smart young cuss would do. Go on. You met with old Malcolm's right hand, Phillip Penguin, then old Malcolm himself not long after you called and arranged for this kaffee klatch."

"The DA told me to get on the plane and go home, there was nothing I could do to help Nat."

"Malcolm tell you why that was?"

"The Weasel." The lawyer's expression showed he didn't understand. "Kern Posey, one of Nat's roadies. What everyone calls him, the Weasel." Hubbard nodded and signaled Danny to continue. "They have a signed affidavit from the Weasel, saying he brought Mae Jean Minter to the motel suite at Nat's direction, for the express purpose of illicit carnal relations with Nat. The Weasel also swears and will testify he was present when the cops searched Nat's suite and found an ounce of cocaine, a large quantity of grass, and other illegal substances—"

Hubbard interrupted him. "Enough marijuana cigarettes to lift a space shuttle and enough of everything else to wake the dead and make them waltz. What do you say to that?"

"Nat used, but he never carried. The Weasel squirreled for him. Always. Just in case of a situation like this one, where the cops showed up unannounced. I think the shit was planted in Nat's suite, Mr. Drummond."

"By your Weasel?"

"The thought hasn't escaped me."

"By the police?"

"You tell me."

Instead, Hubbard said, "Did my client make a habit of taking girls to his room as concert souvenirs?" The lawyer watched him struggle to come up with an answer. "I understand they're called groupies, and it's quite the thing out in your world."

"Not like some rock musicians I could name, who think fucking is part of the encore."

"You haven't answered my question, Manings." Danny hesitated. "If I'm going to be his lawyer, I'd prefer working with the whole truth and nothing but, even if it stays our little secret."

Hubbard's eyes were studying him.

Danny sighed. "A girl in his suite, it could have happened."

"I expect Malcolm told you how Mae Jean Minter's father corroborates some of your Weasel's story. Huck Minter says he caught them fornicating outside his home hours after the concert was over. In the backseat of a limo. The sound of a car driving up woke him and, after five or six minutes, when Mae Jean wasn't inside, he got worried, threw on his robe, went out, and was shocked to find her fighting off my client in the backseat. Huck says the limo tore off like a scared rabbit once he started hammering on the door, stopped about a hundred yards away to dump his precious child. Says Mae Jean was screaming something awful and was all bloodied and beaten, the way she looks in the photos the DA will introduce into evidence when this ugly business gets to trial, as well as Mae Jean's own sworn statement against Mr. Axelrod. I expect they'll have dug up the limousine driver by then. We don't have so many of either hereabouts, so it won't be much of a haystack."

"You think this will go to trial?"

"Not if my client confesses, and I don't suppose that's in the cards." Hubbard rose slowly, removed the Dodgers cap and slapped it back on Danny's head, yanking the brim and giving the crown a few friendly taps. "No plea bargain, either. I already asked. Old Malcolm has an eye on higher office and sees this as a high-profile case that will get him a lot of headlines and, down the line, a lot of votes, especially after the jury returns its guilty verdict."

"You're saying it's open and shut?"

"With the testimony from your Weasel, Posey, and Huck

Minter, himself a garden of garbage? Trust me. I'd say the state's case against Nat Axelrod is as tight as a hangman's knot." He moved decisively with their empty cups and platters to within a couple feet of the trash bin, dumped them with an overhand shot, and returned to the table to sweep up the cream containers and low-cal packets into a flap pocket of his huntsman's jacket.

Danny stood to leave. "Sounds like you've already thrown in the towel, Mr. Hubbard. If it's a matter of your fee, more money, I can—"

"I'm court-appointed, not anointed, Manings, but I don't need your money and I don't throw in towels. I'll be marching into court like one of them old sods in the Good Book, hauling Nat Axelrod's version of the Word, whatever it may be, the way David trod after Goliath."

"Do me a favor, then? Listen to Nat's music. You'll discover his lyrics are full of love, not violence. That's what Nat is about, Mr. Hubbard. Love. Not violence. Believe me when I tell you that."

Hubbard planted his elbows on the table, rested his chin on his clasped hands. He seemed to be making up his mind about something. "Tell me something first." He caught Danny's eyes and held them. "You're married?"

"What does that have to do with anything?"

"Is that your answer?"

"Married, happily married, and I don't beat my wife, if that's your next question."

"Youngsters?"

"Three. A girl and two boys."

"The girl, you mention her first. I would suppose that makes her the oldest?"

"Dory. Yes."

"How old?"

"Teenager."

"About Mae Jean Minter's age?"

"A few years younger."

"You love your family a lot?"

"More than life."

"You ever let Nat around your wife and Dory?"

"Of course. All the time. Anytime. He's my best friend." Danny held his gaze.

"Whether you're there or not?"

"I see what you're driving at, Mr. Hubbard. Yes. Whether I'm there or not."

"Then I am happy to believe what you say about him, Manings. However, the judge and jury will be harder to convince unless your friend, my client, climbs out of his coma with a better story to tell than the stories we've already heard from Kern Posey and the Minters."

Lightning Dickie Porterfield was behind the Columbia Club service desk, waving a message slip at him as Danny moved toward the lobby. It was from Joe Wunsch and marked "Urgent." Danny called him from the pay phone near the registration desk.

"Game, set and match, Captain."

"Tell me what that means."

"Drummond confirmed that Nat's going to be hit with a rape charge and got right back on the phone with Stoker. A wire's on its way to you there, telling you to shift your ass home damn quick."

"Not before I talk to Nat. He's out of intensive care, but still in a coma."

"For Christ's sake, Captain. He could be that way forever. It's not like it's Vickie or one of the kids."

"It's Nat, Joey. For Christ's sake. Nat. He's family. The way you're family."

"Stop wearing your heart up your ass. Stoker's already sent off the kiss of death telegram to Nat's management. Decade's officially dropped him from the label. Morals clause boilerplate bullshit."

"Bullshit is right. Nat's contract is ironclad, pay-or-play for another four years."

"Captain, you know any jury in the land that would order decent folk to pay-or-play with someone who could have been pay-or-playing with their teenage daughters?"

The police officer outside Nat's room was black and built like a small truck, but like the others was armed and sat with his chair tilted against the wall. As Danny approached, footsteps echoing in the corridor, the cop looked up from the thick law book he was reading. He said, "Mr. Manings?" Danny nodded. "Dr. Heidemann's secretary called ahead," he said, tapping the two-way clipped to his shoulder, and aimed Danny through the door with a thumb.

Nat was asleep inside a jangle of tubing extending from his arms, which rested outside the coverings drawn loosely to just below his neck. He didn't look to have moved in the twelve hours since Danny's last visit.

Danny moved a chair to the bed. He sensed someone behind him, turned to see a nurse easing the door closed. She recognized him and formed a greeting with her lips, glided over and stood alongside the chair to observe Nat. "Just fine," she said to herself. She walked around the bed to the utility table and prepared a hypodermic.

Nat winced as the needle pressed into his vein. His eyelids fluttered. He made a moaning sound that turned into a grunt. His eyes opened and closed again, then his eyelids fluttered some more. They stopped and stayed shut. His breathing resumed an even pattern.

The nurse smiled and made a moving circle of approval with her thumb and forefinger. "He's been like that since about six this morning," she said, her voice as squeaky clean as the room's antiseptic smell. "He's rounded the corner."

Danny waited for her to leave. He leaned forward and called softly: "Nat?" No response. He tried again. Nat's eyelids moved. A harsh purring rose from his throat. "It's Danny Manings, Nat."

Nat made the grunting noise again, straining a large blue vein at his temple. He began to work his mouth. The pink tip of his tongue became visible as it dug through the crevice.

"Danny?"

The sound was so faint, Danny wasn't sure for a moment if all he'd heard Nat utter was another rumble.

"It's Danny Manings, Nat."

Nat's mouth opened and he strained to make words happen. He seemed to reach for Danny. Danny took Nat's hand in both his own. He felt Nat's tight grip lock onto him before whatever energy remained slipped away and Nat fell back inside a deep slumber.

"Manings!" Danny turned. Dr. Heidemann was waving him to the corridor. "Come. We have phoned for the taxicab you requested, but it will be fifteen minutes or so."

Danny followed the doctor to his office, where he was directed to a guest chair by the desk. He declined the offer of a cigarette.

"I know, I know, cancer," Dr. Heidemann said, working a filter tip into his ivory holder.

Danny lit the cigarette for him with the pirate's pistol lighter. The doctor nodded thanks, stood with military correctness and blew out smoke toward the ceiling, watching the white trails curl and rise.

Danny said, "Nat was showing a little improvement."

"A lot of improvement." The doctor walked around to his side of the desk and looked out the window, turning his back on Danny. "I understand the taxicab, it will be taking you to the airport?"

"Yes." He started to explain, but Heidemann waved off his words, turned around to look down at him, his face flushed with polite irritation.

"Then I have caught you in time," the doctor said. He balanced the cigarette holder on the edge of his desk, removed from the middle drawer the check for ten thousand dollars Danny had given him three days ago and displayed it between them. "I wanted you to understand something, Manings."

"If it's not enough, I already told you—"

Dr. Heidemann cut him short. "You be quiet . . . I want you to understand that you do not know everything there is to know." He reached for the pirate's pistol. The flame caught. He put the check into an ashtray overflowing with butts and watched it burn. The doctor leaned forward, rocking slightly, balancing himself by his fingertips on the desk. "Now, so," he said. "Now, you go catch your damn taxicab."

A storm front along the Eastern Seaboard played havoc with flight schedules.

Danny spent most of the day in the airport, including four hours trapped in a jet on the runway with two hundred other passengers, swilling complimentary champagne. It was after eleven o'clock when the 747 landed at LAX and nearing midnight by the time the limo got him home.

Although he'd called Joe Wunsch before boarding, he wasn't counting on a car waiting for him, but a limo driver at the arrival gate inside the terminal, lean and long-haired in a scruffy makeshift uniform and black cap, held a square of cardboard on which somebody had scrawled "Decade Records" using a thick, black marker.

Except for the security lights, the house was dark when the limo pulled up.

Danny left his luggage in the entrance hall and tiptoed up the stairs, by custom stopping briefly to look in on the boys and Dory. As always, Danny Jr., and Darryl were lost inside their blankets. Next door, Dory needed covering. She rolled onto her back while he was adjusting her blanket, half opened her eyes and, with a glimmer of acknowledgment, squeezed out a smile. He leaned over and kissed her forehead. She stirred and made a slight kissing sound before drifting off again, leaving him to wonder if she would even remember the moment come morning.

Gliding across the hall into the master bedroom, Danny padded quietly to their canopied bed. Vickie's nightstand lamp was on. She had fallen asleep propped up against her pillows in a reading position, the book still open on her lap. The new Sidney Sheldon. It had kept her up late the night before he left for Indianapolis.

Danny pushed a few strands of her lush brown hair behind her ear, touched her temple with his lips and closed his eyes and his mind to the slight odor of gin. He picked up the glass among her prescription vials on the nightstand and sniffed; the gin smell again. Shook his head and retreated to the bathroom. After a lingering shower, he slipped into a fresh pair of pajamas and slid under the covers.

Vickie hadn't moved at all in the last twenty minutes. He tried inching the book from her, but her grip resisted him. He wondered if she was faking sleep, teasing him a bit. He shook her gently by the shoulder and asked the question in a playful tone of righteous indignation.

She didn't respond.

He attributed it to the gin and reached a hand across her, stretching to turn off her lamp.

His body nudged against hers.

She tilted awkwardly from the waist, still clutching the book.

His hand prevented her from falling farther.

"Vickie?"

He leaned in closer to listen for her breathing and only heard his own, already racing.

No pulse.

He began to cry, understanding the truth of his worst fear for dear, sweet, darling, loving Vickie.

The LA County coroner's autopsy, required under certain circumstances in home death situations, revealed a deadly mix of prescription drugs, alcohol and cocaine in Vickie's system. Given her long history of substance abuse and lacking sufficient cause to rule a suicide, her death was ruled accidental.

Danny blamed himself.

"If I hadn't been in Indianapolis, she wouldn't have had the opportunity to start up with that shit again," he said. "Or, if the fucking plane had taken off on schedule. If I made it home only a few hours earlier, before she—"

"Captain, that's a crock," Joe Wunsch said. "I loved Vickie, too, but let's face it, crack was too high on her Hit Parade for her to let go. Vickie was hardly out of rehab and she was already finding ways, even while you were around."

"She was trying, really trying, Joey."

"In your dreams. Jesus, I don't mean to come down on you like some goddam Reality Commando, but—"

"I said Vickie was really trying. She promised me. Not for me or even for herself. For the kids."

Joe rolled his eyes. He flung his palms heavenward, pushed out a sigh and conceded: "For the kids."

Danny saw the truth on his face. "Leave it there, okay?"

"Yeah. Okay."

The burial service had concluded a half hour ago. They were alone at Vickie's grave site, on a rolling slope of painted grass at Forest Lawn in Glendale that had a view of nothing special, but nevertheless a view. That was the only special request Danny had made of Joe, who'd taken charge of making arrangements over the past week, not needing or waiting to be asked, leaving Danny to his grief. Vickie loved her views. A reason they vacationed in the mountains and not on a beach, despite his own preference for the ocean.

Danny said, "The boys went from here with Bert and Carrie?"

"Yeah, on their way back to the house. Dory went with Manny Goldenberg's kid, her best friend Ally. The two of them spent most of the day crying in each other's arms."

"Been that way since . . ." He closed his eyes to count the days. "And Dory ducking me, like she also knows it's my fault."

"Captain. For Christ's sake!"

"Kids know these things. You can't fool the kids, Joey, especially not the sensitive ones, like Dory."

"Suit yourself, man," Joe said, beyond arguing. He wheeled and headed away. "I'll wait for you in the car. Take your time."

Danny watched him angle down the lawn to the new BMW that was one of Joe's more visible company perks. The kid deserved it and anything else Danny could make come his way.

There could never be enough to repay Joe's loyalty and friendship, the two qualities he admired most in anybody, the standards on which he had based his own career. His whole fucking life, it seemed.

Their relationship had begun when Joe was barely into his twenties, a kid off the streets of New York, who talked himself into the offices of Decade Records and onto his staff. "And talked and talked and talked," Danny added whenever he told the story, insisting good-naturedly that hiring Joe had been the only way to shut him up. The kid was loyal from Day One, routinely proving it through the long sieges of office politics, where gossip and gospel coexist like identical twins and so many others fell for the lines of crap laid out by Harry Fucking Drummond.

"Kid!" Danny called as Joe was about to slide into the car. Certain he had his attention, he threw him a finger kiss. Joe caught it midair and grinned broadly before he flung it away like it didn't matter, but Danny knew better. They both knew better. Danny knew that, too.

He still knew it after Joe told him he was fired.

They were halfway to the house, cruising west past Crescent Heights on Sunset, when Danny said something about going to the office tomorrow. "I'll just get more nuts than I already am sitting around the house feeling sorry for myself," he said. At once it was as if cabin pressure had changed in the BMW and oxygen masks would drop any second. "What is it, kid? What is it I don't know?"

"It can wait, Captain."

"No. It can't, Joey. Tell me."

"You got enough grief right now."

"Drummond, that it? He's winning?"

Joe let the questions simmer before answering. "Won," he said. "The son of a bitch had Stoker convinced you should be history before you took off from Indianapolis, He was looking forward to personally serving you your walking papers. Would've by now except for—"

"Don't tell me *decency.*"

Danny glanced at Joe, whose face had flushed and showed more emotion than Danny could muster for himself. He was already too drained and saturated in self-pity to respond with more than a nod and passive acceptance.

"Decency?" Joe blasted out a laugh. "Not on that prick's part. I even got a feeling he was thinking to drop the bomb at the chapel today, so I tracked down Stoker in New York. Stoker made like he couldn't believe Drummond would do such a thing and was I being too emotional? Not ten, fifteen minutes later, Drummond slithered into my office and told me the office was too busy for anyone to time out for the funeral."

"Explains why nobody from the label was there."

"The place has been in a state of chaos since Nat was shot and the word about you began leaking out. Nobody dared stand up to that miserable fucking—"

"Except you."

"I did it the easy way. I told him to go fuck himself where the sun don't shine and I resigned."

"You shouldn't have, Joey. I would have understood."

"I resigned for me, Captain, not for you."

"Then un-resign for me, okay?"

"And go on working for the slimy bastard after what he pulled on you?"

"He didn't accept your resignation, did he?"

"How do you know that?"

"Because I'm still older and wiser than you."

"Older," Joe grunted.

"Drummond is a first-rate politician. He needs you for now. Because of what you know about our operations that he doesn't and to make it look to Stoker like the ship continues to sail a steady course with him at the helm. In six months or a year, maybe, you're gone, but not now."

"Drummond gave me a death laser look and then all of a sudden he swallowed my shit like it was one of his favorite dishes and told me to send flowers and be sure to include his name on the card. Don't go looking too close for it, okay?"

"It's pay me back time, Joey. I want you to stick with the gig. You owe me that much, so promise me."

Joe stared out the window for the next minute or two, hand-patting a melody on his thighs.

Danny said, "Until I've settled in somewhere else and we can be a team again, how's that?"

"Better," Joe said.

Chapter 4

Throughout the trial, Nat stayed resident at the hospital, under round-the-clock guard; transported the twenty miles into town by ambulance, accompanied by a pair of armed guards; dressed daily in one of the inexpensive blue collar suits purchased for him at a local thrift shop by Benjamin Harrison Hubbard. At Hubbard's insistence he had allowed a tight military haircut to replace his mass of shoulder-length black hair, but refused to lose the beard entirely, allowing the barber to trim it only to the pimple line.

Judge Clyde Staton Dirst had ruled favorably on DA Malcolm Benedictus's motion to have Nat removed from the hospital to a jail facility, but Hubbard prevailed on appeal in district court, contending his client required constant monitored attention based on the recovery regimen established by Dr. Wolf Heidemann.

In fact, Nat's safety was the actual albeit unmentioned issue in Hubbard's brief.

When Nat put the question to him, Ben said, "I've heard rumblings, so I want you where accidents are not so likely to happen, watched over by the federals, not our locals."

"Are you suggesting the cops—"

Hubbard arched an eyebrow. "Mr. Nat the Axe, around these parts the police preference is for country music, not your brand. Keeping you at the hospital, out of town, out of sight, out of mind, shifts the odds somewhat in our favor of keeping you in one piece for the duration."

In court, from the outset, Nat sensed the hopelessness of his case, the inevitability of a guilty verdict. He tried to remove himself mentally from the daily proceedings, using a trick of the brain Ringo called floating and had spent hours teaching him. Every day, once unshackled and led to his seat beside Ben Hubbard in the courtroom, he lost himself in the solitude of desire and tried floating.

As often as he tried, he floated only once.

Nat thought he might the day the Weasel's statement was read into evidence, after the judge denied the meticulously expressed objections of an angry Ben Hubbard, who roused like a distressed grizzly from seeming slumber to respond to what he branded Kern Posey's "prejudicial poppycock, a means for saving his own eternally damned soul by any means."

He thought he might the day Mae Jean Minter's father, Huck, took the witness stand and never looked at him while answering the questions of the assistant district attorney, Phil Penguin, except when asked if he could identify the defendant. At that, Huck fixed a stare and pointed his index fingers like *banderillas,* screaming to the walls: "It's him there what made my precious girl damaged goods."

He thought he might the day Mae Jean took the stand to tell her version of the story. She kept her eyes on him while the DA sang his damaging questions like lullabies and several jurors cried at her damning responses, while Nat took solace from the different message he believed he saw flashing in her transcendental gaze and urged Ben to go easy with his cross-examination.

Finally, Nat managed to float the day the jury returned guilty verdicts on both counts of the indictment and lingering hopes he had for the outcome evaporated.

He squeezed his eyes closed as the court clerk read the verdicts on the pieces of paper handed over by the tall, arthritic jury foreman. When he reopened them, he was swimming in air on his belly, arms and legs outstretched, free-falling without a parachute.

He looked down and saw everyone in the immaculately clean, birch-paneled courtroom in a state of suspended animation, including himself, sitting at the defense table, eyes wide and staring blankly; heard Ben Hubbard whisper in his ear: "Son, no matter how the judge carves up the verdict, figure your next ten years belong to the sovereign state of Indiana."

Ben pulled him onto his feet by the shoulder, said his client waived the mandatory time for an appeal and requested immediate sentencing. "Faster isn't better, but nothing can be now," he whispered side of the mouth.

Judge Dirst wagged a finger at Nat's face and said he would use this opportunity to sound a challenge, whereupon he urged the youth of America to abandon their false idols and build a better world on a foundation of real idols. He explained that possession of an ounce or less of cocaine was a Class C felony in Indiana and carried a minimum sentence of five years, plus or minus three for mitigating circumstances, and a ten-thousand-dollar fine. Rape that didn't involve a weapon or extreme physical force was a Class B felony carrying a ten-thousand-dollar fine and a ten-year sentence that could be doubled in the event of aggravating circumstances.

Judge Dirst prescribed the minimum sentence on the cocaine charge. He doubled the minimum term on the rape offense because of Mae Jean's testimony relating to the use of force, as corroborated by her father. He ordered that the twenty-five-year terms be served concurrently in Indiana State Prison, payment of the twenty thousand dollars in fines a condition of any parole consideration.

Huck Minter, nursing the repulsive grin he had worn throughout the trial, let out a whoop when Judge Dirst finished.

The judge hammered for order.

Mae Jean stood and began screaming. Huck turned, as if getting ready to slap her quiet, but Mae Jean slapped him instead, hard across his savage face, one cheek and then the other; then screamed again. She stepped into the center aisle and fell to the floor and her body erupted into spasms.

"Leave her alone, don't touch her, you lying son of a bitch," Nat heard himself yelling in a blind rage.

He moved in Mae Jean's direction but was easily overpowered by a bailiff, who wrapped both arms around him and dragged him off.

Struggling recklessly to free himself, he caught sight of Huck shaking his head; racing an index finger across his mottled neck to signal the verdict wasn't harsh enough.

Saw Dr. Heidemann jump from his seat in the rear of the courtroom. Rush forward and settle on one knee beside Mae Jean. Begin administering aid.

"Help her," he called to Heidemann. As anxious as he was for the doctor to take care of Mae Jean, he felt a surge of hatred for the man who had saved his life but now dared to touch her body.

Was the doctor pressing his lips to hers?

Why did it matter so much to him?

Nat stopped floating and fell to earth.

The stories the marshals fed him on the way back to the hospital from court played on all his fears. They all had the same hook: *You're white, you're rich, you're famous and, best of all, you're virgin chicken. You won't survive long in the joint.* In his mind, Nat sketched the music and lyrics for survival at Indiana State Prison. He'd show them, he'd show the world, that even prisons have their stars. Nat Axelrod was going to be one of them.

That night, he was startled awake by the sound of metal clanging against metal. He tried moving his hand, but couldn't, and remembered he was handcuffed to the bed. He had made the noise trying to turn over on his back.

Not the next noise, though—

—the squeak of the door being thrown open.

In the combination of light and shadows, he recognized Decade's local promotion kid, Laddie, who'd come to visit a few times. More than he could say for anyone else from the label.

Even before Laddie reached him, Nat saw his eyes were frantic with concern.

Laddie made a hard stop on one foot and held on to the end table to keep from falling and seemed relieved to find him awake.

"Dr. Heidemann said for me to get you up and ready to get out of here," he said, half out of breath. "He'll be here in a minute. He's calling the police. I already told the marshal outside there, the door."

Nat was groggy, feeling the effects of his sleeping pills and the bonus dose of something that was supposed to dismember his tension, but alert enough to understand the danger being explained by Laddie.

"I was hanging loose at the radio station with my jock friend, The Fake Jack Blake, you know?" Laddie said, stumbling over his words. "Helping Jack do 'Two for the Turntable,' when the call come in. Some drunk talking out of turn. Saying Judge Dirst's sentence never give Nat Axelrod what he deserved by half again. Saying he and some of his friends would make up the difference while there was still time to do something about it."

There was a furrow of sweat on Laddie's hairless upper lip and he radiated hyperkinetic panic that wouldn't quit. He kept pushing his hair off his face and fiddling with the noisy zipper of a Warner Bros. Records Windbreaker that had a supine Bugs Bunny chewing a carrot inside the stitched breast emblem patch. He bounced from foot to foot.

Nat said, "Do something here?"

Laddie threw up his hands. "When I heard the call, I just got scared and come on over. The doc said get you moved and then we'll worry about the rest of it." He stepped closer and reached out, as if he were planning to help him from the bed, when he saw the handcuff and stopped. Slapped his forehead. "Jesus! I was supposed to tell the marshal to unlock that damn thing." He made an unintelligible gesture with his hands and raced from the room.

An instant later, Nat heard an angry commotion outside in the corridor.

It ended as abruptly as it began.

There was a momentary silence before the door swung open and banged hard against the wall, swinging halfway back again before the marshal raised a hand to stop it. He came into the room squeezing his shoulder and moaning. Laddie followed, stumbling clumsily and clutching the left side of his face like it might fall off. Blood drained through his fingers. He was sobbing. His legs shook violently.

Both were being prodded forward with baseball bats poked harshly into the small of their backs by two men wearing latex costume masks, pullovers with Richard Nixon's face. Another Nixon followed behind them, brandishing a revolver.

The light snapped on.

Nat winced at the sudden brightness.

Turned for a better look.

Speculation sent his pulse soaring.

He felt the clutch of dryness in his throat and a vacuum sucking inside his stomach.

While the Nixons moved closer to his bed, the doorway filled with a fourth man in a knit ski mask, who rested a bat on his shoulder with one hand and used the other to grip the wrist of a young girl who was resisting him.

Mae Jean.

He yanked her inside and pushed her violently into a chair, pointing at her to stay there and grumbling almost incoherently in a voice Nat recognized immediately from court, from his hotel bedroom in the lifetime before that.

Huck Minter.

"Now we got us some unfinished business needs tending," Huck announced. "And I do mean you, you long-haired pile of vanilla shit." He moved the baseball bat from his shoulder and pointed it at Nat.

Nat looked from Huck to Mae Jean. She was sitting at rigid attention, gripping her hands in her lap, knuckles white, knees pressed hard against one another. Her eyes floated nervously, and her tongue traced the circle of her lips, alternating direction.

Huck called, "Ain't that right, Mae Jean?" She said nothing. Huck moved closer to her, dragging his bad leg behind him, and poked the baseball bat under her chin, making it go up so he had a better look at her face. "I ask you a question, Mae Jean?"

Nat saw her trying to speak, but she couldn't get a word out.

"I said I'm asking you a question, Mae Jean."

She nodded.

"That's my good girl."

Nat struggled to swallow and couldn't.

"You agree with what we're doing here is for your own damn good?"

"Yes," Mae Jean said, almost imperceptibly.

"Yes, what?"

"Yes, Papa," she whispered.

Huck Minter turned from her and pushed past the others in his hurry to reach Nat. As he leaned over the bed, he began to cough uncontrollably. Phlegm burst loose past the mouth of the ski mask.

Nat felt it land on his cheek.

That made Huck laugh. He reached down and rubbed the coarse spit into Nat's chin. Nat smelled the alcohol on his breath and leaking through his mask and his clothing. The look he saw in Huck's eyes was uglier than the rest of him.

Nat glanced at Mae Jean and saw her look married to his. Even at a distance of nine or ten feet he saw her eyes were filled with fear and surrender. Her face was bruised and there were small rips at both corners of her mouth. He felt a desperate need to say something to her, but his throat was too constricted.

Huck took a step back.

Removed the mask and gave Nat a wink.

Tested the bat for weight before swatting at the air.

Nodded approval at the men who had come with him, then looked straight at Nat again. His smile exposed the decayed state of his teeth.

"Nothing fancy now, Mister Nat the Axe. First, I am going to take this here bat and start hammering your brains to horse piss, unless you think you might be able to beg me out of it. You got some words to try with?"

Huck replaced the bat on his shoulder, grip in place, waiting for him to respond.

He cocked his head and Nat saw his bad eyelid start flapping. He'd first noticed it when Huck took the witness stand to recite his litany of lies.

Huck froze his false smile.

The three Nixons chortled among themselves.

The marshal and Laddie huddled together in shock.

"You might start with *please*?" Huck said *please* in a soprano voice, giving it a dozen extra syllables. A sneer that looked more natural on his face replaced the smile. "But I ain't promising it can do you no good anymore."

Hearing nothing from Nat, he made a gesture of helplessness and lifted the bat above his head with both hands, preparing to bring it down like an executioner's axe.

Nat closed his eyes, so he only heard the gunshot when it rang out.

His eyes bolted open as Huck moaned.

The bullet had hit Huck somewhere in his back.

He relaxed his grip on the bat and it fell behind him while he pitched forward and landed across the bed face down, trapping Nat's feet under the weight of his body.

Nat saw Dr. Heidemann bracing himself against the back wall, gripping an automatic in both hands. His position gave him a full view of the room. He called out, "You gentlemen are a little too early for Trick or Treat, are you not?"

The armed Nixon turned toward the doctor, bringing up his pistol. He was too late. Dr. Heidemann took aim and squeezed the trigger. His shot caught Nixon in the chest. The next shot tore through Nixon's throat. Nixon gripped the wound with both hands and fell backward. One of the other Nixons flung his bat at Dr. Heidemann. It struck the wall within inches of the doctor and bounced away harmlessly while the doctor took calm aim and put a bullet between the man's painted eyes. The last Nixon dropped his bat and threw his hands high. The doctor shook his head, fired with a determined precision, caught his target directly above the heart.

By Nat's quick calculation, less than fifteen seconds had passed.

The marshal and Laddie had been facing away from the door. Now, as the killing silence settled in, neither seemed capable of moving until Dr. Heidemann inquired if they were all right.

They turned to look at him.

"Thank God," the marshal said, and sank onto the edge of the bed, next to the motionless body of Huck Minter.

Laddie eased himself down to a sitting position on the floor, his arms gripping his knees, his head buried between his legs, and began crying.

Mae Jean moaned.

Dr. Heidemann seemed to become aware of her presence for the first time. He turned toward her with alarm, not yet ready to relax his grip on his weapon.

Mae Jean screamed, the same kind of screaming noises she had made in the courtroom, sirens of wild outrage. Her body pitched sideways onto the floor, banging into a chair as she fell. She quaked uncontrollably. Dr. Heidemann tossed his weapon aside and hurried to her. The gun hit the floor with a clang. He began administering aid calmly, methodically, his whole universe tied to the sadly contorting figure staring abstractly at the ceiling.

Nat experienced a sudden, sharp pain in his stomach, as instant as the despair he felt seeing the doctor's hands touching Mae Jean again. He closed his eyes. There was nothing else he could do—

Except wish they were his hands, one last touch, one last feel to take with him to a lifetime at Indiana State Prison.

* * * * *

Nine Years Later

* * * * *

Chapter 5

Laurent Connart didn't know about her problem with Bertha and Sam Mendelssohn, even suspect there was a problem, until the phone call this morning from Rabbi Cohen, telling her it was important they meet today at the Anne Frank Home, where she was underwriting a comfortable retirement for the Mendelssohns. They had known Mama in the camps and Papa almost as long as Mama, God rest their souls, and had treated her like their own daughter in all the years since.

There was no mistaking the urgency in the rabbi's voice or on his face after she arrived and was ushered into his modest office. He invited her to sit down and make herself comfortable. Parked a chair across from hers and took it for himself, his back ramrod straight, strong hands on his thighs.

"Your dear Bertha's Alzheimer's has reached a critical point and shortly will be beyond the medical capabilities of the Anne Frank Home," he said, speaking with a quiet dignity meant to take the sting out of his words. "It will become necessary to move her shortly to one of several available facilities. All are expensive, probably four times what the monthly bill runs here, where the rise in operating expenses is making it necessary for us to increase our own monthly fee by a minimum thirty percent."

He paused to study Laurent for some indication. She gave him one of her brave smiles and urged him not to be concerned.

"I suppose there are welfare agencies you might go to for assistance," Rabbi Cohen said, testing her, "but even such agencies have their limits."

"I thank you very much for your concern," she said, "but you just continue to look after them and leave the rest to me."

"Sam and Bertha are blessed to have someone like you in their lives, Miss Connart, but you already have fallen far, far behind in your obligation and this poses a problem for us, given the home's present financial condition."

Laurent shook her head. "What does that mean, *behind*?"

"Behind means behind, Miss Connart," he said, offsetting any hint of sarcasm with a gentle smile. "Our records, and you are certainly welcome to review them for yourself before you leave, reveal you are behind in your commitment in the amount of thirty thousand dollars."

"*Non.* Nonsense. That can't be."

"I don't mean to upset you, but it has become so."

"Thirty thousand dollars," she repeated, struggling not to get angry at the rabbi.

Rabbi Cohen nodded. "An oversight, maybe? I know what it can be, like that, how the mail piles up and bills get misplaced, and I understand your work as a journalist takes you away quite often, besides."

Laurent shook her head to let him know that wasn't the case. It was that damn Aaron, she thought, nothing she intended to share with the rabbi. Aaron. Damn him. How could he let this happen, knowing how much the Mendelssohns meant to her?

"I'm sure you understand how it will be necessary for you to bring your account current before we can consider keeping Mr. and Mrs. Mendelssohn here?"

"Otherwise, what? Throw them out on the streets?"

"Like always, Miss Connart, survival carries its own consequences." The rabbi shrugged and turned his palms to the ceiling. "Shall we go and look at the accounting before you go, how it all added up?" He rose and extended a hand toward the door.

Laurent understood his signal that their meeting was over and got to her feet. "That won't be necessary, Rabbi . . . How soon do you want the money?"

Rabbi Cohen assumed a thoughtful pose, arms across his chest, head tilted, squeezed eyes studying the ceiling. "Today would be nice," he said, a bit of sing-song punctuating his tone. He glanced at his desk calendar. "I suppose a week, ten days, if that's comfortable for you?"

"How much of it?"

"All of it."

She studied him for the joke. He shrugged and said quietly, "I don't make the rules, Miss Connart. Bad enough I got to be the one to tell people what our board of directors decides."

"You'll have it, all of it, the entire thirty thousand dollars, just keep taking care of them, you understand?"

"So, I'll see you in ten days," he said, giving her no sense of option.

"Tell me one more thing, Rabbi. Whatever happened to the concept of charity?"

"Reality, I think."

Laurent left his office dazed, wondering in what corner God was laughing at her and for what reasons this time, but was again in charge of her emotions by the time she had steered her BMW back to town.

She turned off Sunset onto Sunset Plaza Drive and into one of the open garages behind the four-story white stucco building that came with the apartment when she took possession three years ago. Her one-bedroom was on the top floor, a corner apartment with a lovely view in two directions, one of them south over the city to a bleak horizon of smog banks that often, in her rampant imagination, hid exquisite Technicolor paradises.

She charged into the apartment and pounced onto the phone,

kicking off her heels while dialing Aaron's private number. He answered on the first ring, and she immediately tore into him in two languages, overriding his pleas for her to shut up and listen until she was out of breath and had no choice.

"I know, I know, baby. Dammit. I know I shudda told you I was falling a little behind."

"A little behind? *Merde!* Thirty thousand dollars is not a little behind!"

"Okay, a lot then. But—Jesus!—don't think for a minute I did it on purpose. I would never do anything like that to you on purpose."

"When you want to fuck me, Aaron, you just fuck me, right?"

"Don't talk like that, baby. Please don't talk like that. I swear, I'll make it up to you."

"The only way you can make it up to me is to write a goddamned check for thirty thousand dollars and get it over immediately to your friend the rabbi."

"I can't do that, baby."

"Oh, I forget. God forbid the rabbi should know about us or your wife, she should see how you spend money on another woman. A cashier's check. A money order. Like other times. So, you tell me when I can meet you to pick it up."

"Not this time, baby. This time, I can't."

Laurent sucked in her breath and asked Aaron the question, although she didn't want to know the answer. "Tell me what that means, Aaron."

"Not that I don't want to or wouldn't if I could, baby. I can't, but I can't talk about it now. Later?"

"If now doesn't work, don't count on later, you prick, you bastard, you son of a bitch," she exploded, and slammed down the receiver.

★ ★ ★ ★ ★

Laurent sat staring at the phone for what seemed like hours, feeding herself one Camel after another. Beads of sweat rimmed her forehead and chills ran through her as, one after the other, she discarded possible solutions.

The tension became unbearable.

She pulled up her silk skirt, slid forward a bit on the straight backed chair, and spread her legs, then began to play with her clit. What better way to relax? It was a trick she had learned from the young whores of Nam when she was reporting from there and it never failed. It did not fail her now. Generous bolts of warmth attacked the chills and drove them off. She closed her eyes delightedly and wondered if she would have discovered the trick without ever having been in Nam, certain of the answer. She popped her fingers free and ran the hand around her face and past her nose while her eyes searched everywhere for thirty thousand dollars.

And the answer came to her:

The Tab.

Why hadn't she thought of the *Tab* before?

Of course!

All she needed was front page fodder, a story the *Tab* would find irresistible. When she was certain she had it invented, had practiced the lie to perfection, she squashed what remained of her Camel in a Tiffany crystal ashtray already overflowing with her daily ration of butts and lit another, inhaling until she felt the tar and nicotine tearing through the pit of her stomach. As the twin jets of smoke steam cleaned her nostrils, she picked up the phone and dialed Knobby Packwood's direct number at the *Tab*'s main office in Florida.

While the private line rang, Laurent visualized all three-hundred-plus pounds of Knobby defying physics while he balanced his tight ass on the high bar stool that functioned as his desk chair, stuck two or three sticks of Doublemint into his mouth, and adjusted the pilot's headset before clicking on, practicing one last time the lie she would tell him.

He answered with his name and Laurent promptly filled his ear with something sexy and sweet. Knobby always liked that.

"Frenchie," he responded cheerfully, as if they had spoken only days ago. In fact it had been almost six months. "How's the sunstroke out there in Lotus Land?"

They made small talk until she felt he was ripe for the pitch.

"I have something for you, *mon cher,*" she said.

"Didn't think you were calling because you're hot for my body, Frenchie. Then, again, you're usually the one's hot for anybody, as I recall."

"Fuck you, *mon cher,*" she said sweetly, not denying the suggestion, however much in jest Knobby may have meant it. It was her reputation, after all, and more than once it had helped her get a story and photographs after everyone else, the best of her fellow photojournalists, had failed—

Her reputation and what truth it contained.

"I got a big one, for sure, Frenchie, but it doesn't stretch three thousand miles," Knobby said, laughing hoarsely at his wit. "So, what's up? Besides my cock, I mean."

She told him the story she had invented.

Knobby thought about it, for what seemed to Laurent like an eternity. "How much you asking?"

"Sixty thousand."

"Jesus A. Bloody Fucking Christ. You think we're made of money here?"

"Of course, I do, *mon cher.* And, you are."

"Pictures, mate?"

"Of course, pictures," she said, aware she had him hooked by the way his gum chewing sounded, like lava overflowing the volcano.

"I'll go for fifty," Knobby said finally. "All rights."

"US only."

"US, and we split foreign, fifty-fifty down the middle."

"US only." If she made it too easy for him, Knobby would know she was scamming the *Tab* again.

He took his time thinking about it. "Okay, then. The rest of the world at fifty-fifty, but we let you hold on to the copyright."

"The rest of the world and I hold on to the copyright, but it's sixty thousand."

"You are one tough bitch, you know, Frenchie?"

"You're just too used to dealing with men."

"I guess it's your *cojones* fooled me for a minute."

"I need the sixty thousand tomorrow or the next day after, the latest, Knobby. You can FedEx a cashier's check."

"Out of the question."

"I have expenses on this one, Knobby. Payouts. This exclusive doesn't come cheap."

She listened to Knobby chew away, waiting out his counteroffer, expecting to hear him say thirty in front, the balance on delivery. That's what she was angling for. What she needed. Why she had asked for sixty. If she had asked him for the thirty she needed, Knobby would have capped the advance at half that, fifteen.

His chewing stopped abruptly. "No deal, Frenchie."

Her gasp escaped her mouth before she could clamp a hand over the mouthpiece. She recovered quickly, faked laughter. "Okay, I will pretend you are miserably cheap instead of a miserable bastard and make you a present for thirty."

"Here's the deal: No advance. Sixty on delivery."

"No good, Knobby. Thirty is bottom or you can kiss my sweet ass."

"Sure, Frenchie. Feel my lips?"

Laurent wanted to slam the receiver in his fat ear, but knew this was no time for ego.

If she needed the money for money's sake, for herself, some new whim—*merde!*—she would have told Knobby to swallow his dick.

"*Merde!* Knobby, *mon cher,* you know better than anyone that this is much too big an exclusive for me, for anyone, to do on spec, without an advance, for Christ's sake!"

"Anyone else, yeah, but I think this story sniffs like more of your piss, mate. Remember me saying the last lie I fell for was the last lie I'd fall for? It cost me dearly the last time. Jackie took the advance out of my paycheck."

Jackie was Jackie Searle, Knobby's boss. She had had a one-nighter with him years ago, while they were hunting wayward astronauts in Houston. Jackie looked like a goat and fucked like a pig, but he made her laugh, and that was better than another night of recreational fucking with a total stranger.

"When Jackie hears about this, *ça va chier dur, Monsieur* Packwood. The shit is going to hit the fan."

"*Ça me donne la chiasse,* Frenchie. Truly. You are scaring the shit out me. Pardon my yawn."

"Transfer me to Jackie, and we'll see."

"Uh-uh. Standing order from Jackie. He'll call you, not the other way 'round."

"Fifteen thousand, Knobby. Wire fifteen and you'll have it all, including foreign. I'll sign off." Her mind was working in a whirl. If she could pull fifteen from Knobby, she might be able to go down the street to the *Star* or the *Enquirer* and peddle the same lie for the other fifteen she needed.

Knobby said, "What would you say to the thirty thousand you wanted two minutes ago, mate?"

His question caught Laurent off-balance and silenced her. Her fingers twitched for a fresh Camel. *Certainment,* Knobby was pulling something here, but what?

He didn't make her ask. "Frenchie, you remember a rock and roller named Nat Axelrod?"

Remember him?

Of course, she remembered him.

The image that flashed into Laurent's mind was swift and fully rendered, as set as all her precious memories, although it had been years since she'd thought about Nat Axelrod or played his records. Other albums had been dumped as she moved around the world, but Nat's were part of the small collection she kept, the way other people save snapshots. Not since Nat Axelrod had anybody else but the Boss inspired her *a juter* like a soda fountain.

She remembered being unable to connive an assignment for Nat's infamous concert at Wembley in London, so she'd paid a black market fortune to engineer her way inside and, later, backstage. She found a good location, kept her cameras ready for hours and was the last of the paparazzi lurking when Nat finally darted from his dressing room inside a sea of bodyguards and headed for a limo about ten yards away with a young woman who should have been her trapped inside his hug.

She hurried forward, snapping shot after shot and calling Nat's name, so quickly she was able to break through the human barricade to within five feet of him, the strobe illuminating his surprise and, she believed then and to this day, Nat's appreciation for her determination.

"Leave the pretty little lady be!" he ordered the bodyguards after they'd pinned her arms and grabbed the Nikon.

He shunted his groupie aside and held his hand out for the camera, took a half dozen shots of her, had one of his bodyguards shoot the two of them together. "Now we're even," he said, and sent a boyish laugh into the night wind as he pushed his groupie into the backseat of the limo and ducked in after her.

None of this she told Knobby. She said, "He was sent to prison for raping a girl and for drugs, *oui*? I was not yet here in this country, but it was big news all over the world."

"That's the prick, yeah. You say the word, Nat Axelrod can be your ticket to the thirty thousand you're hankering after."

"Any word you want, *mon cher.*"

"Look at it this way, Frenchie, we're coming up on the tenth anniversary of the prick's conviction and everyone loves a celebration. Get me a story that will light a fire under all those Baby Boomers who once treated Nat Axelrod like King Shit royalty until Axelrod became the king of rock and rape. That should give us a nice little boost in newsstand sales, well worth the thirty, not to mention that me and Jackie Searle are hopeful our Laurent can wrangle a confession out of Nat during the face-to-face. After all, you're the best there is at wrangling, especially with that face of yours."

Laurent wasn't satisfied. There was something Knobby wasn't telling her, but it was clear he didn't intend to tell her. "Sixty thousand," she said.

Knobby stopped chewing his gum. After a moment, he wondered, "What's that about?"

"It's about a bonus for me, *mon cher.* I'll get you your tenth anniversary story for thirty thousand dollars, but it doubles to sixty thousand if I come back with Nat's confession."

Knobby laughed. "You have always been the prettiest, sexiest highwayman I ever come across." He laughed again, only it was more forced than before. "Done."

No blustering.

No negotiating.

No crying he had to check first with Jackie Searle.

She was certain now there was something Knobby was holding back on her.

Before she could challenge him, he deftly cut her off, asking,

"A five-thousand-dollar expense advance okay with you, Frenchie? I'll post it end of the day, so it's there tomorrow."

"Ten would be better."

"Ten it is, then."

Too easy, she thought.

Too, too easy.

What wasn't Knobby telling her?

The answer, maybe, waiting for her in Indianapolis?

Laurent spent a week on the Internet and downtown at the main branch of the library. By the time she flew to Indianapolis, she was confident she knew as much about Nat Axelrod as he knew about himself. More, maybe, figuring he had no opportunity to see a lot of the material that followed his descent into the hell of Indiana State Prison.

There were major magazines from every part of the world, the obligatory tell-all books, one ludicrous novel that showed more imagination than a Brothers Grimm fairy tale, the to-be-expected, sensationalized tabloid television segments, and three movies-of-the-week based on court transcripts and other documents of public record, two on the networks and the third on HBO.

With time, as the public moved on to fresher music scandals, Nat disappeared into the anonymity of the penal system. What chance for attention did an aging rocker behind prison bars on a mundane rape charge stand?

Not that "Nat the Axe" craved or solicited attention.

For all the coverage she came across, there was no indication that Nat had ever given a public interview or statement beyond his courtroom plea of not guilty.

That certainly could account for the *Tab*'s interest.

But what else?

Laurent was unable to shake her belief there was something

else that had Jackie Searle ready to shell out high-end dollars.

If it was there, she was confident she'd find it.

Somewhere.

From someone, if not Nat Axelrod himself.

Before leaving, she sent a cashier's check for half her advance to the Anne Frank Home as a show of good faith after Rabbi Cohen agreed to extend by a month her deadline for paying the entire thirty thousand dollars. On her Day Runner expense log she showed it as a payment to *confidential sources.*

As an offset, she flew coach instead of her usual first class, but her choice of the Airport Holiday Inn in Indianapolis had nothing to do with budget. Almost ten years ago, Nat had been sleeping soundly there when the police stormed in like terrorists. Laurent wanted to absorb as much as possible of the history she would be writing about.

She asked for the suite Nat had occupied, said she didn't care when the slope-shouldered clerk said it had been refurnished and redecorated at least twice since the rock-and-roll rapist was captured there. The clerk shrugged and, without losing his painted smile, talked about other Baby Boomers who occasionally dropped by with similar requests, usually slipping him a dollar or two for a fast glance at the room, and another dollar, maybe, for him to take a picture of them there, usually holding up the cover of one of Nat's albums.

Laurent told the fuzzy-cheeked bellman not to worry about her overnighter, the heat or more lights, tipped him a five, and double-locked the door behind him. Kicked off her shoes, stripped free of the casual outfit she had worn on the plane and headed for the first order of business, a luxuriant bath, to rinse away the sweat of the flight.

She didn't get as far as the bathroom. She became excited when she saw the bed Nat was sleeping in the day he was shot. Warmth almost as gratifying as a real orgasm exploded between her thighs. Impulsively, inspired by a vision of Nat at Wembley Stadium, she crawled between the covers. Felt his presence. Heard his infectious laughter. Felt her body burning. Pretended her fingers were his fingers and let Nat explore her body.

He was a gentle lover.

She told him so.

Called out his name and gave herself over to him completely.

Later, in the tub, still consumed by thoughts of Nat, she wondered what was behind the attraction. Except for one chance meeting, there was nothing about their lives to provoke this kind of response in her. Nothing she could point to with any authority and say, *This is why I feel as I do about this man!*

Nat Axelrod had not been a conscious thought before Knobby said his name.

Maybe she would know better tomorrow, when they came face to face at Indiana State Prison. Maybe she would see something in his eyes or hear something in his words, his manner of speech that told her she was being more than a mistress to memory.

And, what would she be to him?

Laurent dried off and studied herself in the full-length bathroom mirror.

Tres bien!

As usual, she liked what she saw.

Laurent stood almost five-three barefooted. While her shortness contributed to a cherubic quality men invariably found appealing in their fantasies, her full, perfectly proportioned body precluded confusing the little girl they might want with the woman she was. She might escape a second look, but never a third, being one of those French women who seem quite plain to the glance, but only to the glance. Over time, she had worked on an insouciant manner that took her innate, charismatic charm and transformed it into magnetic, indefinable good looks and—*be fair to yourself, girl*—an astonishing attractiveness.

Laurent kept her red hair tight-cropped, never hid her matching freckles under makeup. Her satin brown eyes were too wide and her nose, to some, too flat, as if it had been put on her round face by a cookie maker.

Her mouth was her best feature. Most often, she kept it locked in a mischievous grin that hid a slender gap between the front teeth and disguised the more serious ambitions of her mind. She usually accentuated her lips with a light coating of gloss in a color to complement her outfit of the day, succulent lips that more than one lover had compared to a bee drawing honey from a bottomless well.

She wondered what Nat might think.

Enough to confess to her the crimes that sent him to prison for twenty-five years?

The silly notion brought curls to the corners of her mouth. Of course not. Any more than she would confess to her schoolgirl crush. *Merde!* A grown woman, forty-two her next birthday, and she was carrying on like the moonstruck young thing she'd been more than a dozen years ago.

So, what would Nat think?

Would he remember her as clearly as she remembered him?

At all?

He did, later, in the fantasies that occupied her sleep. He remembered everything, and told her how he wished he'd pushed aside his little groupie of the moment and instead ushered her into the waiting limo. The fantasies became a nightmare as the groupie became, not Laurent, but Mae Jean Minter, the girl Nat was found guilty of raping in the backseat of a different limo in a different time and place.

Laurent woke up in a cold sweat, her naked body swimming on sheets so damp and warm she thought for a moment she might have peed in her sleep. It would not have been the first time, only before it had been brought on by different kinds of nightmares about the ugly world she left behind when she fled Europe after surviving the terrorist bombing that killed her precious Papa, at the West Bank café on Boulevard Saint Germain, where they were celebrating her twentieth birthday. She found pillows and blankets in the closet and finished the night on the couch in the sitting room.

When the phone rang in the morning, she was startled out of her sleepy haze by a man's voice apologizing for waking her at so early an hour.

"Barely seven o'clock, Miss Laurent, but—"

"Seven o'clock?"

She had left her wake-up call for ten. That would compensate for the time difference between Indianapolis and Los Angeles, leave plenty of time for the hundred-and-twenty-mile drive north to Indiana State Prison in Michigan City, which the *concierge* told her would take about three hours in her rented Toyota.

"Sorry about that, but I was afraid of waiting too long and missing you."

His voice had an annoying nasal quality.

"Who the hell is this?"

"Flotsan, Miss Connart. Jay Flotsan. I'm the deputy warden at Indiana State?"

"Mr. Flotsan, tell me what is so important that it couldn't wait until I arrive there for my three-o'clock appointment with Mr. Axelrod?"

"Just it, miss. Boss said to track you down and save you from making an unnecessary trip? Boss was anxious to get word to you your appointment's off."

"Impossible! I called before leaving Los Angeles to make this appointment."

"Well, that was then and this is now, Miss Connart. Don't

know what else I can tell you besides that."

"Listen, Mr. Flotsam, I—"

"Flotsan, miss. Name is Flotsan?"

"Whoever you are!" She realized she had shouted at him and took a moment to catch her breath. Getting angry would get her absolutely nowhere. She apologized and said, "I followed all your procedures in preparing for the visit, Mr. Flotsan. I have the identification and credentials I was told to bring, and—" A thought crossed her mind. "Mr. Flotsan, has something happened to Mr. Axelrod, is that why? Is Mr. Axelrod all right, or—?"

"I suppose he's fine, miss, only it's like this . . . Warden said to find you and tell you just that Nat don't want to see you or no one. Warden said to tell you, if you happen to drive on up here anyways, don't be expecting Nat to come forward."

"I'd like to speak to the warden. Please transfer me."

"Sure would like to oblige, only the boss, he's gone fishing. Left about forty minutes ago?"

"Fishing?"

"His passion, miss. We're on Lake Michigan, you know? Lotta swell places hereabouts where the fishin's mighty good, long as you never no mind all them pollutants."

"Mr. Flotsan, who else can I talk to?"

"You just did, miss."

Chapter 6

Laurent dressed for war and drove to the prison.

She expected her pursuit of an interview with Nat to be resisted again, but she could not take the first *no* for an answer.

Ever.

She was incapable of losing without putting up a battle.

Sometimes, she won.

Other times, not.

But it would be never if she didn't try.

Papa had taught her that while making her a photojournalist in his image.

He had instilled the philosophy in her like a Marine DI, and it had brought her some of her best stories, prize winners, especially when she was still young enough and zealous enough to traffic with warmongers and terrorists, earning the respect and envy of her peers, whose own bravery seemed rooted in betting on her chances of survival every time she headed for another hot spot.

Sex, of course, was her ultimate weapon, an extension of her reporter's arsenal:

Notebook, Nikon and nooky.

All three ever ready for action, as now, when she stepped up to the next available guest registration counter clerk and slid her request form through the opening in the thick glass safety screen. The clerk's smile froze in place when she saw the name of the prisoner Laurent was here to see. She directed her to a seat instead of asking for photo ID and processing the information into her computer, as was being done for the dozens of others here during visiting hours, mainly anxious, worn-down women and restless children.

Many of the women clutched heavy grocery bags that were given thorough inspection by the expressionless security guards before they were allowed to pass through metal detectors that looked more sophisticated than any Laurent had seen at airports in Israel, Frankfurt and Munich in the old days, in recent years at the Kennedy and LAX international terminals. She settled on one of the benches that lined the large but uninviting room and watched as the clerk whispered something into her phone, cupping the mouthpiece, as if she might be overheard, and trying not to be caught stealing sideways glances at Laurent.

Within minutes, Laurent was approached by a man in a cheap brown suit with out-of-date lapels, one of which carried a small gold badge in the button hole, a garish tie, and spit-shined black shoes, whose rubber soles squeaked news of his arrival on the worn linoleum. She guessed correctly it was Jay Flotsan, who introduced himself with a smile and one of those strong, manly handshakes meant to prove something.

He led her to a small, sparsely furnished, windowless room twelve or fifteen feet from the registration counter. Held the door open for her and waited until she was seated at the rectangular table before closing and locking it behind them. The room smelled from body odor, baby vomit and cigarette smoke residue that clung to the walls like a thick layer of yellow paint, despite a No Smoking sign precariously taped to the inside of the door.

Flotsan straddled his hand-me-down chair, offered her a Marlboro before popping one into his mouth. She took one of her Camels instead and leaned forward to take a light from his Zippo.

He studied Laurent and licked his lips, his eyes sweating over her low-slung braless tits under the scoop-necked silk blouse. That and a quiet tic told her what she needed to know about the assistant warden.

She crossed her legs and leaned provocatively, so her skirt hitched high above her knees, to give him a better look.

"We got a red flag on Nat Axelrod's name, is why Miss Kling come after me," the deputy warden said, volunteering the explanation too easily.

"Does Miss Kling have all the red flags memorized?"

"Meaning what, Miss Connart?"

"She barely had time to read my application before she was treating me like a virus and on the phone to you."

"Maybe she took one-a them speed-reading courses?" he said, pushing smoke out a corner of his mouth, and laughing big enough to show two rows of teeth stained almost as dark as his shoes.

Laurent smiled to be polite.

"Matter of fact, the boss figured you for one-a them cagey news types who might show up here anyways and try to bluff her way inside," Flotsan said, boasting as if it were a correct guess worthy of Nobel Prize consideration. "So I suppose that's—how would your people say it?—*touché?*" Only he pronounced it *tushy,* and so did Laurent in acknowledging him.

"*Oui, tushy.* One smart boss, your warden; I did think to bluff," she said, plotting her next move as she angled to give Flotsan a better show of flesh. She was certain he had caught sight of a nipple when his tongue flitted out of the corner of his mouth, almost dislodging the Marlboro.

"Maybe, since I have been found out, I can beg you a favor, *Monsieur* Flotsan?" she said, her voice baby-girl soft, narrowing the ridge between her eyebrows.

Flotsan cocked his head with anticipation.

She said, "It was such a long drive, so I would hate for it to be for nothing?" pouring on the accent. Men were suckers for a French accent, except for Frenchmen, of course, who like the Italians were suckers for a woman under all circumstances. She pretended to drop her cigarette. In bending over and reaching for it she made certain Flotsan couldn't miss her nipple and made a modest show of adjusting herself back into the blouse.

He was breathing noisily now and, Laurent was betting, close to being ready to shove his dick inside anything round and warm. *Sex is power,* she thought. That was one of the first things she had learned without any help from Papa. If she could wank her way inside the highest levels of the IRA, what chance did this wart-nosed cop have?

"I don't know, miss," he said, having trouble with the words. "This ain't Disney World, where tours are going all the time, you know? Boss is one of them only goes by the rules, you know? Something like this requires his permission, and he's off fishing, you know?"

"I know," she said, nodding to the truth of it. "*Tres bien.* So, maybe some other time."

"Yeah, better some other time."

"A time and place for everything."

"Everything." He squeaked the word and choked on his smoke.

"Although, it could have been so special, just you and me on this tour. A chance to learn more about the work you do and put it in my article I would write."

"About me?"

Laurent laughed heartily.

Men and their egos.

"*Monsieur* Flotsan—"

"Jay."

"Jay. I can hardly take your photos for the article, as you

show me here and there around the prison, and not mention your name, can I?" Flotsan's eyes darted left and right as he squashed the cigarette on a heel, pocketed the butt and immediately lit a fresh smoke. "I would even spell your name correctly," she said, and winked, confident she had Flotsan as hooked as any fish the warden might catch today.

It was time to reel him in.

"Unless, of course—Jay . . ." She said the name like a squirt of Chanel No. 5 and paused to be certain he noticed her sending him the kind of look even a blind man could not miss. "If you don't know enough to guide such a tour, maybe I should just go anyway," she said, dropping her voice a throaty notch.

Flotsan's mouth contorted. "I been up here a good twelve years longer'n anybody else, including the boss. Nobody comes close to knowing more about this place than yours truly."

Laurent nodded appreciatively.

Flotsan studied his cigarette and seemed to weigh her against the consequences. Finally, he gave her a longing look. Shook his head. "Rules is rules," he said.

Laurent buried her surprise under an expressionless stare, refusing to believe Flotsan was going to let her leave. Her mind scrambled for the next move as he mashed out his cigarette, rose and came around the table to help her up.

She accepted his hand and gave it a squeeze as she stood, then tripped over her own feet and fell against him, as if it were an accident. He caught her before she could slip to the floor. She clung to him like a life preserver, didn't resist as he locked his lips onto hers.

His kiss was sloppy wet and his breath smelled, but at least his dick was hard. She rubbed it and made it grow. The grunting noise he made broke the seal on the kiss. "It's been a long time since I have had a real man," she whispered at his ear.

"Door's locked," he said, struggling with the words.

She shook her head. "No. We shouldn't. I can't."

She pressed her hands against Flotsan's chest and pushed him away. He was about a head taller, but probably didn't weigh much more than she did, and almost fell stumbling backward to the wall. He used it for support and studied her like a hunting dog watches the bird in the tree.

Laurent straightened her blouse and her skirt. Made a show of catching her breath. All the time kept her eyes locked on him while he watched the hunger building on her face.

"*Merde!* How does one explain such things?" She touched her breast. "You are my kind of a man. There is something dark and exciting about you." She squeezed her eyes, as if trying to keep the demons out.

Flotsan cocked a bushy eyebrow that took up about half of his slanting forehead. "Think you should know I got strange tastes my wife ain't ever understood." He ran his tongue over his lips waiting for her to respond, probably reminding himself he was the sexiest man in the world. God's gift to women.

Merde!

Men and their egos.

She said, "Are you trying to frighten me, Jay? Maybe it is you who should be frightened of me?" Then she shook her head and scrambled her hands, as if shaking free of the devil. "I should go," she said. "We are talking fun, but foolishly."

She stooped for her tote bag and started for the door.

He called after her, "Before you get the grand tour?"

Laurent stopped and turned to face him, suppressing a smirk. "What about the warden. You said—?"

Flotsan threw a hand at the opposite wall. "Fuck the warden and fuck the white horse he rides in on!"

He was an artless lover, but she made all the noises and said all the words to make him believe otherwise and shouted his name and begged for more, finally for mercy, and, afterward, while he lay moaning *macho* boasts on the stained cot mattress, she showed her good faith by squeezing his balls and sucking him off while she made his limp little thing grow one last time and, so he would never forget her, used a trick she had learned from one of Arafat's lieutenants.

They were in a filthy room in a remote area behind the stage of the prison auditorium. The pitiful little pervert had brought her here about twenty minutes into the tour, after guiding her through the administrative area, an enormous kitchen large enough to prepare properly for a small army, a mess hall cafeteria out of all the gangster movies Laurent had ever seen, and a sad library overrun with old, well-thumbed westerns and mysteries, classics like *The Count of Monte Cristo, Les Miserables, Treasure Island* and *Robinson Crusoe,* comic books, picture books and magazines, and row upon row of worn, out-of-date law books.

The room, an oversized utility closet that Flotsan said had been converted into a dressing room for the occasional celebrity who came to play for the cons, was furnished in early filth. A sagging cot was pushed against one of the graffiti-covered, stone block walls. An empty milk crate functioned as an end table, near a stinking, seatless toilet and a porcelain sink, whose rusted pipes dripped orange tap water and had put a thick green crust on the basin.

She washed herself off carefully. The paper-towel rack was empty, and she had to tamp herself dry with what remained of a roll of toilet paper, aware that Flotsan was memorizing all her moves through the haze of his Marlboro, wearing the triumphant smirk he had adopted since first screaming at her to come when he came.

Laurent dipped into her tote bag for her makeup kit and the palm-sized .35-millimeter Canon she always hid inside a cigarette pack, the way cops kept a small spare tucked inside a boot or an ankle holster. When Flotsan's lids faltered shut for a few moments of recovery, she grabbed some candids.

She sat carefully on the edge of the cot and, taking his flaccid dick in hand, to show she truly cared, she asked about seeing some of the prisoner's areas, a cell block, maybe? "It will be so important to the story, *mon cher.*"

All along, Laurent had been hoping Flotsan would take her there, without her having to ask. It was her plan for locating Nat Axelrod and, at the least, long enough to pull from him one or two of the thirty-thousand-dollar quotes she needed. Hardly a great plan, not even a good one, but the best she'd been able to quickly conceive under the circumstances. And, she did need the damned quotes. They were a primary part of the package Knobby proposed.

Would the *Tab* write a check for the thirty thousand dollars without Nat's quotes? *Non.* A deal was a deal with Knobby and with Jackie Searle. They might negotiate the price down if her story, without quotes, had a revelation or two, but she needed the full thirty thousand in order to rescue the Mendelssohns.

Flotsan stared complacently at the ceiling. "What you was hoping for all along, ain't that right, Laurent?" He pronounced her name as if she were Humphrey Bogart's widow.

So, he was smarter than she had thought. "Okay, *oui,* Jay. You have found me out," she said, smiling as if it were no big deal and lighting up. She left him and moved across the room, leaning against the wall with her arms crossed in front of her.

Flotsan said, "You was figuring you could screw your way into seeing Axelrod, and I was gonna be dumb enough to fall for it."

"Oui," she said, playing the word for pity at her stupidity, feeding Flotsan's ego while she stumbled after another idea that might get her to Nat. "But I swear not the screwing part, Jay.

Not that part. Fool you, *oui,* but there was something I saw in you—"

He wheeled around on the cot and into a sitting position. "Stow it where the sun don't shine," he said. "Been long enough since I pulled my plug outta there, so there's plenty room."

Laurent sighed with the weight of what she had to do now, offer Flotsan a bribe for his help. She saw no alternative. She clenched her jaw at the thought of parting with the thousand or two it always took to rope in bastards like this one.

"I could make it worth your while, Jay."

"You mean money, honey?" He pushed himself off the cot and wandered over to the sink, but only to water down his hair, and began dressing. "Forget about it, Laurent. That's a criminal offense, you know? Neither of us wants to risk winding up behind bars, like the shits I gotta look after here, day in, day out."

"What then, Jay? What can I do to convince you to take me to see Nat Axelrod?"

Flotsan pretended to think about it for a minute or two before he looked her squarely in the face and showed his black teeth. "Tell me where he is, is all, and I'll oblige you best I can," he said, bursting out with laughter that bounced off the walls.

Laurent stared at him hard.

"He's not here, girl."

Harder.

He shrugged.

Stared at him with total disbelief.

Flotsan raised his right arm like he was preparing to take an oath. "Swear. Last time I see'd him, Nat Axelrod was on his way out of here in a plain pine wood coffin."

Voice mail from Knobby was waiting for Laurent at the Hyatt when she returned from Indiana State Prison, telling her he wanted an update, as well as some indication she was earning her keep on a story the *Tab* had invested five thousand dollars in. *Non,* Laurent decided. It had to be something more than that, something else Knobby might hope to hear from her.

Why else would he have left his unlisted home number and said call him as soon as she got the message, no matter what the time? Knobby prided himself on being *a twenty-five hours a day, eight days a week* newspaperman, but he had never done this for any of the other stories she had worked for the *Tab,* including dozens bigger than the Nat Axelrod story.

His message convinced her Knobby had withheld something when he tossed the hungry bitch a bone. Thirty thousand was too much to pay out for what Knobby called an anniversary story, yet he was ready to double the thirty thousand to sixty thousand if she managed to wring a confession from Nat.

Why?

Was this a cheap prank engineered by Jackie Searle, getting even with her for her past shenanigans, personal and professional, knowing there was no way possible for her to interview Nat Axelrod, much less get him to confess he raped Mae Jean Minter? Knowing what Flotsan proved to her by pulling up Nat's archived file on the prison computer? Knowing Nat was dead, murdered during a prison riot? Cremated. His ashes scattered to the four winds at Graceland, in keeping with a request he was barely able to make while being wheeled into the prison hospital surgery room, where doctors unsuccessfully fought for hours to save his life.

If so, how did Knobby and Jackie Searle come to know this?

None of her research turned up stories about the riot or about Nat's death, not even an obituary in her CompuServe scans. Had her usual thoroughness eluded her this time, or was it because she had focused on the tenth-anniversary angle, in order to intelligently approach the people who played roles in

Nat's arrest and trial and the attack on his life that followed in its wake, who could help her flesh out details she might not be able to pull from Nat himself?

Certainment, this was the case, and—

She laughed at herself.

Ego, she thought.

Where was it written that only men were entitled to ego?

And, as for *Monsieur* Knobby Packwood—

Two could play the game.

She had no doubt she was better at it than he could ever be. She stripped naked, dropping garments recklessly while padding to the bedroom, stretched out lazily on the bed after propping up the pillows to give her a better look at the TV, snapped on CNN, muted the sound, and tapped out Knobby's private number.

He answered with a gruff *Yeah* on the first ring, as if he had been parked on the phone waiting for her call and sounding like he'd had several too many, but snapped to sobriety when he heard her voice. "Hey, mate, how's it going out Indy way?"

"First day, first problems, Knobby."

A momentary silence. "How's that?"

"I could not get inside the prison to see our anniversary boy," she said, enjoying the lie in her truth.

"What's that piss all about?" Knobby said, sounding like he already knew the answer.

"Shot down by the warden. Insisted Nat won't see visitors. Not anybody. I argued my damnedest, but hit the stone wall."

"Place is full of 'em, I expect," he said, washing down his chortle with a giant swallow of something, probably a Foster's, which Knobby routinely drank by the bucketful.

"Even tried the backdoor approach, but that didn't work," she said, choking on a laugh she didn't want him to hear.

"So, you calling it quits?"

Laurent thought she detected a real concern in his tone, not the sound of someone ready to reveal the practical joke and lord it over her. "You know better, Knobby. This is the start, not the finish. It won't be over until you have your story and I have all my money. The whole sixty thousand dollars."

"Knew we had the right girl for the chase in you," he said after another swallow, clearly relieved. "Told that to Jackie first we considered you for the story."

"I called you, remember, Knobby?"

"Fate, Frenchie. Don't mind telling you now that you're into it, we had you in mind for the bloody Nat Axelrod piece all along. Another day or so and I would have been tracking after you."

In fact, it was not the kind of story the *Tab* ever called her about. It was an easy ride that even a beginner journalist fresh out of college could handle, maybe not as well, but *certainment* for less money.

Knobby said, "So, where do we go from here?"

"Where do you think we go?" she said, testing to see how much he knew. When he didn't answer, she volunteered, "In the morning, a call to Nat's old lawyer would make sense—"

"Dead," Knobby interrupted, too quickly. "Benjamin Harrison Hubbard. Bought the ranch years ago, like—" He stopped abruptly.

"Like who, Knobby?"

Was he about to say, *Like Nat Axelrod*?

"Like all lawyers should, sooner, not later," Knobby said, recovering quickly. If he knew Nat was dead, he was keeping it a secret. "Didn't the in-depth research you're always boasting about show you as much, Frenchie?"

"Oui," she agreed. "If you had not interrupted me, I was going on to say it made sense, except that *Monsieur* Benjamin Harrison Hubbard had the misfortune to die of cancer too soon

to be of value to us, which is why I am thinking about Phillip Penguin."

"The assistant district attorney who tried the case against Axelrod."

"Yes. He's the district attorney now."

Knobby made an *It's news to me* noise she didn't believe and said, "Penguin might be persuaded to help get you in to see Axelrod, that you're thinking?"

"Yes," she lied. "This Penguin is one of the few from the cast of characters still around here. The old district attorney, Malcolm Benedictus, is the governor and already campaigning for a Senate seat that won't be vacant for another two years. The judge who tried the case—"

"Clyde Staton Dirst."

"You have a good memory, Knobby, for nine, almost ten years ago."

"Funny name, Dirst, easy to remember," he said, not missing a beat this time; his guard up. "Come across sorting out pictures for the spread. Funny-looking geezer. Fire in his eyes. Not one I'd want deciding my fate on so much as a parking violation."

"Sits on the state court and is supposedly a first choice for the US Supreme Court when and if the other party comes into power."

"Appears like everyone's done well since Axelrod played hide the sausage with the girl. Any sight of her or the doctor she upped and married soon after the trial?"

"Wolf Heidemann. Not yet."

"Girl's father, he still around, I suppose? Huck Minter's not one likely to make governor or the Supreme Court, that one, unless it's on a skid row somewhere."

"For Jesus Christ sakes, Knobby, I'm here only one day!"

"Okay, okay, mate! But Jackie needs to be informed, well as me, so keep in touch. We got deadlines staring at us."

"I've never missed a deadline, Knobby."

"No time to start now, eh, Frenchie, not with sixty thousand dollars waiting here for you?" He sounded like a football coach in the locker room at halftime, trailing by a goal and trying to inspire his team.

Laurent hung up and headed for the bathroom thinking maybe she had been mistaken about the *Tab* underwriting a practical joke at her expense, but still convinced something was going on that Knobby wasn't sharing with her.

She filled the tub, climbed in and, scrubbing herself hard to remove Jay Flotsan from everywhere but her mind, she worked on resolving other puzzles that the day had brought:

When he called her this morning, why didn't Flotsan just tell her Nat was dead and be done with it?

Later, why the sham about Nat not wanting to see visitors?

Why the look from the visitation clerk, when she learned who Laurent had come to visit, and Flotsan's explanation about a red flag on Nat's name?

A red flag?

Since Nat was years dead, why was he even on the clerk's computer to find?

She could think of logical answers to that one, except she remembered how Flotsan had made such a show of having a secretary dig deep into archived computer records to retrieve Nat's file.

So, was the red flag really for her?

Or for *anyone* who came asking about Nat Axelrod?

The questions continued hounding her long after she crawled into bed, until at last she was able to slide into the quiet mist beyond the flickering TV and the fading sound of the CNN newsreaders, convinced she was not yet through with Jay Flotsan or Indiana State Prison.

Chapter 7

The same day in Los Angeles, Nathan Greene was awakened by a banging in his mind that refused to quit. Ana Maria was gone. He was alone in bed. The rhythms changed, the beat got louder. The pillow over his head was useless. He realized the noise he heard was somebody banging on the front door. He wheeled onto the floor and headed over.

The lock was still busted. Pete, the young Mexican kid from the Nam, was standing just inside, working the door like he was *salsa*'s answer to Buddy Rich. Pete was maybe fifteen, short for his age and sway-backed, with a bad scar falling down one cheek to his neck.

He was anxious to tell Nathan that the Tune King had sent him to say Pogo, the regular engineer, had clocked out with the flu again, and it would be okay for Nathan and Jimmy Slyde to work off more credit against their bills. Slyde was already setting the board for some girl who had come in with cash.

Nathan hurried through the aerobics that kept his hips lean and his butt tight but were doing absolutely nothing for the little hill forming between his blades and jumped into a cold shower. Ana Maria had left a clean T-shirt and freshly ironed denims for him before heading to work. He went after his master cassette among the work tapes and papers he kept in the bottom dresser drawer and took off.

The Nam was within walking distance, about a half mile west of Paramount Studios on Melrose. He made the trip quickly, his eyes working the territory and his mind ready for any kind of problem. Even in high-noon daylight, this was a neighborhood of deceptive appearance and sudden gunfire.

The recording studio stood out between an antique store and a television repair shop, as wide as both of them together. The Tune King once told him how it had been part of the Decca Records operation in the old days, and it may have been. Windows had been covered over with stucco years ago. More recently the entire front wall was spray painted by a local artisan who specialized in colorful stick figures and signed his work *El Frito Bandito.* The mural obscured the studio's name on the wall, but the Tune King liked it and kept it because he figured anyone who had to know already knew this was the Nam and a recording studio.

The iron security gate clicked open once Nathan identified himself at the wall intercom. He walked the angles of the musty corridor heading for the control booth, past walls filled with rows of faded photos of forgotten acts, frames askew from occasional dusting, many inscribed to the Tune King, thanking him and urging everyone to look for them soon on top of the *Billboard* charts.

The Tune King was sitting at the board with Slyde, trying as usual to figure out the first-generation computer board that had replaced the old four-track, but ignoring the secondhand synthesizer that fell off the back of a truck after he saw the problems Nathan had handling the sixteen-track. Years ago, somebody had good-naturedly pinned the name "Tune King" on him, because he was absolutely tone deaf, and it stuck.

Nobody remembered his real name and the Tune King was long past telling. He looked like a retired postman, exactly what he was. He had cashed in all his bonds and securities and taken a small mortgage on his house, using the proceeds to purchase the studio as a welcome-home gift for his nineteen-year-old son, a Marine serving in Vietnam. So far as anybody knew to this day, his son was still serving there.

When the boy turned up missing in action, the Tune King took an early retirement and began operating the studio himself, against the day his son would return to pick up his dreams where the war had put them on pause. He named it the Rose, after his wife, and changed it to the Nam when she died, explaining to Nathan once, when he needed to talk and there was nobody else around to listen: "We spoke about it and she told me to. Said it was always better to honor the living than it was to just remember the dead."

Slyde was leaving his mid-thirties, richly tanned and plain looking. He wore clothes out of the *LA Weekly* and a full head of hair styled to his shoulders. He was sucking deeply on a joint he knew to make disappear when Nathan arrived. The kid, Pete, was over in a corner, studiously quiet in a decrepit folding chair he had tilted back against a wall of peeling brown grass mat.

Through the thick glass separating the booth from the narrow studio a young girl, street pretty, maybe twenty, dressed in everything tight, sat under the boom mike, her eyes closed and her lips moving. She still wore her headphones, although she could not possibly be getting sound from them yet. Her body danced in the chair.

The Tune King threw up his hands in one of those gestures that meant *finally* as Nathan entered the booth. He said, "Slyde, put on the playbacks for Nathan, please. Nathan will want to hear he is working today with the next Celine Dion." The Tune King aimed his eyebrows at the ceiling and searched for low-flying aircraft.

It was a little past eight o'clock when Nathan headed home.

He hurried along, his hands in his pockets, in and out of shadows thrown by oaks and Chinese elms and the old movie studio building that was there before acres of surrounding fruit and vegetable orchards were plowed under and became rows of flat-roofed California stuccoes with neat lawns and two-story apartment houses that anyone passing in daylight would see had two things in common, a depressing antiquity and clusters of unemployed men forever engaged in foreign dialogue on the front stoops and lawns.

He kept his focus straight ahead, his body language telling anyone watching that he knew where he was going. He heard a noise and then dogs barking somewhere inside the apartments. He tried not to show concern, but knew the streets were too dark and he was too light-skinned to assume that none of their Latino neighbors might emerge from some hidden corner to barter his loose change or his life against some switchblade or Saturday Night Special. Or, in these days of community warfare, a spanking new Uzi or AK-47.

He reminded himself as he savaged those thoughts that he was not a bigot. He had been around too long and seen too much for simple bigotry. He was a realist. Were he now walking the empty streets of South Central Los Angeles, he would be playing nervous mind games about the blacks.

Besides, who knew who the bad guys really were?

They came in names, not colors.

Some of those names were in his own arsenal of friends.

He kept a steady pace. The dogs kept barking, a serenade of yelps that stretched the length of the block and began to rise ahead of him. He shut his ears to everything except the sound of the new song he was writing. He and Slyde had spent three hours on it after the next Celine Dion impulsively kissed him on the lips and left with her master reel and two sides of ambition, a voice and a dream out of synch with reality.

He let his melody and lyrics boil in his mind while he kept moving, increasing his speed when he spotted two men across the street step out of a doorway and pause to discuss, maybe, if he looked worth the opportunity. Trouble was never his middle name.

Nathan worked the lyrics around in his mouth, like pieces in a puzzle. In his heart, in his mind, in his ears, he knew what he heard now was better than anything he had heard on the radio in months, except on the Golden Oldies stations.

What he had become himself.

A Golden Oldie.

Worse.

Stepping into the apartment, Nathan whistled a curious melody, low, on pitch, and then he whistled it again, signaling Ana Maria he was not an intruder on the prowl for drug money or worse. Ana Maria had had both before. He saw her outline shadowed by the flickering television screen. The movie dialogue floated toward him. He thought he recognized Gary Cooper.

She stirred in the Salvation Army armchair that was getting more and more unstitched with each use. She sat up and turned to look at him. Her smile was the first thing he saw after switching on the light. She blinked the last of the sleep from her eyes and stretched, checked to be certain he was following the spring of her small breasts as they rose to challenge his senses and pressed for release against the tiny bra that barely hid them.

He said, "That's the flick where Gary Cooper kills Burt Lancaster, remember?"

Her panties were as skimpy as the bra and her hips moved with natural lubrication as she untangled herself from the chair and came to him, catching her arms around his body and locking him inside a tight grip, then rising on her toes to bring her lips to his. He watched motionless and didn't help when she tried to work her tongue into his mouth. She released him and stepped back, her forehead creasing and a frown developing, wondering what was wrong this time.

"You been . . . ?" she said, letting the question drop. There was trepidation in her voice. She hugged her arms underneath her breasts and waited for him to say something.

He studied her for a few moments, then said grimly, feigning indignation, "Wouldn't you think just once, once, they'd let Burt Lancaster win that damn shoot-out with the Coop."

Ana Maria's face filled with sullen irritation. She hated to be teased, especially when she was asking a question.

Nathan no longer could prevent the grin from cracking his stern facade. He pulled the small wad of bills from a pocket as if drawing a revolver and aimed it at her. He said, "Bang!" Then opened his fist and let the money drop to the floor.

"Que' cono!" Her mouth went slack with surprise and her eyes darted between him and the bills, some of which had come loose and hung like giant green snowflakes on his shoes. She saw a five among the singles and, no longer able to contain herself, let out a squeal, dropped to her knees and crawled close enough to pull the money to her with both hands. She counted out loud, slapping one bill on top of the other as she created a neat pile on the carpet, exalting with each number after twenty.

Nathan took silent enjoyment from her pleasure.

Ana Maria's expression abruptly turned to concern again. Her eyes shifted and her back arched. She grabbed the pile of money in her fist and shook it at him, angrily accusing, "You went out and stole another car stereo?" He grinned at her and winked. She was not amused. She jumped to her feet and stepped up to him, barely an inch separating them, her lower lip jutting, her voice and her irritation mounting with every word she growled. "You promised me no more with the stealing, no matter what. No more Blaupunkts!"

She threw back a fist, as if ready to pound his chest. He caught her by the wrist and held her like that long enough to read the genuine concern raging in her large, coffee brown eyes.

"I worked today, the Tune King," he said.

She studied him hard, trying to cleanse her doubts. When he saw traces of acceptance and little pinches of tension erasing from the corners of her eyes, replaced by glimmers of belief, he relaxed his grip. She moved a step away, her stare rigidly in place. She took a defiant stand, her arms once more folded under her breasts, waiting for his explanation.

"Damn, you're a good woman."

"No baseball bats and broken windows with *El Diablo,* Carlos? Enriqué the shit? Morales and the other bums?" The accent, otherwise invisible, crept into her voice as it always did when she was angry.

Nathan shook his head. Watched her eyes trying to find the lie in his and shook his head again. "No radios. No reason for me to break my promise to you." He smiled.

Her head bobbed approvingly, resolutely. She took his right hand in hers and brought it to her mouth, kissing the stub of the joint where his index finger ended abruptly. She let the tip of her tongue linger and lick on the scar, turned and dragged him into the bedroom, began wrestling with his jacket and undoing the buttons of his shirt.

"Should I be Burt Lancaster or Gary Cooper?" he said.

She said, "Gary Cooper, and I'm going to kill you anyway," then she reached for his belt as she bit deep into his shoulder, deeper than simple playfulness. She stuck her tongue in his ear and whispered, "Please, try and like it this time. Try to do it, please. Please, Nathan? *Por favor? Por favor, mi querido?*"

Nathan didn't try, knowing it would make no difference if he did.

Later, in the yellow glow of the bed lamp on the night table, he studied Ana Maria while she slept effortlessly by his side, her breathing unlabored in contentment.

He sat up and stared across the room, going deeper into his

thoughts, dragging heavily on the Lucky, wishing he could learn to stop smoking the way he'd quit everything else a long time ago, reminding himself all over again, convincing himself one more time, how fortunate he was to have stumbled into her—could it be?—more than a year ago.

Stumbled?

It had been a calculated walk into possible disaster, then a few shared moments of terror still frozen in both their minds as a souvenir of the fate that put them together.

In the minutes before she stepped into the parking lot of the 7-Eleven, he had been asleep on the bus bench. Teenagers in a Cad amused themselves at the red stoplight by honking him awake. Ignoring their taunts, he wandered over to the Dumpster and rummaged for leftovers. He was closing in on a half-consumed ham salad sandwich on whole wheat bread when a sweeping glance took in her, first, then the man in the shadows against the wall. There was no moon and the night was like ink. Except for them, the lot was empty.

She emerged from the 7-Eleven carrying a fat bag of groceries. The man headed for her, bouncing up and down on the balls of his feet, one hand hidden inside his Windbreaker. At once, Nathan recognized what he was feeling as the breeze of familiar danger. She turned and saw the man about the same time and looked around, as if getting ready to run, but the man was already on top of her.

The man pulled his hand out of the Windbreaker and exposed what Nathan guessed to be a snub-nosed .22 automatic. He pressed the weapon into the woman's waist, just underneath the grocery bag, then maneuvered it onto her stomach. He lowered it and began playing a poking, probing game against her cotton dress, rubbing the gun against her twat. Nathan heard her make a small cry of embarrassment. Her legs began shimmering in the reflected light of the 7-Eleven. Ribbons of pee trailed down to her shoe. That's what decided him to help.

Until then, he was holding fast to one of the first lessons he learned in the joint: treat the problems of others strictly as the problems of others. It kept life easier and longer and left plenty of room for his own problems, but he knew what it was to pee like that. To be so frightened that the bladder opens up like a rain cloud. Back in prison, Chalky Ruggles had seen to that.

He moved in a way that didn't draw attention, quietly and quickly, and stopped about ten or twelve feet away, bending over as if prospecting for stray butts. He looked up and caught her eye. Her mouth opened, as if she wanted to say something. He shook his head, looked down and, still on his haunches, still pretending to search for butts, did a little shuffle forward.

When he looked up again a few seconds later, her eyes were shut, and he knew the woman had to be waiting out the sound of a gun exploding. He guessed there was more than her in her panties by now. He saw he had guessed right about the weapon. It was a .22.

Her eyes flickered open. Again, she seemed anxious to say something. The man sensed something was happening. He gripped her arm, at the same time glanced backward to discover Nathan.

He turned and moved beside her and aimed the automatic at Nathan, who by now had risen and stood with his feet a few inches apart, his body angled slightly forward so that his balled fists swung awkwardly in front of him, like erratic pendulums.

"Go away, old man. I don't want to blow your insides out," the man called at him. He dug his nails into the woman's skin and brought up the .22 so that it aimed squarely at Nathan. He ran his tongue nervously over a trim little mustache.

Nathan was close enough to see the burned-out edge of the junkie in the man's gaze. He decided to gamble and shook his head, knowing any maneuver was chancy and could work against him as easily as it could work for him. Just then the woman let go of the grocery bag. It fell with a noise that startled the man. His finger jerked on the trigger. Nothing happened. The automatic had jammed. He pulled the trigger again, as if examining a mistake. The woman rammed an elbow into his side. Still no explosion.

Nathan leaped forward and wrestled the man to the ground. The .22 went flying. The woman circled while they struggled and, finding a clear target, kicked the man in the head. The man's body jerked and he quit struggling. He was unconscious. Nathan worked an arm off his chest and freed himself from the tangle of limbs. She kicked the man another time in the head.

Nathan stood up and surveyed the moment. The struggle had attracted attention. He saw the store's manager staring anxiously through the plate-glass window while a clerk behind the checkout counter hollered something into the telephone.

The woman found the .22 where it had landed on the asphalt, almost hidden in the tire shadow of a Ford van. She knelt by the man and pressed its mouth under his chin, then looked up at Nathan as if appealing for permission.

She called to him, "The prick would have killed you, too."

"He didn't," Nathan said, quietly, almost appreciatively.

"I'll blow his brains out for both of us."

"I take care of myself," he said.

He turned and started walking away in a hurry, heading for the side street.

He didn't need more police in his life.

Glancing back, he saw she had left the man and her broken bag of groceries and was charging after him.

She insisted on taking him home, to feed him and let him enjoy a hot bath; to say thank you. Something told him to let her. It was the right thing at the time. She was offering an act of gratitude to repay an act of courage. And he was starving. And he was filthy. And, maybe, she wouldn't mind his sacking out for a few hours of real sleep.

The smells of Mexican cooking filled his mouth with saliva as he followed her into the apartment, a comfortable place kept spotlessly clean. The living room had a high ceiling and was full of well-kept budget furniture, with evidence of her religion and family on the walls and surfaces. Through the archway, he saw a smaller dining room off the entrance to the kitchen. A doorway connected to a narrow hallway onto the one bedroom and a toilet full of powdered soaps and sweet scents.

He knew he would stay if she asked, as she did because she was a compassionate person, but—

All this time later, he still wasn't sure why he stayed.

Nothing was holding him here.

Ana Maria was not even his type.

His type got him into trouble.

Ana Maria's body arched, disturbed by some small spasm. He moved his hand over and pressed it softly on her cheek. Her body went still again and a small smile crept onto her face as one of her hands found his and took hold. Through it all she remained asleep.

He inhaled deeply, continued to ponder a relationship he'd neither sought nor encouraged. Ana Maria had taken him in and given him the kind of love he'd forgotten existed anywhere but in lyrics. Her goodness restored two traits he thought he had lost forever, kindness and affection, but not as much as she lavished on him and not enough to set church bells clanging. There were times she made him wish dearly he could add love to the bargain, but they passed quickly.

Maybe someday?

No. Not now. Not someday.

Someday he would be gone.

He would leave Ana Maria when his work at the Nam was completed, and, maybe, he would even remember to tell her goodbye. *Thank you, and goodbye, Ana Maria.* He had tried explaining that to her, more than once, but Ana Maria did not want to listen and nothing he said would make her believe, so he'd stopped.

It was bad enough climbing into bed and acting while she pressed hard to teach him the difference between sex and love. Even if she succeeded, he didn't know if it ever again would matter to him. Ana Maria was too good for him, a dear creature who deserved better, who was still crawling out from under the rock of a life that would have killed someone weaker. She had shared her stories with him after she came to believe she could trust him enough to know.

Know about her upbringing in a second-generation Boyle Heights Mexican family, with parents who operated a small grocery store on Brooklyn Avenue; two older brothers, Jesus and Angel, gang members, street *machos* forever in trouble with the law; a younger brother, Juan Pablo, slow, the neighborhood good-luck charm. Know how her parents were shot and killed during a daylight robbery, murders quickly revenged by her brothers and their band of homies.

Know about the rape at knifepoint that left her pregnant, the baby boy she gave birth to at County General and never saw, having already signed the adoption consent forms; the baby boy she named Eduardo in her mind, after her father. Know about another child and an abortion that left her insides too rotten to remain there.

Know about a succession of lovers, her conversion to alcohol and an enchantment with drugs that led her to put her body on a paying basis. How she began to hate the touch of a man and experimented for a while with women. Know how stealing landed her in prison, where the beatings and other abuses and indignities from the guards was often worse than she remembered getting from some of her tricks on the outside.

Know how she finally chose to hate all men. Hate them the same way she hated her life and the fortress of loneliness she had built for herself. Even hated the priests, some of them too obvious and disgusting in their own pious lust after her, the one exception Father O'Bryan, her boss at the Church of the Blessed Bonaventure.

It was a while before Nathan came to know why she swore Father O'Bryan was the only one who made a difference in her life before him, before Nathan Greene, the stranger who saved her life and somehow was meant by God to become her life.

She cried and carried on and proclaimed more than once: "I would die for you, *querido.*"

"It's something I want to do for myself, Ana Maria."

"Not if I have the choice."

"We'll see," Nathan said to end the conversation, knowing he would leave her one day, before there was any choice to be made.

What he wanted her to know, he told her.

He made sure she learned early not to ask him questions.

He let her witness how questions turned him into a different person from another world, not a pretty place for anyone. She told him she wanted it to be beautiful wherever she went with him, only beautiful, like the scrapbook of her prayers. "Oh, dear, dear Ana Maria," he sometimes thought, "give me someone else to hurt, someone like—"

Meanwhile some of the songs he wrote were for her and about her.

Beautiful songs.

Beautiful music.

Sometimes, when he came home after a day at the Nam, he would tease her affectionately before playing the new tapes for her on a cheap deck the Tune King insisted he take home after he began cranking out the music at the Tune King's place. He would watch Ana Maria listen and weep for joy over the music. That gave him a pleasure better than any of the sex she offered him out of her own needs.

Nathan's thoughts shifted to the newest melody rolling in his head. It seemed louder and stronger than ever, still had the haunting quality present when the melody came to him like a gift. He longed for morning and another session at the Nam. He thought about words again, patiently fitting them to the lyric line like a carpenter with a mouthful of nails, and drew contentment from the knowledge he was building another chariot to the stars.

Ana Maria's body shuddered again under the thin cotton sheet and her hands clamped tighter onto his. He heard the sliver-thin moans passing quietly from her. They were now more familiar than frightening to him. He leaned over to croon the secret fears from her sleep.

Tired, but still unable to sleep, his lyrics blurred out of focus by the hour, he rolled from the bed and moved quietly to the bathroom. He lowered the toilet lid and sat down to study his hands.

The diagonal crack to the knuckles of both hands, broken; smashed flat more than once.

Missing: the middle finger of his left hand, not even a nub to mark where it had been.

On his right hand: the index finger gone down to the second joint, pinky missing the top joint, thumb curved permanently into the palm.

He allowed a few minutes to feel sorry for himself before returning to the bedroom. He sat on the bed with his feet on the floor and his arms folded, imagining his hands as they once were. He felt the ghostly sensation of his missing fingers coming back, as they did sometimes, the fingers and his old hands, and they let his memory play better than he ever could, improved with ten years of aging, the phantom music of the mind.

With his eyes shut tight, he was again performing in front of thousands of people at the Indianapolis Speedway, making rock-and-roll history, taking the crowd's roar for love and using it as inspiration to achieve a new height of perfection.

His left hand ran effortlessly along the Stratocaster he called Eric, the one Clapton gave him as a gift a couple years earlier, and his fingers sneaked in new thoughts among the finely knit phrases the fans expected. He couldn't shake the band. The band felt the same rush he felt, and the crisp night air punctuated their emotions and put a special joy into their performance.

The smell of the rain was still everywhere, rising like a natural aphrodisiac from the infield grass and sending messages to Nat's sinus passages, but at least they were past fearing another downpour. He didn't mind the rain personally, even when it gave his allergies a good workout, but he dreaded the normal Strat problems a casual injection of lightning could cause outdoors. The guitar could go dead, with it everything his show aimed for. Clapton had warned him about that, and Mayall had told him a personal horror story that flashed into memory like a jinx a year later, when Nat opened for Elton in Dallas.

The storm exploded out of nowhere.

The sky lit up, and the whole power plant went dead. The Strat, amps, cords, everything.

He began sweating the sweat Mayall had described to him bead for bead while the crew went crazy looking for the problem, which turned out to be a small piece of tape on the shielding that the humidity had curled loose. It took eight minutes to get back to the business of music and, afterward, Nat called it the longest eight minutes of his life.

Now he worked out a new movement of hand through freewheeling association, mind to hand on automatic pilot, pivoting the left hand in a style others tried to imitate but could never duplicate, the way he had played at being Hendrix and then Eric before he became Nat the Axe.

He kept bending the strings, going for something his mind had hummed over earlier that day. He did not quite have it, but the crowd didn't seem to care, washing him in cheers while he focused his emotion on licking the problem.

Nat knew it was not greatness, only a momentary challenge as he and the band neared the closing number of the greatest concert of his career.

It was the night he discovered Mae Jean standing in the doorway to Gasoline Alley, the moment he came to recognize as the beginning of his next life. Mae Jean smiling at him with her eyes, the dream princess giving him an irresistible, incandescent stare that made them old friends even before they met, lovers before they climbed—

Nathan opened his eyes with a start.

His body was drenched in sweat.

The sweat ran down his forehead at the same time that a chill snaked upward through his body.

Disoriented, he turned and saw Ana Maria asleep. Her back was to him. He ran around the bed and dropped to the floor, studied her sleeping face and reassured himself it was Ana Maria, not Mae Jean, before he could make the explosive pounding in his chest go away.

He crawled back into bed and pulled the covers up around him.

He turned away from Ana Maria, so she would not wake up and find him crying.

He felt his hands and remembered when they did what a Van Halen could not even have attempted. Except for the prank of destiny that directed Mae Jean Minter into his life, he could still be Nat Axelrod, Nat the Axe, confident of his election one day into the Rock and Roll Hall of Fame.

Finally, too tired to think anymore, Nathan fell into a restless, haunted slumber.

Chapter 8

The cabbie spun off the I-5 and made two quick turns that led into one of the many small industrial parks bordering on downtown San Diego. He braked in front of a rundown entrance at the end of a cul-de-sac. A peeling painted sign identifying the building as a metal welding plant was visible above a display neon flashing KJIV.2. One side of the entrance had *Jimi lives!* spray painted in large, red block letters and underneath, in black script by another hand, *With Elvis in T.J.*

On the cabbie's radio, Rap Browning was signing off the air over Simply Red's "Holding Back the Years," his boom-box baritone missing in action, nowhere near as powerful as Danny Manings remembered it from twenty years ago, when the "Dapper Rapper," as he called himself then and now, was the undisputed king of Chicago broadcasting.

Danny paid the cabbie, adding a healthy tip, and at the reinforced door identified himself and his business on the com phone. The door lock clicked open, and he aimed for the receptionist who was grooving to the overheads pumping out the station's signal while Billy Ocean faded out on "There'll Be Sad Songs (to Make You Cry)" and Tina Turner charged in with "Typical Male."

The receptionist was an overweight bleached blonde in her late twenties who wore her hair frizzed on one side and shaved on the other. The shaved side had a heart tattoo and, inside the heart, the word "Available" in curlicue script. She cooed Danny's name into the phone and almost instantly he heard shouting.

"Where is my man? Where is that honky motherfucker? Where is that homeboy?" Rap Browning's distinctive, rasping baritone echoed on the other side of the plyboard wall.

Danny wondered how many others knew Rap's old vocal voltage was missing, or cared, as he called back: "Eat shit, nigger!"

The bleached blonde whizzed her head at Danny, fast enough to get a whiplash, shouting angrily: "We don't use that word around here, man!"

"Cool down, Cupcakes," Rap said, dancing through the doorway. "This brother, he paid some heavy dues. He can say shit 'round here all he want."

"I meant the N-word, Rap."

Rap looked at Danny conspiratorially and cupped the side of his face to hide the wink from her.

"Cupcakes, I know this man since the N-word and after, then when the N-word become the other N-word, straight through the C-word to the B-word. I am gonna be knowing him when it gets to be the A-word on top of the A-word to be the AA-word and, you mark my word, we be going through the whole alphabet together before him and me get to the E-word. You know what word I mean by the E-word, Cupcakes?" Cupcakes showed she didn't have a clue. "The E-word is 'Dead,' you hear, Cupcakes? D-e-a-d Dead. That's the word gets everyone E for Equal."

Rap was still talking like he graduated from the University of Street. None of the stories that dug into his past during any one of the payola investigations, not even *Rolling Stone,* got as far as his BA in communications from UCLA. Rap always had an easy explanation for friends like Danny: "When your white society has need of a badass nigger to parade down Main Street, it know what lyrics belong to the melody before the people will march."

Danny's hand moved automatically through one of their old eight-part handshakes and they embraced before Rap took two steps back to have a good look at him. Rap studied him and motioned for him to turn around.

"You are holding it together, bro," he said, as solemn as a Sunday sermon.

Danny turned to face Rap again. "You, too, Mr. B."

In fact, Danny had never seen him looking so bad. Whether for business or socially, Rap had always dressed like pages 111 to 134 in *GQ*, favoring custom-made suits, silk monogrammed cuffs and shoes of soft Italian leather, but today's pinstripe suit seemed two sizes too large and showed signs of heavy use. The collar was fraying and stained by hair sweat along the ridge. A stain on his silk Sulka tie had defied the dry cleaners.

It was Rap's physical appearance that most concerned Danny. Besides the weight loss, his hair was gone, except for stray white tufts that looked borrowed from a carton of minute rice. His skin was parched, the pores salted, and he had lost the cobra sheen the sun always loved to dance on. He had emerged toting a golf club, but was using it more like a cane, always poised, as if his legs might go at any second.

"Say wha'? You shitting me or something?"

"You haven't aged a day since the last time."

Rap let him know with a look he wasn't buying the flattery. He dismissed Danny with a gesture and said, "We'll talk," then called to the receptionist: "Cupcakes, anybody come calling on me, you get a name, a number and a cash deposit. Me and this nigger, we going anywhere but here for the duration."

Cupcakes nodded as if she understood any more than the air-swilling pauses that came like station breaks at Rap's commas and periods. Rap headed for the door, wearing the golf club on his shoulder, urging Danny to fall in behind.

Rap drove in a pink Cad convertible older than their friendship to a revolving restaurant atop a downtown San Diego high-rise, where they drank too much and ate not enough in a booth with a view of the bay. The hostess knew Rap and treated him like a celebrity, disturbing them a few times to ask Rap to sign napkins for fans at the bar. Rap responded with a smile and enough conversational humility to show he cared, while Danny glanced out at the white sailboats gliding around private powerboats and US Navy traffic heading to dock ahead of dark clouds rolling in from the sea.

They took turns drawing from a shared treasury of brown memories and lies that were starting to sound real, like kids trading farts. Whatever ailed Rap—not a subject he intended to volunteer—it didn't affect his memory of the bad times that led to his exile from the big time, for keeps, if KJIV.2 was any gauge. They got to giggling again after Danny insisted on seeing the photo of Mariah he knew Rap always carried in his wallet.

Rap gave him a sweet look and had it out in an instant.

Mariah was the pet monkey Rap kept in diapers and diamonds, who had the run of his home on the south shore's Gold Coast like she was Cheetah and Rap's mansion was Tarzan's tree house. Only the true insiders knew Mariah's job.

Rap would point to her as soon as the promotion man pulled out his latest batch of 45s and the pay envelope that ensured the records he was working a place on the station play list, saying, "I don't want that. That's for Mariah." Rap would whistle one of Bird's riffs, and Mariah would come swinging and bouncing across the room, land two feet in front of the promo man, her paw outstretched in anticipation. To this day, Danny could remember the expression on Joe Wunsch's face when he took the kid over there the first time, to let Rap educate him to playing the game at WBAB, "Home of Heaven with a Beat."

By actual count, according to *60 Minutes,* Rap sat on the witness stand nine times in four trials and swore three hundred eighty seven times: "There's nobody what can ever say he saw me touch any moneys from any promo man, whether he be working a record company or a indie label." He said it under oath, straight-faced, his thick eyebrows bearing down on the federal attorneys, none of whom ever thought to call Mariah to the stand.

The industry got nervous and closed ranks against Rap and pushed him out and down, but Rap never got bitter or had a bad word for anyone. Danny saw him sad only once, briefly, shortly after Mariah died. Rap told him before her funeral that Mariah died of a broken heart, believing she had been abandoned by all her old friends in promotion. She was laid to rest in the clean dirt backyard of the South Carolina one-watter where the Dapper Rapper was working drive time, in her prettiest silk diaper, a pay envelope in both paws. Danny contributed a hundred.

Their day tripping down memory lane never lagged, but Danny kept waiting for Rap to spring whatever it was he had treated like a mystery when he surprised him with his phone call yesterday, urging him to make the trip down from LA, close to begging after Danny faked some excuses why, much as he'd welcome a reunion, he couldn't get away. Rap wouldn't quit, wearing him down finally with words like *friendship* and *for old times' sake.*

The sky outside their picture window was filling with silver-colored clouds while, below, turbulence was rocking the lighter crafts aiming for port, when Rap said, "One more for the road, then two for the road, my man." He signaled the waitress for another round.

Danny seized the opening. "And that road leads where?" he said.

"Got a singer I need you to hear tonight, bro. She a star, this one I find playing her dime piano in a nickel lounge. Somebody else's meal ticket I don't get me something going with her soon, dig?"

"I don't think so, Rap. That life is history. Dead and buried. I work in an art gallery now, selling pretty pictures instead of pretty voices."

"So I heard when last I checked, and not doing so well in the legal tender department."

"Well enough."

Rap ignored him. "Which is one other reason I got on to scouting after you instead of some choices still plugging away, but not so needy as you."

"Or you, from the looks."

"Well, it ain't Chicago." He traded glasses with the waitress and rewarded her with an upraised thumb for remembering two olives and an onion. Leaned across the table, his hands gripping the edge, and challenged Danny with his expression. Said, "You would not deny me back in the olden days, homeboy, when we tighter than a nun's ass. Same as I would not deny you or your crew nothing back when."

"Don't do this to me, Rap." He checked his watch. "You good for the drive to the airport or should I call for a cab?"

Rap shook his head and, like a football ref announcing the penalty, directed Danny's eyes to the picture window. "The ceiling outside there dropping faster than your goddamn jockeys ever did," he said, cackling over his glass. "By now flights probably grounded, likely nothing moving in or out again until five-thirty or six tomorrow morning. Way the weather works around here."

Danny recognized the smile dancing in Rap's eyes. He said,

"You son of a bitch! You've been doing a number on me! Brought me here to stall for time."

"Good news is I booked us a primo table for her first show."

"Fuck you!"

Rap shook his head. "Uh-uh. Had me a regular for that. He done so good he wore knee-pad holes in my carpet a long time before he split on me for good." He signaled the waitress for the check. When she arrived, he passed it off to Danny, saying, "Give Mariah the envelope, my man."

There were a dozen or more parties ahead of them when they walked into Buckingham Palates, an Americanized version of an English chop house. The decor was heavy on framed oils and prints of landscapes and sporting scenes by nondescript genre artists, and off to the side were the obligatory toilets labeled "Kings" and "Queens." Rap jabbed an elbow into Danny's side and joked about his never knowing which to use.

The maître d' greeted Rap warmly. He waved away the captain and personally escorted them inside the show lounge to the only empty table in a room designed for about three hundred, removed the Reserved card and snapped his fingers, while heads swiveled and diners tried to put names to their faces.

A waitress dressed like *Playboy* magazine's concept of Maid Marian trotted over with menus. Rap ordered a Stoli straight up and, when Danny said coffee, he frowned and muttered something unintelligible under his labored breath.

The table gave them an unobstructed view of the baby grand centered against the used-brick wall and guarded on both sides by suits of red-rusted armor that looked as authentic as the fire simmering behind them in a fireplace large enough to roast a pig.

A key light played on the sign above the empty piano bench advertising:

SONG STYLINGS BY
PATRICE MALLOY

Danny could tell the minute she dropped the first lyrics onto the Gershwin melody that Patrice Malloy was everything Rap had promised. He found himself caught up in her voice as she steered the set through a catalog of chewable pop, standard rock, the blues, R&B, and down-home country. He understood there was nothing that could compromise her pipes when she did the staple of lounge pianists, *Happy Birthday to You,* and had the crowd applauding like she was Garland at the Palace going over the rainbow. Her voice was white on white, blue collar silk and the kind of white for black that carried enough soul to set Ray Charles blinking. He didn't argue when Rap, who was studying him as tightly as he studied Patrice Malloy, leaned in to brag, "She carries any tune the way Jesus walks on water."

Rap drank through the set. Danny was halfway through his King John cut of prime rib when it ended. She did a false exit and a single encore, a "Bridge over Troubled Water" that put away Art Garfunkel forever and made Danny wish Larry Knechtel was up there backing her for this one number.

Patrice Malloy acknowledged the sustained applause all the way to their table, where she grabbed Rap from behind and popped a kiss on top of his head before slipping into one of the empty chairs. She seemed to notice Danny for the first time, although he had had the impression she was playing most of the fifty minutes straight at their table.

"Who's this?" she asked.

"He used to be somebody," Rap said.

Patrice Malloy reached over for what was left of Rap's Stoli and said, "I've never been anybody."

"This is the shot, man. Your meal ticket back into the music business. You heard it for yourself."

"Rap, I honestly don't know if I want the shot."

"Look me straight in the eye and say that, bro."

Danny averted his stare.

Rap pushed out a pound of air and insisted, "Of course you want it. You scared man, is all. You scared, and I do not blame you. You get the shot, you want it to be right. Me too, my man, or you think I enjoy playing first rate music in a second rate market? Patrice Malloy is big time. Us again with her."

Patrice was gone. She had done a second set as remarkable as the first and split after joining them for another ten minutes of small talk, displaying the face of her Mickey Mouse watch.

"She got herself a man problem back at home, him the ugly in her pretty," Rap had said, frowning, making Patrice laugh as she leaned over and kissed him good night on the cheek, but she didn't deny Rap's observation.

For a moment, Danny thought she was going to kiss him, too. Instead Patrice offered a warm hand and, squeezing his tightly, maybe too tightly, smiling brightly, volunteered, "It was all my pleasure, Mr. Somebody."

Now, the club was closing up around them and a couple other stragglers, a few waitresses wiping up after spilled drinks, a kitchen helper indifferently piling coffee mugs and glasses into a plastic laundry basket.

Danny said, "Patrice Malloy is good enough for anyone to pay attention to you. You don't need me for that."

"Patrice is, but I ain't, bro. Too many markers out against me. Too many memories gone sour."

"You think it's any better for me? You know how long I've

been out of the loop? I'm a decade removed from the business, Rap. The business has passed me by. Your name became the game, man. It's become a rapper's paradise."

"Shit, man. It didn't pass you by. The industry threw you out and the key with you, but they didn't take your ears away. You hear what I hear tonight? You hear the Gold? You hear the Platinum?"

"Others will hear it, too, you get them down here."

"Don't care, man. You and only you I want, the one was there for me from beginning to whenever, even when it was roughest for you. Say *yes* to me, my brother, and let us get our show on the road."

Danny was tempted. He was more than tempted. He wanted to say yes, but he couldn't. Rap was right. He was scared. As much as he wanted the taste again, as much as he wanted to show them all, especially that bastard Harry Drummond, that he could come back Big Time, he had spent the last years cleaning up his act, making a new life for himself. He sold art and was damned good at it.

Rap pushed out a fat sigh and said, "What is it, bro? Was I misinformed? You made out of money nowadays, you can afford to pass on the Golden Goose?"

Danny shook his head. "I get by, Rap. I paid my debts the way I paid my dues, so there's always enough to live on and some left over."

"You settling, man. I hear you settling." He slammed a palm on the table. "Never thought I'd live to hear Danny Manings settling for anyone, much less hisself."

"You're trying to shame me into the answer you want, but it won't work, Rap." Danny said it appreciatively, patting Rap's forearm.

"Not gonna let you leave me saying *no,* Danny. You owe me."

Danny snorted a laugh. "Owe you? What do I owe you for now?"

Rap pursed his lips and puckered his face. "Ain't you been hearing me out? The Golden Goose. There's your *owe me,* homes. The Golden Goose. Goes by the name Patrice Malloy. She what'll help you bury your past and give you a fresh future." He dipped into a jacket pocket and pulled out a cassette, pushed it at Danny. "Her demo. You can't see to do it for yourself or for us, go and do it for me."

It felt strange, eerily uncomfortable, to Danny—

—coming back to Decade Records, a roost he no longer ruled.

It had nothing to do with Joe Wunsch heading all West Coast operations now. He was proud of Joe for what he'd managed to accomplish in the years since Danny convinced him to set loyalty aside and stick with the label under that rancorous bastard Harry Drummond. Joe was superior to anyone else at the label out here, probably everywhere. He deserved the prize after Stoker dropped dead during a shareholders' meeting and Drummond consolidated the debts he'd picked up during years of politicking to move to New York as the new top dog.

Credit where credit is due—

Drummond always did know a good thing when he saw it.

Joe had routinely made Drummond and the label winners, signing and promoting acts that sold like monsters and kept the price of the stock spiraling upward. He was confident Joe would be in line for top dog when Drummond dropped dead from *his* fatal heart attack.

His fatal heart attack.

Danny laughed at the idea as he eased from the elevator on the executive floor of the Decade Records Building on a back-street west of Century City.

Drummond had no heart.

Common industry knowledge.

Danny was announced by the attractive brown-skinned receptionist in thigh highs sitting behind the misshapen piece of white plastic in the middle of the room. A minute later Joe raced out to greet him, calling as they embraced, "Captain, my captain! Welcome back to Cemetery City."

The receptionist studied them awkwardly, almost embarrassed as Joe dissolved the hug into a noisy kiss on Danny's forehead. Joe led Danny away, telling her, "It's okay, m'lovely. Me and him, we're engaged."

"She might believe you," Danny said. He felt a memory pain in his side, sharp enough to cause him to wince, as Joe opened the connecting door and ushered him through to his old office.

"She knows better," Joe advised, expanding for emphasis a tight-lipped grin. "M'lovely's been here about a month. She wants to be a record producer."

"Everybody wants to be a record producer."

Joe bounced his head and smiled. "Yes, but it takes longer for the ones especially female and don't know enough to keep their mouth open." He danced his eyebrows. "Talent is talent and lips is lips, Captain."

"So nothing ever really changes around here."

"You mean the sex harassment thingie?" Joe shrugged. "Trust me on this—the guys can keep their little Richards inside their zippers a whole lot better than some of the girls know how to keep their legs tighter than Phil Collins's drum kit."

Danny laughed, the way Joe always could make him laugh, all the way back to the years he was running the store, and surveyed the office.

The French provincial furniture he'd favored, faithful reproductions comfortably meshed alongside notable antiques he searched out on various trips to Europe, were gone, replaced by a clean, contemporary Danish look, sleek pieces in a blend of primary colors. Oversized cushions fit right in, some for seating and some only for decoration, some creating a mountain of comfort on what Danny presumed to be the couch.

He avoided it for a simple, hard-backed chair facing a picture window view of Century City and Joe's clear plastic desk, whose surface was almost entirely covered by CDs and tapes. Framed Gold and Platinum records lined the walls, except for the wall behind Joe, where a clean-lined purple breakfront held magazines, framed family photographs and assorted high-tech audio components to feed the wall-mounted Sony midget speakers smaller than the professional studio HKs Danny had preferred, but powerful enough to ream the most hardened of eardrums.

"You know I had Greta call and fit you in the minute I got your message," Joe said, like an apology. "Was in Paris for another of those *farkakteh Billboard* summits or you'd've been up here the same day you called."

"How is Greta?" Danny said, waving off Joe's excuse as unnecessary. Greta was a bird-like relic from eleven prior administrations, Decade's good luck charm, who worried about dying before reaching mandatory retirement age, when she intended to escape with her pension and her eighty-seven-year-old mother to a condo in Hawaii.

"Died last year, but nobody has the heart to tell her," Joe said, gesturing grandly. "You know you could have called me at the house yesterday?"

"Didn't want to take you away from the family your first day back home, Joey."

"Christ, Captain. You are family."

Danny felt a surge of emotion, another watching Joe ease behind the desk, thinking Joe was now the same age he'd been when he was dumped by Decade. The years had put twenty or twenty-five more pounds on Joe's five-foot-six-inch frame, some sagging face, mostly a belly that refused to hide underneath a stale Aerosmith T-shirt that barely reached his ill-fitting Guess jeans.

Joe was sufficiently bald that he had taken to shaving his skull completely, offsetting that with a lush reddish-brown beard that flowed wildly in all directions and halfway down his chest. He was already losing his hair when Danny hired him, given Joe's encyclopedic knowledge of music and the record business and one of those golden ears that could siphon out special sounds.

He had proved it quickly, prowling the small rock clubs of Southern California and signing Mickey Neel, who had been overlooked by all the labels, including Decade, where Harry Drummond had taken a fast pass after listening to Mickey's garage demo. The demo shortly turned into the *Dead Dreams* album and, long before it hit the ten million mark in sales, Danny had made Joe his personal assistant.

Joe stared at the world through a pair of thick, ill-fitting metal-framed specs that were always sliding down the bridge of his nose. When he would notice, he'd push them back with an index finger, as he did now while swinging around to throw on a tape, a woman rocking to an electronic track. She was okay, overtones of Courtney Love, but her voice better suited to ballads and nowhere near the quality of Patrice Malloy. Only the guitar sounded real. The rest was being served up by computer magic.

To be polite, Danny said, "She chases the base line a few times, but she's not so bad."

"Gimme a break, Captain. She is not so good, either," Joe said. "A hundred years ago or so, before the great unwashed record-buying public decided rap answered a question that wasn't being asked, Darby Brown brought it to me. Like as not she was someone he was poking. Poor Darby. Still wandering around the business like a fugitive from an Ed Wood movie.

Still trying to make a go, like he still knows the score. Christ! Darby hardly recognizes the game anymore."

"I thought Darby had exiled himself to London."

"Well, he got back here somehow after that nasty business with illegal returns, disguised as a decent human being. Talked up a storm about the vocalist and her tits, not necessarily in that order, not that I believed anything he was saying. Even when Darby walked in here and just said *hello,* I didn't believe him."

Danny gave him a mirthless smile and, unable to wait any longer, neck sweat soaking his shirt collar, he pulled Patrice's cassette from his pocket. "Here's what I called about, something to turn you into a true believer," he said, tossing the cassette to Joe, who made an easy one-handed catch.

Joe's eyes got serious. "Patrice Malloy, huh?" he said, reading the label on the box. He cracked it open and slipped the cassette into the deck. "Will I be hearing about her tits, too?"

"Just play the damned thing."

Joe sailed a giant wink at him and poked the start switch. Patrice Malloy's voice blew out of the speakers like a force of nature. Joe turned his back to Danny, stayed that way well into the second of the four cuts on the demo.

The first cut was an up-tempo number Danny had instructed Rap to put at the head of the tape, to catch the listener's immediate attention. Joe's hands were thumb-locked to his jeans, so there was none of the finger-popping or breakfront strumming that would convey a message, but Danny saw Joe's foot catching the infectious beat.

Was it the singer or the song?

The song was proven material, somebody else's hit, as were the others on the demo.

What Joe had to hear and understand was the raw power and originality of Patrice's voice.

Joe turned to face him.

His stoic look gave away nothing.

But only for a few seconds.

His eyes narrowed, then opened enough for Danny to see a glimmer that was not there a few minutes ago. He grunted a laugh and touched his heart like he was about to pledge allegiance to the flag. His voice stretched past a choke. He said, “Welcome back to the record biz, Captain.”

Chapter 9

Laurent spent a morning searching the files of the *News* and a Scotch-filled lunch with the reporter who had covered the trial of Nat the Axe, the notorious "Rock-and-Roll Rapist," a label he took drunken pride in having coined. She picked at her seafood salad while Gary Frisch drank and boasted in garbled spurts about page-one yarns he had broken for the *News* during his thirty-five years on general assignment, how he'd been courted by newspapers in Los Angeles and New York, but they both knew the unspoken truth—Frisch's career would end where it had begun, in Indianapolis.

The truth was as obvious as his frayed collars and his alcohol sweat, but she tried not to show anything but admiration for him, and he was accepting her appreciative smiles and nods.

Men and their egos.

"I got my first-class exclusives in a first-class rag, you know? Not like those scum sheets you favor," Frisch said, making a face meant to convey she shouldn't take offense. "I knew you even before you called to set this up. Know your byline. Read some of your stuff over the years. Not bad, not bad at all, Miss Laurent Connart," he said, managing to mangle both names.

"*Merci,* Gary," she said, sweetly, and rubbed his thigh to tell him how much she meant it. "I take that as real compliment, coming as it does from a fellow journalist."

"I string for the *New York Times,* too, you know? Sometimes. The Rock-and-Roll Rapist yarn, that was one of 'em. Looked for a while I might even have gone off to the Big Apple based on that one; sensed another offer coming. I did not encourage it. Home here, you know, Laurent? You know? Where the heart is?"

"I know, Gary, *oui,*" she said.

She put up with him for two more hours, came away with a few incidental details about Nat's arrest and the trial that had never made his stories and, best of all, the name and address of the victim's best friend:

Nadine Barber.

Because the law protects children from unnecessary exposure in criminal matters, she had not been identified in any media coverage. She was fifteen at the time, about two and a half years younger than Mae Jean Minter.

Nadine's trial testimony was secondary in nature. Phil Penguin, the assistant DA, had her testify as to Mae Jean's character. She also corroborated her best friend's version of events, as related to her the next day, after Mae Jean recovered from the trauma of witnessing the arrest and shooting of her attacker. It was testimony a sharp defense attorney might have kept out, but there was nothing in print to suggest Nat's lawyer, Benjamin Harrison Hubbard, did any more than go through the motions.

Normally, Laurent might not have bothered chasing after this kind of witness, but she fancied Nadine as a stand-in for Mae Jean, who disappeared from Indianapolis a year after Nat went to prison. Better, Nadine might have an idea where Mae Jean was now.

When Laurent pulled up in her Honda rental, Nadine was in the front yard of her cottage-style home in a neighborhood that screamed blue collar, clearing weeds from a sorry patch of flowers. She resisted the idea of being interviewed until she heard the story was for the *Tab,* her favorite newspaper, and would mention her by name.

They were settled over homemade lemonade and brownies in Nadine's pristine *Good Housekeeping* living room, *God Bless Our Happy Home* in framed needlepoint above the floor-to-ceiling brick fireplace, trading girlish small talk until Laurent asked about Mae Jean Minter's current whereabouts.

Nadine shrugged. "No idea. Haven't thought about it almost since Mae Jean left town with her husband, Dr. Heidemann, and dropped out of sight mostly ever since."

"Wolf Heidemann."

"He's the one."

"They just up and left Indianapolis, did they?"

"Like that," Nadine said, and snapped her fingers.

"And you didn't find it strange that your best friend and the doctor would do this?"

"Not at all, Miss—" and Nadine stopped, rather than get her name wrong. "Mae Jean, she told me more than once how Wolfie, she called him that, was talking about pulling up stakes and planning to start out fresh, so when it finally happened, it come as no surprise to me."

"That Dr. Wolf Heidemann would leave behind his successful clinic and go off, not even try to sell it, just sail off the face of the map?"

"Not my business. Besides, Mae Jean and me, we had distance growing between us, you know what I mean?"

Laurent smiled and said nothing. She took another taste of the lemonade and picked out a shard of pulp stuck between her teeth.

Nadine broke the silence. "Well, you see how Ernie and me live? Modest. He works with his hands over to the speedway, Gasoline Alley? It's a living, and we get on just fine lately; kids and all. So, anyway, Mae Jean, she stayed just fine after she and the doctor married up, but he was the possessive sort and always wanted her where he could see her, up on the hill in their big old house. I mean, he worshipped her and all, but he certainly looked down on her old friends in more ways than one, like we weren't good enough for her? Finally, we got to seeing less and less of each other, mostly on the phone?"

"And no call before she and her husband the doctor left Indianapolis?"

"I got a postcard once from her. Maybe six or seven months later? After they were long gone and talk about them from folks who knew them was pretty much over? One of those *having a wonderful time and wish you were here* sort of picture postcards?"

"Where was the postcard from?"

Nadine thought about it, as if she weren't sure she wanted Laurent to know.

"Las Vegas," she said, in a tone that carried a million lost dreams. "There was this wonderful picture of Siegfried and Roy on it with their lion? Mae Jean always did like pets."

"And never since?"

The same hesitation before Nadine counted off the years on her thick, kitchen-scarred fingers.

"Seven, eight, no, seven," Nadine said, dropping back a finger. "About seven years in all without word one."

"May I see the postcard?"

She thought about it, shook her head.

"Tossed out years ago. Not something to save."

Laurent didn't believe her, but let it pass for now.

"Photographs, maybe?"

Nadine smiled eagerly. "Back in a minute."

She returned and cleared space on the coffee table for a thick, tan-covered photo album, taking pains not to disturb the slim spiral pad on which Laurent occasionally jotted a note or two; started turning pages, pausing often to recite a capsule history of some favorite photograph glued neatly to the black paper.

Most of the photos were three-by-four candids. Many caught Mae Jean Minter and her best friend, Nadine, at various ages, reflected in changing hair styles and clothing; little girls growing into young women; generally, at play; smiling with a youthful exuberance that soon enough would be lost to life's realities. Nadine had been pretty once, before the eye bags and the worry lines and the bottled blonde hair, and the sixty pounds that were probably left over from her children.

Nadine tried to hurry past a picture of the two girls with an older man Laurent recognized as Huck Minter, Mae Jean's father. He stood between them, almost two heads taller, arms behind their backs, hands clutching their shoulders; showing an ugly smile. Both girls displayed what might have been school diplomas. Neither looked any more pleased than Nadine did this minute.

Laurent stopped her by pressing down hard on her hand.

"That is Mae Jean's father, is it not?"

"Uh-huh," Nadine said, reluctantly.

"What can you tell me about him?"

"Nothing," Nadine said, and shivered. "I think I have to stop now. I have chores to finish before the children—"

"You think I could have this picture?"

"What for?"

"For the article I am writing. I would make a copy and get it back to you undamaged."

Nadine seemed confused, as if making decisions was not something she was called upon to do much of the time.

"I will even pay you for it," Laurent said. "My newspaper is very generous."

"How much?" Nadine said, suddenly interested.

"A hundred dollars."

Nadine thought about it. "Two hundred would pay a lot of

bills," she said.

"Two hundred, then." Laurent dipped into her bag for her wallet and counted out four fifties.

Nadine cautiously inched the photo off the page and handed it across to Laurent, who made a show of placing it between two thick sections of her Day Runner.

"So, my picture will be in the *Tab*?"

"Oui."

"Ain't that a treat? And my name too, you said?"

"And some of the nice things you said to me about your old friend."

That also pleased Nadine. "The other girls were jealous of us, you know? *Mae Jean Nadine,* they used to call us, like it was one name. *Mae Jean Nadine.*" Her tired green eyes turned wistful and wet. "*Mae Jean Nadine. One's a princess, one's a queen.* How they used to chant, and we'd just laugh and laugh over it, never knowing which of us was the princess and which was the queen."

"Of course, Nat Axelrod is dead," District Attorney Phil Penguin said. "I was there. I saw him."

"Why?"

"Why, Miss Laurent? Because the man had stopped breathing. In my experience that's the definitive sign."

"I mean, why were you there at Indiana State Prison to see him? Nat Axelrod wasn't your friend. He was a man you helped convict and send there in the first place. A drug user. A rapist."

It had taken Laurent two days to get Penguin to see her. So far he had given her less than ten minutes, answering routine questions about Nat's arrest and trial without a trace of attitude, but Laurent could see the wheels of his mind turning, weighing every response before he spoke, like this case was today and far from settled.

The question about Nat's death had produced the only sign of emotion on his remarkably strong face. Penguin hadn't aged much since the file photos and still exuded a youthful vigor to go with a full head of wheat-colored hair worn neatly clipped to complement his Brooks Brothers suit and tie and the impression of a solid, no-nonsense citizen. His voice fit his six-footer's frame: deep, well-modulated, balanced for maximum effect.

She understood why Penguin's conviction rate was so high. What jury would be able to resist Jack Armstrong, the All-American Boy?

"I went to Indiana State Prison to supervise the removal of Nat's body as a favor, Miss Connart." He glanced at his watch.

"Not a favor, *certainment,* for *Monsieur* Axelrod."

Penguin shot her a dismissive look. "A favor to Benjamin Harrison Hubbard. You know that name? Nat's lawyer. A legend in these parts. Ben was too sick to go. If you've done your due diligence, you know he died of cancer around the same time."

She corrected him. "Shortly after."

"Shortly after," Penguin said, cracking a brief wistful smile. "Ben had grown attached to Nat, so when he couldn't go he asked me. I suppose you're going to ask why. He was my hero, Miss Connart. Ben and I were adversaries, not enemies, and I respected Ben and all he stood for. Honesty. Integrity. Survival of the human spirit. I became a lawyer because of Ben Hubbard. So did a lot of lawyers in these parts."

Penguin choked on his words. They seemed to bring a change to him, as if he wanted to tell Laurent other thoughts. Instead, he needlessly shuffled some papers on his desk, waiting for the moment to drift away.

"But *Monsieur* Hubbard asked you, not any of the others. You must have been someone special to him."

Penguin looked past her shoulder. "Ben paid my way through law school, Yale, because he saw something in me others didn't.

We were poor as church mice, my family, but he found something in me, God rest his wise soul."

"And he saw something special in Nat Axelrod?"

"Ben was always finding something special in everyone. His favorites were the helpless strays and Nat Axelrod was one. He had been cheated out of all his money and abandoned by his managers and accountants, who took advantage of powers of attorney after Axelrod was shot and charged and left him flatter than a Kansas prairie."

Laurent said, "You know this for a fact?" She had not discovered this in her research. She was not about to let the information go, although Penguin looked like he had spoken out of turn and regretted it.

He raised his hand as if ready to throw away the subject, as quickly settled it palm down on the desk and told her, "Ben told me. That makes it better than a fact."

"What else did your sainted mentor tell you? On or off the record. For attribution or not, as you choose."

Penguin brought his wristwatch closer to his face. Shook his head. Pushed up from his chair. "I really must be going."

"Like a white rabbit."

"I beg your pardon."

"What the white rabbit said to Alice in Wonderland. *I really must be going.*"

"I don't understand."

"And I am trying to understand, just like Alice. I have fallen down a hole and I'm trying to find my way out, *Monsieur* Penguin."

The comment didn't stop him from helping her from her seat. This close, Laurent saw a sadness in his eyes she had not noticed before.

For Benjamin Harrison Hubbard?

For Nat Axelrod?

For himself, Laurent decided. A look she'd seen before. The look of someone who wants to unburden himself and can't. She'd had it once or twice herself.

She said, "If Nat was robbed of all his money, then who paid for your wonderful man's services, that he should be so involved ever afterward? He was, *oui*? His name was on an appeal that went nowhere."

"*Pro forma.* The filing was automatic. I suppose he got paid with taxpayer dollars, if he even bothered asking. More than that I couldn't say. You'd have to ask Laddie."

"Laddie?"

"Laddie Parriott." He stepped away from her and moved to the door.

Laurent thought that might be who he meant, the promotion boy for Decade Records, who had been in the hospital room when Huck Minter and his brutish friends came after Nat wielding baseball bats. His warning to Dr. Wolf Heidemann was credited with saving Nat's life that night.

"Why would Laddie Parriott know?"

"I can see you're familiar with that name. Somebody else Ben inspired. Laddie took over Ben's practice, what was left of it, before Ben passed on, so he might have access to information Ben had no truck sharing with me." Penguin reflected on some inner moment he didn't share with her and said, "Call Laddie. Tell him hello for me. Tell him you're calling at my suggestion."

"Does that make for special significance?"

Penguin shrugged. "*An' the gobble-uns'll git you ef you don't watch out!* Also tell that to Laddie."

Shortly after five o'clock on a day that went from bright sun to burdensome rain. Laddie Parriott met Laurent in the oak-lined bar off the two-level reception hall of the Columbia Club. He was late, but he was there, the meeting set to her time frame after she repeated the message from Phil Penguin. The sudden downpour had compacted traffic on the downtown streets, and the young lawyer apologized after crossing the narrow room to join her at the round table she had selected in the farthest corner.

The television set was turned to a newscast and, waiting for him, Laurent had given it some attention. The lead story reported how GIA terrorists were creating deadly havoc in Paris as part of the Muslims' ongoing problems with the French government. Laurent tried convincing herself she didn't miss covering stories like that, but she did, and if it had been years ago or if her beloved Papa were alive, she certainly would still be at it, rather than groveling in *le merde,* shit, for supermarket tabloids like the *Tab.*

Laddie bowed slightly and winked. "I talked to Phil after you called," he said, settling across from her. "He sort of told me what this is all about. I'm really happy to help you out if I can, Miss Connart." She smiled, wondering to herself what else they had talked about and how constructed or rehearsed Parriott's conversation with her would be. He said, "I see you have a drink. Ready for a refill?"

Laurent shook her head. "This vodka tonic will be fine. A little end of the day relaxing." She'd ordered the vodka light, rather than the double she might have asked for if she were only relaxing, not working. She always kept a clear head in interview situations, where the slightest nuance of word or body language could be valuable information.

"Relaxing, good to hear," Laddie said. He sent the bartender a signal. A minute or two later, a waitress set down an oversized beer mug in front of him. "Cheers," he said, lifting the mug. Laurent joined him in the toast and took a discreet sip. "I suggested the Columbia Club because it was one of Ben's favorite haunts," Laddie said. "I think he may still be haunting it." He laughed, a sweet laugh to go with his sweet, open face, eyes burnished with enthusiasm, a carryover, maybe, from his days promoting records. "Also the drink. Ben's invention. A bona fide *Hubba-Hubba,* as in *Hubbard.*"

"Containing?"

"Secret recipe. Only Ben and the bartender knew. Ben used to say it contained wisdom, truth, beauty, knowledge, understanding, comfort, joy, and happiness. And a tiny hint of Grand Marnier. He used to say you're not aware of the Hubba-Hubba until into your third one, except for the beauty part, which leaps out for your throat immediately, like a vampire's purpose. Then all of it begins to ring out with an astonishing, overpowering, soothing clarity, like the magical, mystical bells of Notre Dame. I can picture him now, raising a toast to another of his local favorites, besides Benjamin Harrison—James Whitcomb Riley. He would rattle off the poet's life span, eighteen hundred fifty-two to nineteen hundred sixteen, raise his mug and recite, *It hain't no use to grumble and complane. It's jest as cheap and easy to rejoice; when God sorts out the weather and sends rain, w'y rain's my choice.*"

Laddie's smile showered her with charm. He said, "Sure you won't try one?"

Laurent held up the vodka, signaling him it would do, and sipped again.

"*An' the gobble-uns'll git you ef you don't watch out!* Mr. Riley also wrote that. Ben used it with all of us, to remind us to be careful in matters of life affecting us or any living creature."

"I don't think I have ever met a man like your *Monsieur* Hubbard."

"I try to be that man, and so does Phil, Miss Connart. He sent that reminder with you."

"To warn you about me?"

"Is that what you think?"

"Do lawyers always answer questions with questions?"

"The good ones do, especially when they don't know what the questions are."

"When you called him, did *Monsieur* Penguin say I was asking about Nat Axelrod?"

"Nat the Axe. One of the great ones, you know?"

"I saw him at Wembley Stadium in London."

"Then you do know. Good for you. I don't ever expect to find Nat getting elected to the Rock and Roll Hall of Fame, but anyone who remembers knows he belongs in there before a lot of dudes who are already polishing their nameplates."

She said, "I could not agree with you more." The tips of Laddie's smile almost touched his earlobes. Men and their egos. "You helped save Nat's life, I know that, too."

Laddie ignored the compliment. "I sometimes kidded the doc after that, Dr. Heidemann, that he should have had a better aim and that prick Huck Minter would be in hell already, instead of wandering the back alleys after serving hard time."

"I tried to locate him here in Indianapolis. He was not to be found."

"Huck is somewhere. He served his time for coming after Nat, attempted manslaughter, and some extra time for doing nasty business while incarcerated."

"His daughter, Mae Jean, also missing, and the doctor, her husband, Dr. Heidemann."

"Old news. Never did understand that marriage, but the doctor, he was a strange bird. No sense of humor."

"You think *Monsieur* Hubbard ever heard from either one?"

"Hardly. They were at the DA's table, not his."

"So, tell me something else. Who paid *Monsieur* Hubbard for his services on behalf of Nat Axelrod?"

"A great guy, actually, from my old business growing up,

before I fell under Ben's spell. A guy named Danny Manings, who'd been running Nat's label, Decade, out in Los Angeles. Paid up to a point, anyway."

"What was that point?"

"Danny discovered Nat and brought him to Decade Records. He was the person who engineered Nat's success, believe you me. My late father, he could have told you stories . . . So, anyway, Danny and Nat were as close as brothers, closer, like this—" He crossed his fingers to illustrate. "Danny paid Ben and I heard later he even paid Heidemann's bills. That's what cost him his gig at Decade. Danny got run out of the record business on a handrail. Not to mention the poor bastard's wife did herself in. Suicide. Sad. Danny couldn't pay anymore, so Ben carried on anyway. Ben had got to know Nat and liked him. Besides, he didn't believe Nat was guilty."

"Didn't believe or knew?"

"A little of both, maybe? Ben used to say to me sometimes, *You know what Nat Axelrod was really guilty of, Laddie?* So, I'd say, *What, Ben?* And, he'd say, *Nat Axelrod was guilty of rock and roll.*"

She responded with a look telling Laddie she understood the message.

"Nat was guilty of rock and roll," he repeated. "Jesus, you check out there now and you see what those rappers are up to and it makes you wonder, doesn't it? Ben always figured it was that roadie who testified, that turd named Kern Posey, who turned on Nat with lies to save his own greasy scalp. Ben also believed Kern Posey was the one did the nasty to Mae Jean Minter in the backseat of that limo."

"He had proof?"

"Ben had theories. He also had the instinct of a bloodhound."

Laurent was convinced he was holding back. He had a habit of looking away from her, staring into his Hubba-Hubba, when he made his pronouncements. *Merde!* He was another one who for all his honesty and his Crest smile was shuffling through the truth.

Laddie said, "I did bring you proof of *something,* Miss Connart."

He pulled a photocopy from an inside jacket pocket and offered it to her. "Phil said you had questions about Nat being dead? I searched out a letter Ben wrote around that time to Danny Manings."

The letter ran two single-spaced, typewritten pages:

Dear Danny,

I am sorry to add to the burden of your own problems, but I have sad news I am certain you would be equally distressed not to receive.

Prison plays tricks on the best of men in these worst of circumstances, and our friend Nat Axelrod is the newest victim. Nat is dead in the wake of a minor riot that could have claimed more lives than his if the prison authorities had not acted so quickly and decisively to quell a disturbance Nat himself helped precipitate.

As I reconstruct the sad events, Nat brooded for some time about the curious turns fate had taken with his life. His inmate friends, names he may have mentioned to you while he was still communicative, Chalky Ruggles, the "Mayor of the Yard," especially, said Nat became increasingly despondent when he thought about the lies and distortions of Huck Minter and others that had transported him to this sad state.

The thoughts became too much for him and there came the day when he was provoked in the mess hall by a band of inmates with a grudge, who taunted him about his former glory and cast aspersions one would not wish on anyone remotely civil. Nat is said to have gone crazy.

In a mad frenzy, he leaped across tables and attacked the

convicts using his simple eating utensils and his fists. One of the detractors was armed with a handmade blade, which he plunged deep into Nat's midsection and then, according to accounts, pulled upward to his neck, with the net effect of ripping the poor man almost in two. The entire room was agog with fistfights and worse before guards were able to restore the peace. Nat died in surgery, during a meritorious but futile effort to save him.

As executor of Nat's estate, there being no immediate family surviving, and myself unable to attend to such matters, I have requested that Phil Penguin act in my stead. He is seeing to it that Nat, according to the wishes he communicated to me at one time, be cremated and his ashes taken to Graceland, to be scattered in the ghostly presence of Elvis, whom Nat so admired and, as you know, often cited as a major influence on his career.

Phil, of course, is the district attorney who prosecuted Nat in that dark yesterday, but he also is an honorable man who has my complete trust and confidence.

Suffice it to say once more to you, I came to know and to admire Nat Axelrod. I believed him innocent of all charges and to this day nothing has convinced me otherwise. I believe that, with time, we could have sought and achieved our friend's release and return to a productive life. Such thoughts only add to the burden of grief we must now carry.

I now will proceed to close my files on this matter and suggest you do likewise, although we both will doubtless preserve the memory of Nathan Greene, the boy who fulfilled a dream by becoming the person the rest of the world came to know and for a time revere as Nat Axelrod.

Stay proud you were his friend, Danny. Circumstance drove the two of you apart, but only in life, not in truth. Be well and remember to watch out for the gobble-uns.

As Laurent read through the letter a second time, her reporter's sense centered on two names: Chalky Ruggles, the

"Mayor of the Yard" Ben described as Nat's friend at Indiana State Prison, and Danny Manings, the record-company man in Los Angeles to whom Ben's letter was addressed.

CHAPTER 10

Two days later, Laurent arrived at Indiana State Prison during regular Sunday visiting hours, applied to see Chalky Ruggles, and was told he was unavailable. Reluctantly, she asked for Jay Flotsan, who showed up in the crowded waiting room after twenty minutes wondering, "The Mayor of the Yard? Why in hell would you want to spend time with that species of feces?"

She had a lie ready. "With Nat Axelrod dead, my editors now want a story dealing with people who knew him, like you, and what they might have to say. The name of Chalky Ruggles came up in my research yesterday at the library, and—"

"He's in the hole for the duration and pulling him out could mean my ass, not the way I got it from you before, you read me?"

"Rules are manufactured to be broken, *oui*?" She ran her tongue around her lips, finger-massaged a nipple out from hiding inside her spun silk cardigan.

Flotsan broke into a smile that bared his nicotine breath and tobacco-blackened teeth. "It would be a shame you traveling all the way up here for nothing, besides, you already know the drill," he said. "First I drill you, then you can drill Chalky. C'mon, I got family waiting home for me."

He led her to the same windowless room they'd shared before, dropped his pants around his ankles and plowed into her for the minute that took another day out of her life. She moaned and groaned, feigning orgasm to feed Flotsan's ego and at the same time sent silent apologies to God.

After Flotsan left to get Ruggles, Laurent straightened her clothing and applied a fresh coat of makeup, wandered the room impatiently until she heard the echo of footsteps and keys turning in the door locks after about fifteen minutes. She mashed out her Camel on the sink and settled onto the cot, which creaked modestly under her weight.

Chalky shuffled inside ahead of Flotsan, wrists and ankles cuffed, squinting in the poor light. He studied her as hungrily as she viewed him while Flotsan removed the handcuffs.

Laurent thought, *I understand this man.*

As well as prison blues, Chalky was wearing the stale look and scent of captivity. She had learned about both from Papa, who carried them with him all their life together, until the moment the bomb exploded and robbed her of his love.

Chalky was in his mid-sixties, squat and ordinary looking, the kind of person put together in a Waring blender. He had escaped a Queens, New York, ghetto in his mid-teens by graduating from the Police Athletic League to professional boxing as a bantamweight, although he had two left feet and no left hook and depended on his quick wits in the absence of quick reflexes. *Ring* Magazine laid the nickname on him early in his career, based on a large white resin stripe it said appeared down his back by the end of a bout.

Chalky carried a pair of Silly Putty ears, a broken nose reduced to shapeless clay and a mouthful of ill-fitting dentures that caused him to lose arguments with long words and made his mumbles harder to decipher. His hands were oversized and, when he made fists, they suggested a brute power directly connected to the brain. He had a reputation for being good-natured and easy to kid, but quick to turn nasty and dangerous if anyone at State soured one of the deals he closed with his word of honor and a spit handshake.

He ran the prison like a cult. A long time ago, life had become too cushy for him inside to consider parole or, as he put it, "take early retirement." Sometimes, he was sent down to solitary for a brief period, but it was mostly the warden's show to the other prisoners. Even the warden and his uniforms looked for help from Chalky whenever there was a problem that could not be resolved by the book.

The warden denied this, of course, and so did Chalky.

He didn't need to brag about the power.

He had the power.

Chalky rubbed his wrists and, without taking his eyes off her, awkwardly crossed over to the milk crate, which he used as a seat. He sucked in the Camel smoke drifting between them and said, "A woman. And a looker. Congratulations, boss." He winked at Laurent and waved off her offer of a cigarette.

Flotsan flashed irritation and settled against the door, arms folded across his faded blue blazer.

Laurent said, "You think you can leave us alone for a while?"

Flotsan shook his head. "Against the rules."

"*Merde!* We're already breaking the rules."

Chalky said, "Do what she asks, boss," soft as tissue paper.

At once Laurent saw the power. Who truly was in charge here.

Flotsan grumbled officiously, but a minute later he was outside, locking the door, and she was alone with Chalky.

"So, what's this all about?" he said, as quietly as evil ever gets.

Chalky Ruggles was not someone to bullshit, so she told him, pulled out her copy of Ben Hubbard's letter and let him read it for himself. He focused hard on every word, biting his nails the way one of the articles on CompuServe had described, habitually. His expression reflected the need for extra time to absorb all the sentences and their meaning. Then a smile whispered across his face.

"Nat Axelrod," Chalky said. He looked around the room like a landlord inspecting his property. "Lady, the stories I could tell you about Nat."

Laurent lit up a fresh smoke. This time Chalky went for the Camel when she offered him the pack. He sucked down a heavy drag and blew out a string of doughnut-sized rings while she settled at his feet, retrieved her cassette recorder from her handbag and pressed the Record button without asking permission.

Chalky seemed amused, almost as if he welcomed her intrusion on his authority, and swiped the recorder from her. He drew it to within a few inches of his mouth and, before she could ask a question, began talking with the casual ease of a born storyteller, his eyes studying her for reaction as he told the machine:

I liked the kid the minute I seen him, not that I was some starfucker, or like some in here who'll fuck any hole served up between two cheeks. I once had a wife on the outside and I still have a daughter out there somewhere, so call me old-fashioned.

The kid didn't want no special attention, and he was a fast learner in most ways. Stayed to himself. Played by the rules. Never above signing an autograph for some con was a fan or had people on the outside to impress. He even come to pay me respect soon as he understood how the joint operates.

I had my own interest in music, runs in the family, so we struck up a conversation and we got along fine, so I made him a deal. He learn me about making songs out of words I sometimes put on paper, he got my protection.

"Glad to help you with lyrics, Chalky, but I can take care of myself."

Nat says that and I know he means it. He just don't know how ugly a joint can get. Thinks working out with the weights and power-

ing up would tip off anybody who saw Nat for soup. I shrug and go along with him. Some things you gotta learn for yourself, you know? Way of the world, inside and outside.

So, one day I'm TCOB—taking care of business?—out by the baseball bleachers, where I always hang with my toadies, and here comes Nat.

"My man's here," I announce. "My man, he's learning me how to write songs like I was a regular Irving Berlin, ain't that right, champ?"

"Like a regular Bob Dylan," he says. Like I could care a turd about this Dylan when I know from Irving Berlin, but it impresses my toadies, so what the fuck? Like I say, If the rock in rock an' roll stands for rock pile, fine by me.

Nat smiles and I got a big hug for him, and he's got a smile back that shows me his wheels turning; something on his mind. I don't ask. He'll tell me, he wants, which is a couple of minutes. He inquires about a dude name of Horace Morace Maynor.

Now, unnerstand, I ain't no bigot, but in the joint niggers are niggers. They keep to themselves because they like it better that way. I'm the mayor of the yard, but I respect their piece of the turf, too, because it keeps the peace, and I make it a point to get along with their own boss. Was a guy named Rufus Hardaway. Doing major time for pushing heroin and some pimping on the side. Big red-haired dude, big and fat, black as coal, eyes without a soul, and where the word ugly *comes from. Rufus, he would just as soon off you as have you looking at him, he didn't want nobody looking at him.*

So, I tell Nat Horace Morace Maynor is one of Rufus Hardaway's main men and no one to be playful about. Horace Morace got a reputation as a genuine scrambled egg, black or white. A degenerate leftover from a Tarzan movie. About six-foot-three of solid stone starting a quarter inch below his hairline. Why?

Nat says he caught Horace Morace Maynor staring at him once too often in the showers, trying to hang a hard-on, so he finally put the question to him and Horace says he wants some cream of ass for dinner and Nat Axelrod is the name on the soup can.

Nat tells him, "Look for a different brand."

Horace Morace, he says back, "Found me the one to my taste."

They stare down each other a while, but nothing but words comes of it, so far. Only arguing over music. Horace Morace putting down rock and roll. Saying music is rap now. Rap coming in and going to take over. So, what good anyway is Nat, except for soup?

Nat, he don't see it that way, of course, and he tells Horace Morace so. He says rock and roll is forever, same as rap could be someday, same as Horace Morace Maynor's people invented jazz and jazz ain't ever going anywhere away. Me? Give me Irving Berlin any day of the week.

So, I says to Nat, "It ain't gonna end there, Nat. You don't answer this guy, you're soup. You want I should talk to Rufus Hardaway, try and keep it from getting any worse? Besides, I owe you for the songwriting."

Nat says back, "You don't owe me nothing, but let me think on it, Chalky. I hoped you was gonna say it wasn't so bad with this loudmouth faggot."

Jesus Christ on a crutch! Thinking is like the Black Plague in here. Lady, I can't count high enough how many cons bought it while they were thinking. Do unto others before they do unto you. I wasn't the first one to say it, but I know emmes when I hear it. Truth.

So, I'm nervous for my man, what's got to fucking do thinking. I'm working with him on some of my best lyrics ever and now he got me thinking—Nat is gonna be thinking so hard about Horace Morace Maynor, he'll be finished before my lyrics are, if you catch my drift?

So, that same night, I only hear tell, because I wasn't anywhere near—

—Nat is lathering up in the showers and senses someone charging for him. It's Horace Morace, of course, and before Nat can move

Horace has him gripped solid under the arms and trying to make magic with his wand.

Nat immediately struggles to free himself. He pounds his fists overhead and into Horace Morace's face, but the blows have no effect. They're like trying to bring down an elephant with fly spray, and Nat's figuring he's soup for sure when all of a sudden he hears Horace Morace crying out something awful.

Nat feels Horace Morace's hands being stripped off him. He drops back against the wet tile and strains to keep his balance in the soap water puddling down at the drain, and sees—he tells me the next day—he sees a trio of bare-ass cons dragging Horace Morace off—

—the last time Nat or anyone ever sees Horace Morace around the joint again.

And Nat and I are talking about it privately over to center field and he says, "Chalky, one of them bare asses looked a lot like your toadie Frankie Visconti."

I shake my head, the way I'm shaking it at you now, and I tell him, "Champ, I never paid any notice to Frankie's ass and I ain't gonna start now."

Nat says, "Was your doing, wasn't it, Chalky."

I say back, "Let me think on it."

He gives me a smile and a hug.

Of course, it ain't over yet.

There's still Rufus Hardaway to deal with.

We met on neutral territory, just me and Rufus. Wasn't the first time, wouldn't be the last, you know what I mean?

Rufus, he puts on his growling act for anyone watching, same as me, but we're talking clean, because we know what it takes to stay on top in the joint.

He says, "Mayor, you wouldn't have no idea where my man Horace Morace Maynor is missing to, would you?"

I show him my palms and say, "Mr. Hardaway, if you have to believe anything you hear, I would very much like you to believe that's the truth."

"And I want you to believe I have to do something about my man who's missing," he says, and his eyes pop all around us, carrying on like he's James Earl Jones on speed.

"Me, the same in your boat, Mr. Hardaway."

"Christ, fuck, Chalky," he says, and his gestures got nothing to do with what he's telling me in a voice lower than a casket. "Horace ain't been seen since he and his big nigger dick went chasing after that music man of yours last night."

"Heard that rumor, Rufus, so whaddaya say?"

"I got a bone of my own says my man Horace gonna stay absent," Rufus says.

He wonders if Nat is under my wing, my protection, and I have to be stand-up, tell him no. *You lie, you die. It's not a rule around here. It's a fact of life. I tell him how I made the offer to Nat, but Nat is still thinking on it far as I know.*

Rufus says, "You didn't tell him about thinking?"

My face answers for me.

Rufus says, "Think I gotta make him a lesson, this Nat the fucking Axe, you know? You do the same, you in my case, bro."

So, he got me there.

Rufus is one black nigger, but he's brighter than a lot of white men I ever met.

I tell him, "The kid is learning me to write music, and that means a lot to me, *Rufus."*

Rufus says, "You asking to owe me a number?"

I says, "What are friends for?"

"You not careful, friends gonna be the death of you one day," and he gives me this attitude that makes me wonder if Rufus is talking about Nat or about himself.

So, anyway, for a while longer we make out like we're arguing, but what we're doing is coming to terms. I turn a hit into hurt, so it will look good for Rufus and ain't any dirt off my mountain.

Wasn't to be, though. You know what it's like, you try and do some good sometimes, and it up and bites you in the ass?

The notion is, Nat's gonna be scratched, which is a far cry from being blotted, or so I hear, you know what I mean?

So, it's dinner mess, and one of Rufus Hardaway's goon platooners hunkers by Nat, who knows none of this. Nat is talking music over his cow and mashed with some of the boys who play in this prison band he's been putting together for the warden, "Pros & Cons" it's called.

The nigger stoops over and whispers something in Nat's ear and then he kisses Nat on the cheek. Nat, he goes crazy nuts. This goon platooner is two people taller and stronger than him, but he don't care. He elbows the nigger across his kisser and draws first blood.

The nigger staggers back and Nat jumps to his feet and some other niggers are at him already. Nat is tearing loose, getting in some useless punches, when this sound—like

—like Phhp—

—like that.

You know?

The sound of a shiv eating into flesh?

I'm at the table acrost from the action, where I can see a piece of metal about three inches long sticking out of Nat's side.

I hear the noise again—

—like Phhp.

I hear it a third time—

—like Phhp.

It's louder than the goddam noise been growing in the mess. Now what we got here is more than a scratch to settle a score. We got James Cagney himself going nuts, you know what I mean?

Chalky heaved a noisy sigh, clicked off the recorder and settled it on his lap. He appeared disturbed by his memories. He picked anxiously at his thumbnail with what was left of his other thumbnail.

Laurent thought she knew why. "You're still sad when you think of Nat dying that way?" she said. Chalky's eyebrows went up and he rubbed his mouth with his fingers while turning over the question in his mind. "You maybe even blame yourself?" He latched his hands on top of his head, stared at the stained, time-warped ceiling as if it were clear sky and he was counting clouds.

"I have seen more tragic death sometimes than even you, maybe, *Monsieur* Ruggles. Tragedy happens out of our control, and no one is to blame but fate."

He nipped at a hangnail and turned to spit it on the floor, trapped her gaze and shifted his head left and right. "That letter you have, the one from the lawyer?"

"Ben Hubbard, *oui.* I already hear differences in his version from yours, but I think some of it has to do with memory after so much time has passed, so we should talk about that more?"

"Lady, it all gotta do with the truth." His voice had taken on a paternal confidentiality. "I said what I hadda back when. The warden says he'll owe me a big number, so I take it. Gladly. I give up the story he needs and no skin off my dick. The things I could tell you . . ."

He let the thought trail off.

"Tell me, and maybe I will owe you a big number."

Chalky said, "You'd owe, all right, but I ain't no Jay Flotsan. Don't need you fuckin' with my body any more'n you cudda got away fuckin' with my head."

She feigned objection. "I didn't try to like—"

"You saw better, only reason. Same as I saw you were a broad what could do me some good down the line. The fact you offer up a number shows how good I sized you up."

Men and their egos.

"*Oui, Monsieur* Ruggles, so now where are we?"

"First, I'm gonna tell you how Nat didn't get killed in the mess hall that night."

Laurent felt her spine grow three inches.

"And how it really happened?"

"Not *how*. What."

Suddenly, she understood.

Her pulse quickened. She nervously lit a Camel.

She said, "Nat is alive, isn't he?"

"Nat is alive," Chalky agreed, punching the air with a fist for emphasis.

"Tell me everything," she said.

He said, "No tape, just ears."

"No tape, just ears."

He dropped the recorder into her handbag, spit into his palm and held it out to her for a handshake. "Now it's legal," he said. He patted her on the cheek, filched the Camel from her lips and drew in enough smoke to reach his toes.

Laurent brushed her palm dry on her skirt. Her hands were shaking with an excitement she couldn't suppress.

The door opened noisily and Jay Flotsan stepped inside barking something about running out of time and having to get Chalky back to solitary.

"Not yet!" Chalky said menacingly.

Flotsan's mouth opened, but no words came out, and he quickly retreated.

Chalky laced his fingers on top of his head, his arms akimbo, took another deep drag on the Camel and sent a smoke cloud drifting. "So," he said, "where were we?"

Chapter 11

On Sundays, even when they were not expecting her brothers or Father O'Bryan, her boss at the church, for dinner, Ana Maria prepared a meal large enough for the neighborhood. Nathan enjoyed watching her as she went about the ritual of preparation with the precision of a master mechanic. She clearly loved working in the kitchen, maybe because it let her recall the happiest days of her childhood in the Heights.

The food was traditional Mexican, laid out for display on a kitchen table covered with an elegant antique damask cloth that Ana Maria used only on special occasions and for their Sunday feast. Otherwise, she folded it neatly and stored it away in an old bedsheet.

He surveyed the table and found the usual steaming assortment of tacos and enchiladas, rice, beans, a tall stack of homemade tortillas, and a deep bowl of Ana Maria's chili that Nathan was sure had the exclusive, cumulative effect of corroding his stomach.

It was never too hot for Ana Maria's brothers, and she was always experimenting with her secret recipe, blending in different combinations of green peppers and red chili pods. Nathan had come to believe the secret was how to get it hot enough to turn his face the color of the Mexican flag. It made him long for the heartburn of his late mother's *gefilte* fish and potato *latke*.

Today it was just the two of them.

They sat down at the table in late afternoon, after the edge of the heat was gone and the lack of air-conditioning in the small apartment was less oppressive. It was intolerable during the summer, when most everyone in the neighborhood was driven to the streets and they sometimes made a picnic on the front porch, eating cold dishes from paper plates.

Nathan watched Ana Maria say the small prayer that always managed to touch her entire life, including theirs together, her head downward and her eyes shut, until just before the *Amen,* when she slowly, hopefully, drew them open to see if he had participated.

He never had in all the time they had been together. It would have been against his faith, if he had any faith left, although sometimes he thought he heard the melodic voice of his late father chanting in his ear the traditional prayer of the orthodox Jew. *Hear, O Israel; the Lord our God, the Lord is One . . .* Was it just that he had given up religion, but could never entirely shake his upbringing or his God?

"How are you coming with your songs?" Ana Maria said, spooning a mound of rice onto his chipped plate. It was from a set of stoneware she'd acquired at a seconds shop.

"Slow." He didn't like discussing his music with her.

It wasn't Ana Maria. He had always been this way about his music.

When the songs were finished and recorded was when people should listen and make up their minds. He knew the songs he was writing and recording now would never be heard outside the Nam, but old habits were hard to break, even if he'd wanted.

"I know they will be wonderful, *querido,*" she said, and changed the subject, as usual trying hard to please him. Her harsh life on the streets, where knowledge can corrupt and kill, had taught her it's usually better not to chase after answers. Safer.

Nathan used the metal church key to pop another bottle of Cerveza. The higher cost of the Mexican import kept him drinking Bud most of the time, but Ana Maria had purchased a six-pack as a special treat when she stopped for last-minute items at the 7-Eleven, en route from Mass.

"If things stay slow at church, I told the father today I will need to find something else somewhere," she said. "I think they need part-time at the Kentucky Fried Chicken."

Nathan stared across the room. "It can't always be you bringing in the money."

"It can, especially with work slow for you at the Nam."

"I don't think so." He sucked at the lip of the bottle.

"Father said it was okay. He knows you are not simply a lazy bum like so many of the others, including my brothers."

"Father knows best," Nathan said offhandedly.

Ana Maria made a face to show she didn't appreciate the humor and asked, "Will you go out later? Be with them?"

She meant the Blaupunkt *bandidos.*

Had known intuitively what was on his mind.

They were going to make a few hit-and-runs at the mall in Sherman Oaks, maybe the Glendale Galeria. Enriqué had invited him along.

Nathan passed, thinking he and Jimmy Slyde could do some work on the new material tonight, but the Tune King had dropped by shortly before Ana Maria arrived home to explain apologetically that the studio had a late booking, gangsta rappers from South Central.

"I tried to discourage them," the Tune King said. "I told them the rate for a weekend, even with their own engineer. They laughed and threw bills at me like it always rains twenties and fifties."

Nathan shrugged it off good-naturedly, although disappointed. He was on the verge of resolving two problems that had plagued him the last couple sessions, one involving tempo, the other a stronger hook to the lyrics of another ballad inspired by memories of Mae Jean Minter.

"You should hear them," the Tune King said. "Sampling from everyone and his brother, with words not even Richard Pryor ever knew, and full of kill, kill, kill, like there's a special for killing going on today at the Safeway, and a lot of screw, screw, screwing, only they got another word for that. Nathan, tell me, please—whatever happened to music? You make music. These people make noise."

Nathan answered good-humoredly, "Music goes by a lot of names, Tune King, but it's always music. Rap. Gangsta Rap. Hip-hop. Punk. Grunge. Heavy metal. Retro. Rock and roll." He couldn't help laughing. "Rock and roll. Remember that one?"

"Maybe better than you, Nathan," the Tune King said, and for a moment his heavy-lidded eyes traveled somewhere else. He recovered quickly and smiled wistfully. "I'd rather remember swing."

"And jazz isn't so bad, either."

"It don't mean a thing if it ain't got that swing," the Tune King sang in a croaked voice barely meant for speaking. "And it ain't gonna mean a thing for at least the next week or two, Nathan." He shrugged and turned his palms up. "Maybe longer. How long the gangsters think they want to be around, in advance. Why I wanted to come and explain personally."

"I appreciate that, Tune King, and I understand."

"Especially since I think you and Ana Maria could use some cash in hand. I don't mind lending you some, if you—" Nathan shook his head against the idea. "No offense. I know you're good for it and besides, I like what I hear when you're working in the studio."

Nathan showed he appreciated his generosity. "I'll let you

know, okay?" he said, wishing the Tune King would leave—

There might still be time to get hold of Enriqué.

There wasn't.

Ana Maria tapped her plate for attention, signaled she was still waiting for his answer about the *bandidos.*

"Staying home with you is a better idea," he said, and raised the Cerveza bottle to toast her. It wasn't exactly a lie.

Ana Maria let the words sink in, then flew from her seat into his arms. She cuddled in his lap, kissing him long and tenderly, making him feel guilty and wishing he were able to return her love, but that would be a lie.

She deserved better than him.

And he deserved?

Would he ever know the answer to that question?

After a dessert of sweet tamales and flan that helped Nathan through the anguish of too much chili, Ana Maria announced she had a special surprise.

She leaped from the table and disappeared into the living room, returning momentarily with her purse. She settled on his lap, placed the purse on the dining table and pulled out a state lottery receipt with ten rows of random numbers she had purchased at the 7-Eleven. She also had the page from the *Times* that reported the winning numbers.

"I didn't see yet. I wanted us to look together. It is forty million dollars. Imagine!"

Her joy at fantasizing how they would spend the money stopped him from reminding her they really couldn't afford to spend ten dollars this way. Instead, Nathan teased her. "You forget nobody from Los Angeles ever wins. To win, you have to go buy your tickets somewhere you've never heard of, like Hemet or Brea-Olinda."

"Lompoc or Needles," she said, falling into a game they'd played before, and raised her fist in a victory salute.

They had one winning combination.

Worth five dollars.

Ana Maria sighed.

Nathan stroked her cheek and said, "Next time."

She agreed. "Better luck next time," she said, and moved his hand to her mouth and kissed what was left of it. "Although with you, *querido,* I have all the luck in the world I will ever want or need."

Later, in bed, sometime after Ana Maria was asleep, her quest for his body unfulfilled, his nightmare returned, as it always did, in full detail. Nathan floated high above the scene, the way Ringo had taught him years ago. He watched the ultimate tragedy of his life happen again, as if it were not happening to him, although it was, God damn it. It was.

He was on stage at the joint, performing with the Pros & Cons, their debut after months of practice and rehearsal. It wasn't the worst band he had ever played with. The worst was the first one he had put together in junior high, when everyone wanted to be a rock-and-roll star, but none of his classmates had any of the skills that seemed to be Nathan's birthright.

The warden had approached him with the idea of forming a band shortly after Nathan arrived at the joint, presenting it in a way that let Nathan know it would be a mistake to refuse. Also at the warden's urging, he taught guitar and songwriting, mainly to cons who found it a soft way to spend time, and to the Mayor of the Yard, Chalky Ruggles, who insisted on getting private lessons, as befit a mayor, and showed a poetic flair for expressing his emotions in words.

The Pros & Cons consisted of a couple professionals who had turned bad habits into hard time and some well-meaning amateurs with an aptitude for rock and roll. He put together a repertoire of rock standards, songs written by his students and some of his own, composed on lonely nights, when his mind was full of despair over

Mae Jean Minter, who no longer came to visit him.

He had never shaken the belief some indecipherable bond existed between them and it only grew stronger after he got to the joint and Mae Jean began showing up once a month, on a Sunday; always on a Sunday. She never wrote, but she never missed a month, either. Or wore the same outfit twice.

Mae Jean dressed modestly and with seeming indifference to effect, ignoring—if she bothered noticing at all—how heads turned as she hurried to the seat opposite him in the cubicle that put them together and kept them apart. She had a long-legged stride that displayed her body and put fantasy in his mind no matter how she dressed.

He was incapable of letting his gaze waver from the crystal complexion of her face. Her expression was always melancholy, and he decided early it was sadness that held a lien on her luminous green eyes. Mae Jean constantly wet her lips, keeping a line to her mouth so firm it made her despondency seem like lipstick.

Where he kept his hands flat on the dull wooden surface on his side, she clasped hers on top so tightly her fingers seemed to blush. The thick clear plastic prevented them from touching, but in Nat's mind there never was a wall between them, only the sin of omission.

They never spoke, not once during any of the visits, as if Mae Jean knew as well as he did there was no reason to; there was no difference words would make so long as he was inside and she was beyond his reach.

The only Sundays Mae Jean missed, until the last one, were because of illness. A screw would bring the message to his cell, looking as despondent as Nat would after a moment. Her monthly visits had come to form almost as much a welcome part of the screws' routine. Nat was quietly pleased when he heard they routinely bet on what she'd be wearing or how she would have fixed her hair for him.

On the days she did not come, he woke up knowing. These days always followed the worst of his nights and nightmares so real he could smell them and, sometimes, reach out and feel them. On these days, he would not bother with any of the elaborate preparations that were normal for her visits; the fastidious grooming, the fresh uniform. He stayed in his cell and played mind games that always included Mae Jean, not rousing off his bunk until visiting hours had passed.

The last Sunday Mae Jean missed, there was no message from her. And, of course, it wasn't really the last Sunday. It was the first of the last Sundays. She never came again, and Nat never learned why. He tried to find out through Ben Hubbard, but all he heard back was that Mae Jean and her husband, Dr. Heidemann, were gone from Indianapolis. They simply up and left, seemed to disappear into thin air, Ben reported, leaving no forwarding address.

It was confirmation of what Nat already knew.

He would never see Mae Jean again.

He was sick for a week, a temperature that burned as harshly as the pain of losing her. He instructed the bosses, no more visitors, and retreated deeper inside the joint and what happy memories he could salvage.

Music gave Nat some solace. Not always. Certainly never enough to dilute her memory.

He played the first Pros & Cons concert for her, as if Mae Jean were sitting in the center of the front row, not Chalky Ruggles.

There was sustained applause after the band ended the hour-long set with an acceptable version of the old Eagles hit, "Take It to the Limit," and he had each member stand and take a bow before launching into the special encore he had planned.

It was a surprise for Chalky, based on a song lyric the mayor had completed after weeks of trial and error, a simple poem that talked about his love for a daughter he had never seen. He had put a melody to it in the days leading up to the show, as a way of saying thank you to Chalky for the business with Horace Morace Maynor, which Chalky denied knowing anything about, of course.

Nat performed the song as an acoustic solo, sitting on a stool center stage, illuminated by what passed for a pin spot. Not everyone got it.

They wanted something heavier and muttered objections through the first words, but Chalky knew at once what he was hearing. He leaped up and confronted the cons with his wagging fist. Captured in the pin light, his fist was more than enough to turn the house as quiet as a turn in solitary.

Nat wasn't certain, but he thought he saw Chalky dab at his eyes once or twice during the number and elbow Frankie Visconti quiet at one point, when the toadie leaned in to remark something. He was on his feet again afterward, to lead a chorus of applause he challenged to quit before he willed it to quit. The applause was burning in Nat's ears as he followed the Pros & Cons offstage on a false exit and—

—noticed a trio of hulking cons he recognized as part of Rufus Hardaway's inner circle. Chalky had pointed them out to him the day they talked about Horace Morace Maynor.

Rufus himself was nearby, holding up a wall. Loitering was never permitted, but the screws either hadn't noticed or were choosing not to notice.

Nat wiped at the sweat with a towel and led the band back on stage. After a few words of cautionary instruction, he launched into Clapton doing Muddy Waters' "Rollin' and Tumblin'." Hardly waiting for the din to peak, he switched from Cream to Blind Faith and went into Winwood's "Can't Find My Way Home" with a passion that went beyond Clapton and shut down the noise.

Nat felt his hands back on automatic pilot, sending out notes no one had yet mastered like the master himself, Nat the Axe. He opened his eyes briefly and looked down at Chalky Ruggles, who made a circle with his thumb and forefinger.

Nat took the applause graciously, then tore into a little John Fogerty Creedence paired with a lot of Robbie Robertson. It climaxed with "The Night They Drove Old Dixie Down." Nat's wallowing delivery had the cons on their feet, all whistle and cheer like the good ol' boys most of them were, hooting and stomping like he hadn't heard since the Indianapolis Motor Speedway.

When he exited, this time, for real, Rufus's people swarmed him and, still with the screws taking no notice, Rufus pushed his face at Nat and said, "We don't need no trouble outta you, so you just come along quiet like."

"Quiet like," Nat agreed. He had no choice.

Nothing was made to seem unusual about the way they strolled to what was called the Johnny Cash dressing room. Legend had it that Johnny Cash himself, in the years before he was born again, hosted a heavy load of prison population there prior to a performance. Admission for a handshake or an autograph was one pill, either direction, and Cash ended the concert cantilevered, or so the story went, with enough stash left over to stoke a regiment.

The room was unlocked and unoccupied. Rufus entered last, checking the hallway for traffic before he closed the door and turned the bolt. One of his people went after a milk crate in the corner, by an old sink, and turned it the long way.

Rufus motioned Nat to sit down. He pulled a homemade blade from its hiding place inside his pants, at the base of his spine, and used the backside of his arm like a barber's strop, running the blade back and forth slowly and gently. Nobody said anything while he satisfied himself.

He swung his gaze to Nat and said, "What happen my man Horace Morace shun not a-happen."

"He made it happen, not me," Nat said, trying to sound calm as his throat tightened around the words.

"He also made hisself disappear, I be listening to you explain it away, that right? Is what you be thinking, Mr. Thinker Man?"

Nat didn't answer. He knew nothing he said would make a difference. Rufus was strut-speaking to impress his people.

"So, then, after I go and try to do the right thing and take a number, settle on a scratch, you go and show two of my best the way to the dark side of the moon forever, pig-sticking 'em the way you done. Bad, bad, bad. Plain mean for somebody wasn't cut where it

could kill him, only give him a rest in sick bay. What you think that was gonna get you?"

Nat stayed mute. If he had been able to talk, he would have reminded Rufus that he was the one who was attacked. He defended himself, for Christ's sake! That's all he did, what anyone would have done.

"No answer? What you doing, Mr. Thinker Man? Thinking on it some more?"

He held out his hands to his people, looking from one to the next, offering them the opportunity to answer for Nat. One by one, they swiveled their heads and answered back with their hands.

"See how confused you got not only me? Well, we gotta do something about it, don't we? Can't let anyone think one minute more that Rufus Hardaway, he gone soft in the head or anywhere."

With that, Rufus placed the blade cautiously on the flat lip of the porcelain sink and explained what he had in mind. "Was all them Jap movies I seen gimme inspiration," he said. "Yakuza stuff."

Nat felt the color leave his face and his expression fold into flat horror as he grasped the full significance of what Rufus was telling him. Terrified, he was seized by the idea of making a dash for the door, screaming and banging until somebody came, but he knew without trying that his legs no longer were working. He felt a pant leg soaking, but was beyond embarrassment.

Rufus said, "Move him over to the sink, boys." Two of them took Nat by the arms. The third prodded him unnecessarily hard. "See you starting to cry, Mr. Thinker Man. You go on right ahead. We finished with you, you cry plenty more. You played your last concert ever here tonight, Nat the Axe. Anywhere, I expects."

Nat managed to call out, "Kill me!"

"What, and miss the fun?" Rufus said. "You all hold on just one minute now. I wants me the first piece of this here pussy."

Rufus came around to where Nat could see him while the cons wrestled his left hand onto the sink. He held out the sledge hammer he was holding for a better look, then brought it down on Nat's knuckles. The force was sufficient to crack the porcelain. Nat screamed out Mae Jean's name before fading into blessed oblivion as swiftly as he now—

—stopped floating.

He tumbled down from the ceiling, back into the bed, screaming—

What?

Mae Jean's name?

As he had so often on the roads that led from Indiana State Prison to Ana Maria?

His scream awakened her.

It took Ana Maria a few moments to remember where she was and, understanding what she'd heard, roll over to comfort him. If she had heard him calling for Mae Jean, she did not tell him that. She cradled Nathan in her arms, patted his shoulder, assured him soothingly that everything was going to be all right. "You'll be fine, baby," she cooed, stroking his hair. "Mama is here to take care of you. Mama is here to take care of you. You'll be fine, *mi corazon.* You'll be fine."

Chapter 12

When she phoned Monday morning, District Attorney Phil Penguin told Laurent another meeting was unnecessary, adamant he had nothing to add to what had been discussed between them earlier. Before he could disconnect, she said, "I know Nat Axelrod is not dead. I know Nat is no longer behind bars at Indiana State Prison and has not been there for years because of you, *Monsieur* Penguin."

The DA caught his breath. "Of course he's dead. I told you already. I was there. I saw him myself. Check the records and you'll find—"

"I saw the records. I have copies. The real records and also the records that were falsified under your direction."

"Preposterous!" he said, full of bluster, then, more cautiously: "These alleged documents. Where did you allegedly get them?"

"Allegedly at the prison. I was there yesterday."

"Impossible! Nobody would—" He stopped himself. Made an unintelligible noise. "I'm in court most of the day. Make it four o'clock."

"Ask *Monsieur* Parriott to join us."

"Laddie Parriott. What's that about?"

"Four o'clock," she said. *"Merci."*

Promptly at four p.m., Laurent was ushered into the DA's wood-paneled conference room. An anxious Phil Penguin and a curiously sedate Laddie Parriott were waiting under the Great

Seal of Indiana.

She settled at the table facing the two lawyers.

Penguin kept shifting his gaze, trying to read what he didn't yet know, but Laddie was a cipher. She wanted them to stew for a few minutes, keep them on edge for her questions, so she made a show of fumbling through her handbag for her spiral notepad and a pen; checked to be sure the salmon-colored, matchbox-size, mini-cassette recorder was there.

Penguin could not find a comfortable position. The air conditioner was pumping a cold breeze into the room, but he was sweating like he had just come off the hot sands of Malibu. He noticed her noticing and scoured his face with his hand, then dried the hand on his pocket handkerchief.

He cleared his throat and said, "So, where are we?"

Laurent said, "Arriving at the truth?"

Laddie said behind a flat expression, "Phil told me something about documents when he called. You have documents to show us, is that it?"

"I have no documents to show you," she said.

"You said you would have these alleged documents with you," Penguin said, immediately recognizing she had used a ruse to bring them together.

"*Non.* You have been as clever at suppressing the truth, *Monsieur* Penguin, as you were at manufacturing it originally. I was unable to see them or secure copies during my visit."

The DA looked at her sarcastically. Rising, he said, "Well, Laddie, I believe we can consider this meeting concluded."

Laddie looked from Laurent to Penguin and shook his head. Gave the impression he saw she was working on more than a lie. Said, "Hold off a minute, Phil . . . What else, Miss Laurent?"

Penguin settled back in his chair and stared at her maliciously.

"*Monsieur* Parriott, I was hoping you would tell me."

"Give us one good reason?"

Laurent reached into her bag for her spinal notepad and cassette recorder and placed them on the table.

Seeing the recorder further upset Penguin. "I'll ask that you not tape this conversation," he said, ready to snatch the recorder away.

"For you to listen," Laurent said, answering his discomfort with a smile, and pulled the recorder out of reach. "For now it is better than any documents."

She pressed the play button.

The tape began at the point where Jay Flotsan was trying to control his excitement as she glided her lips along the silky length of his miserable prick, playing it like a harmonica:

"That's it, baby, oh, yeah, ride 'em, cowgirl . . . Yeah, no, Nat, he weren't killed in any riot or no ways . . . Suck it, baby. The tip, okay? A little on the tip . . . He, no, Nat come through alive, and them boys got him out right after that . . . That DA, Penguin, and the other one—God. Oh, God! This other guy who sometimes come around to visit and talk music . . . Maybe two months sooner and Nat, he wudda come outta here whole . . . Yeah, pull back the skin and gobble that tip, you cunt you . . . Oh, God! Oh—"

Laurent snapped off the tape and looked quixotically at the lawyers, whose expressions told her they recognized how she was extracting the information from the frantic, tinny voice on the tape. "One must make sacrifices to get at the truth," she said. "Jay Flotsan. He is the assistant warden and a lousy lay, but he likes to talk as much as he likes to fuck."

Laddie cleared his throat. "The tape is about as hearsay as hearsay gets, Miss Connart. Inadmissible evidence in any court in the land."

Penguin interrupted him. "And Jay Flotsan to refute it, he knows what's good for him; if he damn well wants to keep his job!"

"*Bien, Monsieur* Penguin. Now *you* are fucking with Flotsan. I have no objection. It will serve the bastard right, but I will publish his statements anyway. The tape is admissible in my court, the court of public opinion. How he assisted the two of you when you came to take Nat Axelrod away, and how, afterward, he helped the warden hide the truth, exactly as you directed them to do, *Monsieur* Penguin. *Merde!* There could be the devil to pay."

"We'll get an injunction. Sue you and your damned paper for millions, you go and pull that crap!" He was scrambling ineffectually.

"The *Tab,* it has very deep pockets. By the time your lawsuit gets to court, the damage will be done. You have thoughts about higher office like your predecessor, Governor Benedictus. I don't think so anymore, any more than I think the governor he'll be too pleased with the scandal."

Penguin pressed his nose inside the finger pyramid he had formed, elbows on the table, thumbs supporting his chin. Laurent saw beyond his eyes to the wheels turning inside his head.

"An' the gobble-uns'll git you ef you don't watch out!" she said, and turning to Laddie, "Isn't that so, *Monsieur* Parriott?"

Penguin's eyes receded and he released the pyramid to show a mouth brimming over with distaste. "I guarantee you, by tomorrow there will be nothing, no files, nothing, that anyone can locate to support anything that moron Flotsan might think of saying."

Laddie placed a hand on Penguin's shoulder to calm him and wondered, "Scandal? All I hear so far is a tempest in a teapot, Miss Connart. A fib. So, Nat isn't dead? The state respected his wishes for privacy and confidentiality."

"And put back onto the streets a convicted rapist of a young girl many years before his mandatory sentence is up? Because it worked out so well for California when it released that son of a bitch Lawrence Singleton?"

Laddie gave her a blank look, like this would be enough to make the questions go away. Studied his half-moon glasses. She sat impassively, patiently. Finally, he shrugged and gestured her to continue, as if they were in a tennis match and he was a point away from winning.

Merde!

Men and their egos.

"Now *you* are trying to fuck with *me, Monsieur* Parriott? Let me tell you how the game is played, all right?" She looked at him coldly. "The question is not about Nat Axelrod being alive or dead." She moved her gaze back to Phil Penguin. "The question is also not about a convicted rapist. *N'est c'est pas?*"

Laddie said, "Ben Hubbard also had a saying for what you're trying to pull on us now, Miss Connart. He'd say, *Please, stop with the punching already and give me the punch line.*"

"What was his saying for when people like the former district attorney, Governor Benedictus, and Judge Dirst, who tried and sentenced Nat, and the chief of police and, of course, *Monsieur* Penguin—when they got together to frame someone all the way to prison, the way they did Nat?"

"Screw you!" Phil Penguin said, so loud that a moment later a secretary was poking her head through the conference room door, eyes wide with concern. "It's okay, Marybeth," Penguin told her—barely—laboring to catch his breath, his face turned beet red, blue veins stretched out at his temples and just under his inflamed eyes.

Marybeth retreated as quickly as she had materialized.

Penguin sank into his seat, still far from calm. Laddie patted his forearm and grasped it encouragingly, shot Laurent a defiant look. "More hearsay, Miss Connart."

She lowered her voice to barely above a whisper. "I will write about this conspiracy and this cover-up, what happened to Nat

Axelrod, an innocent man, in the sad aftermath," she said. She arched both eyebrows. "The old district attorney, the judge, the others can answer or not as they see fit. Even you, *Monsieur* Parriott, are welcome to talk about this miscarriage of justice and get your free publicity while the public is making up their mind."

Laddie said, "You've done a wonderful job of assassinating by association the governor, a federal judge, a chief of police, and Phil Penguin, one of the few prosecutors Ben Hubbard ever had any respect for. I was just a kid promoting records back then. What am I guilty of?"

"Loyalty," she said, serving the word like an ace. "Your loyalty to Benjamin Harrison Hubbard, who was also part of the conspiracy and the cover-up that sent Nat Axelrod to prison."

Laddie was still for a moment that seemed to stretch forever before he said in a voice that undercut her own, "That simply is not true, Miss Connart."

Penguin said, "For Christ's sake, Laddie. This whore of a woman is not interested in the truth. She's out for a garbage story in her garbage newspaper." He appeared to be on the verge of tears.

"Phil, please, let me," Laddie said, sounding like a parent dealing with a distressed child. He reached over and briefly placed his fingers in front of Penguin's mouth.

The gesture brought back to Laurent images of her own papa comforting and counseling her. In a way, she felt sorry for Penguin, for what she was putting him through, but the way Laddie Parriott contorted his face told her she was closing in on more than the story that brought her to Indianapolis.

The reward that comes with the story?

The thirty thousand dollars?

Sixty thousand?

Non!

Nat Axelrod had become a story worth far more since her first inklings that people had engaged in a silent conspiracy for almost a decade.

Laddie's voice pulled her back into the room, telling her, "Ben Hubbard knew from the first Nat didn't stand a chance, but he did not participate in any railroad. He always believed in Nat's innocence. So did I. So did Phil here."

"I believe Phil, like you, is a good and decent man, also with great loyalty to *Monsieur* Hubbard. But Phil here did participate."

Penguin slammed his fist hard on the glossy surface of the conference table.

Laddie glued it to the table with his own.

Laurent said, "Here is my offer. You speak to me the truth and I promise you Benjamin Harrison Hubbard will not be tainted in any way by my story."

"He's the reason Nat Axelrod got out a free man, you know?"

"*Oui, Monsieur* Parriott. I know." Laddie arched back in his seat, not quite sure if he should believe her. "I have known all day," she said. Laddie looked for the lie on her face.

"And pigs can fly," Penguin hooted from a corner of his mouth.

"Nadine Barber, *Monsieur* Penguin?" Penguin took a sharp breath. "I visited with Nadine Barber, and she had interesting things to say. I will report about these interesting things, and you won't be a happy man. On this I give you my word."

Penguin couldn't find a place for his eyes to land.

Laddie showed he understood what Nadine might have said to her. "Miss Connart, we cooperate and there is nothing in anything you write that tarnishes Ben's memory."

"*Oui.* Yes."

"Phil here?"

"Anything you tell me now in this room will be off the record.

Neither of you will be mentioned by name in the story. Only you will know who, when I write about my confidential and unimpeachable sources."

"Not for attribution, I think. Phil, how about you?"

"What makes you think we can trust this bitch?"

Laurent made a show of taking her cassette recorder, the spiral notepad and the pen and dropping them into her bag. She displayed both sides of her hands. "No tape, no notes, no quotes. Done."

Laddie said, "Phil, be realistic. The story she's threatening us with won't do anybody any good, except maybe to sell more of her newspapers. Sweet Lord Jesus! It's a lose-lose situation. You don't give a damn about yourself, then do it for Ben."

Penguin traded a helpless stare for Laddie's sincerity and looking away, said, "For Ben," like he was examining the concept.

"For Ben . . . Tell her, Phil."

Penguin geared his head left and right and, after blowing away a deep breath, said, "Ben was too smart not to see all the signs, but he never took part in the railroad."

Laurent suppressed a smile. She had won, but there was no purpose in gloating.

"You did, though, *oui*?"

"I closed my eyes and did what I was told. I only followed orders." He closed them now.

"I know from my papa all about people who only followed orders," she said, unable to control her sarcasm. She took a few seconds to let the flash of anger pass. "Go on, *Monsieur* Penguin. Tell me the rest."

Penguin tilted his head back and pushed his hands through his hair. He cast his eyes about the room as if searching for a starting point.

Laddie saw the difficulty he was having. He settled his glasses on the conference table and suggested: "Kern Posey?"

Like a witness under oath, Penguin began explaining how Posey was Nat's key roadie and designated caretaker—

—the roadie known as "the Weasel," who brought Mae Jean Minter to Nat's dressing room at Indy and, later, the only member of Nat's entourage still at the Airport Holiday Inn when Nat was shot. Because Nat never wanted to roll out as early as the others, someone had to stay behind and play nursemaid, get him awake, cajole him into reality, and pursue a checklist of maneuvers toward getting Nat on the glide path to the next city on the tour.

His duties as Nat's key roadie gave Posey a certain celebrity status in their underworld and he enjoyed the attention, although not when Nat would joke, "You know why they call Kern 'Number Two'? Because he's such a little shit!" It made Posey wince, even though he knew the boss was kidding and would never say that unless he had had a couple pops or a few toots too many.

While Nat slept across the corridor from Posey's own room, the Weasel had checked his watch and given himself another ten minutes to linger downstairs in the coffee shop. He was still optimistic as he took one final pass at a pimple-faced waitress, "Corrinne" on her Howdy badge, who had spent the night playing personal room service with one of the backup singers.

She looked worn out and half asleep on her feet, but showed more than marginal interest once he mentioned the chance of her being introduced to Nat before the limo spirited him away to the airport. For sure, the Weasel knew all the magic words that worked.

He did not see the two officers hurry through the main lobby with Huck Minter and his daughter, although he was within fifty feet of them. At that precise moment, his eyes were closed and he was concentrating on the hand he had managed to run under the hem of Corrinne's faded yellow uniform and now used to massage a hole in her pantyhose.

Corrinne was leaning over Posey's booth and clearing dishes in a way that let one of her breasts rub against his face. She smiled sleepily and pushed closer toward him, pressing her breast harder on his cheek while checking to be sure her body was turned in a way that hid his playful arm from the few other customers in the coffee shop.

The gun exploded loud enough to get everybody's immediate attention.

Corrinne pulled back so quickly that Posey's hand ripped a larger hole in the panty hose and sprang free only after two buttons popped loose. She managed not to drop the dishes.

The Weasel sensed he had a serious problem. He pushed Corrinne aside and jumped from the booth, pausing momentarily to throw down a ten on the table. He ran straight for the stairs rather than bother with elevators.

Bounding into Nat's suite and through the bedroom door, he heard a woman screaming and saw Nat drenched in blood, his eyes staring out blindly, and heard himself shouting a confusion of profanities.

Posey felt hands grappling with his body, holding him tighter and lifting him off the floor as he struggled to reach Nat, his arms flailing desperately until a grip turned into the snap of cold metal around his wrists, first one and then the other. He realized he was battling two police officers and froze. One of them shoved the Weasel into a corner and pointed a service revolver at him. The other officer, older, a sergeant, gently directed two people out of the room. One was an old man with a limp. The other person he recognized as the groupie from last night, Mae Jean. She was shouting and crying.

"What the hell is going on here?" the Weasel called indignantly. "Don't anybody care we gotta be on the four o'clock to Dallas? We got a show to do tonight!"

The officer stepped right up to Posey. He cocked back the hammer on his service revolver and stuck the barrel under Posey's chin. Said, "Show me some civil obedience, you little hippie fart-face."

Later, a police search of Posey's room uncovered more than a full ounce of cocaine, a baggie stuffed full of tightly rolled joints, and a collection of outlawed prescription pills and capsules. Before police released him on his own recognizance, he signed without reservation a sworn statement for District Attorney Malcolm Benedictus.

In the statement, the Weasel admitted being present in Nat Axelrod's room and observing the investigating officers discover a series of small brown bottles, each one containing at least an ounce of a substance that later proved to be cocaine; a supply of illegal pharmaceuticals; and a large stash of hand-rolled marijuana cigarettes.

At the airport, the officers accompanying him watched as Posey cashed in his book of tour route tickets for a one-way flight to New York and take a travel voucher for the balance of the refund, rather than permit the difference to be returned to the tour's travel agency.

Phil Penguin said, "The Weasel said he thought about calling Dallas and letting the tour manager know Nat wouldn't be making it, but decided to let well enough alone." He gestured he was done and rubbed his eyes.

Laurent traded looks with Laddie Parriott before asking the DA, "Where the railroad of Nat began, with Kern Posey's false statement?"

"False? I don't know that it was false," Penguin said, with barely a trace of his earlier belligerence. "I wasn't there when he made it or swore to it, but I had doubts. It seemed too pat. Too efficient. And you overhear conversations. Small talk. Hallway gossip. Officers winking at one another. That sort of thing."

"You shared this with Ben Hubbard?"

"As much as I ethically could. Ben tried to shake Posey at the trial, but the little creep stuck by his story."

"Do you know where Posey might be now?"

"That was going on ten years ago. No reason ever to keep track of that sort. Bad enough I remember him."

Laurent looked at Laddie, who also shook his head.

"Huck Minter?"

Penguin said, "Another wart on the ass of humanity. Missing and not missed since he got out of prison," telling her Huck Minter was well known to the police and to the district attorney's office—

—long before the alleged rape of his daughter by Nat. He had a long history of arrests for being drunk in public places, sometimes including indecent exposure, and a long series of nine-one-one incidents, his common law wife Elizabeth accusing and later recanting allegations of verbal and physical abuse.

At the time, he was forty-three, a sullen, stone-faced man of medium height, stocky and balding, exhibiting what Phil Penguin came to characterize in the transcript of his preliminary interview as a simmering hatred for society. Other than a chronic drunk, Huck was a widower, another situation of his own making.

Three years earlier, heading home with Elizabeth and their only daughter, teenaged Mae Jean, after a full day at the state fair, where the beer was as plentiful as the popcorn, he missed seeing a stop light and plunged into an intersection. His pickup plowed into the side of a feed carrier, bounced off backwards into a station wagon and a van, burst instantly into flames.

Huck was thrown clear, and a quick-thinking pedestrian rushed to pull his unconscious daughter from the fiery wreckage, but Huck's wife was trapped in the crush of the truck. The fire climbed too fast and too defiantly for anyone to reach her before her screams of pain turned into pleas for help, then anguished begging for God's forgiveness.

A four-year-old girl and a six-month-old infant boy in the station wagon also were killed.

Huck sustained a concussion and two legs that cracked loudly and splintered through the skin, gushing blood as he hit the concrete pavement and bounced several times while rolling into a temporary peace of mental darkness.

The DA's file indicated that Huck had all the time he needed to think out the details of his story before the doctors finally permitted police at his bedside for the purpose of taking a statement. He told them Elizabeth had been driving. They didn't believe him, but couldn't shake him into any other truth, and he was never charged.

Huck left the hospital six weeks after the accident, his bills covered by state and federal aid, carrying as a permanent souvenir a wide strip of pink scar tissue that ran down the left side of his craggy face and kept the eyelid at permanent half-mast. Doctors said his noticeable limp would be with him for the rest of his life.

His daughter suffered no visible scars.

When the police tried questioning Mae Jean, she screamed until they left her alone. When they tried again later, she sank inside silence, swooned into a spasmodic seizure. They retreated after settling for a statement they framed and had Mae Jean sign. In it she said she remembered nothing. Unable to locate relatives who could care for her while Huck was in the hospital, the authorities temporarily placed her in a foster home.

Father and daughter were ultimately reunited in the small, decaying house northeast of downtown Indianapolis that had been Elizabeth's inheritance and now passed to his daughter under the inviolate terms of her grandmother's will.

Huck was not an educated man. He had never gotten past the fifth grade and could hardly read or write, but he had a native intelligence that told him the house was his as long as he held on to Mae Jean—

"Or so he inferred when he sat down with me to talk about the rape of his daughter," Phil Penguin said, recreating the meeting for Laurent and Laddie Parriott:

"Penguin, huh? You look young to be a lawyer." Huck's voice had a derisive sound built in, and its thick, coarse tone told of years of hard whiskey abuse.

Penguin smelled the booze on his visitor's grimy clothing even before he looked up and saw him standing across the small utility of-

fice, just inside the door, an arm resting casually on the filing cabinet.

Huck looked like a pit bull to him, fresh from one battle and ready for another.

Penguin sensed the challenge and braced himself to resist. He also resisted any courtesy. He already did not like the shabby old man, and there was no sense now that something could happen to change his opinion. He stayed seated while gesturing Huck to have a seat, meanwhile, closing the Huck Minter *file on his desk and dropping it out of sight onto his lap.*

Huck crossed over, pulling his bad leg after him.

He repositioned the only guest chair so it was to one side of Penguin's desk, sank into it, and lapped the bad leg over an arm rest. He looked around smugly, then straight at Penguin. "You gonna get that rapist bastard for me?" He covered his mouth with a hand, calling attention to the side of his face that was distorted under a patchwork quilt of gauze squares and strips of adhesive tape.

Penguin said, "I'm twenty-six and a graduate of Yale Law School, Mr. Minter." He indicated the framed evidence on the wall and managed to keep his smile from faltering. "Should the facts in the case so merit, I will be doing everything within my capability to see that Mr. Axelrod is convicted and sent to state prison for the term prescribed by law."

"Myself, I'd turn him into one-a them dickless wonders, like in a harem, you boys let me have him to myself for five minutes. That's one long-haired singer would come away a high soprano, and hard-pressed to grow whiskers no more."

"Yes, I've already seen your act on the TV news, Mr. Minter. Two or three times so far."

Huck cocked his head and gave the deputy district attorney a critical once-over with his good eye. He made a face and said, "You mean something insulting by them words?"

Penguin cleared his throat before answering.

"I mean, I wish you would stop trying my case on the six-o'clock

news, Mr. Minter. The net result of your statements to news media may be to make it impossible for Mr. Axelrod to get a fair trial here."

Huck opened his mouth and made a silent laugh that sent the acrid, whiskey smell of his breath sailing across the desk. "Don't want no fair trial. What I want any more is justice."

Penguin turned to avoid the smell and ignored Huck's answer. "Those interviews are why I requested this visit today. I'd like you to stop. It doesn't help our case, Mr. Minter."

"Go fuck yourself," Huck said. He sent another jet of bad breath in Penguin's direction. "You need to respect I'm only doing like Mr. Malcolm Benedictus, your boss, says is fit and proper for a father to act."

"The district attorney said that to you?"

Penguin stirred unintentionally, and the Minter file slid off his lap and onto the cold hardwood floor. The loose pages scattered.

"Yeah, your boss. You don't believe me, you just go trot off and ask for yourself."

Huck's smug look returned, elevating his cheeks. It pulled loose corners of the adhesive tape that already were curling, pushing some of the gauze aside like flaps and exposing purple and red masses of wounded flesh.

"Excuse me," Penguin said. He ducked below the desk to reassemble the Huck Minter file, glad for the distraction that hid his astonishment and anger.

Penguin leaned back and stared down at the conference room floor, like the file might be there now, then lapsed into silence again.

Laurent said, "So, after this, you asked Malcolm Benedictus what Huck Minter meant by acting like a fit and proper father, or you decided to forget about it?"

"What do you think?" Penguin said. "I was pretty certain my boss had Minter playing the trained parrot for his own political ambition. A victory here, high profile and all, would give a big boost to Malcolm's ambitions. How the system works in this country. I didn't put it that way to him, though. I didn't have the chance."

Clearly, the memory was painful to him.

"Malcolm took me aside, over to the Columbia Club, and he spelled it out, but not exactly in those terms. Just enough. I would do the grunt work and he would be around for the kill, and I could come out ahead, too. Just like some others would. He did not say Judge Dirst specifically, or anyone, but there was no way to mistake his meaning. I was trapped. It was go along to get along. I was fairly fresh out of law school, green behind the ears, and already had started on a beautiful family. The old story. So that's how it went. Kern Posey and Huck Minter stood by their sworn statements and not even Ben Hubbard could shake them on cross."

"Even after Nadine Barber came to you?"

Penguin propped his elbows on the table and turned his palms to the ceiling.

"This little schoolgirl friend of Mae Jean's came asking to see me when it was looking real bad for Nat, close to the point of no return. She had this fanciful story she swore came from Mae Jean herself. I listened real good—"

"And you went to Malcolm Benedictus again, to tell him what you had found out."

Penguin winced audibly. "I didn't bother. It wouldn't have made any difference. To make any difference, it would have to be Mae Jean Minter herself taking the witness stand and telling."

"Did you go to Mae Jean and talk to her. Ask her?"

"Of course I went to Mae Jean. It was my sworn duty as an officer of the court. I told her what I told you—the only way for her story to help Nat Axelrod would be for it to come from her. She said she could not do that. I asked her why, and she began shaking something fierce. I saw if I pushed any harder she would fall apart, that's how fragile she was, so I let her be."

"And what did Ben Hubbard do when you told him?"

Penguin gave Laurent an appreciative smile. She supposed it was for understanding that was his next move, the right thing to do.

"Ben thanked me and said he would try to make more headway than I had been able. That was the only time it came up between us, except for a look he gave in court the next day, too fast for anyone else to understand, Ben telling me he also had struck out with Mae Jean."

"And, shortly after, Malcolm Benedictus called Mae Jean to the stand."

"Malcolm called her, yes."

"And her testimony sealed the case against Nat."

"Mae Jean testified like her first statement, nothing like Nadine Barber had told it to me, like Nat was guilty as original sin."

"And after, so did Nadine Barber."

"Said it was exactly how Mae Jean had told her the story the next day, how she had been forcibly raped by Nat twice, first in his suite and second time in the back of his limousine, when he dropped her off to home. Like she had never heard otherwise from Mae Jean or said otherwise to me. And that was all she wrote."

"And the forensic evidence?"

"Forensic evidence?"

"The results of the medical examination of Mae Jean?"

"There was no medical examination. Mae Jean would not sit for it and went into one of her frenzies every time we asked. Neither would her daddy, Huck. That scumbag raised a loud enough racket that, finally, Malcolm told me it didn't matter. We had Mae Jean's testimony. That was dandy enough."

"And it was dandy enough."

"As dandy as Yankee Doodle, with Nadine Barber a bonus."

"And the jury brought in a guilty verdict."

"Faster than any Five Hundred."

"And Nat would still be serving his sentence at Indiana State Prison today if it weren't for—"

"—Ben," Laddie cut in. "Ben Hubbard."

"And you, too, *Monsieur* Penguin?"

Penguin thought about it and made an *I suppose so* look.

"And Mae Jean Minter."

"Mae Jean Minter, yes, especially Mae Jean Minter," Penguin said, and turned to Laddie Parriott for confirmation.

"The way Ben told it to me," Laddie said—

—and began painting a picture in a way that showed off his courtroom skills, full of rich details that could impress and sway a jury by the clean truth of the vision.

Momentarily, Laurent was back in time with him, as Benjamin Harrison Hubbard studied the handwriting, a childish scrawl full of misspelled words.

Ben looked from the letter to the envelope and reflected on the postmark: Las Vegas. Judging from the date, it had arrived about a month earlier, while he was in the hospital, and was shoved inside one of those obedient stacks of mail that wouldn't be going anywhere until his return to work. His hands pressed hard on the desk as he pushed back on the swivel chair and eased up, pretending not to feel the million razor blades taking small slices from his skin.

He was barefoot and let his feet enjoy the softness of the thick pile carpeting crossing the office to the liquor cabinet. He poured himself another straight Scotch and held the glass up to the light. The color satisfied him, but not the amount. He added another turn of the wrist.

"Cheers," the lawyer said, toasting himself. He nodded approvingly at the flavor, took another swallow, then fished ice cubes out of the

small refrigerator and dropped a bunch into the glass before retracing his path back to the desk.

Ben settled down and placed the glass on the wet surface of the coaster while adjusting for comfort. His other hand moved by radar to the humidor and connected with a giant Havana. He fiddled with its preparation and, after the cigar was lit, contemplated its flavor and fragrance as white smoke floated like miniature clouds in the modest natural light of late morning.

He picked up the letter to read again, sipping cautiously and occasionally sucking one of the cubes. Traces of moisture clung to his mustache. Where the half dozen pages of penciled words had shocked him on first reading, they saddened him now. Not because the truth came as a surprise, but because it came at all.

He reached for the telephone and dialed the district attorney's number from memory. Chatted briefly about the weather and her blue-ribbon winning hot apple pies with Judy on the switchboard. Asked for Phil Penguin. Was put straight through.

"How're the ulcers holding up, Ben?"

"Doctors tell me I don't have to worry about the bleeding anymore."

"That's great news!"

"Not to be confused with the not-so-great news. When they cut me open this last time, they found a slight case of pancreatic cancer."

First there was quiet, then Penguin said, "I don't think that's funny, Ben."

Ben swirled the ice cubes in his glass and took a hearty swallow, catching one cube on the rebound. "It doesn't exactly have me bending over with a million laughs, either, Penguin."

"I'm sorry."

"You want to make it up to me, find a miracle cure. I'll give you sixty days. Not quite as good as the doctors give me, but more than generous, considering."

"I don't know what to say, Ben."

"First, you forget what I just told you. Privileged. Then you listen. Indulge me for a couple of minutes." He put down the glass, cradled the phone, and reached for the letter. *"Of course, you remember the unforgettable good doctor and missus Wolf Heidemann, however long it's been since they vacated our fair city?"*

"Of course."

"The good missus doctor has communicated with yours truly, esquire, from Las Vegas, and she's telling old wife's tales out of school."

"I don't understand."

"Mae Jean Heidemann nee Minter has written to confess all. Maybe just some. In the modest mea culpa I hold before me, Mae Jean says you folks put Nat Axelrod away on a bum rap. She says he never laid so much as a guitar pick on her."

"Who, then?"

"Mae Jean says it was our original contestant number one—Kern Posey. A lot of chapter and worse to what she's reporting."

"Jesus! Do you believe what you're reading, Ben?"

"More so than her spelling and punctuation."

"What are you suggesting?"

"Mae Jean's formal education was severely lacking. It's more than a suggestion."

"Hah, hah. Very funny . . . You didn't call only to share the letter, Ben. What are you suggesting?"

"As a matter of fact, lad, the impossible dream of the legal fraternity. Let us go out among them and do something right for a change."

Laddie looked at Phil Penguin for verification.

"Sounds right," Penguin said, as if he begrudged Laurent the fact. "I remember you hanging around him almost from the time the trial was over, already caught up in his spell, the way a lot of us were long before you. An inspiration, that man."

Laurent was anxious for knowledge, not overripe sentimentality. "So, when he said do something right for a change, what did you do right for a change for this wonderful man, your inspiration?"

Penguin gave her a harsh look, found things to do with his hands for a minute or two, showing it would not be her who controlled the situation.

Men and their egos.

"I told Ben what he already knew. The DA would not be about to give him what he wanted, Nat's freedom, on the strength of an unsubstantiated letter that could have come from any one of the millions of cranks out there. Ben was satisfied, though. He was certain, even if we couldn't find Mae Jean in Las Vegas—and we never could—we could find handwriting specimens that would prove she'd written this confession.

"He accused me of talking law when he was busy talking justice. He reminded me that Malcolm Benedictus would never let anything or anybody contaminate the conviction that had made him a leading contender for lieutenant governor.

"He said, *Believe me, Penguin, unless this gets done and soon, I will raise a stink that will consign your boss and his ambition to the garbage heap. You find a way. Think of it as a going-away present for me or, so help me, the gobble-uns'll git you when you least expect.*"

Penguin grew wistful at the memory. "With Ben riding herd most of the way, it took us a little over three months to work it to where the State Parole Authority commuted Nat's sentence to time served. Parole was waived, provided he agreed to leave the state and the jurisdiction of Indiana within twenty-four hours.

"Appearing on behalf of the DA, I vouched for the prisoner in this regard. There never was discussion for the record on the rape charge, not that it mattered any. The Nat Axelrod file was closed and ordered sealed, part of Ben's tradeoff with Malcolm. You hadn't come looking, nobody ever would have been the wiser."

"And the other guy Jay Flotsan told me about, who sometimes visited and talked music with Nat, that was Ben?"

Laddie shook his head and poked his chest with a finger. "Me, Miss Laurent." His throat closed explaining, "Ben died a week before the Parole Authority met. I went with Phil in Ben's place, the way he made me promise, and the same way I promised him about law school."

"Tell me about Nat's hands. Jay Flotsan said they had been horribly maimed. He said he didn't know how. Do you?"

"You get off on horror stories?"

"I have lived enough of them not to be bothered by one more."

"He was never going to play a guitar again," Penguin said. "His hands had been crippled beyond repair."

Laddie shook his head. "We only saw photos. Horrible."

Penguin said, "We heard Nat had some serious problems with the black faction, but any details are locked away in that file. It happens all the time, not just in the movies."

"Nat never told you?"

"Never a chance. He wasn't at the hearing and he didn't want visitors then or anytime afterward. The last I heard, he got his cheap suit, whatever money he'd banked working in the library and teaching music classes—some band he put together—and a one-way bus ticket out of Indiana."

"To where?"

"Vegas. I think. Laddie, that your recollection?"

"An overnight stop in Indianapolis and a transfer to Vegas."

Laurent thought: Las Vegas again.

Mae Jean's letter to Ben Hubbard. From Las Vegas.

Her postcard to Nadine Barber. From Las Vegas.

Nadine Barber.

Laurent's instincts screamed it was time to pay another visit to Nadine, whose importance to the emerging mosaic had become a concept to pursue when Chalky Ruggles spoke of the love Nat wore on his sleeve for the girl whose sworn testimony sent him to prison, yet who showed up every month to visit until she disappeared from his life.

Why had Mae Jean done this?

Was it a question Nadine could answer for her?

CHAPTER 13

Tuesday.

Nadine was playing in wet dirt that passed for a front yard garden, doing something to the flowers with names Laurent would never know or care to know—only orchids and roses mattered to her—when she looked up and noticed she had company again.

"I have something here for you," Laurent said, displaying a check.

It was for a thousand dollars and would be making a major dent in what was left of the *Tab* advance, but Laurent figured she would need this large an incentive to inspire Nadine to talk to her this time. Besides, if the story coming together was as big as she had begun to suspect, she was confident Knobby would gladly wire more money.

Merde!

Her recurring thought:

Had it become too big a story to waste on the*Tab*?

Nadine's puzzled look turned curious as she rose and, after putting aside her tools and mud-encrusted gloves, wiped her sweat-drenched forehead dry with the checkered bandanna hanging from a back pocket of her overalls. It was only mid-morning, but already the sun was burning a hole through the haze of a rain-threatening sky.

Nadine moved the check in and out until she found a good reading range, almost to her nose, swollen this morning, as red as the skin of her left cheek was a bulging bluish purple.

Perhaps her marriage to Ernie was not as idyllic as Nadine had painted before, and—

—how many other truths hadn't she shared?

Nadine's eyes widened. "What's this about?" she said, holding the check between them.

"Mae Jean Minter. Again. If you tell me what I need to know, I will sign it for you. One thousand dollars."

"Like what?" she said, not ready to commit. Uncomfortable. If not for the check, Laurent sensed she already would have found some excuse to flee inside the house, locking the front door behind her. "I told you I only heard from her that once? From Las Vegas?"

"Before that."

"Before?"

"*Oui.* The trial."

Nadine acted a smile. "As much as I could surely use this money, Lord knows, anything I said to you would already have been in the newspapers. Go and look there and—"

"I want to hear what wasn't in the newspapers." Nadine looked puzzled again. "How Mae Jean visited her convicted rapist after he was in prison."

Nadine's eyes blinked with astonishment and settled into a defiant stare. "I didn't know that," she said and handed back the check to Laurent, shoving it at her before she could change her mind.

"Of course you did," Laurent said. "You were Mae Jean's best friend and it's something best friends would share."

Nadine opened her mouth to say something, but any thoughts emptied unspoken into the air. She glanced at the check, dropped her hand to her side.

Laurent said, "It's been ten years almost. What trouble can there be in telling the truth after ten years?"

Silence again fell from Nadine's mouth.

Laurent took a chance. "They might know you lied for your friend on the witness stand? The authorities? How you lied under oath?" Nadine chortled and turned and tilted her head, as if she were studying Laurent for lunacy. "They don't care now after so long. Nat Axelrod is gone from prison, a free man."

"The authorities?" Nadine said indignantly, almost spitting out the word. "I give them what they wanted and they got off my case anymore."

"Who, then? Who or what is keeping you from all the truth now?"

Nadine thought about it for a long time. "I get to keep all this money? It's all mine?"

"Answer all my questions and there may be more."

"Maybe two hundred and fifty dollars more?"

"Maybe five hundred dollars more?"

Nadine shut her eyes momentarily, signed in surrender to temptation, and held out a hand.

Laurent flushed a pen from her handbag, hastily scribbled her signature on the check, and pushed it at Nadine.

Nadine folded the check and slid it carefully into a pocket. Searched over both shoulders. Dropped her voice to barely whisper, "Huck Minter warned me, if I ever told on him, he'd come back and kill me for sure, no matter when or how I might try hiding from him."

"Huck Minter."

"Mae Jean's go-be-damned daddy? You ever see him, you would know you just looked Lucifer, the devil himself, right square in the face."

"Told on him what?"

"What Mae Jean said? Right after it happened?"

"Mae Jean said what to you? She told you something?"

Merde! Nadine was one of those people who need to be

guided thought by thought until she caught the rhythm of the story she wanted to tell.

"Let me think how to tell you."

"Take your time."

Nadine did for the first five or six minutes, after which the story came gushing out like a catalog of troubling memories she was glad to be rid of, a jumble of thoughts accompanied by expressions that ranged from disjointed smiles, especially when she talked about Mae Jean, to borderline panic whenever she had to deal with Huck.

Mae Jean, following her ordeal, had spent a week at Nadine's home, where she was a frequent and welcome guest. In fact, the second twin in her room was routinely referred to as Mae Jean's bed. Nadine's folks liked Mae Jean despite her sometimes quirky behavior, which they blamed on the tragic loss of her mother and the daily trauma of living with a lowlife father.

Mae Jean slept round the clock the first day, a sleep more fitful than Nadine had ever experienced with Mae Jean, who rolled noisily through many a nightmare on most nights. This was different, she knew, because her dearest friend had been brutally assaulted by someone she had fantasized over. Nat Axelrod. Whose eternal soul should rot in Hell for what he had put her through, a mind-bending, life-changing misery.

Nadine told her so when Mae Jean showed signs of wanting to talk about the night Nat Axelrod's road manager, Kern Posey, singled her out of the crowd of jostling fans hoping for a glimpse of Nat before the concert, shunted Nadine to one side without so much as an *Excuse me,* maneuvered Mae Jean past the wooden horse barriers, and led her off.

"Not so, not so, not so, Nadine," Mae Jean said. "What they all say, but it's not the truth. It's not the truth."

"What are you saying, girl?"

"Nat was sweet and loving and good and kind to me, just the kind

of man we talked about anymore. It wasn't him. It wasn't Nat."

"Who was it, then?"

"Was that horrible person who took me to see Nat. He's the one what did me something awful. Twice. Back at the hotel after Nat told him to take me on home. First in his own room, grabbing onto me, saying he knew what girls like me was always after. Once more in the car, getting my legs spread and him all over me in a hurry, the greasy pig."

"But you said to the police it was Nat. The newspapers say you did, and it's all over the television about Nat and how he treated you."

"Daddy made me."

"Oh, sweet Jesus, Mae Jean. Why did he go and do that?"

"Daddy never tells me no reasons, does he? I just do or I get stomped. I got stomped anyway that night. Huck come out of the house when he heard the car pull up and the motor idling and he seen enough. Would of killed that boy he had the chance, but the car got away too fast."

"Then you have to go and tell the police the truth."

"Can't, Nadine!" she said, her voice verging on panic. "Can't, can't, can't! Can't go against my daddy 'cause I know what's good for me!"

She swore Nadine to secrecy and Nadine carried the guilty secret with her for weeks, long into the trial, until it became clear that Nat was going to be convicted.

On an afternoon they were at Nadine's preparing posters for a pep rally, Mae Jean seemed unusually fitful and preoccupied. Nadine was getting ready to ask her why when she blurted out, "I can't let them do that to Nat!"

"What do you mean, Mae Jean?"

"You know, you know, you know!"

"About who did it to you?"

"Yes, uh-huh. I need for you to go and tell someone the truth.

Tomorrow. While there's still time."

"Me? Better it should come from you."

"You know about Huck and what he said to the jury. I can't make him out to be a liar. It would be my skinny ass, clear to the bone. If it comes from you—"

"Then it's my skinny ass."

"Huck wouldn't dare. He wouldn't, wouldn't."

But, of course, he did, shortly after Nadine told Mae Jean's story to Phil Penguin.

Nadine was grabbing a smoke in the alleyway behind the Big Burger where she worked part-time and alternate weekends when she heard approaching footsteps crunching gravel behind her, and turned expecting to shoo off a bum.

It was Huck. He came upon her so quickly that he had a hand locked on her upper arm and was snatching the cigarette from her mouth before Nadine had time to be startled. He leaned in so close she could almost taste the liquor on his breath and, pushing smoke into her face, said:

"I hear tell you been going around spreading lies about business what concerns only I and my daughter?"

Nadine was too frightened to answer.

Huck coughed up a wad of phlegm and spit it by her shoes. "Girlie, I'm going to tell you this once and only once," he said. "What you told was a damned lie and, when anyone comes and asks you again, that's what you say—if you know what's good for you." He pushed her face up with a forefinger under her chin and leaned in so they were nose to nose. "You follow me? You follow me, girlie?"

Nadine wanted to scream, but she was speechless. Huck was pushing up so hard, she could not open her mouth to answer him, even if she thought she could get words out. He licked her neck and sucked at her throat before taking a step back. His bloodshot eyes were doing worse things to her, uglier than the pink scar on his face.

"Tell me you follow me, you little cunt."

Nadine nodded.

"Say it. Mae Jean said it already and I want to hear it from your dick-eating mouth, too, Nadine."

"I follow you."

"Louder."

"I FOLLOW YOU!"

"Good."

He took the cigarette from his mouth and Nadine thought he was going to hand it back to her. He jammed it so hard against her right arm, inside her elbow, that she heard her skin sizzle. And, still, she was too frightened to scream.

"That was just a sample, girlie. What you're in for you ever tell a living, breathing soul about this little chat we had. I'll come back and fuck you and kill you and fuck you again, you try fucking with me. For sure. No matter where you are, how you try to hide, you won't ever again be safe from Huck Minter."

Nadine's legs started to buckle and she began gasping for air as she told this to Laurent, who quickly steadied her with one hand around her waist and the other supporting her elbow.

She managed to pull an inhaler from her overalls and took four deep shots.

"My asthma," she said, replacing the inhaler. "It comes on whenever I got too excited."

"I'm sorry. I didn't mean for—"

"No need. Happens anytime I think too hard or long on Huck Minter. Here, look for yourself."

Nadine pushed up her right sleeve and showed a round scar about the size of a dime, red and mottled like a vaccination mark. It was not the worst wound Laurent had ever seen, but it made her wince. She had no use for any man who would treat a woman this way. The last man who had tried to hurt her against her will, a senior member of Castro's government, would never again have children of his own.

"I know from my research how you and Mae Jean testified at the trial."

"Now you understand why," she said. She rolled the sleeve back down and fought the metal button back into the button hole. "It wasn't any better the second time."

"The second time?"

"After he come out of prison for trying to kill Nat Axelrod in the hospital, like he did. I suppose you know about that?"

"*Oui.* Yes. I do. Three years and eight months before he was let out on parole."

"Somebody pulling strings for him, because it should've been a whole lot longer . . . So, he finds me again, only this time at the house. I'm alone. The folks, they're off at some PTA meeting and I'm watching a movie on TV, *Nine to Five* with Dolly Parton?

"Somehow, Huck's got inside . . . He's drunk as a skunk, so what else is new? He wants to know what has become of Mae Jean. I tell him like I told you before. All I know is she's been gone a while since marrying Dr. Heidemann; how the two of them just upped and disappeared together. I tell him the last I heard they're in Las Vegas. Huck gets blacker and angrier. He says I better be telling the truth, or else, and I know what he means by that. I know, all right. Not like as to ever forget."

Laurent saw something new glide across Nadine's eyes before she turned away, a mixture of fear and pain.

"Huck hurt you again, didn't he?" she said, knowing what the answer would be.

Nadine didn't hurry to respond. She looked past the property line, like she was checking for traffic. Turning back, she said, "Hurt me? Yes, but not so's I can show it to you." She made a little noise. "Don't know why I answered you. Never told a soul before this, except—"

She waved off the rest of the thought.

Laurent was also certain of the next answer.

"Mae Jean. Is that who you were going to say?"

No response, except for an effort to regulate her breathing.

"Tell me, Nadine. You can trust me. You kept in touch with Mae Jean, didn't you, and Mae Jean with you? Best friends don't disappear from best friends . . . How often? How many times over the years? Do you know where she is now? Where is she, Nadine? You told Huck, you can tell me, *certainment, oui*?"

Nadine started trembling. She wrapped her arms around her body for warmth, although the day defied cold. Her arms shook, too. Laurent knew she should ease up before the poor woman had another asthma attack, or worse.

She couldn't.

Losing the moment might cost her answers. She understood without yet knowing entirely why that it was important to find Mae Jean. Go there, wherever *there* was. Talk to her. And Nat? Was Nat with her? If so, what about the husband, Dr. Heidemann? Questions inside questions inside questions, like those Russian eggs.

"You reached Mae Jean afterward, didn't you, *non*? After Huck was here?"

"If he ever learned . . . A long time, but if he ever learned, he would—you know? Find me and kill me." Her voice was barely audible. The color had drained from her face.

Laurent persisted. "Is that why you didn't have the postcard from Las Vegas when we talked about it? You showed it to Huck and he took it from you? Huck left you to go to Las Vegas, so you got on the phone to warn your best friend he was on his way to find her there? You feared he would do to Mae Jean what he had done to you."

Nadine's eyes filled with disgust for Laurent, for throwing her secret back in her face.

Through thinned lips, her expression hard as stone, she said,

"He already done that to Mae Jean a hundred times before. He done that the night with Nat, not just the roadie. Huck, also. Her own father. Learning Mae Jean a lesson, he said, for being in the backseat like he found them."

Laurent pounced, too astonished by the revelation to do anything but what she knew by years of training and experience. "You told this to the authorities?"

"Mae Jean wouldn't let me. She was that a-scared for both of us, so she said to only tell them about the Kern Posey fella, so I did like she asked."

"That's why Huck came looking for you behind the Big Burger and frightened you so badly? He wanted to be certain you did not go back and tell them the whole truth?"

"Huck Minter is the devil." She found her inhaler and gave herself another shot.

"Huck took the postcard and went to Las Vegas. Did he find Mae Jean? When the two of you spoke eventually, what did she tell you?"

Nadine looked at Laurent as if she were a bug in the flower garden. It was not the first time Laurent had known that look.

"Five hundred dollars more, you know, Nadine? I will write you the second check before I leave here."

Nadine's high-pitched laugh was full of scorn.

Laurent wondered, was it aimed at her or inwardly, for reacting to the reminder?

Nadine's hand grazed the pocket where she had put the first check.

She shot another disgusted look at Laurent, said in a voice flat with anger, "The postcard was long gone by the time Huck come around. I give it to Nat, when he come searching for Mae Jean. He got his own letter from her, saying was where he could ever find her, he wanted. Or, to come ask me, her best friend, who'd know. So, I showed him the postcard to prove it, because he looked so unsure about the world. One other thing?

"His hands? Lord have mercy. I could hardly find new ways to keep my eyes off them. I wondered if Mae Jean knew, and I thought about telling her. In the end I figured she had to find out for herself. Didn't have the heart, not for someone who loved him and his playing as much as her."

Laurent charged into her suite at the Airport Holiday Inn, jumped onto the phone and called Knobby Packwood, giving him just enough background—the sizzle, not the steak—to win his promise that another five-thousand-dollar advance would be waiting at the American Express counter when she landed in Las Vegas. She made flight reservations, then called the Anne Frank Home to check on Bertha and Sam, as she had done several times since coming to Indianapolis, and was reassured by Rabbi Cohen.

She threw off her clothes and jumped into a shower, discovering that, while her hands caressed her body, her mind was transfixed by images of Nat Axelrod well beyond the magical memories of their brief encounter at Wembley Stadium.

Laurent recognized she was developing a strange fascination for him, this sad man sentenced to prison on a political whim, for a crime committed by others on a girl, a woman now, with whom he shared a strange and implausible communion that somehow made all the sense in the world to her.

Were they together?

When she found Nat in Las Vegas, would she also find Mae Jean?

And what about the husband, the doctor, who saved Nat's life and took Mae Jean for a prize?

Indeed, a Russian egg—questions within questions.

Laurent settled in bed with her mini-cassette recorder and depressed the playback button, fast-forward to her voice assuring Laddie and Phil Penguin, *"Anything you tell me now in this room will be off the record."*

And, they had believed her.

After another thirty or forty seconds, *"No tape, no notes, no quotes. Done."*

They always believed her.

Phil Penguin's voice: *"I closed my eyes and did what I was told. I only followed orders."*

The maneuver, subtle sleight of hand, always happened too fast for them to notice Laurent snap the recorder back on before dropping it into her bag.

Laddie's voice: *"For Ben . . . Tell her, Phil."*

Was she guilty of lying or were they guilty of believing?

She was guilty of doing whatever it took to get the story, and damn the rest of it.

Right, Papa?

Isn't that so, Papa?

You always told me, Papa, "The real journalist gets the story first and worries about any consequences after. Always the story first. Whatever it takes."

She pressed her fingers to her lips and aimed her eyes and a kiss to the ceiling, telling him, "For you, Papa."

And closed her eyes to concentrate on the tape.

And found her thoughts drifting back to Nat.

Chapter 14

Bad news comes behind the protective wall of the US mail, good news by phone and great news usually in person, or such is common wisdom in the record business, why Danny's anxiety began running at Olympian speed when Joe Wunsch phoned him to suggest they meet for drinks at the Peninsula at five o'clock. Danny arrived first, about a half hour early, to score one of the coveted quiet booths off the hotel's main flow of traffic, inside and to the right of the lobby entrance.

Joe charged in like it was a china shop and found him with a Tarzan yell. He settled in the booth alongside him, scooped up a handful from the bowl of mixed nuts, washed it down with a swallow from Danny's Scotch, and told the server to bring a tap beer. His body language, a smile too big to be believable and the way his eyes played hide-and-seek after launching a story about David Geffen and Clive Davis at the Grammy Awards party told Danny that Joe had not brought common wisdom with him.

Joe quit the story short of a punch line, like he was breaking for a commercial, focused on a starlet-type redhead selling visibility at the bar and said, "Captain, I can't make the Patrice Malloy deal." He appeared on the verge of breaking into tears behind a smile of despair.

"It was that miserable fuck Drummond," Joe said. "I spent the week mustering support here and in New York. Raised lots of excitement in all the right quarters playing the demo. Patrice

Malloy. That voice. Christ all fucking mighty! Promotion went dip shit. So did marketing, everybody, until—"

Danny said, "I know you did your best." There was no need to make Joe feel worse than he was showing. He toasted Joe, emptied what was left of his Scotch-rocks double and signaled for the server. "How about you?"

"This'll do me for now," Joe said, hoisting his draft beer. He erased a foam mustache with an index finger. "You really don't want to be hitting that stuff too hard, do you, Captain?"

Danny said, "I was a junkie, not a drunkie, remember? I'll be fine, Joe. You caught me a little off guard is all. A whole lot off guard, as a matter of fact."

Joe smiled acceptance. "Drummond got wind of what I was up to. The usual spy in the corporate ointment, you know? He waltzed into my office this morning, shot me down. He said he knew what I was up to, trying to blindside him, and there was no nine yards in it for me. Try it again, he said, and he'd dump me from the Decade team. He'd toss me out of the stadium and see to it I never get back into the game, just like he did my old teammate Danny Manings."

Danny tried covering the noise of his labored breathing.

He made what he hoped looked like a smile.

Joe said, "Jesus fuck! I came this close to slugging the cocksucker and quitting once and for good." He showed about a quarter inch between his thumb and forefinger.

"But you didn't. We've played that scene out before, lots of times, Joey. Drummond can't last forever. One day you'll be the guy running Decade."

"Yeah, yeah. You never stop reminding me, do you?" He let his attention drift.

For a moment, Danny thought Joe was tracking the progress of a statuesque brunette with Betty Boop eyes and invisible boobs in a silk shantung blazer and matching everything, who had glided in from the lobby and was heading for the shopping arcade entrance at the rear through a Red Sea of admiring suits.

"There he is," Joe said, and called, "Mason!" The man crossing past the brunette signaled back and headed over. He slid in on the end opposite Joe, putting Danny in the middle. "Mason Weems, Danny Manings, and vice versa." They shook hands. "I think you guys know each other already."

"Been years, Danny. How are you?" Mason Weems said. His grip was as tight as the look he gave Danny was relaxed and friendly. His manner and his clothing were decidedly New York, the suit off some store's sedate and safe businessman's rack.

"Pretty good, Mason. I see by the trades and the tip sheets things are going well for you and Shoe Records."

"Beat SoundScan at its own game a few times," he said, his voice warm and ingratiating, full of unreconstructed Jersey. "And you?"

"Which lie do you want first?"

Mason smiled his understanding as the server arrived. He asked for an Evian and this time Joe agreed to another beer on tap. Danny stuck with his Scotch. They continued to make small talk, playing catch-up with industry names that had dropped from sight over the past ten years, until the server returned with their drinks and a fresh silver bowl of nuts.

"He's still one of the good guys," Joe volunteered, and neither Danny nor Mason looked like they knew who he meant, but joined in the toast he offered: "To all the good guys, past and present . . . and no future to all the fucking bad guys."

Mason took a swallow and sorted out some nuts. "I ain't even going to speculate on who you got on your short list of bad guys, Joey."

"My usual list of one, Mason. Danny, you know we distribute Mason's label, your basic P-and-D deal, but he's never been a member of the Harry Drummond Drum and Bugle Corps."

Mason nodded. "Strange bedfellows. Made the deal with old Stoker on a handshake, but got it in basic black and white when Harry took over. He likes to think he has me by the balls. If he could read, the boilerplate my lawyer put in would tell him better."

"Danny, when Horrible Harry pulled his fuck-you stunt with me this a.m., I thought of Mason. I knew he'd be in town for this fucking party Drummond is tossing at La Bamba end of the week. I begged him to give a listen to Patrice Malloy."

"He didn't have to beg, Danny. Everybody knows about Joe's ears. Yours never were so bad, either." He smiled sincerely and held up the cassette he'd pulled from somewhere. "The girl sings up a storm. I'd love her for Shoe Records."

Joe drummed his fists on the table. "I knew it, I knew it, I knew it. Mason, I knew you were the right man for my man here."

Danny recognized that, in his enthusiasm, Joe had missed the edge creeping into Mason Weems's voice. He gave Mason a nervous, quizzical smile. "Was that a *but* I detected, Mason?" Mason's overgrown eyes considered him carefully while he ran a hand over his head, pressing down the few remaining long strands that strained to reach the back of his neck. "What's the bad news?"

As Mason worked out a way to answer Danny, Danny studied him without staring in the dim light and took quiet pride at looking so much younger than someone he knew was about his own age. Mason always did worry too much, he remembered, but what does a little worry matter when you have money machines like Keen McNamara, Blood Spot and the Jerkies on the label?

"How honest do you want me to be, Danny?"

"What's a hundred percent of a hundred percent?"

Mason smiled appreciatively.

"Okay, then . . . She's great, this Patrice Malloy. That's a given. As many times as I've played the tape, I hear a winner. I hear a little Wynona. I hear a lot of Celine. I hear Cheryl Crow. Some Tina. Some Janet Jackson. Ella even, for Christ's sake, and a touch of Billie on some of her riffs. You get my drift?"

Danny motioned him to continue.

Mason said, "What it tells me is this girl is a Go Gotta Have, but only if she cleans up her act and gets rid of all those influences. There's room at the top for a Patrice Malloy who sounds only like herself, and I'm betting that's one of a fucking kind."

"You don't think it's because of her choice of material on the demo?"

"Definitely part of it, Danny, but that tells you what I'm getting at for another part of the problem."

"The songs suck," Joe said. Danny looked like he'd just been wounded by friendly fire. "It didn't matter when it figured to be you and me, Captain. I expected we would make the deal and then go and find us some stronger material than Patrice is writing for herself."

"She's written stronger stuff since the tape was put together," Danny said, on the defensive. "I like two of the cuts on there."

"So would Top 40 radio, Captain, if Top 40 radio was still around. That was ten years ago, maybe longer. Think back. They were already on the down elevator, those sounds, when you got shafted out of the business. It's wah-wah under the bridge, unless you're a Joni Mitchell or a Carole King riding the history and nostalgia wave."

Joe shot a questioning look at Mason.

"On the money," Mason said. "No one spends a dime promoting that kind of music today. There's no section for it at Tower Records or Virgin or any of the chains."

Joe framed an invisible display placard with his hands. "In Fluke Releases. Those bins over there, between Fat Chance and

Fucking Forget It."

Danny realized Joe and Mason had already discussed this. He wasn't going to argue the point—besides, they were more right than wrong—when the major point of conversation was closing in on a deal.

The deal first, always.

Nothing else mattered without a deal in place.

He threw the negotiating edge to Mason, who had it anyway. "What do you suggest, Mason?"

Mason didn't hesitate over the answer. "Bring me a demo I can live with and it's a done deal. Not even a master. Just enough to tell me we're all right about Patrice Malloy."

Joe said, "Don't worry about material, Captain. I'm owed favors, even Diane Warren, and you know what she is capable of, that girl. Also, primo stuff I stole out from under Quincy when Q wasn't looking. It's been locked away in my safety drawer waiting for the right artist."

Danny said, "You'll cover the session costs, Mason?"

"Front it? No. It'll be built into the advance when we get that far."

"How much of an advance?"

"I tell you, you'll tell me it's not enough, so let's save it for after you bring me something really worth fighting over." He held out his hand. "Shake on it?"

Danny hesitated. His mind calculated the money it would take to go into a halfway decent studio and produce the kind of cuts Mason wanted. Joe saw him struggling and understood. "I've got the dollars covered as part of my game plan, Captain."

Danny gripped Mason Weems's hand.

"Shake on it," he said.

After Mason was gone, apologizing that he had to check arrangements for Puddy Katz's performance and autograph party tonight at the Borders in Westwood, Joe spread a smile the size of Texas and signaled the server to bring another round and a split of Cristal. He said, "It's time to celebrate, Captain, figuring you're gonna forgive me for starting with the bad news first."

"Something else first, Joey—what you said about the dollars to cover the studio. I would never let you be cute with the company treasury, try to finesse a Decade check past Drummond. My underwriting of Nat Axelrod's medical and legal expenses with corporate dollars is what got me tossed out of the company and—"

"Stop there," Joe said, his voice as urgent as the open palm he raised between them. "That was your mistake. If I make any, they're going to be my own." When he was sure he had Danny's full attention, he said, "I'm talking about a few dollars I stashed away on spec."

"With another kid coming, I'm not going to let you—"

"It's not your call. Besides, it's not the money I'm talking. There's already enough in a trust fund to send Future Kid through college and med school and have enough left over for a used stethoscope and a dozen tongue depressors. The other kids are already handled, and there'll be no more to worry about if my vasectomy doesn't grow back. These bucks are rainy-day bucks, like the Christmas Club, you know? Becky started it when she saw how this business eats its old alive. It's against the day I might be out on the fucking street or ready to take my own shot, like I am now going to do with you and Mason."

The last thought caught in Joe's throat. He washed it down with his beer.

Danny said, "Not a chance if your plan calls for you to leave Decade, kiddo. I won't do that to you or Becky or—"

Again, the crossing guard's hand. "Sure, the plan does, but not yet, not immediately. Let's us get this show on the road first. Let's us get Patrice on top of the charts, then I'll show fucking Harry Drummond the label I have for his ass—called Go Fuck Yourself—and offer to personally tattoo it there."

"Becky agreed to this?"

Joe laughed a bit too strenuously, and Danny saw something he had not noticed before. It was more than Joe drinking too much. He was enjoying it too much. A maniacal glisten to Joe's eyes made Danny wonder if he also was doing too much of something else. It had been years, but Danny remembered the look from his own eyes, looking in the mirror and seeing a coke-inflated Mr. Hyde staring back. He could not ignore his concern.

"Are you on something, Joe?"

Joe showed he understood the question by the way he jarred back against the soft leather of the booth and considered how to answer. "Captain, a natural high is all what I'm on. What you see is a fucking natural high. And that's all you see."

"You worry for me, I worry for you, Joey."

Joe's tone, now his look, insisted Danny not push the issue.

Danny nodded and made a gesture of acceptance, covered the awkward moment by taking a marginal swallow of Scotch. He put the glass back onto the table and finger-stirred the ice cubes. They clanked against the glass and the sound briefly overpowered all the other room noises. He changed the subject. "How did Becky react when you told her what you had in mind for the money?" he said.

A grin flashed up one side of Joe's face and he relaxed.

"How did she react? Shit! It was her fucking idea, Danny."

"Before I asked Mason about front money, she knew? Kid, you never were a good liar."

"And fuck you very much, too . . . Listen, Danny . . . We had our little louse and his spouse talk the night I got back home with your fucking Patrice Malloy tape. Becky's got ears, too, you know? She heard the future. She knows how long I've been yearning for us to be together."

"And she told you to offer me the Christmas Club?"

"Not until I called to tell her about Drummond. Then, yes. Good thing, too, or I would have never offered it, even though you are a close second in my heart, behind the family. But Becky is always first in my life, irregardless, and that takes precedent. Mason plays it straight, but cheap. I knew he wouldn't spend a dime before its day."

"If you pay to play, you share."

Joe pushed his metal specs back up the bridge of his nose and gave Danny a hard stare. "What did you think, you're like the fucking UJW and I'm making a contribution? Of course I share. Love is love, Captain, and business is business."

"Did Becky also suggest what our deal should be?"

"Yeah, but I told her, *Honey, we have to give him something for his time and efforts.*" Joe threw back his head and laughed outrageously. "That's my Becky. Generous to a flaw."

"Rap Browning and I split a twenty-percent management fee he worked out with Patrice before I got involved. You're in for half of my half."

"Keep it. Don't want it." Joe's eyes gave no clue to where he was heading. "I've dealt with too many managers to ever want to be one. Wake up in the morning and fucking hate myself? No thank you. I'll make my deal with Mason, taking a half of the record end. He might try pushing me down to forty. Fair for starters. He and I, we can renegotiate after we've made history with Patrice. You're in for half of my half, making it sweet all around . . . What about publishing?"

"What will Mason want?"

"The whole enchilada, of course. He knows where the real money is."

"Patrice keeps half on all her copyrights. We're talking the other fifty."

"Of course. Mason gets half of that on both the ASCAP and BMI companies we have somebody like Buddy Martindale or Al Tunney set up for us and Mason administers. We can trust him for an honest accounting; there's never been a bad rap on Mason in that department either."

Danny said, "We split the remaining twenty-five three ways, Rap, you and me. Rap will go for it; it's straightforward enough; no boilerplate."

"You make it fly with him and Patrice while I navigate us through the paperwork."

"Who picks up the lawyer's tab?"

"ASCAP or BMI. That's where I think the advance can come from, don't you?" Danny nodded. "If the other songs Patrice has are good as you say, there might also be enough to cover us on the new recording sessions."

Danny chuckled good-naturedly. "Meaning, all things considered, you'll have wangled your way into this deal on a promise and a few phone calls."

"Bet your ass! Pretty good, huh? I learned at the feet of a master." Joe blew Danny a kiss. "Once we get a producer, I'm thinking Rancho Musico. Pricey, but I throw a lot of serious dollars their way. I'll have Greta call over in the morning and apply some heat." He jiggled his eyebrows like Groucho Marx and tipped the ashes off an imaginary cigar. "Dig?"

"Of course I dig, Joey. I know that ditch well, but I don't want to lose time in the studio because we're out hunting for a producer. Patrice isn't half bad as her own producer and we'll do just fine with a halfway decent engineer."

"Spoken like a true manager, Captain . . . It won't be the case, swear." He held up his hand to take an oath. "This show is on the road. If Greta can't score fucking Rancho Musico for us, or even second or third best, she'll call around until she gets us a decent room with a decent board."

Danny felt his heart charging with excitement as reality continued to set into what only a short time ago had seemed like disaster.

Back home, Danny called Rap, to share the news and make certain there was nothing he had agreed to that Rap could not live with or felt he could not sell to Patrice. He didn't want any bad news falling from the sky after it was too late to change a commitment.

Rap was on the air at KJIV.2.

Danny squeezed in the details and answered questions in the musical gaps between Rap's delivery of record IDs, music trivia, station tags, and assorted commercials aimed at the station's target demographics, which he guessed from the spots' content stretched from the prepubescent to graying baby boomers.

Rap's delivery, while beautifully enunciated, was no longer faster-than-light. There was the weary quality of someone easing through motions he knows as well as his name and, Danny decided, a worrisome frequency to his coughing to clear his throat.

He said, "Flu hangover is all, bro," when Danny put the question to him. "So what more from you? So far I'm hearing only the baddest in the bestest sense of the word."

Danny told him about Mason Weems and how Joe had fit himself into the deal.

"Sounding like your boy has done you proud since you first time brought him on by to meet my dear, sweet Mariah," Rap said.

"He's like us, Mr. B. Honest and loyal to a fault."

"Which is why I gotta tell you something now, my man."

There were mumbles to the way he confessed that made

Danny ask, "Why do I think I don't want to hear this?"

"Same as I wish it was nothing needed telling. Hold on a minute-sixty. Time to raise the rent here." Danny listened in on two minutes' worth of commercials. "You still hanging, man?"

"I'm here, Rap. All that's missing are a few more of my fingernails."

"We got a partner who you ain't yet worked into the fine equation you got made with old Mason Weems and your boy, Joey."

Danny let the words sink in, as deep as the breath he pushed back into the air. "Tell me about our partner, Rap. The one you forgot to mention before now. One, right? You're not going to spring more than the one on me, are you, homes?"

"He the righteous one and oney. Name of Brian Malloy."

"Brian Malloy? The husband. You or Patrice mentioned him that first night in the club."

"One and the same."

"In not very flattering terms."

"Like it is, bro."

"And he's our partner?"

"Patrice, she our community property with him." The sinking feeling in Danny's stomach began to ache while Rap spent a minute-twenty with his listeners. "So, we was saying?"

"Rap, I remember asking if you had paper with Patrice. You said you did. I told Joe this. I told Mason Weems. Tell me again you do. Paper. A contract. Something, that allows us to follow through on the deal."

"Yes." Danny closed his eyes and whispered a thank-you to God. "But not exactly, you unnerstan' my meaning? Brian Malloy, he the one what got the paper with Patrice."

"And you got your paper with Brian Malloy."

Rap crowed into the phone, "Now you on the right frequency, Daniel. Why you ever been my main man."

Danny knew what the flattery meant. "I'm not going to like the paper, am I?"

"See? Why I hook up with you in the first place. You get there, you know how to turn up the volume onc't you arrive."

"Tell me about the paper, Rap."

He was back in a minute-sixty to say, "Paper simple enough. We can do what he wants and Brian, he can do what he wants."

Danny covered the mouthpiece with a hand while he searched around the apartment for his composure.

"Rap, will he want to do what we want to do?"

"A good question, my man."

"Try me on an answer, okay?"

"When it's 'splained to him the way you 'splained it to me."

"Do that then, right now. I'll hang up and you call and 'splain it to him. Then, call me back?"

"Danny, you don't have to get insulting with that 'splain jive," Rap said, exposing his UCLA degree. "Find your own jive street to walk down."

"You haven't answered my question."

"Brian Malloy is a first-class prick, a cop here in San Diego. Works vice. Thinks that cop who fucked up the O.J. trial, Fuhrman, is the next best thing to the Ku Klux Klan. He and Patrice live their life in one big brouhaha and it will end in divorce court one of these days. He slid paper under her the second he got wind I was high on her talent, afraid of being cut off at the pass from a pot of gold, demanding protection, telling Patrice she should know better than to trust an uppity nigger, especially an uppity nigger in show business.

"Patrice asked me what to do. I told her to sign the damned paper. The fifty percent he was screaming about was fifty percent of nothing, I said. I said we would negotiate our way out of it when her career was a hundred percent of something special and we had the bread to bury the mongering bastard deep into her past. So, she signed, and that's it, what you want to know."

Resigned, Danny said, "Any suggestions on how to get rid of this guy now?"

"We could be talking another kind of contract," Rap said, "but maybe you meeting him makes more sense."

"Set it up."

Chapter 15

Danny's home since reversals had cost him the Beverly Hills estate was in an apartment in a three-story eyesore in West LA, near the Sunset and Crescent Heights intersection, built around a courtyard dominated by a kidney-shaped swimming pool and unemployed actresses in skimpy bikinis, in an architectural style he'd dubbed California Neanderthal.

The corner where Schwab's Drug Store once stood as a magnet for tourists who believed the legend that Lana Turner was discovered there was a Virgin Records Megastore plaza. What glamour there was came in the form of street corner hookers, shopping cart beggars, and foreign movie buffs racing to the next starting time at the plaza's multiplex.

Across Crescent were low-end fast-food stores that took over for the savings bank that replaced the legendary Garden of Allah apartments created by the legendary Alla Nazimova, the legendary Rudolph Valentino girlfriend, and occupied by F. Scott Fitzgerald, Robert Benchley, Errol Flynn and a raft of drinking, philandering movie stars.

Danny had furnished the place like a practical joke. Furniture had always been Vickie's thing, not his. One of the two bedrooms housed his neatly cataloged and indexed albums, eight tracks, cassettes and CDs. What wall space there was featured the tastiest of the Platinum and Gold records he had accumulated over the years and some colorful and inexpensive County Museum posters bought already framed in cheap plastic.

Brian Malloy looked at Danny like a traffic cop with tickets to spare, at Patrice like the vice cop he was, and surveying the apartment said, "Bad enough she's hanging with the spook, now she's got a certified loser to complete the set."

Malloy was a six-footer, about Danny's height, but maybe four or five years older; late forties. Large black eyes under a thick, single ridge of eyebrow and graying black hair razor cut in sleek military style; no sideburns. Heavy five-o'clock shadow to match a voice as deep as a well. Muscle tone turning to flab and a ton of it settled on his belly. Looking uncomfortable in a blue blazer he had no possibility of buttoning. A bulge underneath, at his waist, that could have been a holster.

Patrice said, "Brian, you promised not to start that crap with Danny—Mr. Manings."

"Did I ask you, sweet thing? Shut the trap door, okay? I'm trying to make a point with—who?" He wandered the living room with his head, searching. "Is it Mr. Manings or is it Danny? You already got something going on with this here one, too?"

Patrice showed Brian the middle finger of her right hand. "In stereo," she said, adding the left hand. Turning to Danny, she said, "I want to apologize again for my husband."

"Nobody has to apologize for what I say."

"I'm apologizing for what you are," she said, her voice as nasty as a hornet's sting.

Danny sat like the Invisible Man, a closemouthed smile locked between his cheeks while they continued bickering, harsh words and accusations rumbling back and forth, wishing now he hadn't agreed to the meeting when Rap suggested it three nights ago.

When Patrice quit to take a breath and threw Danny an apologetic look, her husband said, "The spook told me you have a big fucking deal for my wife, Manings. Said you'd tell me more, fill me in, I drove up. Great. I want to hear it from a pair of white lips."

Danny squeezed his throat to keep his temper from escaping. Under other circumstances, somebody spoke that way, he'd deck the guy on the spot. Bigotry had never sat well with him. In the music business, color was something they put on album jackets and racists lasted only about as long as a blink in his presence.

Rap had prepared him for it, given it as his reason for not making the trip to LA with the Malloys, saying, "Believe me, bro, we're better off with you going at this asshole redneck one on one, white bread to white bread. Me in the same room would only remind him that the bullet that took out Martin King didn't wipe all us coloreds from his woodpile."

Brian pushed up off the soft couch he and Patrice were sharing and wandered the room, studying Danny's poster art and the peeling wallpaper, while his wife shouted her latest demand for him to be courteous.

"Courteous?" He made it a dirty word. "Didn't you tell me how wonderful this guy was, a prince among princes in the record business?" he said, swinging around to stare Patrice down, a sweeping gesture and a sideways glance for Danny, who occupied a stool he had pulled in from the dinette counter that broke the room from the kitchen. "How come the prince is living here in this two-by-four instead of in Beverly Hills and Malibu, like all of them princes I read about in your God damned *Billboard*?"

"He did. Once," she said, indignantly, defiantly, pounding her thighs with her fists. "Rap told me so. Isn't that right, Mr. Manings?"

Danny would not have dignified the subject with a response, except for the need he saw in Patrice's flaring green eyes. Her desperation had also brought a pink flush to her lightly tanned complexion and a curious set to her face that made her prettier than how she had lingered in his memory. She had let her reddish brown hair grow longer since the club date, to just above her shoulders. It made her look younger and fresher than the twenty-nine-going-on-thirty years she had declared in that candid way she had of talking, her voice as soft as a cloud; also like a cloud in the way it drifted lazily from topic to topic.

But not in the last twenty minutes.

In the last twenty minutes she had been as hard and direct as a bullet to the brain.

Danny said, "This, Brian, is evidence of what happens to a man who goes through a divorce after uttering the wrong words to the wrong lawyer," pausing to be certain of Malloy's attention as he moved to his feet from the stool and opened his arms to the room in a gesture worthy of a Barrymore. He was lying to him, but easier than trying to deal the truth in this situation.

Brian gave him a curious look that signaled he didn't know what wrong words Danny meant.

Danny said, "And those words were: *Give her anything she wants.*"

"I'll never make that mistake," Brian said, controlling his smile until he could replace it with a scornful look. "I hear tell you had a bow-coop big-time drug problem. How much of your prince-sized bankroll went up your nose, Mr. Manings?" He said the word *Mister* like it was biting his tongue. "How many of all the hundred-dollar bills you think to make off my wife will you use to suck up the coke off your mirror?"

"Brian, you apologize to him or I'm leaving." She turned to Danny. "I'm truly sorry. If I had known he was going to behave badly . . . I mean, he gave me his word on the drive up, and—"

"Just to shut you up," Brian said. "Either that or put up with your yap-trap of a mouth the whole hundred and twenty miles."

Patrice seemed about to leap for him.

Danny restrained her with a look.

"It's a fair question," he said, trying to calm down the son of a bitch enough to get him back on track. "Brian wouldn't want his wife associated with some drugged-out record-industry crazy, Patrice. For your sake, and because he's a police officer."

"Detective third," he said proudly. "Spend about a half of my time putting down the drug trade comes creepy-crawly over the border, not to mention pond scum laying all over our streets and anyplace worth hiding out in over to Balboa Park. Christ! We got little kids in that park all the time, going to the zoo and that art museum deal."

Patrice frowned and faked a yawn. "In case you haven't figured it out, Mr. Manings, Detective Third Grade Brian Malloy gets off on *N.Y.P.D. Blue* and *Miami Vice* reruns." She couldn't have been more scornful saying *Detective Third Grade.*

Before Brian could vocalize his contemptuous look, Danny said, "I've been stone-cold clean for almost five years, Brian. Friends, and then the Betty Ford Clinic."

"Not the way I hear it," Brian said.

Danny looked through his eyes and saw more dirt than that had been put in Malloy's mind. Certainly not by Rap. Who then, and when?

"You been checking me out, Brian?"

"Uh-huh. What the good cops do. You're known by the company you keep, you know?"

"Somebody told you I was still trapped in the snow?" Brian hid any emotion like a hole card. "Then you better go and check again, because somebody has been handing you worse shit than I ever found in a dime bag."

"You know, you sound a lot like this one here whined away, first time I find her looking to trade a blow job for some blow." He blew Patrice a kiss. "I don't know why I took her out of the life, wonder often and a lot, but she carries on like this much longer and I'll throw her back like an undersized trout." A snap of his fingers. "Like that."

Patrice could no longer contain herself. With a scream loud enough to frighten Dracula, she threw herself at Brian, somehow attached her legs around his waist, and began slashing his face with an open hand, first one direction, then the other. When he managed to grab her by the wrist, she leaned back and used her other hand, beating wildly on his chest and almost catching his nose a few times before he managed to push her off and onto the floor.

She moaned.

Her eyes slid into momentary unconsciousness.

He hauled back a foot, meaning to kick her. Danny moved in to stop him and wound up taking the metal toe of Brian's boot on his left calf. Another ten degrees and the kick would have hit leg bone and cracked it for certain.

Danny reeled back and crashed to the ground, almost on top of Patrice. Falling, he saw satisfaction smeared across Brian's face. He set his jaw hard, determined not to cry out in pain and give him further satisfaction.

As Danny rose to a half-sitting position, anchoring himself with a rigid arm, Brian said, "Listen up, Manings. I really came here just to say about the deal you and the spook think you got for my wife with some guy named James Mason or something at some pissant label. Ain't gonna happen, *amigo.* Man enough to be here in person and let you know. That's my decision and the one that really counts—"

"Fuck you, Brian!" Patrice screamed at him. She had roused back to consciousness and was on her hands and knees, trying to use the coffee table as a crutch back onto her feet.

"Fuck me? Sweetheart, been there, done that . . . Anyway, I know you know I can do that, Manings. Know I got the right.

Why ever else would the spook even offer to pay for my gas up here?"

Recognizing Brian was preparing to leave, Danny tried to stop him by insisting, "I doubt that Rap told you the half of it. It's a better deal than you can find anywhere else, Brian. Mason Weems is one of the most respected—"

Brian signaled him quiet.

"I already found something better. So, it's goodbye to you and no hard feelings. That's how it is, okay? If you're finished picking your ass up off the ground, let's go, my honey." He pulled his jacket as far as it would travel around his belly and tugged at the seams, exposing a flash of holster.

"I'm not going anywhere with you. Fuck you."

"Suit yourself. It's a long hike back down to San Diego, but maybe the prince here will front the cost of an Amtrak ticket for you, or you could earn it?" He winked at Danny. "The little woman don't give out Frequent Flyer miles, but she definitely knows how to get you 'round the world better'n anyone else I know, Manings."

Patrice grabbed for the water glass she'd been drinking from and hurled it at Brian. He angled his body. The glass sailed past him and shattered and rained against the wall.

Brian blew her another kiss.

"I'll see myself out," he said.

Patrice calmed down the moment Brian was out the door. She sucked in a deep breath, extended her lower lip over the upper one, and pushed out a mountain of air before easing into a corner of the couch between the back and the armrest. "Pretty spooky, huh?" she said, screwing on a smile. "The Brian and Patrice Horror Show. Always playing at a theater near you. Check local listings for time." A shrug and a curious twist of face marked either regret or acceptance. She needed some sort of acknowledgment.

"I've been in a few of those pitched battles myself," Danny said.

He thought back to Vickie's descent into oblivion after creating her own demons and letting them destroy the good life they had had together, even when he embraced her and said none of it mattered, get off the shit the way he had gotten off the shit, and she said she would, only it didn't work out that way. She could be so loving when she wasn't so irrational, screaming away her personal demons in the night, accusing him of her own sins, always accusing, at the top of her lungs, swallowing her Prozac the way she loved to make him swallow his pride, which he did gladly, anything for Vickie, everything for Vickie, and what did he accomplish?

An end to a marriage.

The loss of the family he so desperately loved.

A slide back into the madness of drugs, and what life they hadn't taken away from him he threw away for himself.

But he had friends, strangers who became friends, people who cared and helped him lift himself back onto his feet and start to move forward again.

Curiously, through all the dark days, every one of them, he never quit.

Somewhere in the back of his mind he knew he would battle his way back onto his feet, and a day would come when it would be better than that.

These days?

With Patrice Malloy?

Yes.

Absolutely, he thought now, in spite of Brian Malloy and the sense that opportunity was blowing away in a windstorm of malice that might be beyond his control.

Patrice said, "They're no fun, the battles, are they?"

"Never. How long before Brian shuttles back here for you?"

Patrice shook her head. "Not how he plays the game. He goes, he's gone. It's up to me to find my way home."

"You're joking."

She shook her head again. "How he gets his rocks off, but don't be concerned. He hasn't lost me yet. We can finish up our business and I'll get out of your hair."

"How will you get back to San Diego?"

"A cab to LAX. I carry mad money wherever I go. A trick my mom taught me. Up from a quarter for the phone, though. It's a hundred to cover the cab and the plane, sometimes the bus or the train, depends on where the jerk plays out his big scene."

"I'll drive you to the airport. The least I can do."

"No, that's okay. Wouldn't want to get spoiled by too much nice-nice." She closed her eyes and retreated into herself.

"It's an hour max there and back. No big deal."

Her eyes flashed open again. She studied him somber-faced, searching for something it took a minute to find. Satisfied, she said, "Okay, then. Thanks. You're okay, Lone Ranger." Her voice turned husky. "I've always been big on the Lone Ranger."

They spent an awkward moment staring at one another before Danny excused himself to clean up the broken glass. He realized for the first time how hard Brian's kick had been. He was limping and the pain was throbbing something awful. When he got back from dumping the glass in the kitchen trash basket, Patrice was exploring the rows of titles on his music shelf, humming something he recognized as one of her own songs.

"Very eclectic," she said.

"My taste has always defied labels."

"Only in music?" Her look suggested the answer she had in mind. After another moment, she said, "Can you tell I've been dangerously attracted to you since we met, *Kemo Sabe*?"

"No," Danny said, taken aback by the declaration.

She turned and smiled at him, wetting her lips and parting them just enough for him to see her tongue probing outward, and swept back onto the couch, sitting with her legs crossed under her in a way that put the focus on her crotch, like in the Ralph Lauren ads, and gesturing with her eyes for him to join her.

She was wearing a Counting Crows T-shirt with her jeans. It was a size and a half too small and gave a succulent curve to her breasts and dimension to nipples the size of thimbles. She let a hand stray from her thigh onto her crotch and an itch she wanted him to notice.

Danny crossed over to the CD player and snapped it on, then settled back onto his stool. The room filled with Frank Sinatra.

Her head shifted up and down, accepting his unspoken answer, and she said, "The *Come Fly with Me* album."

"Songs for Swinging Lovers."

"Don't think so."

Her look was as challenging as it had been inviting a minute ago. "I know them like the front of my back, Danny. All those old Capitol albums."

He moved back to the player and popped out the CD to check, expecting to waltz the disk over to her in victory. Instead, he sank the carrier back inside, restarted Sinatra, and sheepishly returned to his seat.

Patrice patted her shoulder. "Mom played those Sinatras all the time," she said. "Mom said they reminded her of my dad, who was a big, big Sinatra fan. If you insist, I can give you the running sequence on all twelve of the cuts, album by album, and even the running times of every cut. And lyrics? Don't start me."

"From the sound, your dad is deceased?"

"Mom, too."

"I'm sorry."

"That's okay. I suppose about my dad." She did a nervous thing with her fingers through her hair. "I never really knew him. I knew my stepdad, though." She grimaced reflectively. "You wanna know about him? Think Brian Malloy. I guess it's true what they say, about girls marrying their fathers."

"Not their stepfathers. Anyone who loved Sinatra the way your mom said your father did couldn't be all bad."

"Go tell that to Woody Allen," she said, and shards of laughter diminished Sinatra's voice for a few seconds.

"Was your father the musician of the family?"

"Maybe, I couldn't say. Mom never talked about Dad too much, like he was a mystery she didn't want to share. Frank there was an exception, and sometimes a song by Irving Berlin. He loved Berlin, too." She lapsed into a few lyrics: *I'll be loving you, always. With a love that's true, always* . . . "That's the song that always got Mom going. We could do a load of laundry with those tears."

Danny smiled reflexively and so did she, like two strangers who've reached the end of one conversation and don't know how to continue. He wanted to ask her about the management papers she'd signed for her husband, see how she felt about the Mason Weems deal, about Joe and his involvement, and, of course, there still was the matter of her music.

Brian Malloy wasn't the only hurdle.

How would she react to the suggestion she needed stronger material for the deal to fly?

Hopefully, her own, but maybe by others.

And commitment to a style that would distinguish her from the pack, the way nobody else could be Garland or Streisand, not her composite of myriad singers' tones and tricks and, listening now, yes, there was a lot of Sinatra, too, in who Patrice thought she was.

Maybe she was reading his mind, because she said, "I promise you Brian won't keep this from happening, Danny." She studied him studying her. "Go on, ask me anything. I won't mind. I've always been too honest for my own good. Maybe that's why I'm here now, instead of in my trophy room polishing all my Grammys." She laughed her rumpled laugh and lit the room with her eyes.

"I told Rap to be discreet in what he told your husband and absolutely no specifics, but Brian knew more than he should have. About Mason Weems and Joe Wunsch and—what was it he meant when he said he had found something better?"

"Not the anything kind of question I had in mind," she said, letting her expression tell Danny the rest. She flicked away her fingers. "Something better? I think that was Brian spouting off like he does a lot. The other was Rap, but not his fault. On the phone to me and neither of us knew Brian was listening on the extension. I didn't know he'd come home. I no sooner hung up, he was on the attack, demanding to know everything, calling Rap every name in the book that he wasn't using on me."

Patrice lifted up her T-shirt as if it were as natural as brushing her teeth, exposing high-strung, painters' white breasts and welts and bruises that stood out like purple shields against her delicate tan. "Record deal or no record deal, I'll never lack for a hit as long as I'm with that son of a bitch. Usually he leaves no visible marks; one of those cop tricks. This time he was flying high on a couple vodkas, so his stress medicine wasn't working, but his fists sure were. If you want to know what a leather belt can do, we can move on to my ass next. Brian certain as hell did, while he's screaming about me and Rap keeping secrets and who wants to be with some second-rate label."

Her voice barely betrayed emotion talking about the beating in details so exquisite they almost overshadowed the real pain radiating from his leg. When she stopped to look nowhere in particular, pulling down her T-shirt in the process, Danny said,

"If this happens as often as I think, why do you stay with him?"

"You think I don't ask myself the same question every day? Where? You have an answer for that? I don't. He took me off the street when I had nothing, and I still have nothing. He sees to that. I'm his love slave and his sparring partner. Once or twice I tried to run away. The first time I came back. The second time, Brian found me before I could go back. I lost the baby that time," she said, her throat clogging. "That time I . . . I suppose I keep thinking the son of a bitch is bound to change one day and things will get better. I know they won't, but—"

Patrice stopped abruptly and looked away from him, fighting back tears.

Impulsively, Danny moved next to her on the couch and took her in his arms.

"We're going to make our deal and it's going to get you away from him once and for all, Patrice. You're going to be a giant star and Brian Malloy is going to be history, out of your life for good. I promise."

"I don't need your promise, I—"

She was giving him the same penetrating look she had before, only this time it ended with her crisp lips pushing hard against his. Her tongue found his. It had been a long time since Danny had experienced so much passion. His erection was immediate. Patrice grabbed for it, resisting his efforts to pull her hand away or release his mouth. She gripped one of his hands, forced it onto her breast. He felt the hard nipple dig into his palm, arched back with the pleasure and panic brought on by the sensation. Her rubbing had him ready to burst through his pants. He couldn't make his voice work. When he looked into her eyes, all he saw was her desperation and his—

His what?

What, Danny?

His desire?

His need?

Maybe even his own desperation?

It had been too long since anyone needed him the way she needed him; wanted him the way he had to have her now, although it was wrong.

Wrong.

Brian Malloy was a bastard, but he was her husband.

Patrice had managed his zipper down and was pulling down his jockeys, momentarily exposing his cock, until—

She stopped abruptly.

Jumped to her feet, frantically undressing.

"You, too," Patrice said, barely able to speak, begging him, "Oh, God, please, Danny. I just need somebody to love me. Just for tonight. Please? Just for tonight? Just for tonight?"

Patrice made noises through the night, often a sound at the base of her throat that rolled into a hum against the roof of her mouth, one of many in her arsenal. She seemed to have one for every part of her body, wherever and whenever he touched her, even for an unintentional breeze from his fingers by the down on her face, which trapped the light like an angel in flight.

Her expressions belonged more to Michelangelo, especially when she was crying out of need or shame, he was never sure which. Especially when she called *Oh God!* he couldn't tell if it was for the pleasure or some pain her mind eliminated through her body.

Danny wondered if she was the Mona Lisa in disguise.

And feared he was falling for her, even after she roused that morning full of apology, urging him to believe her when she said, "I didn't mean for this to happen, Danny."

"Makes two of us," he said.

Patrice leaned over and kissed his cheek.

He reciprocated with a kiss that caught the corner of her

mouth while he gave the back of her neck a few gentle rubs and made her coo.

And they fell back into bed by unspoken mutual consent.

Morning, sitting naked over a makeshift breakfast of instant coffee, toaster waffles and day-old bagels at the dinette counter, close enough for their thighs to touch and deliver tingles while Sinatra sang in the background, Patrice was more relaxed, as if he'd shut the nightmare of Brian Malloy out of her dreams.

She said, "I should feel guilty or regret or remorse, I suppose, but all I feel is wonderful, honey. I hope you can understand that. Even if it never happens again, wonderful knowing that a decent person like you still exists in the world—"

"Never happens again?" Danny said, shutting her off.

"What do you think?"

"I think we have to find out if we're running to something or away from something."

"For me that's more than a marathon and carries a lot of baggage. There are things you should know."

"Same with me. I'm willing to take it a mile at a time, if you are."

"Yes, but I need you to travel the first mile with me. To see if the rest of the run makes sense for you. Besides, I already heard from Rap about your wife and losing those poor kids of yours." Danny winced. "I can imagine how a caring person such as yourself carries that kind of tragedy with him. And I heard about your troubles at Decade Records over Nat Axelrod that cost you your job. I heard about your brushes with drugs. See? You went the first mile with me already and you didn't even know it."

"Rap always did have a big mouth."

Patrice tore off a piece of bagel, swiped it in the margarine container and chewed slowly, thoughtfully. She screwed up her face and said, "I think what I want you to know most of all is that I am not now or ever have been a whore . . . Mom died when I was in my teens when I married for the first time, to escape my stepfather, who made Brian Malloy look like a leading candidate for sainthood. My husband was old enough to be my father, a good man who loved me dearly and died too soon. By this time I was into my childhood dream of becoming a singer in Las Vegas—part-time gigs in hotels off the strip when I wasn't working swing as a *Folies Bergère* showgirl at the Tropicana Hotel.

"It didn't work out with a boyfriend, a bad ending to what should have been magical and forever, and I wound up sneaking out of town with barely more than the clothes on my back, to LA, waiting tables while trying to catch a break in the record business. My choice of bands was about as good as my choice in men, not good at all. Music was going through a transition again. The underground was six feet under, mired in a mosh pit of chaos that wasn't for me. My kind of music was nowhere to be found.

"I fit in with another band, Band Why?, replacing the lead vocalist who deathed out on meth two hours after finishing the band's showcase gig at the Roxy. This thing developed with the bass player, but he was more into crack than me. We had a major blowout in San Diego, and I was left stranded at the Greyhound station with a gym bag containing my clothes and makeup, ten dollars in my wallet, not enough mad money for a bus ticket anywhere worth going, and a vice cop who is shaking me awake on the station bench where I had sacked out for a few hours, getting ready to run me in for hooking.

"I tell him my story and beg him to leave me be. He says he believes me, but I'm in for serious trouble if I hang around the station too long. The station is full of creeps and perverts, he says, and who would know better than a vice cop? A pimp with a smooth line comes along, and they come along as regular as the bus schedule, he says, and I'll be turned out before I know it, with powder up my nose and a dick up my ass. He invites me to go home with him, bunk on his sofa, and first thing in the morning he'll see to getting me back to LA. He's a cop and I believe him—until he's fed me so much beer and bullshit that I'm too relaxed to resist the powder he's putting up my nose or the dick he's ramming up my ass."

Danny said, "Brian?"

"Himself, Danny, and where it began with this whore fixation of his. So help me, God, the closest I ever came was in his mind. Sure, I have loved and I have fucked, sometimes doing both with the same man at the same time, like with you, but not that much and there was always chemistry. Every single damn time. But never for money. Not ever, God damn it!

"The jerk gets his rocks off thinking that way. He can't get it up unless he's gangbanging my mind, too, with those names and the rest of me with his hands, sometimes his belt, and one or two times, when he was really drunk and couldn't even find it to pee out a five-alarm fire, pistol whipped. Whacked real good where it wouldn't show. You cannot believe what it's like to see a man drunker than a skunk, his hands shaking like he's just invented palsy, take a pistol and shove the barrel up your vagina, and say like he means it—*Whore, I'm gonna pull the trigger and blow your brains out!*"

"How long has this been going on?"

"Since he took me in. That night at the Greyhound." Patrice covered her face, rubbed her nose with a finger, and counted off the years with her other hand. "If I'm twenty-nine now . . . and that was four, no—going on three years."

"What possessed you to stay with him, especially after that first night. The lies, then and since. The way he treated you and keeps on treating you . . ."

"I was a fool? Can the answer be any simpler than that? It is more complicated, of course, but that was a major part. The next morning, when he was sober, he became a whimpering slob of a man-child, hardly better than a newborn, crying about how rotten he was for treating me like that. He said he didn't know why, except I was so beautiful and reminded him of one of his exes, the only one of the three he ever truly loved or missed. So I felt sorry for him. Here was this guy on his knees, truly, asking for forgiveness and begging me to move in with him, because he was lonely and he knew we could make a go of it if we gave each other a little time.

"Well, I thought, a cop. One of the good guys for a change. Give me some respectability for once in my life. Sure, we got off to a bad start, but I had worse back home and for sure in Las Vegas, so, why not give it a try? He wasn't so much older, not so bad looking and, besides, what did I have going for me back in LA? So, I said, okay, let's try it, and the same day he drove us up and back for my things.

"It was good for a while. Brian tried, and I was on my way to becoming quite the little woman, but one day he just stressed out beyond redemption and became the total monster you saw." Patrice stared despondently into her coffee cup. "The booze is his real wife, Danny, like it is for a lot of his cop buddies. His medication is for stress and depression, Paxil? Only he refuses to take it all the time and it won't work unless it's always in your bloodstream. It doesn't work if you're drinking booze, either. So he drinks and drinks and, if the ex-Gyrene in him is unhappy with the way I've spit-polished our happy home, he lets me know."

"Three years of this," Danny said, dumbfounded by what he was hearing. Patrice was a complicated person, but she also came across as too intelligent, too independent to permit this kind of treatment. "Why haven't you split already? Picked up and gotten the hell out of there? Why are you going back today, for Christ's sake?"

Patrice looked at him with sympathy and amusement.

"You just don't get it, but I suppose that's the good news for me. There are thousands of us across the country, Danny. We get the shit beat out of us and our self-esteem and confidence. We get to believing we are lower than scum and lucky to have a roof over our head and food on the table and, of course, a man who tolerates us and is willing to put up with us. We're chained by our insecurities and, in some back corner of our screwed-up minds we think, *This won't last forever. I can change him if I hold on, work real hard at it.* Brian lets me scream and rage at him all I want, you saw that, and he likes it. Loves it. It lets him get back at me, feeling he's doing the right thing, teaching the little woman a lesson. But God help me I ever try leaving him for good. He lets me know that, too."

She reached over and laid a hand on his. "You want to hear something truly funny about it all? We never even married, Danny. I became his bride in bullshit only. That talk you heard from Rap about Brian wanting a signed paper from me, because he was scared of what he would lose if we ever divorced? Brian is total bullshit. He talked a lot at first about taking time off and driving to Vegas, making us legal in one of those cute Elvis Presley chapels, where the minister dresses like Elvis, but it never happened, like a lot of Brian's promises."

Danny noticed for the first time she wasn't wearing a ring on her left hand. There was a gold wedding band on her right ring finger. He supposed it was left over from the husband who made it possible for her to break away from her stepfather's indignities.

Impulsively, feeling purer for not having spent the night making love to another man's wife, he said, "I don't want you to go back to him, Patty. Stay here with me."

She inched away to have a better look at his face, almost seemed to mock his sincerity with her expression. A wistful smile appeared as she eased off the stool and started piling the dishes and discards for a trip around the counter into the kitchen.

"I know you mean it, Lone Ranger, but I can't let you." She shook her head and, almost as if he was no longer there, dumped the trash and started rinsing the dishes and stacking them in the dishwasher.

Danny joined her in the kitchen. "Try," he said, wrapping his arms around her bare waist, resisting the excitement of his body pressing on hers. She shook her head. "We'll be working in a recording studio any day now. What are you going to do, travel up and back every day from San Diego? He's not about to give up his day job to become your chauffeur. It makes sense. That's all he has to know—the recording sessions—until we see where else this takes us."

"He's already said no to you, remember?" Patrice said. She eased herself free and moved back into the living room, to the couch.

Danny stared at her from the kitchen side of the counter. "Listen, Patty, I've dealt with these wannabes a million times. I'll call Brian in a while, tell him what I have in mind. I'll tell him he owns your masters whether we ultimately strike a deal or not. As long as he has a signed paper he thinks is worth something, he'll go for it. He may huff and puff, but he won't blow the house down. They never do."

"You can't tell him I'm staying here."

"I'll feed him the address of one of the condos Decade Records leases on the Wilshire corridor for visiting artists and VIPs."

"Will he own the masters?"

"That's for the lawyers to shark over down the road. Until

that day arrives, possession is nine tenths of the law."

"I know Brian's idea of the law better. You fuck with him, he'll go insane. He has said often enough—if I ever get serious about disappearing on him or he ever catches me playing around, he'll come after me or whoever, and won't think twice about what happens next. Not a hollow threat, *Kemo Sabe.*"

"That's why I always keep a supply of silver bullets handy," Danny said, heading for the couch.

She welcomed him into her arms.

Joe Wunsch called shortly after eleven o'clock with the good news and the bad news.

"The bad news first," he said. "We're fuck out of luck on Rancho Musico for this week and maybe into the next. For the duration, the entire studio is overrun by a label that pulls bigger and harder—Danger Funk."

"Aren't they exclusively East Coast?"

"Out here for the Soul Train Awards and using the downtime to lay down some tracks with I.C.U. and the Street Boyz. Juke Daddy B. has been in and out a few times, too. The label keeps armed guards inside the entrances. AKs and Uzis, like all we hear about a quiet war raging inside the kingdoms of hip-hop is more than a rumor."

"What's the good news?"

"You remember the Nam?"

"The Tune King's place over on Melrose. Your lucky studio."

"Where it began for me with fucking Mickey Neel. Like the way the Beach Boys had Sunset Sound until it became a Mexican TV station. I still use it off and on for my low-budget discovery shit, so I called the Tune King. When he heard I was doing this session with you, he said, *You need it, you got it. Anything for Danny Manings.* What's that all about?"

Danny searched his memory. "I don't have the slightest idea.

I was there two or three times the most after Mickey. We talked the usual small talk, hello and where to send the P.O. That was about it."

"Well, the Tune King sounded like he had a hard-on in his heart for you and we're set until we can make the move to Rancho Musico."

"Today?"

"Today? Fucking what today?"

Danny told him about Patrice being in town, leaving out any mention of the problem with Brian. "I'd like to go check out the place, make sure she's okay with it. If the engineer is halfway decent, we can think about moving in and laying down some test tracks on the cheap, before we get into any real money with Rancho Musico."

Joe said, "I'll call the Tune King and tell him. How's two o'clock sound?"

The Nam was pretty much as Danny remembered it, the kind of place that stands on reputation and need, the former stemming from the occasional hits developed here, the latter because it was as much recording studio as a struggling artist or band could afford. He pointed out to Patrice the Mickey Neel Gold and Platinum albums on wall display, framed presentation copies with gratitude plaques engraved to the Tune King, alongside an effusive thank-you letter from Joe raving about the Nam's part in Mickey's success.

The Tune King came rushing flatfooted up the corridor, stumbling over his breathing the way old men do when they try to make their legs move as fast as their desire. "Mr. Manings, you old sumna-gun!" he called to Danny, joyously; locked him in a grip that also signaled his delight. "It's good to have a *mensch* like you back here working." Turning to study Patrice, he said, "This the wonderful girl I heard all about from Joey?"

Danny introduced them. The Tune King released Danny and embraced her. "So lucky you are, miss. They don't make them better than him. Come, come. I'll take you on the not-so-grand tour. It ain't a Rancho Musico, but what is?"

Not the Nam. The gear was older than rock and roll, even a discarded one-track shelved for emergencies in a tiny booth studio built around a four-track that was state-of-the-art when the place belonged to Decca and Crosby ducked in for recording sessions when he wasn't around the corner making movies at Paramount. A relatively new board was in the big studio where Danny would be working with Patrice. The Tune King introduced them to the black engineer fiddling with the dials in the booth, trying to find satisfactory levels on a reel in the play deck that pushed forward and back too erratically to digest.

"Say hello to Jimmy Slyde," he said. "Jimmy, this is Mr. Danny Manings, what I already been telling you about."

They shook hands.

Slyde's grip was strong, as determined as the snap of his eyes.

"The Tune King been carrying on and on about you ever since I got here today," Slyde said, checking Danny out like he was a used car. "Hear tell you're one heavy dude."

"Only as good as the people I'm with, Jimmy."

Slyde liked that and showed it.

The Tune King said, "See what I was telling you, Jimmy? We got a *mensch* here." Danny felt his cheeks flushing. "You remember what I told you was a *mensch*?"

"Not a *zhlob, shlemiel* or *momzer,*" Slyde said, treating his pronunciations cautiously.

"But first of all an honest and decent person, a man of consequence. That's a *mensch* . . . Mr. Manings here." The Tune King rolled his eyes and made a face at Patrice. "Do you know already how modest he is? Like any true *menschen,* they make you find out for yourselves."

"I know, Mr. King, I discovered that for myself," she said, with a taint of mischief that only somebody looking for it might see.

"Then you're a smart girl, all right. You should only have a voice like you have this way to understand?"

Danny said, "You'll hear it soon enough, Tune King."

"So, good, then. When you want this studio for real?"

"Tomorrow, maybe? Maybe Joe told you, we haven't settled yet on a producer and we still have A&R questions—"

"Yeah, yeah, yeah," the Tune King said, throwing a hand at him. "I heard. Is why I'm glad you come down first like this. I got Jimmy to come here special to meet you, because he's your engineer. And a Triple A-OK engineer, what he already knows and what he's been learning working with the other boy I got coming over to meet you. The other, he might be the producer you're looking for." The Tune King checked his wristwatch, bringing its large oval face to within an inch of his eyes and trading his thick lenses for a squint. "I sent over Pete to tell him to come, so he shudda been here by now." He looked at Slyde, who shrugged.

Danny traded glances with Patrice, but kept his smile in place. He didn't want to imagine what the Tune King's idea was for a producer for a singer he had yet to hear.

The Tune King said, "This producer is more, Mr. Manings. He writes and he even been laying down his own material, what I got Jimmy readying for you to hear. Thought it would be nice for the other boy to be here, but we can begin without him, and serves him right for being late. Go ahead, Jimmy."

Slyde jiggled a few more dials, pressed a button, and the tape he had been working with filled the booth.

Danny was trapped immediately by what he was hearing.

By more than the melody.

By more than the lyrics.

By more than the voice.

There was a familiarity of the whole on all the cuts, one as good or better than the next.

It was Nat Axelrod.

How Nat wrote. Sang. Performed.

Flush with unmistakable Nat Axelrod production touches.

The Tune King's missing boy was a Nat Axelrod clone.

Danny didn't want to speculate how many hours of listening the boy had done to Nat's old albums, cut by cut, to get so close to duplicating the unmistakable quality of the whole in ways that captured, redefined and raised to higher levels the music of today. More than merely cloning magic, there was genius at work on these demos.

Even in their present unfinished state, the cuts had a chemistry that matched Patrice's own.

Better, but who could Danny admit that to for the moment, except himself.

Patrice made it easier. "Awesome," she said. "Until now, I thought I graduated from songwriting kindergarten years ago."

"He is something else again," Slyde said, not wanting to be left out of the voting.

The Tune King recognized Danny's excitement. He clamped his arms across his chest and surveyed faces, looking the way Hannibal must have looked when he conquered the Alps. "So I think maybe you wanna meet him?" he said. "Any minute he'll be here."

The minute stretched to almost an hour of repeated listening to the music before Danny said, "Maybe you should call?"

The Tune King said, "He don't got no phone, Mr. Manings. Why I'm always sending Pete after him. Anytime he and his lady make ends meet, there's no middle left, if you know what I mean? You could be good for him and him for you, you know?"

"Where's he live? I'll take a run over."

"He's close enough. But a walk, maybe, will do it if he's not here in ten more minutes. Or, I could send Pete again?"

"Pete can take me there."

"I'll be right back." He was, in five minutes, advising, "I got a missing Pete on my hands now. You see what kinds of days it can be? Come, into my office. I'll look up the boy's address for you."

The Tune King found what he wanted in his Rolodex, scribbled down the address on the back of an envelope and handed it over.

He said, "I know what you are thinking or should be, Mr. Manings. What's this old Yid going to ask me for over this? How big a piece of the pie? A piece of the publishing? A piece of the production fee? What already? He ain't doing this from the bottom of his heart or the good of mankind. So, I'll tell you, you want to know.

"A long time ago, you don't even remember, I'm here after a day nobody should ever have, my beloved wife gone to her rest and me wanting to die and be with her. The call on the telephone is you. You heard the news from Joe, who was working all day and just come back there. And you talked to me, no, you listened to me go on and on for an hour, longer maybe. You were there on the other end of that phone there. Running a big record company, a million things on your mind, a million people a lot more important than an old Tune King you hardly knew in a studio you dropped by maybe two or three times, and you listened. Sometimes you said a few words like the *mensch* you are.

"Later, when Joe would describe the terrible things happening to you in your life. Your wife. Your children. The goings-on with destroyers in this business. You destroying yourself bit by bit on the white crap or the pills or whatever. I knew a telephone call wasn't enough, especially from a *shlepper* like me, so I prayed for you. I don't pray much anymore, even then, but I prayed for you. I reminded *Hashem* about you, how I knew I could never repay you for your kindness by myself. But along comes this boy years later into the Nam, then Joe is on the phone, and I think to myself, *Hashem,* sometimes You take Your own sweet time to make a *mitzvah,* but when You do . . ." His eyes had misted over. "So if I want anything, it's nothing, but you should live well and do right by these people the way you did right by me, Mr. Manings."

The Tune King saw the difficulty he was having and offered a two-handed shrug. "Listen, just go and talk to the boy. What goes around comes around, all right?"

"All right," Danny said, glancing for the first time at the envelope the Tune King had handed him, and—

Nathan Greene.

Danny froze in the moment, paralyzed by a congregation of emotions brought on by the name the Tune King had written above the address.

He got directions from the Tune King. Passed his key ring to Patrice and told her to drive the car back to the apartment. Without explanation, sped out of the Nam flushed with excitement.

Certain the Tune King's other boy was no Nat Axelrod disciple.

Certain the Tune King's other boy was Nat Axelrod.

Chapter 16

Earlier that day, Nathan wandered the apartment in a worried mood. Bills were piling up, the rent was due in four days, and Ana Maria had spent half the night moaning how it was likely Father O'Bryan would be cutting her hours or laying her off at Blessed Bonaventure, because the church had serious financial problems, a victim of the trickle-down theory since the archdiocese slashed its budget the first of the year. The congregation at Blessed Bonaventure was a poor one to begin with; contributions had not made up the difference.

The Tune King also had serious money problems this month, and it was going to make him late with a check for sessions that were no fun to begin with, Nathan and Jimmy Slyde working with one of the Tune King's aspiring superstars, DJ Doom & The Skin Mob, gutter rap masters who dropped four-letter words like they owned the copyright.

Shit. Fuck. Cock. Piss.
Screw her. Do her.
Eat her meat, her
Pussy fur.

He and Slyde had never laughed this hard, especially during setup breaks yesterday, when they challenged one another with their own vamped lyrics and scattered laughter like buckshot.

When he got home from the session, he called *Here's Johneeeeeeeeeee!* to Ana Maria coming through the door she never locked, doing his version of Jack Nicholson in *The Shining,* trying to make sunshine in an alley of bad news.

He had never intended to be the head of this family of two or otherwise responsible for providing, but he was feeling it now. He knew he would leave Ana Maria one day—it had to be—but until the day arrived he had a responsibility and an obligation to pay her back for her kindness, her generosity and a love he had not reckoned on.

Nathan found her curled up like a ball in the armchair, engrossed in the black-and-white images of the movie on the Spanish-language cable channel. She waved for him to be quiet and pressed a forefinger against her lips. She was naked except for her panties and dried tear streams under her soulful brown eyes. He crossed to her and sat down on an arm of the chair that creaked under his weight.

She was watching a dubbed version of a movie starring Glenn Ford and Rita Hayworth he remembered from childhood. The movie stopped for a commercial by a *gringo* lawyer with a passable accent and a round-the-clock 800 number hawking the fantasy of green cards.

She looked up smiling. "So beautiful, that Glenn Ford," she said, "although not so much as you."

"I remember a hot song from that picture. Rita Hayworth is dancing it up in a nightclub or somewhere, throwing around her tits and all that red hair something fierce."

"Put the blame on Mame, boy," Ana Maria said. She began singing the words. There was an exceptional quality to her voice. She was no Selena, but her voice was warm and lyrical, with a memory for notes and near-perfect pitch. He smoothed her hair and pushed stray lengths back off her face. Ana Maria reached for his right hand, kissing the mashed knuckles and sucking the mangled thumb before placing it over the extended nipple of her tiny breast. "My tits are just as good as hers for throwing around," Ana Maria said, proudly, defiantly. "Rita was Spanish, you knew? Her real name was Margarita. Margarita Carmen Cansino."

Her skin felt warm and alive to his touch. She was studying him inquiringly. He shook his head. She responded with a coy look and began walking her fingers playfully across his thigh and onto his crotch. She changed to a slow, circular movement, frequently alternating direction.

Nathan moved his mind out of reach, but it was too late to destroy the erection she had inspired stroking through his pants with gentle patience. The movie began again. She turned to watch, continuing the massage. He rubbed his hand over the refreshing smoothness of her brown skin, squeezing the back of her neck and manipulating her shoulders.

Ana Maria closed her eyes and groaned. "Will we ever make real love, *mi corazon*?"

Nathan pulled back. For a moment she'd made him forget. He stopped playing with her and took her hand off him; moved away.

She crooned after him, "Put the blame on Mame, boy; put the blame on Mame."

Nathan sank onto the sofa. He stared into her eyes and she matched the look defiantly. She sprang from the chair, kneeled between his legs and began working at his belt. She got his denims and jockey shorts to his knees, humming the song while she stuck out her wet tongue, worked the moisture around her lips with erotic delicacy while playing with her hands on both breasts.

Nathan watched until it was impossible to keep his eyes open, hoping this time he would see Ana Maria, not Mae Jean. Mae Jean's image formed anyway. He tried to erase her from his mind by thinking about Ana Maria, the good, loving woman who'd salvaged happiness for him, however modest, at a time he thought he was beyond hope, beyond help, beyond redemption—

> *Shit. Fuck. Cock. Piss.*
> *Screw her. Do her.*
> *Eat her meat, her*
> *Pussy fur.*

Whose face now, Nathan?
Whose face do you see now?

> *Shit. Fuck. Cock. Piss.*
> *Screw her. Do her.*
> *Eat her meat, her*
> *Pussy fur.*

Nathan thought he heard his laughter rising above the lyrics and his own rap:

Love her. Love her. Love. Her.

He screamed a frightening scream and called out for her to stop.

Don't stop. Stop. Don't stop.

He screamed louder and then louder still.

He shouted, *Jesus! God! No. No, don't!* He felt his body shifting like a missile on a launch pad, carrying him to some isolated star.

He began crying.

Ana Maria sprang up and hurried onto Nathan's lap. She comforted him in her arms. He squeezed his eyes to hide the pain and the hurt, but he did not resist. She fit like she belonged there. A series of indecipherable words spilled over his lips. She wiped the layer of sweat from his head, dried his cheek with her hand, kissed him gently; her voice patient and comforting.

He thought: *When do I leave her? I will, I must, I can. I can not, never, do to her what I did with Mae Jean. Never to Ana Maria what I did to Mae Jean.*

When he was calmer, comfortable with her again, Ana Maria told him about Blessed Bonaventure. Her tears this time were for them, not for Glenn and Rita. It became his turn to comfort her, reassure her. He did not add to her burdens by telling Ana Maria about the Tune King and how the money from him would be late.

In bed later, after Ana Maria fell asleep with her face on his chest, an arm across his chest, her breathing relaxed, he sent a prayer to a God who seemed to take constant pleasure from testing him, and—

"Nathan! *Hola!*"

Nathan stopped his tracking the room and flashed on the door.

Pete was standing in the open doorway, wearing an anxious smile on his cherubic face.

"Tune King sent me over," Pete said. "Says he needs you to be over at the Nam at two."

"He say what for? Not the rappers again, I hope."

"Only it was *muy importante*. The Tune King, he said for you not to be late."

Nathan was delayed by the musical horn of Alfonso Morales's canary-colored lowrider as the signal light changed and he could cross Melrose Avenue to the Nam. Enriqué and Carlos, *El Diablo,* were with him. Morales gunned the engine. Enriqué pushed open the Pontiac's rear door and called him over. "Blaupunkt weather, *amigo,*" he said. "Maybe we even catch ourselves a nice Alpine or two. Nice afternoon for catching Alpines."

Nathan zipped up his jacket, tossed his cigarette into the street and headed for the car.

"I don't think so, *amigos,* not today."

"Ana Maria," Carlos said, cackling like a crazed rooster. "She got you like this, *émé.*" He scrunched his hand, like it could be holding a pair of balls.

Nathan had promised Ana Maria no more car-radio heists, but he wasn't about to admit it. Face was everything in the gangster hood they had accepted him into. "Need to work today," he said, aiming his chin at the Nam. "Otherwise—" He shrugged, as if suggesting some other time.

"Can't wait," Enriqué said. "Tomorrow is Open House at school and the kids made me swear on every saint from A until Z. The fat cow would kill me if I didn't get there for Open House. Then, tomorrow night is always our bowling night."

Morales started to say something about Friday and slapped his forehead. "No, is no good for me," he said. "We going to Las Vegas on the bus Friday for Julio Iglesias."

The singer's name excited Carlos and Enriqué.

They appeared envious of Morales.

Morales said, "Three nights and four days we're getting. A complimentary continental breakfast or dinner buffet. Don't come along so often over weekends, so I need to fill up my pockets from a good haul."

They exchanged a few more minutes of convivial small talk before Nathan turned and started from the car. In that moment, while checking the signal crossing window, he recognized the man who had just released his hand from the back of a woman the man was ushering into the Nam.

Even at this distance, in profile, before he turned to enter himself, Nathan recognized it was nobody he wanted to ever see again—

Danny Manings.

"*Amigos!* Wait!" he called at the Pontiac. "I feel the Blaupunkt weather!"

Enriqué pushed open the back door and made room for him.

They decided on the Century City Mall.

The pickings there would be richer this time of day than at the Glendale Galeria. The underground parking garage would be full of the high-end cars owned by visitors to the high-rises fronting the shopping complex, who looked to save on parking fees by cheapskating on the mall's free three hours.

Morales made it there in under a half hour and maneuvered down to the third level, where the foot traffic would be lightest. Found a good getaway spot. Aimed the Pontiac face out, within a sharp left turn of the exit ramp. He got out and strolled off with Carlos. Enriqué hung back for a minute before moving in the same direction, only up a different aisle.

Nathan waited until the three of them were almost out of sight before going to his usual sentry point, a pay phone about fifteen feet from the escalator bank. He leaned against the wall with the receiver cushioned between his ear and his left shoulder while his eyes kept lookout, working the garage the way he used to work concert arena audiences, routinely moving his lips like he was in conversation with the dial tone, a safety habit Enriqué had taught him.

A security guard zipped by on a patrol buggy.

Nathan checked his watch.

The *bandidos* had a good thirty-eight minutes more to shop the cars for the stereos of their choice. The thirty-eight could easily become sixty on midweek days like this if the guard turned down the volume on his Walkman and sneaked off to *siesta* in an out-of-sight corner. It wouldn't be the first time he'd experienced this with the *bandidos*. The attitude of these parking guards seemed a lot like school crossing guards an hour after the final bell: the job is there, but not the work.

Carlos eased by, looking moderately pregnant under his knee-length leather coat, and turned up a thumb. He mouthed the word "Blaupunkt" and headed for the trunk of the Pontiac, glistening clean under thick coats of fresh wax. He raised the unlocked lid. An instant later he slammed the lid shut and headed off again. He gave Nathan a wink.

Nathan knew this was a bad sign.

It meant Carlos already had forgotten about quitting early.

He let his eyes follow two teenage girls who wandered off the escalator. They paused to verify the location of their car. One was pretty. Not the other. The usual combination, he thought. He adjusted the phone on his shoulder and dug his hands inside his pockets. The one who wasn't pretty smiled at him and whispered something to her friend, who sneaked a look at Nathan and then grabbed hold of her friend's shoulder and began tugging her toward a dirty blue Honda two aisles away.

As the Honda headed for the exit, Nathan heard—

Kuh-rakuh.

The sound echoed at the far end of the garage, out of view.

Backfire?

Less than ten seconds later—

Three more echoes from the same place, one after the next.

Kuh-rakuh. Kuh-rakuh. Kuh-rakuh.

The sniff of gunpowder reached him.

Not backfires.

Trouble.

The *bandidos* had stayed too long.

Nathan hung up the phone and calmly moved with the escape plan.

He sauntered toward Morales's lowrider. The rear door on the passenger side would be unlocked. The emergency ignition key would be in the ashtray of the armrest. He would give them sixty seconds to show up, then split. Whoever was still missing would have to walk and talk his way out of the garage.

Nathan had the door half open when he heard the nervous command:

"Don't you give me no trouble."

It came dressed in a borderline baritone that squeaked like a leaking tire.

He turned his head carefully and looked over his shoulder. Three or four feet away, a uniformed guard stood hunched like a question mark over his .45-caliber revolver. He was old, black, skinny as a pork sausage, and frightened ass-wipe silly. The guard's hair billowed from under his cap like coiled aluminum and his mustache was snow white, like the inside of a dime bag. A curious tic kept pushing his left cheek into his left eye.

"I don't want no trouble," the old gent said. He paused to wag the weapon, developing a sweat bag of a face that belonged on the late, late show, tap dancing up a plantation stairway with Shirley Temple. "We gots your friends and no need for no aggravating circumstances from you, so you just raise up your hands," he said.

Nathan remembered one time in Burbank, how Social Security recruits like this one could be as dangerous as loose strands on a rug. At this range, they were also deadly. He turned to face him in slow motion.

"Nice and easy," the guard said.

"Steady as they go, boss."

The guard's grip shook. Nathan thought, *Careful. Do as the man says.* The guard caught sight of his corrupted hands. "Jesus!" he said. His jaw went slack. " 'Pears somebody surely did a number on them hands of yours."

"Number two," Nathan said. He feigned a smile. His eyes shifted casually, searching out the possibilities. Hardly two minutes had passed. The garage was still empty around them.

The first sounds of curiosity and concern were traveling from where he had heard the four gunshots.

Kuh-rakuh.

A fifth gunshot.

The noise level instantly rose, punctuated by a scream and muffled shouts. The guard flinched reflexively, pulled to action by the sounds. His eyes widened and he yanked on the trigger of the .45.

Nathan saw it coming, but it happened too fast to move out of the way.

Kuh-rakuh.

Nathan fell hard onto the concrete of the empty parking space next to the lowrider. He fought an urge to sleep and opened his eyes. He was on his back and the layers of leaked oil felt cold against his shirt. He saw the antique guard standing at his feet, amateur close, pointing the .45 at his belly.

Nathan brought a leg up hard. The toe of his shoe punched into the guard's balls and kept going. The guard grabbed after them, agonizing, in the process dropping his revolver. It hit the concrete with a two-pound clang and bounced.

Nathan rolled after it; sprang to his feet.

He stepped forward and smacked the handle down hard on the guard's head. The guard's jaw dropped and he went suddenly quiet before swooning forward onto the oil-slicked concrete.

Nathan swooped down beside him to check.

The old man was chugging breath through his mouth. It smelled like stale whiskey.

Nathan pushed out a breath of relief. He had feared he'd inflicted greater damage than a headache and a wonderful story the guard would have to tell his great-grandchildren.

Less than a minute later, Nathan was navigating the Pontiac slowly toward the exit ramp. At the tollbooth, he took the parking ticket from the clasped hand of the plastic Virgin Mary on the dashboard and handed it over to the attendant.

He was still within the three-hour free parking limit.

"Have a nice day," the attendant said, waving him forward.

The barrier rose.

Nathan turned onto Little Santa Monica heading east toward Hollywood.

As Century City receded in the background, his adrenaline rush faded and he moved into a mild traumatic aftermath. Transparent layers of shock slid over his face.

He reached down to touch a serious kind of pain he had not felt since Indiana, whenever Rufus Hardaway and his goons came calling. It was radiating from his left thigh. His palm came up blood red. Horns sounded. He looked out in time to twist the Pontiac back onto his side of the line and avoid a head-on.

He pressed down on his thigh, felt the denim soaking up wetness.

He was getting cold.

His eyelids felt like they were soldering together.

Somehow he got through Beverly Hills, where posted regulations made street parking impossible, and into the City of Los Angeles.

He turned off Wilshire and navigated residential streets full of high-rise condos until he spotted curbside space he could slide into.

Nathan found one of Enriqué's headbands and a penlight in the glove compartment. He pulled the headband over his shoe and up onto his thigh, inserted the pen light underneath and, biting his lip against the pain, twisted it around and around until he was certain the flow of blood was stopped.

He held on tightly, afraid to let go, and feel asleep that way.

A rapping at the window woke him.

It was an old woman with blue hair walking her pet Airedale, a lively pile of overfed off-white and tobacco brown. She looked irritated by her discovery. Her mouth shouted words at the window while the Airedale sniffed diligently on a straw bush in the grass island.

Nathan stared back at the woman vaguely. She wore oversized designer frames on a beaded plastic chain. Her tightly pursed lips moved like she had had one face lift too many.

He rolled down the window.

She said, "You get out of here now, you just scat, or I'll call police." Before he could answer, she screamed: "You don't frighten me a-tall. I'm Neighborhood Watch." The Airedale had a leg up and was peeing on the bush.

Nathan let go of the penlight without thinking and raised his hand to reassure her.

She saw the blood on his palm, glanced down at his thigh.

"Oh my God in Heaven!"

The woman backed away a step or two, turned and fled. The Airedale was in the middle of a squat. It barked angrily and chased after her.

Nathan turned the key in the ignition, drove the rest of way home full of pain and anger.

Pushing open the apartment door, he sensed something wasn't right. That, or nerves. His three *amigos* would never rat out one of their own. Besides, even if they had, it was too early for the cops to be here. Or was it? He had lost all sense of time.

Nathan pulled the guard's .45 from his belt and followed it inside. The room was empty.

"Oh!"

His head and the .45 snapped in the direction of the outcry. Someone stood framed in the open bedroom door. Nathan barely heard himself wheezing her name.

"Ana Maria?"

"*Non, Monsieur* Green. My name is Laurent Connart, and I

have come to speak with you about Nat Axelrod."

Nathan tried getting a grip on the .45 as he pitched forward into a black tornado.

CHAPTER 17

In the exhausting week Laurent had spent between Indianapolis and Los Angeles, in Las Vegas, then Fort Worth, then Indianapolis again, she'd made a number of discoveries about Nat Axelrod. One was shocking beyond any of her expectations, if true, but it would require Nathan Greene's confirmation.

She worked out how to ingratiate herself, worm the truth from him, while drifting up the stairs through the mixed odors of Latin cooking to Ana Maria Alfaro's apartment. After a third time knocking to no response, she tried the doorknob.

The lock was broken.

The door swung open noisily.

"Hello!" Laurent called out. "Anybody home? Someone?"

No response.

She began exploring the neatly kept apartment, looking for something to verify Nathan Greene was, in fact, Nat Axelrod, unwilling to trust only the words of the Las Vegas police and Phil Penguin. She was in the bedroom, trying to satisfy her curiosity without moving anything out of place, when she heard the apartment door opening on its rusty hinges.

Moving to the connecting door with an excuse for her random snooping framed in her head, she delivered words meant to disarm and intrigue—

"*Non, Monsieur* Green. My name is Laurent Connart, and I have come to speak with you about Nat Axelrod"—

—when she recognized his pained expression as well as his

face, not so different after all these years, and glanced down to the blood and his gun before he stumbled forward and fell into an unconscious heap.

Within minutes, Laurent was cleaning Nat's wound with rubbing alcohol she found in the bathroom, in the metal cabinet below the sink.

She took off his headband tourniquet, replacing it with strips torn from one of the bedsheets, and made a bandage wrap for his leg from other sections of the sheet.

His condition did not appear critical, not yet anyway, but she was careful not to move him more than necessary going through emergency motions she had learned in the trenches.

Nat had suffered a substantial loss of blood. The slug was still in his thigh, raising the possibility of blood poisoning without antibiotics. His forehead was feverish to her touch. His hands—as horrible as Penguin had described them—were colorless and cold, covered with the thin oily film of shock.

She settled on the floor alongside him, smoothing his hair back, studying his face, and debated with herself over calling a doctor. Paramedics would rush him to hospital. The police would come. Her chances of getting this close to him might at best be remote. Was the story worth risking his life?

Nat opened his eyes and froze them on her. She flashed on a photograph burned into her memory: Bobby Kennedy mortally wounded on the kitchen floor of the Ambassador Hotel, his eyes like Nat's, staring vacantly.

Laurent said, "Not to worry, Nat Axelrod. You are not going to die."

Impulsively, she leaned over and brushed his lips with hers.

Nat's eyelids flickered and closed.

He was asleep again.

She searched the apartment for a telephone.

There was none.

She figured it would be safe to leave him alone for the fifteen minutes it would take to make the nine-one-one call from a strip mall she had passed on Wilton Place, less than a half mile from here, and return.

The .45 he'd aimed at her was still on the floor where it fell, the blood dried flat brown like a cheap one-day paint job. She looked around for a safe hiding place. Changed her mind. If the police came, better they should not find a weapon. A gun was not something for Nat to have in his possession. She moved an ashtray full of butts from the occasional table by the armchair to get at the cheap silk covering, wrapped the gun and dropped it into her tote bag.

The front door banged against the wall.

Somebody called: "Nathan!"

The Mexican boy, not more than twelve or thirteen, overweight and winded, skidded to a stop and froze, confused by the sight of her. His wide-set eyes were suspicious. He looked down and saw Nat. Let out a noise.

"He is hurt," Laurent said. "I have to go for help now."

The boy pointed an accusing finger at her.

He pursed his lips and shut his eyes and shook his head.

Bounced on the pads of his feet.

Laurent measured her words carefully. "I did not do this. I am trying to help, and now I must go and get a doctor for Nat." She gave him her best smile. He glanced around for definition. His movements became more violent and his mouth worked anxiously to catch up with his mind.

"Not doctor," he said finally. "Father says for Nathan to hide."

"Your father wants him to hide?"

The boy nodded. "Father O'Bryan. Father O'Bryan says for me to tell Nathan hide before any cops come. Cops are coming. Somebody told on him and cops are coming."

She had been right about the gun.

She said, "The police will come and take him to a hospital. He needs a doctor."

"Away," the boy screamed. "Father says Nat has to run away." He held his fists ear level and rattled them at her. "Away. Someone told on him. Cops are coming."

Laurent extended her palms between them. She picked up the cadence of his nods and smiled. "Okay. Away. Will you help me?"

While the boy thought about his answer, she hurried to the bedroom. She found a flight bag the size of an overnight case on the floor of the closet. Sampled articles of clothing from the closet and the dresser and shoved them inside the bag. Quit after pulling out one of the bottom drawers where, instead of clothing, she found more audio cassettes like the one on top of the TV, identified in grease pencil as work tapes; folders full of loose papers and envelopes gathered by two thick rubber bands. She liberated a pillowcase, dumped everything inside and sealed it with a looping knot.

The boy was standing over Nat, his fingers laced in front of him, staring tearfully at the motionless figure. The sound of a siren in the distance jarred him.

"You and me, we must be quick about this," Laurent said. She crossed to him and told him to take the bag and the pillowcase downstairs to her car and wait for her. She described her BMW carefully and made him repeat what he had heard before letting him leave. The boy's eyes traveled back to Nat. "I will bring him with me," she said. "We will be right behind you. Do you understand?"

The boy hesitated, his eyes searching for the light, then nodded and fled the apartment, gripping the flight bag and the pillowcase.

The siren grew louder. Laurent was sure she heard two of them now. No time to waste. Her long hours at the health club on the Nautilus were about to pay off. She worked a grip on Nat's body that would make it possible to lift him to his feet. *Merde!* She could budge him, but she would never be able to pull him to his feet, no matter how much Nautilus she had done. He was dead weight to her touch. She would have to do it another way, risking his life like he was another soldier with spilling guts she had to pull from the clearing to the temporary safety of the underbrush.

She got down on her knees and straddled him, leaning forward with her hands bookends alongside his shoulders, and shouted into his face to wake up. Nothing. Nat was hiding from life. She leaned back and slapped him hard across the face. He made a noise. She slapped him again. His eye muscles barely twitched. She slapped him again. He worked his eyes open. They were wet with mucous.

He said, "Did it, Mae Jean, what you asked."

"Nat. We have to get out of here. You have to help me."

"You and me now, Mae Jean. Right?" His words swam in the back of his throat, his lips barely moving.

"You have to help, Nat."

"Out of here for now, while the getting is good, baby."

He worked a hand upward, as if trying to reach for her face.

The sight repulsed her, although she had seen worse in her time. She scrambled off him and took his hand, then the other hand, and, shouting out instructions like a drill instructor, she got him onto his feet.

She came around behind him, strapped one of her arms around his waist and ran his arm around the back of her neck.

Directing Nat out of the apartment, she held on to him tightly, encouraging him to keep moving one foot in front of the other.

Halfway down the corridor, he stumbled and fell to his hands and knees, almost taking her with him.

He stared up at her pathetically.

She shook her head and said, "You do what I say or I won't tell you later or ever."

Laurent half-walked, half-dragged him down the stairs. He tripped on her foot and seemed about to plunge forward. She gave him a hard shove that pushed him into the banister, breaking the fall. They reached the landing between the second and ground floors.

She realized the sirens were right outside the building.

She heard the screech of brakes.

If she didn't do something to hide, in a minute it would be too late.

Laurent looked around desperately.

There was a door on the landing.

She tried the handle and the door gave inwardly. In the dim overhead light of the hallway, she recognized it was a common utility closet: assorted mops and brooms lining the walls; some buckets on wheels; a cheap vacuum cleaner.

She maneuvered Nat into the closet, stepped back onto the landing and pulled the door closed as four uniformed police officers came charging through the building entrance. The boy was right behind them. He appeared bewildered and frightened.

The police sped past, but the boy stopped when he reached her. His eyes followed the cops up the stairs as he started to ask a question. She motioned for him to keep silent. The halls echoed with the determined baritone voice of a cop blurting out instructions for Nat's surrender.

Anticipating his question, she pointed to the closet. "I'm hiding him in there. I'm hiding him from the police." The boy's eyes tracked upward over his shoulder, then back to her. "Where are the bags?" she said. He gave her a quizzical look. "The bags I told you to take to the car. Are they at the car?"

He thought about it and nodded, then stepped around her to

get to the door. He gripped the knob, anxious to open the door and see inside. She stopped him. He looked at her defiantly. She realized he didn't believe her. The cops were still making demands to the apartment door. She opened the closet door enough for him to see Nat propped precariously by the brooms and mops, straining to stay on his feet. The boy nodded.

"There's something else I need you to do," Laurent said. The boy looked at the door. "For him," she said. The boy nodded. She dipped into her tote bag and retrieved the .45. She removed it from the silk wrapping and handed it over to the boy.

"Go upstairs and show this to the police," she said. "Let them see what it is, but do not shoot it. Just let them see it and do not shoot it."

Christ! She remembered she had not bothered to check if the gun was loaded. There was no time now. She would have to trust the boy to understand her instructions, as she would have to trust the police to think hard before shooting at him. She shook her head clear of old headlines presaging otherwise.

The boy held the gun like he knew how to use it.

Without another word, he took quick steps around her and up the next flight of stairs.

She got Nat from the closet and was guiding him recklessly down the last steps as the hallways became charged with the sound of cops reacting to the sight of a boy with a gun. It interrupted a surrender count that had declined to six. Voices were dealing with the problem kindly but sternly, enticing the boy to put the weapon on the floor.

At the arc-shaped entrance, Laurent turned Nat to face her. She could barely hold him upright within the crook of her arm, one side of her face mashed against his chest tightly enough to hear his labored wheezing. While she used her free hand to try getting the door wide enough for them to pass through, she had a sense of Nat's legs giving at any moment and toppling him down on her.

The door would not cooperate.

She became aware that she had not heard a cop voice for at least a minute or two.

At once, she heard the boy screaming at them, "Bang, bang; bang, bang," his voice filled with the delight of a new game. She heard a gunshot and a scramble of shouts, layers of voices calling out orders. There was no way to know who had fired.

Laurent had a vision of the boy being struck by a bullet, dropped in his tracks for refusal to give up the .45.

A chill as cold as Papa's gravestone cut through her chest.

She thought her legs would give up before Nat's.

She sensed somebody step up behind her.

Feared it was more police.

In the same instant realized she no longer bore the burden of Nat's weight.

She heard Nat talking past her, begging, "Just the two of us? Right? Tell me now, Mae Jean. Please tell me now?"

A man's voice marked by a thick accent said, "I help you."

Laurent swung around and looked up at an anxious Latin face. He was wearing a clean undershirt and the tattoo on his bare left shoulder portrayed a traditional Mexican death mask. She obeyed his signal to step aside and ducked under his arm. He was using his forearms like a forklift to support Nat, whose feet were two or three inches off the ground.

The man pulled Nat to him and ordered her, "Get the door; hurry." Laurent gave him a suspicious look. He turned his head and rolled his eyes up to the third floor. "Around here we only got each other," he said. "Quick."

Nat's eyes gazed blindly over the man's brown back. He said something, but the words were buried in the man's chest.

Laurent led the way down the porch, past clumps of gawkers on both sides of the street. Three or four people blocking the steps moved out of the way and neighborhood kids sitting on the squad car hoods whistled and applauded.

Words of encouragement, mostly in Spanish, chased after them as she led the man to the BMW parked halfway down the block, on the opposite side of the street. She took quick steps, not quite running, occasionally turning to verify he still was behind her.

The man kept pace and so did another man, who skip-stepped directly behind.

Crossing over, she reached into her bag for the remote. She got the alarm off and the doors unlocked and stood by anxiously, her eyes trained on the entrance to the apartment, while the two men manipulated Nat onto the backseat and strapped him securely in the seat belts.

The other man slammed the door shut and gave the thumbs-up sign, then both retreated, hands jammed in pockets and laughing as if they were sharing a good joke. She jumped behind the wheel, started the engine and was ready to pull out when her mind flashed on Nat's flight bag and the pillowcase.

Laurent sprang from the car and ran around to the curb side.

Nothing.

What was it the boy said in answer to her question? The boy told her he had left them when he returned to the apartment. She checked underneath. Nothing. Either the boy had lied to her or somebody had stolen the bags, a legitimate assumption in this part of town. *Merde!* But the boy had no reason to lie.

She tried to remember how it was when he came back inside the building.

She didn't remember seeing them; seeing the police was enough.

The clothing didn't matter, but the cassettes, the documents and letters; the gravy to go with her prize turkey in the backseat.

The boy was not the brightest after all. Maybe he set them down somewhere else.

Some other car that looked like her BMW?

Were the bags worth the risk of going back to find out?

Oui.

But the gunshot. What if the boy . . . ?

She started toward the apartment building, halted just as quickly as two of the police officers came out onto the front steps and began shooing back spectators. She heard police sirens and the alternating decibels of an ambulance, a half mile away at most.

Fils de putain! Too risky now, Laurent, even for you.

Laurent jarred the car climbing back inside. Nat made a groaning noise. She pulled away from the curb and made a swinging left turn into the first open driveway, then backed out onto the street and started south, away from the building. Approaching the first intersection, a squad car swept right around the corner and raced past her, its siren loud enough to obscure the pounding of her heart.

For a fraction of a second she forgot how to drive, then she pressed her foot hard on the pedal and the BMW leaped forward.

In the backseat, Nat was groaning again.

The signal at Beverly turned red before she could enter the intersection to make her left turn. She glanced nervously out the window. On the corner, a wind-damaged bag lady wearing a wilted gardenia in her hair seemed blind to the world as she pulled up her flimsy skirt and black coat and squatted to pee by a lamp pole.

She had a grip on Nat's flight bag.

The white crest on the mountain of debris in her shopping cart was the pillowcase.

Laurent pressed down on the brake and threw the car into

park. She vaulted from the car and narrowly missed being struck by a Toyota completing a turn. The driver screwed up her face and gave her a contemptuous middle finger.

She stepped onto the curb, demanding that the bag lady surrender the flight bag. The bag lady stared back defiantly and continued peeing. She clutched the bag in both arms and pressed it tightly against the shabby black coat.

Laurent wrestled her for it.

The light changed and two cars trapped behind the BMW honked angrily.

Cars slowed to watch.

Windows rolled down and Laurent heard the drivers taking sides.

Getting nowhere with the tug of war, she released the strap.

The bag lady fell over backward. Her head hit the sidewalk and her grip sprang open.

Laurent hauled in the flight bag, yanked the pillowcase from the top of the mountain, dodged another car getting back to hers, and heaved the two bags onto the passenger seat.

Nat was mumbling unintelligibly.

An hour later, the city was behind them.

It was approaching sundown when Laurent navigated the last of the curves and caught sight of Dr. Emil Gautier sitting on his front porch swing, gently stroking one of his precious cats. She turned off the dirt road and headed up the cobblestone drive, gentling the BMW to a soft stop.

The single-story stucco house was small, as depressing as the rest of the neighborhood, almost fifteen minutes outside Idyllwild in a remote area not designed for tourists. It ached for fresh paint. Shutters hung precariously from their hinges. A bare bulb illuminated the concrete porch, which carried the faded remains of a large red swastika spray painted awkwardly and in obvious haste. The grass was overgrown and the narrow walkway missing cobblestones.

A polished oak slab hung by the wall, its message gleaming in the bad light: *Here, at whatever hour you come, you will find light and help and human kindness,* a sentiment he had appropriated from Dr. Schweitzer, with whom he had once worked.

Uncle Emil was in his late eighties, but he stood up swiftly and as erect as a pencil at the sight of the car, with one hand jammed inside a pocket of his immaculate frock. He was tall, lean and angular, like a sculpture by Giacometti. A lion's mane of snow-white hair framed penetrating gray-green eyes that seemed to know everything. Liver freckles marked his face and the back of his free hand, which he used like a baton waving her forward.

Seeing her signal for help, Uncle Emil moved with dexterity, in a swift, single motion from the swing, down the broken bench steps, to the BMW.

He opened the back door, ducked inside, pressed his fingers underneath Nat's jaw and used a thumb to peel back the eyelids.

He grunted and, finally acknowledging Laurent's presence, declared in French, in his reed-thin voice, "Congratulations, young lady. You did not kill him getting here."

They struggled navigating Nat from the car to the examination table in the small, sterile room laundered with the smell of alcohol he kept for the last of the patients who refused to go away after he announced his official retirement a dozen-plus years ago.

"Loyalty is such a bore," he told her, whenever an unexpected phone call tore him from her during one of her infrequent visits. "It gets in the way of more admirable pursuits, anarchy, for example." Laurent knew it was posturing; of all her few friends, Emil Gautier was the most loyal. Although she had called him Uncle Emil since childhood, she had to stop sometimes to remember they were only related by history.

Uncle Emil got to Nat's wound with a surgical scissors, complimented her on her first aid and grunted something about morphine. He stepped over to the glass-enclosed cabinet, selected a small vial and fished for a fresh needle.

"Go, go," he ordered her. "You look like shit. You look like you can do with a nap. If it all works out, both of you will wake up. If not . . ." He gave a modest shrug. "Then you and I will still have catching up to do."

Laurent retrieved the flight bag and the pillowcase from the car before settling into the cabin's tiny guest bedroom. She made a warm bath, pouring into the stream a liberal dose of the bath powders she kept in the cabinet under the sink, and passed an hour luxuriating and reading after scrubbing off a day's worth of tension sweat so hard that the skin in places seemed violated by sandpaper. She read Nat's letters and papers until her concentration ebbed and she could not focus her eyes, not even on the postcard Mae Jean had sent Nadine Barber from Las Vegas; only one souvenir of a love gone sour.

She came across nothing that talked about the murder in Las Vegas.

The murder wasn't baggage Nat brought with him to Los Angeles, except maybe like a memory as disfigured as his hands.

Laurent dumped everything back into the pillowcase. She tossed it over to a dry corner of the bathroom and set her mind adrift in hopes she could forget for a while about the man who had come to consume her existence.

When the creak of hinges startled her upright, she had no sense for an instant of where she was, then how long she'd been sleeping in the tub, in water no longer warm or comforting.

Uncle Emil entered the bathroom, somber, indifferent to her nakedness, and settled on the toilet cover. Two cats trailed alongside. He lifted one onto his lap and stroked it absentmindedly while they talked.

"Good, you slept," he said. He glanced at his watch. "Not quite two hours." He pulled something from a pocket of his white smock and flipped it at her. She snatched it from the air and saw it was a spent bullet. Uncle Emil nodded.

"How is he?"

Uncle Emil's gesture said it was too early to know. "The next twenty-four hours will tell the tale," he said. "You know the law says I have to report a gunshot wound?"

"Better you did not."

"Are you asking me to break the law?"

"Fuck the law. You are retired. The law does not apply to you anymore."

He put a singsong to his voice. "That's how it started with the Nazis, deciding to whom the law should apply and to whom the law should not apply."

"The Nazis, the Nazis. You still answer everything with the Nazis, like you are talking to Papa."

"Sometimes, moments like this, I close my eyes and almost believe I am."

"Nobody can know, Uncle Emil." Even she was surprised by the urgency in her voice.

"We will compromise," he said. He paused to make sure he had her attention. "As you quite properly note, I am retired, so I will wait to find a retired policeman and then I will file my report with him."

She sent him a kiss. "Done. What else do you want to know?"

He shrugged. "What else do you want me to know?"

He asked the question smugly, knowing she would tell him everything. There had never been secrets between them.

Uncle Emil carried the pillowcase for Laurent as she moved from the tub to the bedroom while toweling herself dry and let her talk without interruption. He found a comfortable position on the edge of the twin bed, joined by two other of his cats, Flotsam and Jetsam, both brown and white and overweight.

She crossed to the closet, where she maintained a wardrobe sufficient to accommodate these sudden visits, selecting an old velour jumpsuit by Cardin and a pair of Gucci loafers. She fluff-dried her hair with her fingers and settled down in front of the mirror to work at her eyes and her lips.

At first, Laurent got the impression he found her narrative amusing, but he seemed to grow increasingly intense as she tied all the pieces together. He reacted as she expected to the latest news about Bertha and Sam, clucked sadly at her descriptions of the conspiracy that sent Nat Axelrod to prison and, although his life had been filled with worse sights, seemed shaken hearing how Nat had come to have his hands mutilated.

He pressed his slender fingers together and used them to hold up his chin while his mind wandered. "So the good news after all this is that you are not the one responsible for the bullet in his thigh," Uncle Emil said, passing judgment.

"And the bad news?"

"From what I hear, dearest Lorraine, you are the bad news."

Laurent swung around on the piano bench anxiously, tired of confronting a reflection. "You don't approve of my ideas." She felt her mouth harden at the corners.

"I don't judge, either."

"I thought I made it clear enough: there's no way to take care of this emergency with Bertha and Sam except by selling his true story to the *Tab.* To the highest bidder, I think. I'm doing it for Bertha and Sam."

" 'I'm doing it for Bertha and Sam.' " He mimicked her words and swatted the air.

"I expected you of all people to understand, Uncle Emil."

"I would never disappoint you."

"There can be enough money to care for Bertha and Sam for the rest of their lives. Properly. Comfortably. As they deserve."

"And maybe just a little fresh cream for you?"

"That's not why, you devil, and you know it."

"Nat Axelrod, shouldn't he have some say in the matter?"

"Of course."

"What makes you think you'll get from him what you want?"

"Have you ever known me to fail?"

"With men? Never." Uncle Emil gently shoved Flotsam and Jetsam aside and rose from the bed, holding the pillowcase overhead like a water balloon about to be dropped, unsure what she wanted done with it. "Suppose he refuses to cooperate," he said.

Laurent crossed the room and snatched the pillowcase from him, pushed it underneath the bed and out of sight. "I have enough there in a pillowcase. Not as good a story or the whole story, but a story."

Uncle Emil nodded acknowledgment and wandered to the window; Flotsam and Jetsam chased after him.

At this time of night there was nothing to see, but he stared off into the blackness as if something was sending back signals. He opened the window slightly and a modest breeze crept inside. Laurent joined him at his elbow. He clasped her hand like papas do at the zoo. Silently, they surveyed the starless sky for something besides their own thoughts until Uncle Emil said, "He will fight you, you know. You and I, we have seen his kind before."

"I ask you again, have you ever known me to fail?"

"No, only to be the bad news."

"You said you don't judge."

"Judgment? You're a reporter. Don't you know *reporting* when you hear it? Maybe it would have been easier if you left him to die in Los Angeles."

"I guess I wasn't thinking fast enough."

"Lorraine, tell me that was a joke."

Her eyes wandered to his gaunt face. It was as grim as his command. She pretended not to have heard the request and went back to searching out the window for some vision to go with the curious, indecipherable noises of isolation.

Later that night, unable to sleep, Laurent fished out other letters and documents from the pillowcase and discovered more of Nat's sad history after he left Nadine Barber in Indianapolis, bound for Las Vegas, Mae Jean, and the next sorrowful chapter in his life.

Within minutes, she felt like a burglar breaking into a man's soul.

More than once she caught herself weeping.

Laurent berated herself for surrendering to her emotions. She knew she had no business behaving this way over a stranger, somebody who did not constitute more than another pawn ticket in her life, yet she could not contain her tears.

She pushed the material aside and shook her fist at an idea.

She slipped down the hall to the recovery room where Nat was sleeping off his surgery, connected to the examination room by an inner door and less than half the size of her bedroom.

She needed to be certain he was all right.

The only light filtered through the venetian blind covering a window the size of a porthole and threw alternating strips of lightness and dark across Nat's motionless body in the twin bed that was a companion to her own.

His visible eye flickered when she made a noise accidentally pushing against a chair. She held her breath until she could be sure he wouldn't waken. She positioned the chair to watch him and sat that way for what seemed like hours.

His voice snapped her awake.

She had been dreaming about Wembley Stadium, the moment he took her photograph and made it seem like marriage, and Indianapolis, the first trip, when she crawled into his bed at the Airport Holiday Inn, and—

"Mae Jean?"

The painkillers had not stopped his dreams. She debated whether to answer or just leave. She got up to go. The chair scraped against the linoleum.

"Mae Jean?" She kept moving. "Where you going?" She stopped and turned around. He was staring at her. He managed to raise himself onto his elbows. A new band of moonlight slid over his eyes like a mask. "Been looking for you, Mae Jean."

"I know."

"Long time."

"Yes. A long time."

"Remember your promise?"

"Yes." Mae Jean had repeated it often enough in her letters. "When we're together again."

"Now."

"Not tonight. When we're together again."

He made a little hurting noise from somewhere deep in his throat and slid off his elbows and out of the light.

She turned and passed through the connecting door into the examination room and was halfway into the corridor when she stopped short. She stepped back inside, crossed her arms and sank her chin onto her chest. She imagined Mae Jean Minter speaking the words, only the voice she heard was her own, saying, *When we're together again.*

Laurent took off her robe and threw it onto the examination table. The night felt cold and woke her nipples. She went back to Nat and crawled into the bed alongside him. His body was turned away from her, facing the wall. It burned hot, warmer than her needs. She reached inside the hospital gown and began stroking him. There was no response until she thought to whisper in his ear, "Finally, Nat."

"Mae Jean."

"Finally, Nat. You and me."

"Mae Jean." He tried to turn, but didn't have the strength and the bed was too small for her to maneuver. She got out and helped him onto his back, hands fumbling with anticipation. She climbed on top of him and lowered herself onto him. Shut her eyes. Moaned uncontrollably as Nat penetrated her. He seemed to grow larger every time she came, every time, even after he came.

Again. There.

Once more. Yes.

Don't stop.

Oh, God! Oh, Nat!

Laurent leaned forward to feel the thick hairs of his chest electrify her breasts and she let them sway to the sensation. His hands weighed them from underneath, gently, then started up her chest until they found her cheeks and framed them lightly.

Laurent pictured them as they were on the guitar and in all the fan magazines and how they became in her own photographs and how they were now, mutilated grotesques pawing over her body, and she came again.

She opened her eyes, saw him studying her ecstasy.

She whispered, "You and me, Nat. Finally."

"Finally," he said, moving his hands to her throat.

Laurent felt him increasing the pressure against her throat, making it difficult to breathe.

She found his wrists and tried pulling his hands away from her neck, but he was too strong. She wondered if Papa felt this way when the bomb exploded.

Chapter 18

The street was curiously alive as Danny neared Nat's apartment building. Clusters of people milled about on porches and the grass islands, some with questioning expressions and expansive gestures. Pointing fingers aimed at the building he wanted.

A police car cruised past.

Some neighbors studied him suspiciously when he headed up the entrance stairs and past the security door, which had been propped open with a brick.

Ana Maria Alfaro's door was ajar. Danny stepped inside cautiously. The front room was empty. He called out a greeting. A woman's mournful voice responded, *"Aqui, padre; momento."*

In a moment he was facing a petite, pretty young Mexican woman wearing a full-length apron over a plain cotton dress with a bright floral pattern and discreet Peter Pan collar that did nothing to offset her figure or her sensuality.

"Miss Alfaro?"

She wanted more than that.

Danny smiled back at her somber face and said, "I'm looking for Nathan Greene."

Her expression registered a surprise that turned to concern. For a fraction of a second she became ugly in his eyes; then, as if it had been his imagination, she forced her full lips to beam. He saw her mind working overtime. She belonged in a painting by Diego Rivera.

"Not here," she said.

"When will he be back?"

"You more police? Your friends who been here first, they know already I don't know where. I don't know nothing."

"I'm an old friend, Miss Alfaro."

Her look turned dark again. "How you know my name?"

"The Tune King."

"Why would he tell you my name?"

"He's the one who told me Nathan lives here—with you."

"An old friend, you said?" He nodded. "How old?"

"I knew him when he was Nat Axelrod, even before that."

Danny saw at once she didn't like his answer.

A teakettle whistled.

"I was making coffee. You want some coffee?" She gave him another spurious grin. He knew he had to play the game to learn the rules and nodded again. "Instant okay?" He signaled approval. "How you like it?"

"Black."

She pointed him to a chair, turned and left the room through the connecting archway. He clasped his hands behind his back. Wandered about the apartment looking for evidence of Nat. Was studying a framed family photograph on the mantle when he heard her footsteps halt behind him and a metallic click.

Turning, he saw her halfway across the room.

She was holding a cocked revolver aimed at his chest.

"Now, you go on and get the fuck shit hell out from here or I going to kill you," she said, her voice as demanding as a past-due notice. "I got it up to here with cops already." She used an edge of her free hand to set a level at her forehead.

He held out his hands, fingers spread wide and backed away slowly, then wheeled around and sped up in the same anxious motion, too fast to avoid crashing into the priest in the black cassock who had entered the room.

He bounced off the priest's robust stomach and grabbed the

air for balance, dancing like a puppet before something tripped him and sent him sprawling. He pulled himself onto his knees and looked up after a minute, as the priest was insisting in no uncertain terms that Ana Maria put the gun away.

Ana Maria, no less sullen, gave Danny another violent glare before disappearing into the kitchen.

"Please forgive her, Detective. The events of the last hour have her in a terrible state," the priest said, offering his hand to help Danny onto his feet. "O'Bryan's the name. Bryan O'Bryan. Me parents had an enduring sense of the sublime. Bryan Patrick O'Bryan. Family and friends call me Pat, as you probably figger."

The priest's grip was stronger than his outlandish smile, barely a drunk's lie less than his boozy breath. He looked like an overstuffed pixie, a powerfully built man with a Play-Doh face and a moon of teeth above a stained collar and a rumpled cassock that redefined the concept of dirt. Hearing aids grew from his ears like new potatoes.

He explained without prompting, "Ana Maria's brothers are *very* protective of her. They found her that Colt .38 Detective Special after one break-in too many." He dropped his voice another decibel. "The poor, dear child was attacked in her own bed. I will consider it a personal favor if you forget the previous excitement or to inquire about a permit for the gun."

"I'm not a cop, Father." The priest's eyebrows went up, his expression wondering what Danny was doing here, then. "I came here looking for Nathan Greene."

"Well, you certainly picked the right day for it, although I fear, just like our fair minions of the law, you also come up empty handed, Mr.—?"

"Manings. Danny Manings." The priest's eyebrows rose once more, this time as if he recognized the name. "I'm an old friend of Nathan's."

Ana Maria had returned from the kitchen, standing with her back to them, staring out the window that fronted the street and picking desperately at her nails. She turned to stare at Danny, her face a sensation of minor tics. "Father O'Bryan, make him to go! Nathan don't ever want to know from any old friends! You know that, too!"

Father O'Bryan rotated a palm outward and pouted, as if he were wounded by the need to appear inhospitable. "I do have to say she is correct, Mr. Manings. Besides, Nathan is not here or expected back in the foreseeable future, making this visit of yours regretfully ill-timed."

"When do you think he might be back?"

"Is none of his business, *padre*!"

"Not so soon, I expect, if he knows what's best for him." The last almost a mutter, not meant to be heard.

"Do you know where he is?"

"Are you sure you're not a police detective, Mr. Manings?" His smile almost twinkled. "Why don't you allow me your business card? If I hear from him, I'll pass it along, how's that?"

Before Danny could answer, Father O'Bryan took him by the elbow and was escorting him to the door. In a voice too low for Ana Maria to overhear, the priest told him where to go.

The Church of the Blessed Bonaventure was about a half mile east of her apartment, on the northeast corner of Melrose and Wilbur. From the outside, the single-story structure looked like a giant poor box, an architectural eyesore in arrears a couple thousand blessings and a few thick coats of paint. The inside was no better, only hotter. An overhead fan missing two rotary blades passed for air-conditioning and turned more for concept than coolness.

There were a few people in the pews or lighting candles before an altar whose statuary resembled leftovers from the bottom row of prizes at the old Pacific Ocean Park baseball toss. It was crowned by a remarkable stained-glass window that had not been set properly and made the angels look like airplanes. The music of Santana was being piped loudly over a tinny sound system.

After about forty minutes, Father O'Bryan found him wandering about. Full of apologies for his late arrival, he clasped Danny's hands and said, "If you were looking for the toilet, lad, by now you know you're in it." He laughed uproariously and, gesturing lavishly, said, "You can see why Saint Bonaventure is the patron saint of skid-row hotels," making it more evident to Danny the priest was one of those people who treats life as a joke and living as a punch line.

Father O'Bryan took him by the hand and, en route up the vestibule, talked like he was a tour guide at the county museum.

"Should you be wondering," he said, "I'm a fugitive from the blue-collar white-collar school of the Berrigans. A long time ago, it come to anger all the whiter-than-white sanitary collars more than the way I keep my whistle lubricated or bray at full moons, lad. I refused to take popular stands sitting down and ultimately found m'self in the arse-awkward position of being disconnected by Our Holy Mother Church." He crossed himself pronouncing the capital letters.

"Disconnected?"

"The Church looks upon it as suspended animation, not quite excommunication. More like the pit and the pendulum. I choose to be more merciful with my words, though. *Disconnected* almost makes it sound like Themselves dialed incorrectly and my number will be restored to full service at any blessed moment.

"It's how the congregation come to own the property. When those soldiers of the Church come after me with their eviction notice, the good people here saw fit in their hearts to take up a collection and purchase the weed patch of land right out from under the building, not the church proper, what can only rightfully belong to Himself. Right after, my friends in the hierarchy were prevailed upon to help turn all the right heads in another direction. So, here I am, *disconnected.*" He made it sound like four words while gesturing munificently.

"Where did they get that kind of money?"

Father O'Bryan gave Danny a conspiratorial look and stopped at a thick door almost at the end of the hallway, hiding behind a cheap tapestry and protected by three deadbolts. The wood stairway creaked as he followed the priest into a basement crammed full of merchandise.

"Ill-gotten," he said, "should you be wondering. More you don't have to know, except that it pays the mortgage and why on some days the line to the confessional is longer than the ones we see at the 7-Elevens on lottery day."

He pointed Danny up the stairs. A moment later they were settling in the priest's office across the way from the secret door, and Father O'Bryan was again apologizing for having kept Danny waiting. "I was easing Ana Maria's burden best I can," he said, his head twisting left and right. "That beautiful young woman has been besieged by panic since all this appallingly nasty business."

"What nasty business, Father?"

"Of course, how could you know?" The priest looked back at him with a sly twinkle of acknowledgment. "But first things first, you don't mind sparing me another minute or two."

The office was stacked with sealed TV and home appliance cartons in various sizes, some of the stacks six and eight feet tall.

Danny watched while Father O'Bryan, readjusting them, began to sweat. His face turned a deeper red, but he waved off Danny's offers to help, calling him a guest.

Satisfied with the new landscape, he pointed Danny to a chair, oomphed himself onto the ancient desk and sat like an inquiring Buddha, legs dangling and hands resting below his belly while he told Danny about his four Blaupunkt *bandidos* and their misfortune earlier today at the Century City mall, giving the story no more significance than a restaurant review on the eleven-o'clock news.

"So, I patched up two of them here; saw them safely off," he said. "One is still missing. Nathan, wounded, all bloody. Spirited away by a woman little Juan Pablo said he's never seen before. Not Chicano. Drove away in a BMW. Mean anything to you?" Danny shook his head. "One reason I rushed off to Ana Maria after she sent Juan Pablo back to tell me. Knowing she'd need comforting. Not over the woman, mind you, but for Nathan being shot and gone like that."

"He was wounded, you said? Nat?"

"Nathan, yes. At Ana Maria's, did you observe the blood on the floor?" Danny shook his head. "In falling you pushed aside a small throw rug she meant to cover the bloodstains. Imagine, Ana Maria is hardly there before you, a half hour at most, and she's cleaning and straightening. A fetish I've seen with others who rise out of dirt poverty. A real pisser, that one. If I'd been another minute, she well might have pulled the trigger on you and gone after a larger rug."

Father O'Bryan laughed heartily.

Danny shook his head. "Nat steals radios. A common thief."

"More the lookout, and mostly car radios. Stereos and those CD players. The *bandidos* are not exclusively predisposed to sound if they spot something valuable in grabbing distance. Phones. The occasional laptop."

"And you don't know where Nat is?"

"Any more than I know the woman, lad."

"Would you tell me if you did, Father?"

"I don't think so."

"Why?"

Before the priest could respond, there was a knocking and the door flew open to reveal two young Chicanos. One had his arms around a microwave oven and the other was halfway into explaining in Spanish when he saw Father O'Bryan had a visitor and quit with his mouth hanging open.

The priest bobbed an index finger downward and the Chicanos retreated, easing the door shut after their apologies. He hopped from the desk, navigated the cartons, threw the door lock, cleared a path to a small refrigerator on top of a breakfront and withdrew a bottle of wine. Filled two water glasses and handed one to Danny before toasting, "To the truth. *Magna est veritas et praevalet.*" Emptied his glass in one swallow and refilled it. Asked, "Do you know your wines, Mr. Manings?"

Danny shook his head.

"This is a Chalone; Caprone Zinfandel, nineteen eighty-four; unrefined and unfiltered."

Father O'Bryan pinched three fingers to his lips and kissed them.

Danny took a sip. It tasted the way wine always tasted to him, like wine.

The priest swirled the wine and held it up to the light for inspection as he observed, "So, you want to know why I wouldn't tell you where Nathan is, assuming I knew?"

"Yes, especially considering how much you've already told me about him and what goes on here at the church."

"Any more than that I fear Nathan would mind you knowing."

"What's that supposed to mean?"

"Nathan told me about you."

"He talked about me?"

"Often. He told me your history together and how, when it became unfashionable to be associated with Nat Axelrod, the rock-and-roll icon he once was, you turned on him like all the others he'd come to trust, leaving him to rot in prison while you went on with your life as usual, continuing to profit at his expense."

"That's a lie!"

"Please, lad. I'm a priest."

"Then it's a God damned lie!"

Father O'Bryan laughed beyond containment, almost sloshing wine on his cassock. Rearranging himself on the desk, he threw a gesture at Danny and said, "My little joke, that was."

Danny let his temper settle. "I may have been the only one who stuck by Nat, until the day my letters started coming back from Indiana State Prison marked *Unread—Return to Sender* and I couldn't get a call through to him or get any answer to messages I tried leaving, and—"

"You had your own demons to deal with."

"I had my own demons to deal with."

"Not an interesting confession, Mr. Manings, and entirely unnecessary. Truth is, I know all that about you. I know about the role you played in his career and his life."

"Then why—"

"The truth is, Nathan said you were an honest man. Honest and trustworthy. Perhaps the most honest man he has ever known in this life." Danny felt his face flush. "But I also know why he cut himself off from his old life and why right to this minute, wherever he is and whatever his condition, Nathan would not want you or anyone from those days back into his life."

"If you can't tell me where he is, can you tell me why he feels that way?"

"It would be more than he wants you to know, Mr. Manings."

"But not more than you want me to know, is it, Father O'Bryan?" Danny said, suddenly struck by the idea of the game the father was playing with him.

The priest acted astonished, then dismayed.

"Well, lad, you may not know your fine wines, but, like me, you are a connoisseur of the truth," he said, leaning in closer. "If you're threatening to run to the police if I don't tell you about Nathan and disclose my nefarious activities here, you leave me no choice. I will have to tell you everything in order to protect certain members of my congregation from the consequences of my intemperate mouth."

A Cheshire-cat smile crossed the priest's face and a benign twinkle settled in his eyes.

Danny said appreciatively, "Father O'Bryan, you are some piece of work."

"Aren't I now?" he said, raising his wineglass in toast.

Danny phoned Patrice as he prepared to leave Father O'Bryan after an hour, to say he was on his way home. A man answered. "Who is this?" Danny said, his brow knotting with curiosity.

"What business is it of yours?"

"Sorry." Assuming he had dialed wrong, he tapped off and was about to try again when he stopped to disengage a sudden, alarming thought. The man's grating voice was too recent in his memory for him to be wrong about whose it was.

Brian Malloy.

He dialed his number again.

This time he got the machine.

"Are you okay, lad?" Father O'Bryan wanted to know. "You've just turned white as the clouds at Saint Peter's pearly gates."

"Nothing a ride home in a hurry can't cure."

"Not to worry," the priest said.

His building's security door was working for a rare change and Patrice had his key ring. Danny buzzed upstairs and got no response. He trailed a finger down the directory until he came to the name McGarry P. Murray. The little man lived in the apartment unit next to his, and they had nodded at one another over the years in what passed for friendship in LA.

Murray buzzed him through.

When Danny rounded the corridor, Murray was standing by his door, half in, half out, wearing an opulent crimson robe with angled, architectural shoulders and a matching emperor's hat with a dangling gold tassel. A look of apprehension spilled over to his voice while insisting Danny step inside the apartment.

"I was thinking seriously about calling the police," Murray said. "I mean *seriously,* baby, and our crowd never ever gives the local *gendarmerie* so much as a Diet Extra Light thought. Come." He led Danny to a common wall, reached for a water glass on top of the hand-carved Oriental commode and pressed it against the wall. "Put your ear to there, baby; I mean, give a hard listen."

Danny was alarmed by what he heard.

Murray saw it on his face.

"Almost nonstop the last two or three hours, through that shoji screen that passes for a wall," he said, indignant over the concept. "It is noise to die from; to dieeee from, baby, like the whole leather bar moved in."

Murray sank cross-legged onto the floor, crossed his arms and defied Danny with his stare. The visible skin on his body was red and flaked, like crusted dandruff. He sprinkled as he raised his hands in mock surrender.

He said, "It got so dreadful, I charged on over to complain. I noticed a woman sleeping on the floor." He described Patrice. "It was all I could do to get a look at her around this horrible whiskey breath who answered the door. He told me to mind my own business. My own *fucking* business, like he was the queen, not me? I may not know everything, baby, but I know when to pay attention."

Danny explained what he had in mind.

Murray's eyebrows rose to the question and his bloodshot eyes bugged out. His tired mouth trapped a throaty sound. "Aren't you the brave one," he said, trying his hardest to sound like Mae West.

A minute later, Danny stepped onto Murray's living-room balcony and looked over to the smaller balcony connecting to his own apartment's bedroom. The door was open and he thought he heard scuffling. He measured the jump across with his eyes; a matter of three or four feet, he judged. If he fell short, there was nothing to break his fall to the pathway concrete. He winced at the image, took a deep breath and pondered his options until the sounds of a woman in distress pulled him back to the emergency of the moment.

A man's voice was threatening, "Ammonia-D, you cunt! A swallow of this is good for whatever ails ya!"

No question: Brian Malloy.

Without further thought, Danny reached up and grabbed a brick protruding from the false facing of the building and used it to lift himself up onto the railing. He glanced down and knew that had been a mistake. He shut his eyes. He steadied himself, stretching out a hand for balance, closed his eyes again, bent his knees like a pier diver, and leaped. Landed on a foot, maneuvered like Marcel Marceau without the umbrella, caught his balance, and rushed through the entrance.

Patrice was on the bed, her arms crossed in front of her to ward off Brian's punches.

Danny spotted the glint of sunshine reflecting off a pair of scissors on the floor behind a shrouded occasional table he used to display family photographs and other personal mementos. He swooped down for the scissors as Brian backed off the bed, cursing Patrice and seething at him, "Them scissors won't do you any good."

"Try me, you bastard."

Danny sent Patrice a look that said everything would be okay before turning full attention to Brian, who was advancing on him with a Windex bottle for a weapon and a look sufficiently dangerous to strip away some of his confidence.

They circled one another.

Danny bobbed and weaved behind the scissors.

Brian aimed the bottle for his face, grunting to every move, calling him names, begging him to step closer as he looked for a clear shot, then yanked a pillow from the bed and used it for a shield.

Danny reacted to a sudden motion and plunged the scissors into the pillow. Brian gave a yank sideways and the pillow and the scissors sailed across the room. At the same time, he shot Danny in the face with the blue liquid. Danny made a noise and brought both hands up to his eyes for protection.

Through a crack in his fingers he saw Brian throw away the spray bottle and send a roundhouse punch that caught him on the shoulder. Brian aimed a straight fist at his exposed chin and he couldn't move fast enough. It landed hard and the impact pushed him backward.

Danny hit the edge of the glass door with his body and kept going, wrapping around the door and stumbling forward onto the balcony. For an instant he thought he'd go over the railing, but managed to brake himself with a last-second, one-handed grab onto one of the vertical bars.

The sharp pain made him certain his fingers were about to

rip loose of his palm. He clamped his free hand onto another bar with his other hand and slid down into a sitting position with his body vertical to the railing.

Shaking the hurt and confusion from his head, Danny watched Brian lurching forward confidently. From the corners of his eyes, he saw Patrice try unsuccessfully to pull a lamp free from the table next to the bed.

Her face agonizing, she dropped onto the floor, on her hands and knees, and went after the pillow. He guessed she was looking for the scissors. She pulled the pillow to her and the feathers puffed out and gentled downward. The scissors were gone; they had landed somewhere else, somewhere invisible.

Brian stooped over Danny. His hands clamped around Danny's forearm. He was trying to pry him loose from the bars and Danny knew to let go was to be lifted up and tossed over the railing. He resisted, but the pressure increased and his grip eroded. He was holding on strictly from habit.

Patrice got up from the floor and dashed forward. She had pulled something from her robe and held it like a dagger. It was the pointed handle of a comb. She jammed it into Brian's ass. Brian screamed and released Danny. He reached back and pulled out the comb, wheeled to face her. Held the comb like the Statue of Liberty's torch and, covering his wound, hissed, "This time you went and picked the wrong playground, whore."

His hand came down on her shoulder. Her eyes flushed fresh tears as she pulled a cuticle scissors from her robe pocket and jabbed. Brian yowled and pulled back, scissors dangling from the back of his hand. He swore, "No more chances, Patrice!"

"Get the hell out of here," Danny called to her.

Patrice dashed for the living room. Brian started after her. Danny used the railing to pull himself up and dived after Brian. He caught him by his leg, causing Brian to fall chest down. Danny held onto the leg as Brian struggled to free himself. A kick hit him on the shoulder, then another. Another. The leg slipped free.

Brian rose gradually, dusted himself off and kicked Danny in the side. He stood in the open doorway catching his breath, turned to give Danny a cold-blooded look. "I'll be back for you," he said and moved cautiously out of the room, screaming something at Patrice. Anger seemed to have renewed him.

Danny climbed to his feet. Looking around for anything that could be a weapon, he saw the ceramic pots on the balcony and got two of them. Entering the living room, he saw Patrice at the front door, working desperately on the chain lock. Brian was between them, advancing at a nonchalant pace, stalking her as if it were a playground contest. "Too little too late," he taunted Patrice. "The boogie man, he's coming to get you."

She got the lock off and pulled the door open. Instead of escaping through it, she sent a look to Danny and jumped over to the desk, where she picked up a Heizer metal sculpture he was selling and turned to face Brian, who was five or six feet away, poised to charge with the rat-tail comb.

Patrice took a shot-putter's aim and threw the heavy hunk of steel at Brian.

Brian sidestepped it and kept advancing.

Danny reached him and crashed a ceramic pot down hard on his head, giving Brian's shoulders dirt for dandruff as the pot shattered.

Brian crashed to the floor and grunted. Danny didn't wait to see if he was mobile. He cracked Brian's head with the second pot, raining more shards on the carpeting. Brian did a dance step with his body and stopped moving.

Danny looked over to Patrice. "I always heard the second time is the charm," he said.

His looked begged an invitation and she responded, managing the best smile her bruised face allowed. He hurried over and took her in his arms. She did not resist, and he realized how much he had missed her touch. They drew tighter to one another, her hands pawing for attention as eagerly as his.

The phone rang and his machine picked up.

It was Father O'Bryan, calling to see if everything was all right and urging him to call back as soon as he got the message. He thought he knew who the woman who had driven off with Nathan might be, the woman in the BMW, the priest said, and recited his phone number twice.

Danny and Patrice were too lost in each other for the words to connect until Danny heard him say Nat's name. Clinging to Patrice, he grabbed for the phone. "Hello, Father O'Bryan, you still there?" He shook his head. Pressed the playback button that gave the most recent message. Listened intently to the playback to be certain he understood.

When the message ended, Danny turned to check on Brian.

Brian was gone. All that remained on the pile carpeting where he had fallen was busted pottery, dirt, and a few dead flowers.

Chapter 19

Danny raged over the condition of Patrice's body as he helped her into the tub. It was a battlefield of bruises, her face disfigured by swelling that made it difficult for her to speak. He cursed himself aloud for having let Brian escape. Patrice smiled gamely through lips frozen in place and insisted his caring was the best therapy.

He soaped her back and sponged it off gently, but when he applied the liquid soap to her breasts, her body flickered to his touch. She took his hand and turned it away, quick to reassure him her reaction was only temporary.

He told her he understood. In his mind he was not entirely sure he did, but he suspected the worst pains of the experience with Brian Malloy were trapped inside her. He was determined to give her all the loving comfort and support she needed.

He showered, dressed and headed for the kitchen, called Father O'Bryan while the water was boiling for a cup of instant.

The priest acknowledged his greeting and said, "Listen, lad, this woman in the BMW?"

"You do know her?"

"Not exactly, no, but I remembered Juan Pablo saying about how she talked funny. Not Spanish, but not English funny either. It come to mind then, this French woman ringing me up, saying she was from some newspaper and wanting to chat. The *Tab,* I think it was. I'm thinking, maybe it was her?"

"Did she mention Nat?"

"Nathan? No. Didn't give her the opportunity. Last thing I ever need doing is talk to some newspaper or other inquiring into my priestly comings and goings. I told her I already subscribe to enough newspapers and magazines, thank you very much, and hung up quick as a wink. She called back and I politely hung up again. That was it, but I thought to tell you since you got my solemn word I'd share any news."

They chatted amiably for a few more minutes and, afterward, having noticed the pileup on phone messages, Danny pressed the replay button. Sales pitches. The potential Heizer buyer calling back with a counteroffer. Joe Wunsch, checking in about the time he and Patrice headed for the Nam, reminding him he'd be waiting to hear back, and not long afterward—

A woman with a French accent.

"Monsieur Danny Manings? My name is Laurent Connart, and I am calling you about a matter of mutual interest concerning a friend of yours."

No details, just the tantalizing premise, followed by her name again and a local phone number. Danny jotted it down and immediately dialed, guessing this was the same woman who had called Father O'Bryan. The French accent had to be more than a coincidence.

Her machine picked up on the fifth ring. A terse instruction to leave any message after the beep; no identification. Danny hung up, changed his mind and redialed; this time left his name and number.

He headed for the bathroom to check on Patrice. She'd managed to get from the tub to the bed and into a pair of his pajamas, the buttons in the wrong holes. He pulled the covers up under her chin and gave her a soft kiss on the forehead.

Patrice stirred and opened her eyes. Seeing it was him, she responded with the best smile she could manage. "He must have been spying, or one of his cop buddies from up here," she said, sounding groggy. "Knew I'd spent the night. Bullshit his way inside like nothing ever happened; started hammering on me, screaming; calling me *whore;* worse, and—"

"It's over with him," Danny said. "You're not going back to that son of a bitch."

"He won't let it end with tonight, honey."

"Let's talk about it later."

"He was more scary than ever. Never this bad. Worst ever." Speaking was an effort for her. Her face showed pain with every word. "I know what Brian is capable of, Danny, drunk or sober."

"Catch some sleep," he said, caressing her hair. "I'm here for you."

He sent Patrice a kiss and returned to the living room, leaving the bedroom door open wide enough to hear her if she needed anything, and settled on the sofa in front of the TV.

His body felt the way it used to after a football scrimmage, muscles turning to cream of mush. He dozed off to an old Judy Garland and Mickey Rooney musical, *Girl Crazy,* only the songs playing in his head weren't the George and Ira Gershwin songs from the movie.

Danny was hearing Nat's songs.

They were being sung by Nat and Patrice.

Danny wheeled out of bed at six in the morning.

Nat's music was still on his mind, joined by a plan that seemed to have developed full-blown overnight. He felt refreshed, invigorated, although it had been an unsatisfactory sleep, frequently interrupted by Patrice's nightmarish shouts, begging Brian Malloy to stop assaulting her. She was calmer now, asleep in a fetal position on top of a tangle of blankets, arms clutching a pillow as if it were a life preserver.

He went through his ordinary morning routine, including a ritual three-mile jog on the silent, empty streets of a city that would not come alive for at least another hour, passing other runners he knew by sight, who nodded back casually as they charged by on their routes, lost in their own sweaty visions.

Before showering, he phoned Mason Weems at Shoe Records in New York.

An exasperated Brooklyn voice identified the company and enunciated the label's motto through saliva and chewing gum—*If the Shoe Fits, Hear It*—and took Danny through the standard ID drill before revealing that Mr. Weems was out of the office today and wouldn't be available until Monday.

Danny left his name and number.

He dialed the Nam. The Tune King wasn't there, but Jimmy Slyde was.

Slyde had worked through the night, he said, with a three- or four-hundred-pound tenor, "Mickey Moose," who accompanied himself on keyboard to songs from Disney movies, hoping to produce a demo that would land him a job at Disneyland.

Danny told Jimmy what he needed.

Jimmy said, "No problem. I'll clear it with the Tune King after he shows up, around nine-thirty. Figure anytime after that."

That worked fine.

He could meet with Joe by ten or ten-thirty to explain his plan and, if Joe agreed, start preparing Patrice for recording sessions that would be her best therapy, reminding her there was life without and beyond Brian Malloy.

Afterward, he'd bring Rap Browning up to speed.

Just past eight o'clock, confident Joe was up by now, Danny dialed the home number.

Joe listened to him and answered in a yawning voice still not sure of the day, "Whenever, Captain, but better if it's not at the office. Fucking Drummond won't take the hints and go back to New York. He's still rat-holing around here, his usual shit-stirring act."

They settled on a one-o'clock lunch at the Jerry's Deli across from Cedars-Sinai Hospital on Beverly.

Danny dressed and tried Laurent Connart's number again. Got her machine. Left another message.

He slipped into the bedroom and watched Patrice sleep for a few minutes.

She must have sensed his shadow.

That or something startled her awake.

She sprang into a sitting position, hands in front of her face protectively, throwing the word *No* like a ballistic missile. Her face relaxed into a smile when she understood it was him. Wordlessly, she eased back down on her side, palms tucked under her cheek, and was sleeping before he reached the door.

McGarry P. Murray stepped into the corridor while Danny was checking the door lock. His black cashmere robe hung open over a pair of paisley jockeys. "The young lady is all right?" he said.

Danny smiled appreciatively. "She'll be fine. It could have been worse."

"How? Guerrilla terrorists mistaking your place for the Gaza strip?" Murray said, pulling the robe closed.

"She'll probably sleep through most of the day. You mind keeping an eye open?"

"Both eyes, baby, and two ears, too; my pleasure," Murray said, and retreated back inside his apartment.

The Tune King rushed to greet Danny after he was buzzed inside the Nam, only this time the smile was missing. Draping his arms over Danny's shoulders, his eyes and voice as mournful as a funeral dirge, he said, "Slyde, he told me what you need, *boychick,* only I can't, not even for you."

"Maybe Jimmy misunderstood, Tune King. I don't want your

boy Nathan's master tape. I asked Slyde to run me a dupe, for Joe Wunsch and some other people to hear."

The Tune King took a step back and hand gestured hopelessly, like Tevye in *Fiddler on the Roof.* "Nathan, he don't want copies made, except the ones he makes for himself. That's his rule, so I gotta honor it like I honor rules laid down by everyone what works here."

"This could be good for him, Tune King."

"But bad for me, Danny. I break my word, out the window goes my honor. You know? I can't live with myself, I ain't got no one else what matters."

"What if I bring Joe here?"

"What if Nathan don't want him to listen? Probably I should have thought some more when the boy never got here yesterday, before I give you the listen, and maybe I wouldn't of."

"Have you heard from him since?"

The Tune King shook his head vigorously. "Only from *tsuris* he got now, poor sumna bitch. Talk of the neighborhood. Not the kind of talk you ever need hearing about a good person, which he is, Danny; like you. That makes me even more sorry to give you the answer you didn't want about a dupe copy."

Danny recognized something in the Tune King's eyes he wouldn't have been looking for yesterday. He said, "You know who Nathan is, don't you, Tune King." It was less a question than a declaration.

The Tune King gave him a moment of silence. He eased down to pick up a lost guitar pick and stashed it in a pocket of pants at least two sizes too large that hung from his eroding frame by a pair of red suspenders. The faded Simpsons T-shirt should have looked ludicrous on him, but it didn't.

"Don't put me on the spot, Danny, okay?"

Danny slipped out the name under his breath. "Nat Axelrod."

"I'd have to go back on my word again," the Tune King said.

"It's okay," Danny said. "I got enough of the story from his lady's priest to understand why he was trying to put his past behind him."

The Tune King looked at his hands and shuddered. "The music deserved better," he said. "Someone like you again. Can you leave it at that, Danny? Please?"

Danny showed surrender and started to leave.

He wheeled around on a sudden thought.

"Tune King, what if Nathan's lady, Ana Maria, said it was okay for me to have a dupe?"

The Tune King smiled at the effort. "It wouldn't be good enough, *boychick.*"

They shook hands, shared a hug and Danny left.

His cantankerous four-year-old crimson Ford Mustang was parked on the street, about ten yards south of the Nam. He clicked open the door and was about to climb inside when he heard his name called. Looking across the roof of the car, he saw Jimmy Slyde racing in his direction.

Slyde stopped five feet short. "You forgot this," he said, and sailed a cassette at Danny. Danny made a perfect one-handed catch. "You get something going, you remember who's the best new fucking engineer on the street, my man!"

"These two guys are at that Grammy Awards party at The Palace," Joe said, laughing in anticipation of his punch line. "The first guy points out a fucking, drop-dead blonde across the room who's surrounded by a squadron of record execs feeding their fantasies. Blondie has a set of pumpkin tits, a neat little waist the size of your neck, lean, mean legs made for wrapping, an ass designed for drilling, teeth you can land a jet by, and a laugh to end all wars. *Yeah, I see her,* Guy Two says. *What about her?* Guy One brags back, *I'm fucking her husband.*"

Joe roared and palm-slapped the table.

Danny laughed, not as hard, and emptied more Sweet'n Low into the malt-sized glass of iced tea.

"I see you're in no fucking mood for humor, Captain."

"Lot on my mind, Joey."

"Not the least of which brings us here to Jerry's Deli."

"The most of which, if you're ready to listen."

"I am all urine," he said, pouring too much sugar into his coffee cup.

Danny explained about Nat, the tapes, the shooting at the apartment and what he had learned from Father O'Bryan; about Patrice and her husband, and Brian's vicious attack on his wife last night.

Joe was never good at hiding his emotions. Whatever enthusiasm he showed had faded once Danny explained about the tapes. His face registered one pensive moment after another, and he flinched when Danny repeated the priest's description of Nat's hands, sketched a picture of the physical and emotional damage Brian inflicted on Patrice.

He said, "Captain, you ever see me speechless before? Frankly, I haven't a fucking clue where to begin."

Danny reached into his shirt pocket for the cassette he had received from Jimmy Slyde and handed it over. "Where it always begins for you, Joey. With the music."

Joe inspected the cassette from all angles, like a diamond merchant searching for flaws, then back at Danny. "Really good?"

"Does the word *great* ring any bells?"

He told Joe about playing Nat's songs in the car, in the time before their lunch date, how he found himself driving the streets, then the freeways, hungry to hear the songs over and over again.

"It was worse for me than yesterday," Danny said, "when I realized what I was listening to was Nat's, not some remarkably talented kid who'd done his homework. The music was richer and wiser, more adventurous and inventive than anything Nat turned out before, stamped with emotions deeper than Nat ever revealed before; maybe, understood. The hooks were killers on five or six of the cuts. Monsters, Joey. You'll listen to one, I won't say which, and know it's the next Song of the Year. Nat Axelrod is back, big time."

"Except you don't know where Nat is, for Christ's sake."

"I'll find him."

"And then what, Captain? If he was interested in picking up where he left off, don't you think he'd've been knocking on doors by now, instead of getting caught fucking robbing cars and some French broad hustling him away to parts unknown, one step in front of the law, no earthly reason to come back real soon?" When Danny didn't answer, he said, "Okay. Let's assume you find him. Let's fucking even assume we have lawyers who can clean up the mess and make it go away. Are you suggesting we dump Patrice Malloy for Nat?"

Danny shook his head.

Joe shifted his eyes from Danny to the cassette and back. A momentary silence, then a glimmer of a smile, and he smacked his forehead. "Fucking dummy that I am. You mean we have Patrice cut his songs instead of her own."

"Better than that. I want to team Patrice with Nat. That duo performing that music. It's a Number One album by a Number One act straight out of the box. Joey, if I have ever been right about anything before—"

He stopped. He hadn't meant to be selling so hard.

Joe studied Danny's face. "You mean it, don't you?"

Danny nodded enthusiastically.

"The hype aside, aren't you forgetting to wash some dirty laundry?" He rinsed his mouth with coffee and made a face. "Who the fuck makes the coffee here, the sugarplum fairy?" He motioned for the server to bring a fresh cup and after it was served again poured in too much sugar. He took a taste. "Better," he said.

"Ask your questions, Joey."

"Let me start with the most obvious first. Christ! They're all obvious. We got a fucking asshole wife-beater husband trying to kill the both of you . . ." A pause, followed by a sideways look of understanding. "You and Patrice, huh?"

"Finish your question."

"As if this situation isn't already fucked up enough." Joe shook his head. "Brian Malloy has the final say on any deal to do with Patrice."

"What's the question?"

"Danny, the guy not only hates your guts, he tried to spill them last night. You're history with him—kaput!—so Patrice Malloy won't be singing anyone's songs where you're concerned. You don't understand that, I have a book on remedial intelligence I'd like to recommend to you. It begins, *Look, Jane, look.*"

"Let's say I have that covered. Next."

"Let's say you don't, but okay—I'll play your game. You don't have Nat Axelrod."

"But I do. You're holding him in your hand."

Joe treated the cassette like it was on fire and handed it back. "What's in that iced tea you been drinking?"

"Ask your question."

"That was a question."

"Iced tea."

"Thank you. An answer I can accept . . . Listen, Captain, I'm not talking about copyrights or the publishing. I know how your mind works. If Nat didn't cover his fucking ass, you'll do it for him."

"Protect him? Absolutely."

"And who protects us? What if someone got there first and

we have the gigantic smash you're talking? He comes racing in after the fact on clearances and royalties and we are screwed royally."

"It's covered."

Joe squeezed his face. "Again with this *It's covered.*"

"Joey, you're going to have to trust me."

Joe gave him a hard stare. "It's covered," he said, as if offended that Danny might ever believe otherwise.

A tug of emotion constricted Danny's throat. Joe's loyalty was remarkable in a business where backstabbing is limited only by the number of available backs. Danny wanted to reveal the one significant piece of information he hadn't shared, but he couldn't. He'd given Father O'Bryan his word. Instead, he said, "You think you can talk Nat's master away from the Tune King?"

"Probably not. He's a man of honor. I'd hear the same thing he told you . . . Why?"

"We break down the master. We lose everything except Nat's vocal tracks. We lay down new music tracks. We lay down Patrice's tracks, marrying her vocals to Nat's vocals, we have our duo and our album."

"Like Natalie Cole with her late daddy. Sinatra on his duets album, where he never made it into the studio same time as anybody else. Why you said I was holding Nat in my hand. On the cassette. We don't need him otherwise."

"We locate him before we're done mixing, he sweetens the tracks, works with Patrice on the three or four songs where we'd otherwise have to feature her solo."

"Only his vocals? No guitar? No Nat the Axe?"

"Not like before. Some of the runs are stunning and riffs I've never heard before. Others, hardly shadows. If they're on a separate track, we can work with them. Our problem is pulling the master loose from the Tune King, unless you figure someone like Archie at Rancho Musico can get us what we need off the cassette."

Joe sent the idea sailing. "Even with his computers, I don't think Archie could strip away everything but the vocals and leave us with the release quality we need. Good enough maybe for a dummy track, so we could add the band and Patrice, but not for any final mix. I'll fucking ask him anyway, but we both know the master would be better." He absentmindedly added sugar to his coffee. "I'll also take a whack at the Tune King, but don't hold your breath." He sipped at the coffee and made an ugly face. "What is it with them and the fucking coffee here?"

He searched for a server. "Jesus fuck, Captain. I have a new question for you." Something had astonished Joe. "Don't look now, but look now, only not so obvious." He motioned with his head and then leaned down as if searching for something he'd dropped under the table. "Who do you see?"

Danny eased a head turn and glanced over his shoulder toward the deli's entrance.

Joe whispered, "Please tell me you don't fucking see what I just saw, Captain."

Danny couldn't.

His heart had captured his tongue watching the hostess guiding a party of four to a table two aisles over and closer to the front. He didn't want to guess what business had brought Harry Drummond together with Brian Malloy, Rap Browning and Mason Weems.

He said, "They didn't get together to organize any benefits for us."

Joe said, "Nothing to be gained charging in now, Captain. I'll get a read later, back at the office. The minute I know, you'll know. What's it the wise man said, the one you were always fond of quoting? *If you know you're gonna die, what's the hurry?*"

Danny shook his head in disagreement. "He also said, *What*

you don't know can kill you." He started to ease out of the booth. Joe grabbed him by the arm and wouldn't let go. "Later will be better, Captain. Trust me."

"Fine, good enough," he said, like he meant it.

After a few minutes, they ducked out the rear patio entrance.

Three hours later, Danny was at the Beverly Hills Hotel, knocking on the door of the third-floor suite occupied by Mason Weems.

Chapter 20

Laurent examined her throat in the mirror. Almost a week later and it was still ugly and purple, no matter how she covered up the bruises with makeup. Had Nat been able to get a real grip around her neck, she would have been dead for sure, *certainment,* before Uncle Emil came running to hammer Nat into submission and managed to free her.

And what if Uncle Emil had not heard her calls or the bed table rolling and crashing into a wall from the force of her aimless kick, then tipping over; bottles and jars and instruments breaking and crashing like the thunder she remembered from the Boulevard St. Germain?

Dead.

Poof.

Laurent let her fingers dance toward the sky.

For all the death she had viewed in her lifetime, at war and in peacetime, she was ready to admit this was the closest she had come to meeting Death face to face.

And what was Death saying to you as he approached, Laurent?

Death was saying, *Je t'aime. Je t'aime, Laurent. So kiss me and feel my passion.*

Bien, she thought now. *If only I could get Nat to feel the same way about me.*

Nat had awakened remembering nothing, certainly nothing of the photos she had stolen of him asleep. After she told him how she discovered him bleeding to death and hid him from the police and got him to Idyllwild and Uncle Emil, his way of saying thank you was to wonder why she had bothered.

She told him, "You have something I want, *Monsieur* Axelrod."

"Goes without saying," he said.

"The rest of the story."

"What's that mean?"

Laurent explained who she was and what she knew.

Nat gave her a chilling look meant to banish her from his presence.

He said, "Tell your editor Nat Axelrod is dead."

"So you shouldn't mind telling me about his life. It can do him no further harm."

"What business is it of yours, his life? Who are you? God?"

"Maybe his guardian angel, *Monsieur*—"

He shook off the need. "Greene," he said, making it a demand. "The name is Greene. Nathan Greene." He stared hard into Laurent's face with an expression that said those were his final words on the subject. Retreated to squander his time in the woods, pulling his healing leg up the worn, narrow footpath caked with dead leaves.

She waited a reasonable amount of time before trailing after him, not for more argument, but to sneak more photographs with the Nikon.

Cuh-lick.

A picture here, a picture there.

Cuh-lick.

Always when Nat was unaware.

Men and their egos.

The photos, together with her miles of interviews and the research, the contents of the pillowcase—

She would have her damned story with or without his help.

The deeper, darker story she knew was there was the better story, the story she wanted, but it would take winning a contest of wills with this man who had endured some of the worst tortures life has to offer, worse even than her own.

When she told this to Uncle Emil, he laughed as if it was a joke and she already should know the punch line. "He is like you in many ways," Uncle Emil said. "You have fallen in love with yourself."

"Craziness, you old man."

"I listen to this person's silence. I look at this person's face. This person's deceptions run deeper and are more practiced than your own. He is older than you; that accounts for some of it."

"The rest?"

Uncle Emil shrugged. "He will never be mistaken for one of the Three Wise Men, even when he offers you a gift."

"Frustration. You call that a gift?"

"An apple."

"He has said something to you, hasn't he?!"

"Yes."

"Tell me what."

"He said, *Call me Nathan.*"

"Uncle Emil, I try very hard not to hate you."

"Such an exclusive club."

It was clear Uncle Emil had not entirely forgiven her for climbing on top of Nat in bed. He understood the men she'd brought over the years did not come for his *haute cuisine,* so was it because this was the first time he had seen *her* hunger at the table?

"What did you say back to Nathan?"

"I warned him about you."

She pressed her lips gently to his, the way children address a grandparent, and stepped away. "You protect him from me?"

"To protect you from him."

"He will not put those hands to my throat again."

"It's your heart you must protect."

"Again with that foolish theme. Pooh. He has a story I must have, too. That is it. Have you finally gotten so old I must say things to you twice?"

"You asked me. Remember?" He smiled, the way he did whenever he beat her at chess, which was almost all the time.

On Friday morning, when Laurent called home to check her phone messages, there were two callbacks from Danny Manings. He could wait, she decided. He would be important to her, maybe, if she failed with Nathan Greene. He might be able to plug some of the historical holes, especially if Nat had kept up contact with Manings after leaving prison.

Phil Penguin had not thought so, where he was certain she could learn from Father Bryan O'Bryan, who was so abrupt with her on the phone, and perhaps Ana Maria Alfaro, the Mexican woman who took Nat in after he returned to Los Angeles. Rereading Nat's papers, feeling more like a sneak the more time she spent with him, she had to agree with Penguin.

She did not return Knobby's latest call.

It still wasn't the right time, although he was threatening to pull the story from her if she did not check in. He said that on three successive calls, always mentioning the money Laurent would lose if the *Tab* had to reassign the story. The threat didn't bother her. She knew now for certain the Nat Axelrod story was worth more than sixty thousand dollars. And that was before adding in what she might make from a sale to the movies.

Rabbi Cohen had left an urgent message for her, saying it was imperative they speak.

She dialed him immediately.

Past greetings, she heard reluctance in the rabbi's voice as he searched for some polite way to say what was on his mind. She sensed whatever he planned to tell her could not be any worse than her fears since hearing his message, so she asked.

It was worse.

Sam and Bertha were missed at breakfast, the rabbi related. Friends went to check on them and recognized the smell of gas stealing under their door. Staff members broke in and found the gas jets and the oven turned on and the Mendelssohns in bed, half asleep, half dead.

Sam blamed Bertha's memory, explaining she turned on the burners and forgot.

Everybody else was of the opinion Sam had tried to do away with both of them.

Rabbi Cohen made clucking noises with his tongue against the roof of his mouth and directed a heavy sigh into the phone.

He said, "I told you before how helping them is already beyond our capabilities unless we get trained help that makes it unnecessary to"—and here his voice broke—"find somewhere else for Bertha and Sam to stay, Miss Connart . . . I sincerely implore you to find the money"—and his voice broke again—"the balance we require, which you said was only a matter of weeks away when we spoke the last time."

Laurent made up another reasonable excuse, which the rabbi took like a subway strap, and a minute after the call ended was on the phone to Knobby.

"Another advance?" His laugh was as horrible as his accent. "Frenchie, you're lucky we're not pulling the bloody plug on you, wanting returned the money already in your kip for no value received."

"The story is not ready to be written. It's bigger than you or Jackie suspected. The delay is worth every minute, every dollar."

"Where all we've been expecting is an anniversary yarn. Nat the Axe ten years after. One more week, mate, and then it's into the black abyss with you."

The dial tone hummed in Laurent's ear.

She dialed him again.

"Listen, mate," she said, spitting out the word *mate*. "Sitting a door away from me is Nat Axelrod, *mate*. The additional advance or I'll have Nat spilling his guts for the *Enquirer* or *Paris Match* faster than you can fart, and fuck you, fuck Jackie, and you can go sue me for the advance money until your dick falls off."

"He's alive? The *emmis,* mate? Not just trying to get under my skin?"

"For what? To prove you are full of shit and—?" Laurent stopped, recognizing what she wasn't hearing from Knobby. There was no surprise in his response. She challenged him. "You knew already, Knobby, that Nat was alive. Tell me the game you've been playing with me."

The phone went dead in her ear until Knobby erupted in laughter. "Caught me," he said. "If we didn't know, we suspected. Why else dish out as much money as we settled on with you, for a lousy anniversary story that any fuzz-faced J-school grad could give us?"

"Tell me the rest."

Knobby took a hungry breath. "We were following up on a blind lead that come with the postman, unsigned like most, claiming Nat Axelrod got sprung on the sly years ago and was out to exact his revenge. Find and murder the girl who was responsible for him landing behind bars. I had research sniff around enough to know there was a front-page story here of a kind we could feast on for weeks, and none better to ferret it out than you, mate: Revenge of the Rock-and-Roll Rapist."

"You couldn't tell me this up front?"

"Could've, would've, but you were after big dollars before I hardly put the anniversary idea to you. You knew about the tip letter, the sixty thousand you demanded would've been twice that dead cert. Besides, you're at your best starting from ground zero. So what's he had to say for himself so far? How close to truth was our anonymous letter writer, mate?"

"The price is now double, mate. A hundred and twenty thousand dollars."

A deeper breath and Knobby might have sucked the receiver from her hand. "Tell me this one thing now. Has Axelrod confessed he found the girl? Killed her?"

Certainment Knobby would be tape-recording the conversation, the way all conversations were taped by the *Tab;* standard policy. Her answering him now would be enough for them to go to press on the flimsiest of pretexts. An unsigned letter, her response, plus a corroborating source of their invention, and *Adieu, Laurent;* no further need for her at all.

Men and their egos.

"Telling you if Nat Axelrod found and killed Mae Jean Minter is not for now. Wire thirty thousand dollars to me at home by tomorrow, Saturday, and the package price goes down to a hundred thousand dollars, photographs included. Otherwise, no deal, and I go elsewhere with Nat Axelrod's story."

The sound could have been Knobby having a heart attack.

He pushed out a fat sigh.

"You are truly some cunt, you know that?"

"Please, *mon cher.* Flattery will get you nowhere."

Her laughter as she was hanging up the phone was interrupted by Nat.

He had shuffled up behind her.

She almost dropped the receiver.

He said, "Couldn't help overhearing. Did I? Are you going to tell me if I found and killed Mae Jean Minter?"

His eyes seemed flushed more with curiosity than anger.

Laurent's eyes floated nervously. After a moment's hesitation, she said, "It all depends. Am I talking to Nathan Greene or am I talking to Nat Axelrod?"

A smile played at the corners of his mouth. She had the feeling he was memorizing her with more than curiosity. He said, "You're talking to the man who sent a letter to the *Tab* and told them Nat Axelrod got out of prison and went after the girl responsible for him being there."

She said, "Nathan Greene. Nat Axelrod. Whoever you want to be. What the hell is going on?"

He shook his head. "Not so easy," he said. "First, I have some questions for you."

They walked to a verdant corner of the woods surrounding Uncle Emil's property, under weather crisp and invigorating.

Nat stretched out on his back, using his jacket for a pillow, and for a while watched a squirrel navigate a tree. Listened to the birds sending signals back and forth. Thought he saw a dog pause to study him, realized it was a coyote before it skirted the periphery and disappeared into the brush.

She sat nearby on the grass, her legs crossed provocatively, so he could see enough thigh to hold his attention, but sometimes more, like a flashing mound of hair that signaled no panties. Whenever she extended her arms, her tiny breasts pushed against the wool and her brown nipples became visible through the knitting.

Sex was her weapon of choice.

It had never failed her with a man, where men had failed her more times than one.

He said, "How did you find me in LA?"

Her mind wandered back to Indianapolis and Laddie Parriott, so easy to seduce in their brief motel liaison the morning of the meeting with Phil Penguin, getting him to tell her what questions to ask and how to ask them of Penguin, information that led her to Las Vegas, to Fort Worth in Texas; ultimately, to him.

She said, "From Phil Penguin in Indianapolis. From him I got the address. The name of the woman you live with. The name you use."

"The name I use is my real name, the one I was born with. Nathan Greene."

"That truth was all over your jacket at the Las Vegas police, as well as the photos from before you were tried and sent to the penitentiary there."

The cryptic smile slid off his face, replaced by a look of respect. "You're good," he said, applauding her. "Phil had become someone I could trust, to this day. I thought he had squelched that file when he got a court order sealing it from prying eyes."

"Your friend the district attorney also did not need to inform me about the murder of Huck Minter, the father of Mae Jean Minter Heidemann, or your part in the murder, *Monsieur* Axelrod Greene."

"You didn't find that information in any Vegas police jacket."

"*Non.* In Fort Worth."

"Fort Worth?"

"Texas."

"You found Mae Jean, didn't you? Is she—?"

Laurent finished the question for him: "Dead or alive?"

"I was going to say *there.* Is Mae Jean there? In Fort Worth?"

"First tell me about the letter you sent to the *Tab.*" She had the upper hand now and she intended to use it.

Nathan eased into a sitting position with his wounded leg slightly elevated to reduce the pain and discomfort.

He examined the grass, like he could find there what he needed to say.

She didn't rush him.

"The letter to the *Tab* comes later," he said, as if this gave him back control. "There are things I want you to understand first." Laurent arced her arms outward, palms up, stretching the sweater tighter across her breasts.

He touched on Mae Jean's letter to him saying she was in Las Vegas, the postcard she had sent to her best friend, Nadine Barber.

"The letter summed things up," he said. "Mae Jean wanted me to know she had to get on with her life, but she would always love me. Forever. It didn't say where in Las Vegas she was, and there was no way once I was out of the joint that I wasn't going to see her."

"And try taking her away from her husband, Dr. Heidemann?"

"No, just see her one more time. I wouldn't ever wish these on her."

He thrust out his hands.

She treated the view with indifference, signaling she had seen worse before and would see worse again.

He said, "The postcard she sent Nadine Barber was my starting point. It had a picture on it of Siegfried and Roy, from the Mirage Hotel. So, that's where I headed once I found a fleabag rooming house north of downtown that my friend Chalky Ruggles told me knew how to do right by ex-cons. I could keep the pool clean in trade for a cot in the basement storage room until I got back on my feet."

Looking at the sky for guidance, he told her the rest.

There is no listing for a Dr. Wolf Heidemann in the phone book, so Nat hangs out at the Mirage and other hotels on the Strip for weeks, barely supporting himself with odd jobs. Three weeks hauling garbage at the Tropicana after his hands feel healed enough for him to cut open his casts with heavy-duty shears borrowed from a garage mechanic. They are red and sore and there are scabs where he'd managed to wedge a pencil inside the casts to get at the itching, but what there is left of his hands works.

Four months as a busboy in the Circus Maximus at Caesar's, until a Cuban-sucking high roller makes a sour face and complains to the maître d' about friggin' freak hands that make him want to puke and Nat's ordered to clock out permanently.

He is increasingly discouraged and on the worst nights tells himself she's left Las Vegas, but he stays. What if he were to leave and she was still here? On the best nights, he knows she is here, his to find provided he doesn't quit the search. Besides, where else could he be that would make a difference in his life now?

He checks local directories and, desperate, even the photos in the call girl tabloids in the newspaper vending machines. He sends a letter to Mae Jean in care of General Delivery, giving her the address of his rooming house. He systematically checks out the unemployment agencies. Most of the people ignore him and his questions. Those who take time to listen generally respond with an indifferent gesture.

When rock concerts play the Convention Center, he hangs around the backstage door, thinking Mae Jean might still cling to old habits. One time, he spots a Neil Young roadie with a face full of warts who looks familiar, only ten years older. The guy looks up from unloading a sound rig and stares back at him curiously. Nathan flees before it can go further.

Mae Jean appears in his dreams regularly. He knows he can always find her there and the anticipation of sleep helps him survive the waking hours.

Almost a year goes by.

More time.

And then, one sticky afternoon, dragging back home after a temporary double shift on the dispatcher's desk at the Golden Rainbow Limousine Service, Nathan steps inside the second-floor single he has graduated to and immediately senses a difference.

Mae Jean. Her scent. The sweet-smelling cologne she wore on the night he first saw her at Indy, when he played only for her and they made love at the Airport Holiday Inn and—

"Mae Jean?"

"Over here," she says, and he looks in the direction of her voice, by the window, where she is peering cautiously through the narrow space between the draw shade and the sill. She backs off a step and turns to face him. Smiles the smile that has helped keep him alive over the years in anticipation of this moment.

"Did you miss me as much as I've missed you?" she says, her voice sweet as every lyric he has ever written about her.

Little has changed about Mae Jean. Older, of course, and a few laugh lines clinging to the corners of her pale green eyes, sadness melting into relief as they look invitingly at him. Maybe a few more pounds, but still on a figure as succulent as a ripe peach, sheathed in a silk chiffon dress, chambray roses on navy blue, sleeveless and almost to her ankles.

She says, "I really need to love you."

It is both a statement and an invitation.

It is the moment he has lived for, and yet—

There is something wrong about it.

It doesn't feel right.

Or has he just learned a lesson, that there can be a lie in moments of absolute truth.

He says, "Even though you didn't want me to come looking for you?"

He feels his hunger growling inside him.

Mae Jean runs her lips nervously over one another. "I wrote it and I meant it, only I didn't," she says, putting a question mark on her face. "I love Dr. Heidemann so much, and I know what that's supposed to mean, but here you are, and I would've come to you before now, when the post office forwarded your letter to General Delivery telling me you were here, but I could not leave Dr. Heidemann yet to rush on over into your tender arms as much as I wanted and, oh—I know how I must sound to you, sputtering on this way?

Please, Nat, please. Take me to bed and make love to me like before?"

She begins to unbutton her buttons. There are only four of them and in another minute the sheath slides off her shoulders and onto the floor. She steps out of the silken puddle and holds her arms out to him.

"It can't be like before," he says, revealing the hands that until now he's been hiding from her inside his pockets.

A knot of puzzlement pulls her eyebrows to the bridge of her perfect nose and she tilts her head for another angle. She steps forward for a better look, taking his wrists and bringing the hands to within five inches of her sight. Tears well in her eyes. "Oh, my poor, sweet knight. My dear baby. What have they done to you?"

Mae Jean is warm, loving and anxious in his arms, responsive to his slightest whims and encouraging on her own. She makes him soar above his wildest fantasies, with a driving hunger and passion beyond any memory he has of the one other night they shared together—before the best turned into the worst.

Afterward, spent, locked in a mutual embrace on top of the covers, she shimmies up a few inches, pressing closer, so close it's as if her heart is his own, and starts to cry.

"It's about him, your husband, isn't it?"

He knows the answer, so why has he even bothered with the question?

"Oh, Nat, Nat, Nat, my own true special lover," she says, wailing at the walls.

Her body begins quivering. He has an instant vision of her falling into a seizure, the way he's seen before, only this time with no cops or doctors around to rescue her. Does he remember what to do? What was the trick the cop did with a pencil in her mouth? No. A pen. With a pen.

Mae Jean rolls away and into a sitting position, drawing her arms across her breasts. Draping one long leg tightly over the other one.

Dissolving inside herself, and, turning her body into an unassailable temple, divesting herself of him?

Passion spent, has the strange love both carried through the years been reduced to a one-night stand? "My own true special lover," she'd called him. Were they words preparing him for rejection? Had he asked her the wrong question?

"It's about us, not Dr. Heidemann, isn't it?" he says, placing a hand on her cheek.

Mae Jean pulls out from his touch. She leaps off the bed and flies to the window, peers out a corner like a criminal checking the street, bouncing nervously on her feet.

She says, "He has people watching me, you think? I think. Dr. Heidemann is so good to me, so wonderful and sweet, but he's jealous, also, especially since he got so sick. He never likes me to be out of his sight. Oh! There, I think. There!"

He joins her at the window. He grips an arm securely around her shoulders and takes Mae Jean's direction to the man across the street, who is leaning against the lamppost while his tiny Scottie takes a poop on the lawn, pooper-scooper at the ready. No other sidewalk traffic and only a car or two passing.

She understands his look. "Go ahead, laugh if you want," she says. "You don't suppose private detectives show up wearing a badge or carrying signs, do you? They put on disguises all the time."

He guides her back to bed, wondering aloud why Dr. Heidemann would even consider having someone spy on her. She stretches out, seemingly more relaxed once he settles against the dresser.

"Dr. Heidemann just likes me to be with him all the time," she says, as if he should know that already. "Even so, even back home, and I had to stop seeing the friends I got. He is a proud man and now he needs me, also, so it's just the way it is." She shrugs. "But I don't want you to think poorly of him, dearest darling."

"He needs you now? Why is that?"

Mae Jean gives him an of course, you couldn't know *gesture.*

She says, "The Parkinson's, you know, like Muhammad Ali got? As bad, so he needs a lot of attention. Why we left Indianapolis in the first place? It got to a place he couldn't be as good a doc as he always was and he was too proud to let anyone know what was going on with his body, so he just come home one day and says to me, We are leaving, Mae Jean. *And so we did. Here we are and been since, where nobody knows him, the way he likes it. Enough money to take care of us. Me to care after all his needs."*

Her eyes appeal to him for understanding.

"Do you love him?"

"Oh, we used to. Never a lot. Enough to make him happy and me, sometimes, but never like it was with you, precious knight. Now, he can't, really, so we don't."

"That wasn't what I asked. Do you love him?"

"Oh, baby, baby, baby. I know where I'd be without him."

"Do you love him, Mae Jean?"

She thinks about it. "With all my heart. Same as I love you." She thinks some more. "No, different from how I love you. Come here and let me show you?"

Soon, as he slides deep inside of her, seconds before they explode together, Mae Jean struggles out a question. "It ever like this with any others, sweetie baby?"

"Only you."

"Forever?"

"Forever."

"Oh, baby, damn, choke my neck, baby, like you done for me that very first time, baby, sweetie, remember?"

"Forever," he says, gasping over her shudder and silent scream.

They carry on this way for months, Mae Jean rushing over to share his bed at every opportunity, him feeding off her love and surrendering his own; Mae Jean fearing private detectives, him fearing the day the loving will stop and she'll become part of the life forever beyond his reach.

Her presence inspires him to write lyrics again, for the first time since his prison letters back to her, to melodies growing in his mind like wildflowers in eternal fields of sun-kissed beauty.

She arrives one morning grappling awkwardly with a gift-wrapped box large enough to hold a scale model of the Titanic, *squeals delightedly when he gets past the red bow and colorful ribbon and paper and cardboard to the guitar case and, inside, a round-body acoustic almost like the one he had described to her from years ago.*

"I can't," he says, and jams his hands into his pockets.

She exaggerates disbelief and her displeasure. "Of course, you can, honey buddy, and when you're ready we'll get you one like you said you learned to play on, with the twelve strings instead of these here only six."

Time and practice—inventing a way of playing that serves his limitations—and he is playing as well as singing for her, and one day there is another gift-wrapped box and, inside, a twelve-string.

It is his turn to cry, her turn to comfort him.

And he understands he can never let Mae Jean go.

She is not the brightest woman, he knows, and they have so little in common besides each other, but who has ever understood love?

He would die for this woman.

He would kill for this woman.

He would—

—torture himself nights, wandering the apartment with questions about Dr. Heidemann.

No matter what her husband's shortcomings or his present physical condition, the doctor saved his life one way and Mae Jean's another.

Is what he's thinking now any way to repay him?

Is the doctor who he must kill in order to live?

★ ★ ★ ★ ★

Back from hanging out at the Hard Rock, nothing he does on a regular basis, but he'd heard U2 would be showing up tonight, jamming informally after the scheduled sets by the Chieftains, the phone is ringing as he works the key in the lock. He picks up on the fourth ring, no idea who might be calling at three in the morning.

Mae Jean announces herself and says, "You think you can come on over my house now?"

"You okay? Is it your . . . Dr. Heidemann? Is there something wrong with him? If it's—"

"Just come, okay?" Her voice is flat and emotionless.

He has never been to her house, except for one lonely afternoon she didn't know about, when he drove by hoping to catch a glimpse of her, only spied the doctor on the front porch in a motorized wheelchair, legs covered with a blanket and eyes overshooting reality.

"I'll be there in twenty minutes. You okay until then?"

"Okay," she says. She recites the address and hangs up.

Anxiety grips him. He dashes out and hops into the old Chrysler Firebird convertible he bought for two hundred bucks cash from a fry chef at New York New York who should have bet de la Hoya. The roads are deserted and he covers the distance there in fifteen minutes.

The house is located in an exclusive section east of the Strip full of rambling single-story, country-style homes on large lots for well-heeled types like casino execs and showroom, movie and TV celebrities who maintain a Las Vegas address to take advantage of Nevada's other main attraction: no state income tax.

He decides against pulling up the circular driveway and parks on the street, half runs the hundred yards to Mae Jean's front porch. The porch light is on and the front door ajar. He slows down. Enters cautiously. Mae Jean didn't sound right on the phone. Now, this feels wrong.

He calls, "Mae Jean?"

He hears something to his right, past the archway, and heads through to a living room comfortably furnished like he has always imagined a cottage in New England would look, all homespun, overstuffed elegance, large enough for a baby grand in front of the picture window.

The sound again, a despairing noise.

He glances down to the thickly woven rug that centers on the lustrous hardwood and sees her. Mae Jean is naked. Half her face has been pulped beyond recognition. Her body is an island of welts, burns and worse.

"You like what you see, you crap piece of shit dung?" The harsh, whiskey-besotted voice belongs to an old nightmare:

Huck Minter.

Huck is parked casually against the bookcase wall and aiming a .45 automatic at his belly, a pencil-thin silencer jutting from its mouth.

"Come here to finish what I started long time ago," he says. "Even the score. You become the surprise package bonus, like I have been blessed by God to take care-a all at one time. Ain't that so, Doc?"

He follows Huck's glance and sees Dr. Heidemann off to the left, about midway between the two of them and six or eight feet from Mae Jean, caught in the half-light of a ceiling lamp. In his wheelchair, transfixed, staring blindly at Mae Jean.

"Been trailing the girl, waiting for a ripe time, and what turned me on to you in Vegas, Axelrod. Had her call to fetch you onc't I give her a good what for, showing the doc here how it should be done."

He scours the room searching for anything he might use as a weapon against Mae Jean's father. Any hard object. Something to take out the bastard without taking a bullet himself.

"Don't even think them thoughts in your rock-and-roll pea brain," Huck says. "You see him, Doc? This crip thinking he can try something on ol' Huck? Even before, it took a Nazi kraut son of a bitch wimp like you to rescue this ass-fucker. That what you become in the joint? Nat the Axe become Nat the Ass? Doc, you think that's

how he gone on to fucking your wife? In the ass? Same as me just now?"

Dr. Heidemann appears deaf to the question, blind to the realities of the moment.

Huck grunts at him and turns to Mae Jean. "You like it, too, didn't you, daughter? You can 'fess up. You're with friends. You sure got it enough times like that onc't I taught you how. Even your drippy friend Nadine, she got her a taste when I hadda prove something to get her telling me where to come find you."

Mae Jean whines uncontrollably, like a pet dog hit by a car and brokering death in the street.

Huck says, "Give Mae Jean a good one the regular way, too, waiting for you, Nat the Ass. Now it's your turn to take Mae Jean on, show the doc your stuff, or is all you're good for now fancy finger-fucking, judging by them crip hands of yours?" He rolls his head to the sound of his laughter. "Go on now, drop them pants. Unfurl your dick and give her a whack."

He shakes his head just enough for Huck to understand it's not going to happen.

An ugly, black-toothed smile unveils every dark crevice on Huck's ashen face. "No? I don't remember giving you a vote, did I? Here's what's up. Your dick right now, stuck in her pronto, or I'm gonna pop a bullet in her brain, supposing she got even a tiny one, and then another bullet that blows off your dick."

With that, Huck steps forward and, leaning at a slight angle, presses the mouth of the automatic against Mae Jean's temple. Huck studies him frozen in the archway and says, "Gonna give you to ten, shit brain."

His mind is at mach speed, chasing after some solution, some salvation.

"One . . . Two . . . Three . . ." Huck hesitates. He flicks a smile. "Four . . ."

Unquestionably, the bastard will pull the trigger. He's probably drunk, judging by his guttered voice and the slight whiskey odor coursing the room, but drunk doesn't matter. Nathan knows Huck's type from the joint.

"Four and a half . . ."

Thinks he's funny.

"Five . . ."

Killers kill.

"Six . . ."

This type murders equally well drunk or sober.

"Seven . . ."

This type gets drunk on murder.

"Eight . . ."

What happens next seems to happen in slow motion, but it's only a matter of seconds.

Dr. Heidemann propels his wheelchair at Huck. His blanketed knees ram the back of Huck's legs and throw him off balance. Huck falls at an angle and a loose shot cracks into a wall as the wheelchair tumbles on its side in the opposite direction and sends the doctor sprawling. Mae Jean has the .45 in her grip. She springs catlike to her feet and aims at her stepfather.

Huck recognizes what's about to happen. His mouth forms a wide silent O! *as she pulls the trigger and puts a bullet in his shoulder. She shakes her head and pulls the trigger again. The second bullet rents Huck's chest. It's still not good enough for Mae Jean.*

She says, "You ain't got no heart, devil man," and sends the third bullet into his crotch; the fourth bullet through his right eye. She peers at Huck's lifeless form. Satisfied he's dead, she drops the .45 and turns to send a look of triumph in Nathan's direction. She says, "What do you think of your girl, honey bear?"

He thinks about seizing the moment, telling himself: It'll be easy, Nathan. Take the gun and turn it on Dr. Heidemann. Make it look like a shoot-out between them, Huck and the doctor. A roll of the dice the cops will buy, especially when Mae Jean corroborates the story.

Mae Jean has scurried beside her husband and on her hands and knees begun comforting him, saying, You okay, Dr. Heidemann? You okay, honey husband? He ain't gonna harm you or me no more. I just see'd to that."

Dr. Heidemann stares directionless into some other world.

Wherever that world is, Nathan recognizes Mae Jean is meant to stay her husband's guide.

Besides, killing is not what Nathan Greene does.

Not who he is.

But—

Who he almost became.

Nathan said, "You know how you think you're doing the clever thing and it wins you the Nobel Prize for Stupidity? That was me, not wanting Mae Jean to wind up behind bars for killing that SOB. I get her and the doctor packed, pile them into their Range Rover and send them on their way, instead of leaving her to the mercy of the Vegas cops. I tell her to write me in care of Phil Penguin, let me know where she's settled.

"Mae Jean says, *You understand about Dr. Heidemann and me?*

"*Of course,* I said back. What else could I say? She says, *Oh, precious knight of my life, I swear I will. I'll write right away I know. You'll come to us and one day it will only be you and me together.* She kisses me on the lips, softly, like a mother putting baby to bed, and roars off out of my life."

"And you went to prison for her crime," Laurent said.

"I should not have done what I did, hang back and call nine-one-one to do more cover-up for Mae Jean. What the cops heard is what you read in the jacket. How I was invited over by the doctor, who saved my life years ago. The door open and me going inside and stumbling into this dead body, et cetera and et cetera. I got a hard going over, and it didn't take much checking for them to learn about my history with Mae Jean and Huck Minter. The evidence against me wasn't all that strong, less than circumstantial, easy to show I could operate a forklift better than I could operate a .45 automatic.

"Phil Penguin flew in ready to do battle, but I wanted it over and done with and nobody looking for Mae Jean. Phil roared anyway and the Vegas DA, anxious to close the book, went for a bargain down to interfering with an ongoing investigation. I suppose there's a con back in Indiana who's benefiting from the trades these district attorneys buddy among themselves."

"You served how long at the Nevada Correctional facility?"

"Too long. Two and something. I could give it to you in days and hours, but why bother? Chalky Ruggles used to say all counting proves is you know how to count, with no time off for Good Fridays. Phil monitored regularly to make sure I wasn't getting more than the usual share of con shit."

"In all that time, you didn't hear from Mae Jean?"

"Word one . . . I knew she hadn't played me for a fool, so I stayed worried sick about her every day I was in the joint. After Phil steered me to early good time release, I headed to Vegas, thinking she and the doctor might have sold their house and some real-estate guy would have an address. The house was sitting empty behind a wall of weeds. I connected with Nadine Barber, who was no help this time. Et cetera and et cetera. Out of bread and out of tricks, deep into my misery, I caught the first lonely trucker willing for company, not caring where he was heading, and found myself back in the City of Angels, where one day the idea came to me.

"Sorting through a copy of the *Tab* my priest friend Father O'Bryan had been reading, I saw an article about an old songwriting buddy, Jamie Boyd, and how Jamie chose to conclude his downward spiral from the pantheon of rock-and-roll lesser immortals by blowing off half his head. Even though Jamie had done the coward's waltz, the article was written with compassion and a depth of knowledge about rock. I knew at once what I could do. I wrote the *Tab* setting up a fictional premise the editors had to find irresistible."

"Jamie Boyd. That was my article, my story."

"That's why my invented anonymous being also recommended you for the Nat Axelrod story."

"Those bastards never told me that part."

"They probably figured, if you knew, you'd hold them up for big bucks." He ate Laurent with his grin. "Probably an advance in the thirty-thousand-dollar range?"

"You are not amusing, *Monsieur* Greene."

"Only patient, waiting for you to make good on your end of our bargain. Mae Jean is in Fort Worth, isn't she?"

"Oui," Laurent said, sounding like the time for games was over.

Nathan jittered with excitement, as if the smell of the woods had become as intoxicating as the best French champagne. "She's well?"

"The doctor is still alive, and she has thought better of disturbing him before his time comes. There is not much left to him. He is like a blade of grass in the wind, but I could see sparks in his eyes whenever Mae Jean showed him his son."

"His—?"

"A lively boy. Bright and intelligent. Mae Jean plays your music all day long and already he knows enough to sing along."

"Does he have a name?"

"Wolf. Wolf Heidemann, Jr. She calls him Wolfie."

Nathan resisted the news with a look. "How old?"

"Four and something. Not yet five."

Nathan rose too fast and his wounded leg sent him sprawling noisily back onto the grass. He moved onto all fours as an intermediate step, blustering words inside heavy breathing. "I'm going there. Now. Today."

"You'll be lucky to make it back to the cabin, the shape you're in. Maybe in another few days, if Uncle Emil feels—"

"Uncle Emil can feel my ass. I've got to find her and my son."

The time for games was over. "If I can go with you, you won't have to look," she said. "I can take you right to her."

Nathan dissected her with his stare. He managed to get to his feet, brushed himself off. "What's that going to cost me?"

"The pleasure of my company."

"What else?"

"Nothing else."

"Just the story, that it?"

"*Non.* I want to repay a favor." He gave her a disbelieving look. "You were very, very nice once a long time ago to a girl I knew. You took a picture for her."

Nathan's expression turned passive. His head shifted left and right. "I don't want my son in any story you write," he said. "Your word on that?"

"My word, although it means I break a promise I made to Mae Jean—not to say where she was or guide you to her before she was ready to write to you in care of Phil Penguin . . . Two promises . . ."

Nathan waited for the rest, uncomfortable with her pause.

Laurent thought about something she'd once read, written by a philosopher, about life being a game of moments. If so, this moment belonged to her, but it was one she could well do without.

She turned from his troubled stare and said, "Mae Jean also made me promise I would not tell you she is dying."

Chapter 21

"Are you going to invite me in?" Danny asked Mason Weems, whose expression said he didn't quite know what to do with the unexpected visitor who'd come knocking at his hotel door, which he didn't seem inclined to open wider than the safety chain allowed.

Mason falsified a smile. "Not a good time, Danny. I know you called my office and I was going to return it, but—"

"You didn't want me to know you were back in Los Angeles again, not in New York?"

"Not that at all. I . . . That is a bug up your ass flashing through your eyes, isn't it?"

"Invite me in so we can talk about it?"

"Was getting ready to leave, Danny," he said, averting his eyes. Something inside the suite was competing for his attention. "Let's grab some breakfast *mañana,* say seven or eight, Polo Lounge downstairs, or maybe Hugo's?"

"Been there, done that, Mason. A few minutes now should do it."

"Awkward, Danny." He did an appeal signal with his eyes.

Through the partially open door Danny saw that Mason was wearing a royal blue oxford robe over matching boxer shorts. He had the pallid skin of someone who didn't catch much sun and a rise of belly advertising the good life. He said, "I can talk while you dress, Mason, unless you were getting ready to leave like that, in which case I'll tag along for the elevator ride."

Mason didn't bother masking his irritation. He pushed his hair over his scalp, wondering, "What the hell's got into you all of a sudden?"

"Premonition. I see you in town, where you're not supposed to be, at Jerry's Deli sitting with people you're not supposed to be with—Harry Drummond, Rap Browning, Brian Malloy—and, admit it, Mason, I might have cause to be nervous."

Mason's mouth played with a smile. He took a step back and unleashed the door. "C'mon in, maybe we do need that conversation," he said, swinging around and leading Danny into the sitting room.

The parlor had been refurnished and redecorated as part of a multiyear overhaul of the hotel a few years ago. It still smelled fresh. Layers of brown tobacco stain were missing from the wallpaper and the floor-length drapes, but the room had retained the hotel's signature pink and green motif.

"Make yourself comfortable," Mason said, and plopped onto the sofa. On the coffee table were two glasses, one rimmed with lip gloss. Four empty mini-bottles of Scotch from the service bar. A jar of jumbo cashews. A bag of Frizzy Wowie chips. A half-crushed cigarette smoldering in the ceramic ashtray, tipped with the same green shade of lip gloss.

Danny looked around, then back at Mason.

Mason nodded. "My LA regular," he said. He hand sketched a killer figure in the air and wagged a thumb at a connecting door open a crack and probably the source of a drifting, familiar scent, Chanel No. 5. It had been Vickie's favorite. She adored Chanel No. 5. She'd have bathed in it if that ever had been an option.

Mason called out, "Cindy, tied up for a bit. Find something on the boob tube." Then *sotto voce:* "Speaking of boobs?" He flagged a hand.

"You always were the ladies' man, Mason."

"A one-woman man, Danny. One woman per city, anyway." He made a *What else can I tell you?* gesture, settled back and waited to hear from him.

"I'll get it straight out, Mason. Are you trying to fuck me over?"

Mason exaggerated a wounded expression, clutched his heart. "You don't trust anybody anymore, do you, Danny?"

"I trusted you until Jerry's Deli."

"Listen, *putz,* you'd be well advised to learn all over who your friends are. I wasn't there for the hot corned beef san. For that I got the Carnegie."

"Honey, should I get started with the movie on HBO? Patrick Swayze and Demi Moore, Whoopi Goldberg, or what?" Cindy was standing in the open doorway, a lean blonde in a mesh black boatneck bodysuit bulging in all the right spots; at least six feet and stilts for legs; less than half Mason's age.

Mason rolled his overgrown eyes at Danny. "A while longer, sweetheart. You want, go down and wait for me in the stretch." Cindy grumbled something before retreating back inside the bedroom.

Mason popped some nuts and adjusted his seat. "I want to say Cindy'll learn patience and understanding when she gets older, but it would be wasted on you, Danny. You need the lesson, too, jumping on conclusions like you have. What happened is, I got summoned by that fucking prick Drummond. Warning me I better be in LA for a meet. I ask about what. Drummond says book the flight, or he'll come down so hard on Shoe Records I'll be filing Chapter Eleven before summertime.

"Well, the prick doesn't know who he's playing with—there are two sides to a pancake—but I don't play in the dark whenever I'm offered daylight, so I spend some frequent-flyer miles and get to Jerry's as he's pulling up with your friend Rap Browning and this mouthy cop with an attitude, this Malloy.

You don't have to be Einstein to figure what's going down. It's spelled out for me by the time the pickles and the sours are on the table. In a nutshell, this Malloy had put it to Rap that he go with him or with you on Patrice, it couldn't be both . . . You know Rap long?"

Danny turned a palm to the ceiling.

"Well, Rap knows who Number One is and had enough history in the business to pick up a phone and get through to Drummond, tell him he has an act Danny Manings is hot to trot with, a helping hand from Joe Wunsch, and even Mason Weems in on the deal . . . Drummond tells me this and stares at me like he's the Crypt Keeper and says, *I'm a face-to-face guy, Mason.* I say, *Straight arrow all the way, Harry, so what did I fly three thousand miles for, to hear you tell me you're shutting me down on this deal?*

"He says, *Jesus Fuck, no, Mason, baby,* like we been sleeping together. *I'm not cutting you out. I'm cutting myself in is all, in place of that has-been cocksucker Danny Manings, and by the time I'm done Joe Wunsch will be history, too. I've just been waiting for the time when it would hurt that prick the most.*"

Mason gobbled some ice cubes from one of the drink glasses.

"You see what he's saying, Danny? He's saying he's running the deal through me and collecting personally through me, and all the while he'll be guaranteeing Decade puts its whole marketing operation behind launching Patrice Malloy big-time, bigger than I could do it through Shoe Records alone."

"And you went for it?"

"Fucking A. He gives me no choice. He can bury me if I say no, the fucker reminds me, just by being good to me. Press and ship enough of my product to guarantee returns offsetting any profit. A buy on chain listening posts and display caps that puts me in the hole deeper. An imaginative sinkhole budget on videos. The indie promo thieves. Whatever. You understand?"

"I thought you had an ironclad with him that gave you all the options."

"Yeah, but not the six hundred thou in front he's ready to pay as an advance when Patrice puts her name on the contract. By then there'll be a side letter giving Drummond the share that would have been yours. The six hundred isn't all clear. A step deal, two at a time, and recording costs come out of it."

"If Decade ever gets wind of the side letter, Drummond will be out on his ass."

"C'mon, Danny. You know how many side deals are always out there. Everybody blinks and winks about them, just as long as the money comes in black ink. Patrice Malloy is black ink once we get her the right songs."

"So, you're going to do the deal?"

"We spit and shook on it. Tonight, Drummond's throwing a little soiree at La Bamba on the Strip. He'll have our letter ready for signing, and I can be catching clouds tomorrow on the noon flight. Maybe Sunday instead, if the weather is good and Cindy is Cindy." His heavy lids slid over his eyes. He smiled at some secret delight.

Danny said, "You accused me of not knowing who my friends are, Mason. What you just told me makes you my friend?"

Mason thought about it as he stood and adjusted his robe. "What I haven't told you, dig? Leave it at that and let go for now." He headed for the bedroom. "Let yourself out, okay?"

Danny left knowing he couldn't leave it at that or let go.

Friday night.

Danny fought the traffic snarl traveling east on Sunset, past Billboard Live!, the Roxy, the Viper Room and the Whisky to within two blocks of La Bamba. Limos stretched in front of him, waiting to snake onto the nitery's miniscule parking lot, already jammed with limos and the usual assortment of Rolls,

Mercedes, BMWs, Porsches and four-wheel road warriors in garden variety decorator colors.

Mismatched couples waited for their cars or stood patiently in an erratic double line that worked up the exterior staircase to "Ritchie's Room," the exclusive hip-hop club also named for Ritchie Valens. Stray women alone and in pairs were half dressed, begging for attention, trying to entice the beefy security guards into sneaking them inside the private party in progress—

Harry Drummond's party.

The sounds of old disco hits mixed with current hip-hop and gangsta rap smashes sailed above the noise. Ray Parker, Jr., faded into Tina Turner and "What's Love Got to Do with It?"

Danny didn't know the attendant who took his car with a look that suggested it was a vehicle that didn't belong here, even if the driver did. He used to know all of them, but he also used to drive a better car, when prestige, not survival, was the game he played.

He assumed an attitude of belonging, insinuated himself into the Ritchie's Room line and to the top of the stairway. The two hostesses behind the reception table wore harried expressions and not much else. They motioned for security when they couldn't find a "Manings" on the guest list.

"It may be under Wunsch, Joe Wunsch," Danny said, improvising. "I'm supposed to meet him here." They found Joe after Danny helped them figure out the spelling, but were confused over a "Cancelled" reference next to Joe's name. "Mr. Wunsch works for your host, Mr. Drummond," Danny said. "Mr. Wunsch runs Decade Records on the West Coast. I work for Mr. Wunsch. I'm his personal assistant."

The two hostesses gave Danny another once-over and told the guards it was all right to pass him in. He shot them a smile as he stepped inside the club and traced old, familiar steps to the service bar in the back of the narrow room, weaving through and around the tightly packed bodies trying to make impressions and connections in the dim light that passed for atmosphere. There were breasts, breasts and more breasts wherever Danny's eyes stopped. "Tits 'R' Us" in all sizes and conditions always survived the seasons and changing attitudes in music.

Danny thought he'd been busted when a pair of arms grabbed him from behind and lifted him a good four inches off the ground. It was Jamey Hustle, the original keyboard player with Easy Street, a band Danny had helped develop during the pre-grunge "Second English Coming," the one that failed for the British as badly as 1776. Jamey was still a good head and a half taller than anyone, a hundred pounds heavier, and acting like the good times never ended. His smile showed a mouth of rotting teeth as he shouted into his face, "It was more bloody to hell fun then, Danny, all it." His eyes wore at least five coats of shellac and waited unblinkingly for a reply. Danny nodded agreement. Jamey lifted him up again, long enough to smash a wet kiss on his lips before stumbling backwards onto the dance floor, rejoining a sexy thing in white stockings, seventeen, maybe, advertising her breasts in a sheer nylon blouse while moving sensually to the beat of Mary J. Blige; slanted eyes sewn shut and not missing Jamey at all.

Danny got a different reception at the service bar, after the bartender recognized him and automatically splashed together and settled down in front of him a tall vodka and tonic, his drink of choice in the old days here. For a moment, he thought about pouring a few inside himself, but tonight was something he needed to do stone-cold sober. He pushed aside the glass with thanks and indicated the Perrier bottles. The bartender showed surprise and uncapped one after he filled a glass with ice, painted the lip with lime and dropped in the sliver.

Danny poured the Perrier and turned to survey the action, ready to search out his Unholy Three—Drummond, Rap

Browning and Brian Malloy—and found himself staring back at Cliff Berlinger, one of Harry Drummond's disciples. Actually, he was staring at Cliff Berlinger's bad Goldilocks toup, which made him look like Harpo Marx on a starvation diet. Berlinger was not a tall man, but always seemed to Danny the right size for the ass kissing that formed a major part of his job description.

Berlinger had his limited charm on automatic pilot, greeting Danny as if they were costars in a buddy movie. The terror didn't begin eating at Berlinger's expression until he realized who Danny was. He began looking everywhere else, as if fearful of eyewitnesses to the way his sunshine smile had glowed in the dark at Danny.

Berlinger fled, tripping on the one-step down from the bar, but saved from a face on the soiled commercial carpeting by a pair of massive breasts that caught his chin. Danny followed Berlinger's flight to a group of tables in the VIP corner of the cushioned terrace lounge against the back wall. He spotted Drummond there and felt his spine grow six inches.

Drummond was holding court for a slew of celebrities, the *glitterati,* a prince at his leisure, stage-managing false smiles and fabricated toasts for the crew from *Entertainment Tonight,* while one of the program's interchangeable blonde anchors zipped back and forth flashing her microphone.

In the sweep of his glance, at an aisle table outside the gilt, Danny spotted Rap Browning. Rap didn't notice him. He was too busy delivering a load of laughing teeth at an unreconstructed groupie, forty-five minimum, in a crotch-high skirt and a supple hand inside his thighs. He was repositioning her hand when Danny reached the table and said hello. Between the distraction and the music, Rap had not recognized his voice, was saying something automatically cute and polite until he understood it was Danny.

He froze, but recovered quickly.

"Bro," he said.

"Bro as in broken," Danny said, firing an accusatory finger at Rap.

Rap understood. He slid the old groupie's hand off and rose, adjusting his pants, his grim-reaper look back into something he probably thought was sincerity, and said, "Had no choice, my man. Business takes of it what fate makes of it."

"Don't blame fate, nigger." The old groupie gagged on the word. "Our business is what you made it. You dragged me in and then dragged me down, like I was just another pet monkey to you."

"More than that, my man, you know that, nigger." The old groupie cringed. "We have a history together, but that Brian Malloy, he a crazy man he want to be."

Danny's fist came up. It reeled Rap backward and onto and over the table and rolling onto the floor, where he landed at the feet of the old groupie. Her nervous eyes swished from Rap to Danny. Back again. She recognized she had to do something. She took the stir stick out of her drink and poured the drink on Rap's face. He didn't budge.

For a moment Danny thought no one had noticed. The dancers were into themselves and attention otherwise was focused on the *ET* taping. He was mistaken. Drummond was glowering at him. Cliff Berlinger stooped to Drummond's ear and pointed at Danny as a hand slammed on his shoulder and dug in.

"You are out of here, bitch," Drummond called at him, his pronouncement cutting hard through the din. Danny glanced over his shoulder.

Two fuzzy-cheeked, muscle-flexing bodyguard types, one blond, the other an Arnold Schwarzenegger clone. Blondie was the one digging his fingers. "Mr. Drummond says you go, so move it, bitch," he said.

They were at least five inches taller, ten years younger and twenty-five pounds heavier than him. Danny pretended it didn't matter. Leaning his weight on the ball of his left foot, he roundhoused a left into Blondie's aquiline nose. He heard a sickening crack. The blood gushed like water from a broken hydrant.

Blondie screamed, "You fucking cunt!" He swung wildly at Danny, who stepped aside, almost tripping over the prostrate Rap Browning. The old groupie banged a fist on Danny's thigh.

Arnold hauled back a grapefruit fist, aimed at Danny's chin and unloaded. Danny angled; the blow missed him. Arnold was off-balance. Danny smashed an elbow into his ribcage. Arnold let out a howl, grabbing his side. His mouth opened wide. Danny aimed his next punch straight for Arnold's teeth. He landed it with the accuracy of Shaquille O'Neill, scoring two. Arnold sank down moaning surprise and disappointment.

Blondie was trying to get a backside grip on him. Danny's arms were still free. He raised them over his head and grabbed at Blondie's bushy hair, pulling hard as he was lifted four or five inches off the floor. Blondie screamed, but held on to him. Danny pulled harder. Beads of sweat popped on his forehead, and he felt Blondie's blood pouring down onto his neck and shoulders. A hand sprang loose holding a hank of thick, blond hair. He opened his grip long enough for the hair to rain down; got hold on another patch. Blondie cursed and screamed names between moans of hurt until, finally, he let go.

Danny felt his feet on the floor again. He revolved and without hesitation planted a hard foot into Blondie's groin. Blondie bent over and cupped his hands over his balls, accompanying the move with painful murmurs. Danny kicked him in the chest and he fell backward. Sucking and swallowing air, he glanced over at Drummond, who was glowering at him, his face twisted in angry contemplation of some odious desire, his gash of a mouth sending ugly signals.

"Nigger!"

Danny turned in the direction of the voice. Saw Rap swinging a wrought-iron chair, about to use his face for batting practice. It was the last thing he saw. The last voice he heard belonged to Drummond, screaming demands: "Get that motherfucker out of here! Beat the living shit out of him!"

Danny felt his shoulder being nudged, light tapping on his cheek. Heard a voice he didn't recognize saying, "I think your white boy he coming 'round now." Smelled a smell he did know, Chanel No. 5, and flashed on Vickie drowning herself in it before sneaking off to another romp in the hay with Drummond in some seedy little pay-by-the-hour motel past the Hollywood Bowl on Little Cahuenga. Saw Vickie's shame devour her, lead her into depression and suicide, shortly after he confronted her with his discovery. Saw Vickie dissolve back into memory as he cranked open an eye to see—

Mason Weems.

On Mason's right, beautiful, Chanel-reeking Cindy.

To his left, leaning forward at him, a thumb and two fingers gently rattling his chin, an enormous black man in military-style fatigues and a red beret, deciding, "Yeah, Mason, got one eye going now. Be happy they left his face alone, them goon platooners a Drummond's."

Danny started after the crud that had his eyes glued shut. His arms felt heavy and hurt like hell as memories of La Bamba trickled back. He confused the tan color of the stretch limo's lining with the sky before realizing he was peering through the plexi skylight. He tried moving his leg. It fell off the narrow seat and onto the floor. He moved his toes to confirm his feet were swollen inside his shoes. He turned his head for a better look at the three people looking back at him from the jump seats. It hurt to move.

"Don't think nothing is broken," the huge black man said in a voice that could have been trained by Barry White. "You hear me saying, dude?"

"Mason?"

"Here, Danny . . . You couldn't leave it alone, could you?" There was almost humor in the way he put the question. "Sorry I missed the fun and games, but our social hour got to running late, Cindy's and mine."

"What happened, Mason? Where are we?" Danny said over the humming motor and the breath of an air conditioner on low.

"Outside your place, waiting for your nap to be over. What happened? Rufus here saved your ass is what happened. Tell him, Rufus."

"Happened inside with Mason here as them faggots was dragging you over and out some back door, a stairway going from there down to the kitchen. My man here, he says, *That be our partner, Rufus, and he look to be needing a friend.* I gets there, they beating and stomping on you something fierce.

"They looks at me like the North lost the war and say, *Haul your nigger ass out a where it don't belong, black boy.* Not the way to talk polite to me. I got Little Pokey all ready to go and go he do. Little Pokey, that my Swiss Army knife. Corkscrew just right for this, and it say hello to the blond dude. Catch him at the cheek bone; gonna leave a nice souvenir. He take one step on away and down he goes the stairs. Think I hear a bone or two go crack he land.

"The other dude, the dark motherfucker, he come at me like a bear wanting to share his hibernation. I sleep alone and let him know with Little Pokey to the gut. That only slow him, so I shoulder him to a stop and give him a taste of Little Pokey where it mean he remembering me he try for children or slide into some mud pile, faggot that he is. So that was that and here we is."

Danny coughed his throat open and said, "Thank you."

Rufus shrugged and drew his lips back to reveal a dentist's expert workmanship. "Being as we partners, you don't even owe me a number, dude."

"Partners?" Danny shot a look at Mason, who nodded back.

"You ever hear of Danger Funk Records?" he said. "I.C.U. and the Street Boyz. Juke Daddy B. Might-E Ripple. Funky Miss Clunky. Death Vader."

"Tha's me," Rufus said, pounding the 24-karat skull-and-crossbones gold medallion hanging from the thick gold chain around his neck. "Death Vader, aka Rufus Hardaway."

Danny knew who Hardaway was. He'd founded Danger Funk Records about five years ago, as gangsta rap carved a bigger and richer slice of the music industry pie, almost overnight equaling the multimillion-dollar successes of another East Coast label, Bad Boy Records, and Death Row Records on the West Coast.

A spate of gangsta rap murders, among them Death Row's Tupac Shakur and Big Boy's Notorious B.I.G. had helped shove Hardaway into a spotlight he didn't welcome, revealing the onetime street drug pusher as a professional criminal who had spent more time in prison than on the outside.

"Man, he got a right to reformation," Hardaway told Larry King on the one interview he granted. "Clean is better, Larry. Murder never been my territory, and I come to know my urge for music in the joint."

"Weren't you serving time in Indiana around the same time as, I'm trying to remember—of course, Nat the Axe? Nat Axelrod?" *People* Magazine quoted King, and that's what had made the exchange and Rufus Hardaway's name memorable for Danny.

Hardaway had answered King—

"Seem so, Larry, but first you need know I was doing the time without doing the crime."

"How then do you explain the twelve pounds of heroin and twenty-two pounds of crack cocaine police testified they found lining the tires of your Rolls?"

"Planted, Larry, easier 'n my Lord Jesus ever made the trees and flowers grow."

"I notice you didn't say grass, *Rufus."*

"I say grass *even here, likely they come onto us and haul my black ass away again on suspicion a suspicion, Larry. Same as they making me out now to be part of them killings come along, where I as peaceful as a dove. And that the only bird I look to give to the law these days."*

"Performing as Death Vader, your songs are full of evil and violence, Rufus. How do you explain that?"

"That where I leave it, Larry. Moral I put out there is you can own a piece a the dream without giving in to the nightmare, and all my brothers know so. Same as when that Nat Axelrod made some a his music for us. It be full a love in a place full a hate. Hardly ever knew him at all, though. I ruled my roost and whiteys theirs, not much common ground, you unnerstand? But that Nat the Axe with his music show me white and black can live together in peace and harmony, so here I'm at, collecting cars and diamonds, more booty a mortal man can handle, not one a them trying to take over gangsta rap through killing means, or whatever they say."

Mason Weems said, "Rufus co-owns Shoe Records with me and I'm an equal partner in Danger Funk, Danny. Nothing we advertise. A secret mostly between us and the IRS."

"Mason here, he put me in business when it mattered. The two of us too clever to put a white face up front in my yard, you dig?"

"Now, maybe, you get the drift better, Danny? When Harry

Drummond started to fuck with me he was also fucking with Rufus."

"Nobody fuck with Rufus for long," Rufus said. His massive chest shook with the humor of the concept. He adjusted his tightly clipped scarecrow red hairpiece. "Same as when they fuck with you, now they fuck with me."

Cindy said, "All this talk about fucking is making me hungry. We ever gonna go and grab a bite?"

"Shut up another minute," Mason said. "Danny, Rufus knows what I know. What don't we know?"

Danny sorted out the story in his mind and shared it.

Mason and Rufus listened carefully.

Cindy buffed her two-inch ceramic nails, blue now, the same color as her eyelids.

When he finished, Rufus said, "Something, ain't it, about Nat the Axe and me locking up again. Told that to Mason I first heard, how history sometime climb right up your leg and gnaw you a Weight Watchers ass."

"You told Larry King you barely knew Nat."

"Told Larry Nice Guy Gullible King a whole load a shit. You also believe for real the suck hunks Jenny McCarthy carrying?"

Cindy stirred uncomfortably.

Mason said, "Any reason we can't use a studio at Rancho Musico, Rufus? He has the place tied up, Danny."

"I know," Danny said, and explained.

Rufus said, "Come Monday, though. Give me the weekend to soften the screw to Juke Daddy B., Funky Miss Clunky, them thinking to come in Monday and shake up the place."

Danny said, "You're forgetting the part where I explained the Tune King won't let go of the master tapes."

Rufus said, "We go visiting this Nam place beforehand, me and some a my friends."

"You can't hurt the Tune King, Rufus. I won't—"

"Said nothing about hurting."

Danny slid an inquiring look at Mason.

Mason said, "The Tune King will not be touched, Danny. My word. Meanwhile, leave Drummond, Browning and Malloy to me."

He and Rufus slid out of the stretch first, helped angle Danny from the backseat onto the grass island. Rufus half guided, half carried him to his apartment. Patrice opened the door while Danny was struggling with the key in the lock.

She said, "I woke up and you haven't been here for hours. I was so worried. I—" She flung herself into his arms, concern giving way to relief, then uncertainty as she stepped back and took a hard stare from Rufus.

"I know you?" Rufus said.

"Unlikely, unless you spent time in the clubs in San Diego," Danny said. He introduced them.

Patrice acknowledged Rufus cautiously, but it was clear his name meant nothing to her.

Rufus shook his head. "Not San Diego. Patrice. Already was thinking the name got bells on it, too."

"A family hand-me-down."

"Like I also seen your photograph onc't."

"My picture?"

He angled his chin at her, narrowed his eyes and studied her, deciding, "My mistake. A picture I onc't seen is all, but you ain't it. Someone I knew, showing off his kid, like that."

"My mother is deceased and probably my father."

"Prob'ly? You don't know?"

"A long story."

"Prob'ly none my business neither, so go on and take care a our main man here. Monday, Danny."

Patrice took Danny by the hand and led him into the apartment.

"Monday, Rufus, and thanks again," Danny said.

"No thanks and owe me no number, either, partner. No number."

Chapter 22

Saturday and Sunday passed slowly for Nathan.

He was anxious to start for Fort Worth, but his vote didn't matter.

Laurent had control of the car and, even if he hot-wired the BMW, his leg wasn't healed sufficiently to take the strain of constant driving. He had no money and little more than the shirt on his back. Besides, he needed to go back to LA first. There were belongings there he couldn't leave behind—his journals, letters and, most importantly, the cassettes stored at the apartment.

Laurent had her own affairs to put in order in LA on Monday, she said, making it clear she didn't want company, but would happily run his errands. Meanwhile, in trade, she intended to use the weekend to probe deeper into his story.

Nathan was amenable and ultimately casual with his answers, except where a question dealt with Ana Maria, sensing at these times Laurent was more than a reporter digging at the garden patch. He raised the question with Dr. Gautier Saturday afternoon, after Laurent had gone off to the village to shop and run errands for the doctor.

Dr. Gautier was on the front porch and at first seemed oblivious to his presence, applying lemon oil to the carved oak slab above the doorbell, rubbing briskly with the energy of a man half his age.

HERE, AT WHATEVER HOUR YOU COME, YOU WILL FIND LIGHT AND HELP AND HUMAN KINDNESS

"Laurent told me that's a quote from Dr. Schweitzer," Nathan said. "She told me you spent time with him."

"She sometimes talks too much, that girl, and sometimes not enough," the doctor said. He rubbed a bit more while informing Nathan, "She saved my life over there, you know that?"

"Laurent?"

The doctor grunted. His bushy white eyebrows formed two arches. "Who, then? Joan of Arc? Laurent, of course, Laurent. Only that was years later. Laurent doesn't speak much about herself, you may have noticed."

"I've noticed."

"Like any reporter. Get, get, get is what they're all about. I knew her father, too; Kohner. From years before. Peas in a pod. It was through Julian Kohner I first came to meet Schweitzer and properly dedicate the rest of my life, so many years ago. In nineteen hundred and I do not remember. Lorraine was a mere child, perhaps not a year old. Her mother had died in childbirth, so I never knew her, but I remember her photograph. Red hair, the color of fresh strawberries. A brilliant smile. A treasure, like her daughter came to be." Dr. Gautier stepped back and approved his work. "Lorraine always enjoys playing with half the truth. Or less. She is so, so secretive, that girl, but always on the side of goodness. She escapes here sometimes, to me, whenever she has a need to escape her life temporarily, but she never comes with more than half the truth. Like with you this time."

Nathan laughed. "I've come with all the truth, but not even half to share."

He felt Dr. Gautier's stare, as if he were searching for Nathan's soul.

The doctor walked over to a table and put down the bottle of oil and the scrubbing cloth. A cat, brown and white and overweight, moseyed around the corner of the cabin, rubbed against his leg, hopped up to join him.

"There is something *Le Grand Docteur* told me as I prepared to leave him for the last time. I would like you to remember this, Nathan, especially if you should feel you owe me something. He said, *Emil, there is only one commandment, and that is love.*" Dr. Gautier's slender fingers orchestrated the words. "She loves you, you know?"

"Laurent?" Nathan looked for the joke.

"No. Joan of Arc." The doctor was deadly serious. "I tell you that for her own good, not yours. Once you leave, you will become hardly a memory in my life, but Laurent will always be more than a moment. If you do not love her back, I understand. I can see that. But, please, you should not hurt her and you can trust her. Another reason I tell you. I suspect you have to trust someone again, sometime."

"Why would Laurent possibly love me?"

While the doctor was considering a way to answer him, they heard her before they saw her. Laurent honked a warning on the horn as she pulled up the narrow dirt driveway, scattering dust clouds.

"If it matters, maybe better to ask her that question," Dr. Gautier said, and signaled her a greeting.

Nathan decided against it.

Love was a word he had reserved for Mae Jean, an emotion he had refused Ana Maria, a feeling he wasn't about to risk sharing with Laurent Connart.

It was the doctor's custom and habit to watch *Entertainment Tonight* before settling down to dinner, the one brush with fantasy he said he allowed in a life burdened by too much reality.

For Nathan, tonight, too much reality poured over from the television screen.

The program led off with an exclusive special report about a record-company party at trendy La Bamba that roared out of hand like a canyon brush fire. Flashes of celebrities lapsed into fight scenes caught on camera, and there was Danny Manings slugging it out with Rap Browning. As far back as Nathan could remember, the two of them had been friends. Rap had been a key man in breaking the first Nat Axelrod single and other releases that Danny needed springboarded onto the charts.

There was something more startling.

The picture was poorly lit and the figure of the gigantic black man had barely angled into the frame before it disappeared through the same doors beefy security guards had dragged Danny through, but he could never forget the elephantine stride, the red hair, the way his fists clutched around something. Nathan stared at his corrupted hands, remembering the worst of Indiana State Prison and images of Rufus Hardaway that sat like scars on his soul.

"You know people there, *oui*? Danny Manings especially?" Laurent said, breaking his concentration.

"Not Danny Manings especially," he said, and let her see he didn't want to talk about it.

She bought into his reluctance. "Danny Manings is someone I have left messages for, but not yet reached," she said. "We will have a lot of hours for talking about him before we arrive in Fort Worth."

Nathan rose carefully and dragged from the room, a question that had been bothering him grown into a burden: When he spotted Danny at the Nam, why was Danny there? To that he added: Did it somehow connect to La Bamba? To Danny and Rap Browning? To Rufus Hardaway?

He grabbed the phone in the kitchen and called the only

person he could trust who might have answers.

Father O'Bryan answered on the third ring.

Their conversation lasted about ten minutes.

Nathan hung up hoping Dr. Gautier was right about trusting Laurent.

He needed her now to do more than stop at the apartment and retrieve his belongings.

CHAPTER 23

Laurent started for Los Angeles early Monday morning, easing out of the cabin before sunrise, out the door even before Uncle Emil roused, anxious to beat as much commuter traffic as possible on what would be a two-hour drive under the best of freeway conditions. A twelve-car pile-up on the 60 shut down one lane and cost her another hour, time she spent listening to news on NPR when her mind wasn't overrun with thoughts about Nathan.

He had labored over letters yesterday and asked her to deliver them to people she'd not yet managed to interview: Father O'Bryan, who had hung up on her when she phoned, and Ana Maria. The letters were personal, Nathan said, and he was trusting her not to open and read them.

Merde!

Had she given him her word she wouldn't?

Not that giving her word ever meant more than she wanted it to mean.

But for him, for Nathan, she wanted it to mean something.

For her, also.

How do you explain emotions?

Simple, foolish woman. You don't.

What was the word Nathan had known to use when she got him to say a few things more about Mae Jean? *Sforzando.* A thunderbolt. One of the few Italian words that made sense to her. Nathan said he had been hit by a thunderbolt the moment he saw Mae Jean, and that was how it was from that day to this day.

So, Laurent, you too?

Sforzando?

For the French, a *coup de foudre*?

Or foolish girl *voodoo,* because Nat Axelrod was so nice to you that day at Wembley Stadium?

She had come to recognize there would be no future for Ana Maria Alfaro with Nathan.

But, for Laurent with Nathan?

Maybe.

Mae Jean was dying. There would be a void to fill when that happened, whenever that would be, since death does not adhere to a rigid schedule. Was Nathan meant to fill the void in her heart, in her life, since Papa died? If the answer was *yes,* the new question was *why*?

Sforzando?

A *coup de foudre*?

Laurent stopped first at her condo.

The check from the *Tab* was waiting for her. She endorsed it over to the Anne Frank Home and added a note to Rabbi Cohen before sealing the envelope and applying a stamp, in case there was no time later to swing by for a visit with Bertha and Sam. The Alzheimer's was eating Bertha's memory faster and faster. Laurent was anxious to see her one more time, while Bertha still recognized her and understood how much she was loved by her. After Fort Worth might be too late. She resisted crying, but her tears would not cooperate.

Laurent had two cups of coffee, changed outfits and, after packing, checked the machine.

Knobby was among the callers, confirming her thirty thousand dollars was on its way and reminding her about deadlines. She intended waiting until the story was finished and delivered to tell him she was fleeing the scum-filled world of the tabloids, as odious as any war she had ever covered, to find something useful to do with her life.

With Nathan, maybe, but Knobby did not have to know that.

Father O'Bryan was not there when she arrived at the Church of the Blessed Bonaventure.

An old man in a Dodger cap appeared like magic from behind a tapestry, said his name was Old Galindo and explained it was too early for the priest. He took the letter Laurent offered and, while holding it up to the light, nodded and said he would be certain it reached the priest.

The gang of bare-chested teenagers playing soccer on the street outside Ana Maria's apartment building included the boy who'd helped her with Nathan. She sent him a thumbs-up sign as she headed up the front stoop. A cool breeze caressed her face. She tugged up the collar of the silk blouse she wore under the Isaac Mizrahi cardigan she'd bought for herself as a birthday gift.

Nathan wanted her to wait after delivering the letter, while Ana Maria put together some personal belongings, which Laurent was to bring back with her to Idyllwild.

As he described them to her, explaining where they could be found, she almost blurted out the truth, that she'd taken them already, that she'd hidden them in Uncle Emil's cabin, that she'd read them and played his music, and—

She knew how Nathan would react to her cunning.

She would still get her story.

Fort Worth and the promise of Mae Jean guaranteed that.

But she would stand no other chance with him.

Sustain the deception, she ordered herself.

Pull the pillowcase from its hiding place when Nathan isn't

looking and deliver it like it was never there before.

This lie was a better truth, of that she was certain.

There was a new lock on Ana Maria's door and Laurent had to knock.

A moment later, she was staring across the length of a chain into the anxious face of a young woman who fit Nathan's description. She was prettier than he had portrayed Ana Maria and had that curiously erotic aura unique to Latin women.

Sensing she was about to be dismissed like a door-to-door charity, Laurent said, "Nathan sent me to see you." Ana Maria looked startled. She turned away while trying to figure out what the announcement meant. "May I come in?"

Ana Maria continued thinking.

Laurent smelled Mexican cooking through the narrow opening. She was hungry. She had not eaten since breakfast, except for a Snickers bar from a vending machine at Father O'Bryan's church. The sweet aroma was more inviting than Ana Maria, who said, "Why should I believe you?"

"What reason do I have to lie?"

"Where is Nathan?"

"I can explain better inside."

"You're the police again? I already told you police what I know anymore."

Laurent shook her head, and in a faltering Spanish she had rare occasion to use said Nathan's message for Ana Maria was *urgento, muy importante.*

Ana Maria studied her face. "No more police," she decided. "You got something you want to say to me, you come with a warrant." Her nostrils flared and her breath was rushed. She slammed the door and turned a snap lock.

Laurent knocked and kept knocking until she was certain Ana Maria was on the other side of the door. "I have a personal letter for you from Nathan," she said. "I have it here in my hand."

"What does it say?"

"It's for you. I have no idea. I haven't read it." Laurent heard a brief moan, the shuffling of an uncertain mind, before the door opened a crack, enough for her to see Ana Maria's look of disbelief. She displayed the letter. "I suppose Nathan has things he wants you to know before he leaves."

"Leaves?" Another moan. "How do I know you're saying the truth?"

"I think only by reading the letter."

Ana Maria closed the door and fumbled with the chain lock.

Laurent entered and handed over the letter.

Ana Maria turned and plopped into the abused armchair in front of the TV, where two overwrought actors were throwing tears back and forth in one of those *novellas* broadcast from Mexico. She struggled through the letter, her eyes flooded with tears. Read it again, tilted her head and looked back at Laurent from the corners of her eyes.

Laurent smiled and, trying to soften whatever had made Ana Maria cry, said, "Whenever he speaks about you, he only has the most wonderful things to say. He says you are so lovely and now I also think so. *Qué bella. Tu es una mujer bella.*"

Ana Maria's eyes began to shine. She turned back to the TV screen, where the actors were embracing their way toward a giant-sized mattress floating in an ornate, hand-carved frame, then had a glower for Laurent. "Why would Nathan be talking to you about me?" she said. "Nothing about that here in this letter. Nothing about you. Nothing about you at all. Only about goodbye."

"There is someone he must see in Fort Worth, Texas. I'm going there with him."

"You are—?" Ana Maria's fingers moved to her mouth.

Laurent recognized at once it had been the wrong thing to say. To say more now, try to explain, would be foolish. The damage had been done. Only time would heal this woman.

"You been here before?" Ana Maria said. "You the one here when Nathan was shot and got him away quick with my brother, Juan Pablo?"

"Yes."

"Now that I look closer, yes, you are the one Juan Pablo describes to me, even how you talk a funny way, not like us; the accent . . ." Her words trailed off into a cloud of silence. She did not try to hide the tears forming as she rose from the armchair. Her sudden movement drew open her terry cloth robe. She was wearing sheer bikini briefs.

Laurent read her from the ground up. Ana Maria's firm boobs were marvels of desire on a tempting body younger and better than her own, making her wonder if Ana Maria's lovemaking also was better. She felt jealousy rising, as if Nathan Greene were not already a closed chapter in Ana Maria's life.

Ana Maria realized she was being studied. She pulled the robe around her and drew the belt tighter. Her cheeks glowed. She said, "You hungry?"

Laurent feasted on Ana Maria's homemade *polvorones* and *rosquillas* while Ana Maria shared pieces of her early history with Nathan, telling her, "In the beginning I was so curious about him, like a priest about pussy. The way I grow up, though, was never to ask too many questions. Sometimes the answers are more of a burden than the curiosity. That Nathan come into my life, that was important. Not from where. Maybe not even why. I could tell he was a person to let me know in his own good time, he wanted. He did, some of it, so I'm almost right about that."

Her reporter's mind busy, as well as her need to understand

the relationship, Laurent said, "You find that out about somebody only after you have lived with him for a while, what a person is like."

Ana Maria signaled agreement. "Nathan was like a saint to me," she said. "Saint Nathan. I discover that about him before I even let him into my house, the second I lay my eyes on this dirty man at the 7-Eleven, who saves me from attack and maybe even death, but looking worse than a beggar."

"Beggars scare me."

"Men of the street are there to hurt themselves. It is only after they come off the street they can bother to hurt somebody else."

"You are very wise for somebody so young."

"Maybe not so young as you think. I am twenty-seven." She gave Laurent a look that said they could trade womanly secrets, further cement their bond.

Instead of shedding five years, as she usually did, Laurent said, "Forty-one." Immediately felt betrayed by her candor.

Ana Maria leaned back from the dining table and widened her eyes. "The truth?"

"The truth."

"You look so much younger, five, maybe six years. Even my age. Now it makes me sad to think how I look, when I should look like you."

"You are beautiful."

Ana Maria methodically rapped her jutting lower lip with her knuckles. "I see you, I see beauty," she said. "You do not see my worms. They grow inside me, where the beauty should be. There I only have worms."

"Nathan sees only your beauty."

Ana Maria wagged her head from side to side. "He found the worms. Never the beauty, I don't think." She stared off into space. "Some people, they spend their whole life looking for the worms. Even saints. Maybe, especially saints."

"In his journals your Saint Nathan writes time after time about your beauty. Never about worms. Maybe these worms are only in your imagination."

"He lets you read his journals?" The look on Ana Maria's face revealed Laurent may have said the wrong thing again.

Laurent wondered how to answer. Tell the truth? She settled for the lie. "*Oui.* Yes," she said. Glanced at her watch. Said, "It is really past time for me to be going." Pushed away from the table.

Ana Maria stopped her with a stare. "Nathan, he tell me once long time ago his journals were only for him, nobody else. He never even tell me what was in them, the same way he don't let me go anywhere near his music tapes. You, he tells, and you come here before and you take him away and you also take his journals and his papers and his tapes, so you got to be somebody special even then."

"That's not the way it is."

"I'm asking you something," Ana Maria said. She clasped her hands, elbows on the table, gently hammered her thumbs against her chin. Her eyes traveled to the ceiling as she swallowed fresh sobs. "You his new girlfriend?"

"No."

"I think you are, and that is why. I think that is why he says nothing in here, this letter, about you or Fort Worth, Texas, only goodbye and a thing I don't understand. If Nathan got everything of his already, why he write I should put all together and give to you?"

Laurent quickly fashioned another lie. "Nathan told me something about other papers here he needs. More cassettes."

Their eyes locked.

Ana Maria threw together a stack of plates and traded the table for the archway.

She studied the TV screen, laughing with contempt as organ music swelled like a giant ocean whitecap while the *telenovela* lovers embraced. Turning back to Laurent, she said, "Do you believe they will live happily ever after? I don't think so. Happiness will be gone the minute the TV is off and all there is remaining is a black screen. I have my own black screen, don't I?" Her head began bobbing. "So tell me, now when Nathan cries out in the night, whose name is on his lips?"

"Not mine."

"*Collate!* Shut up. You have shown me enough worms already. You don't have to hurt me anymore. He has only the best things to say about me, but he whispers them in your ear."

"Not so."

Ana Maria dismissed her with a gesture. Her eyes went blank. "In a minute we go look and see if his drawers got more in them than you took from here the last time." She disappeared into the kitchen.

Laurent heard the clatter of dishes in the sink, the rush of tap water. She carried the rest of the dishes to the kitchen counter. She tried apologizing, but Ana Maria ignored her, her body hunched over the sink as she scrubbed the same ceramic dish endlessly, humming a tune Laurent remembered from Nathan's tapes. She moved to the bedroom, stooped by the dresser and opened the drawer that had held Nathan's papers, determined to keep her story consistent in Ana Maria's eyes.

Ana Maria padded into the room wearing a dazed, defeated expression, quavering inside her robe, holding a short-barrel .38 revolver casually at her side.

"My brothers Jesus and Angel gave me this for protection," she said, showing it off. "To use against anyone who comes here looking to harm me. I don't think I want any more harm from anyone."

She moved the weapon to her mouth.

Poked the short barrel in and out several times.

Moved it to her temple.

Laurent dropped her voice to a gentle whisper. "That would prove nothing, Ana Maria. It is a mortal sin besides. You would consign your eternal soul to Hell."

"I been there already without any instructions from you," Ana Maria said. She made the sign of the cross. "You don't think it would tell Nathan I love him more than life, no matter how much it hurts inside?"

"What would he do with the information?"

"He could write another song about me."

"Is that all your life is worth, a song?"

"One of his songs . . . Is he good in bed with you?"

"*Merde!* I tell you again, it's not what you think."

"Does he grow large for you? Can you tell me how it feels inside, the explosion, the pleasure that comes from pleasing your man?"

Before Laurent could answer her, a thickly accented child's voice called for her from another part of the apartment. "Ana Maria, Mama she send me upstairs for the *rosquillas* you said you have for her."

Ana Maria lowered the .38 and headed for the living room, where the front door was open as far as it could go with the safety chain in place. Laurent trailed after her, deliberating how best to separate this sad woman from the weapon.

Ana Maria called at the door, "*Polvorones,* too, Julio, but not now. Tell your mama I'll bring them to her later. Soon."

Satisfied, the boy pulled the door shut. The rumble of his footsteps dissolved down the hallway.

Ana Maria studied the .38, an edge of alarm in her eyes.

"You know something," she said. "When I first hear Nathan left with a woman, I know in my heart it was her, whose name he screams in the night, this Mae Jean, and I only wished I had been here to rescue him from his worst nightmares." She pulled back the hammer, rolled out the cylinder and gave it a spin to verify the load, snapped it back. "Now, I look at you wondering if there is a difference between the one who come between Nathan and me before and the one who come between us now. I wonder if Nathan going to scream about you the same way and who is going to be around to make him feel better."

"I'm not the one taking Nathan from you, Ana Maria."

Ana Maria nodded agreement.

Aimed the .38 and squeezed the trigger.

Laurent heard the explosion, then saw the dark light of yesterday and knew it was Papa coming to take her home.

Chapter 24

Monday morning.

Neither Danny nor Patrice noticed the dirty maroon-colored Honda that locked onto their tail when Danny came through the underground parking gate, heading for a meeting commanded by Father O'Bryan. The priest insisted urgency, advising, "We have serious private matters to discuss."

The address was a shabby bar with painted-over hardwood boards for windows and a sign too faded to decipher, between a discount porn shop and a Thai restaurant on Cahuenga, a trash-laden block south of Hollywood Boulevard. He angled into a parking space with a broken meter another half block south, unmindful of the Honda as it tooled by and pulled into a spot another hundred yards down.

Father O'Bryan was already there, carrying on a conversation with the flush-faced bartender, whose name was Al, like they were old friends. "My church away from church," he said, once their eyes grew accustomed to the dark, and he led Danny and Patrice through the tobacco fog to a booth in the back. The priest slid in first, planting the doctor's satchel he carried on his lap, invited Patrice to settle beside him and Danny next to her.

"The other side is for errant parishioners," he said. "I do some of my best work right here with vagabonds from life too lost to find the church, so the church comes here to find them. We keep regular hours each and every Monday, praying the money we gladly share doesn't run out before these dear good people do." He patted the satchel.

Danny said, "This is Patrice Malloy, Pat."

The priest grabbed both her hands and made a face as pleasant as a summer breeze. "Of course you are, and every bit as lovely as our mate here promised." He pressed his lips to her cheek. She flinched hard. Danny wrapped her in a protective arm. Father O'Bryan's face flushed and he apologized. "It's my way is all," he said. "You might say I'm grossly outgoing even when I'm not being gross, so forgive me, you dears?"

Danny said, "You insisted this meeting couldn't wait, Pat. In the back of my head I was thinking maybe you'd heard from Nat?" The priest tilted his chins up and down. "Maybe Nat's amenable to what we talked about, using his songs, the duets with Patrice?"

Father O'Bryan lost his mask of joviality even before Danny finished the question. "Yes, I spoke to him, but not what, Daniel. What I have to repeat is nothing that pleases me any more than it will satisfy you."

The bartender delivered a bottle of bourbon, a half-full pitcher of water, a shot glass and three water glasses to the table. The priest downed a fast shot after Danny and Patrice declined to join him, wiped away the residue on his lips, raised his eyes to the ceiling, and issued a grateful sigh. "Still as good as the first one," he said.

Danny moved around to the other side of the booth to cut off the possibility of visitors after handouts and better observe the priest. "Talk to me about Nat," he said.

Father O'Bryan focused on one of Danny's shirt buttons and cloaked his thoughts inside a disingenuous grin. "He phoned me, you see? Nathan. He said he caught you on the telly in some brawl or other and was pleased to see you trim and fit as ever."

"Enough malarkey, Pat."

The priest shifted his head up and gave him an owl-eyed stare. "It's Nathan's master tapes over to his recording studio, the Nam." Danny suspected where the conversation would head and assumed a blank expression. "Nathan phoned me asking that I retrieve them for him. This was on Saturday evening. Sunday, yesterday, after a weary day pouring God's word to the unwashed and hearing their sins multiplying in the confessional, I went and found they were gone. Missing, like they had been stolen, the masters and the backup tapes, six flat white boxes." He pushed around the ice cubes in his water glass. "Would you know anything about this?"

"Why would I?"

"Loving them so much? Wanting the music so much to be a part of your recordings with the lovely Patrice here, I thought maybe you could have borrowed them?"

"Not me, Pat," he said, honest if he stuck to those words. He wasn't surprised at hearing confirmation Rufus Hardaway had secured the masters, given the way Rufus had confidently talked about *visiting the Nam* with friends, the strut in his voice when he phoned last night to set a noon start at Rancho Musico.

"Wasn't accusing. Only inquiring."

"My swiping the masters. Was that what Nathan thought, too? Why he called you?"

Father O'Bryan poured another shot and, head cocked, one eye closed, tongue protruding slightly from a corner of his mouth, carefully lowered the bourbon bottle onto the wet circle on the table. He cackled triumphantly, tossed back his head and downed the shot in a gulp. Ran his knuckles across his mouth. Inquired, "Sure you won't join in?"

Danny waved away the invitation. He ground out the remains of a cigarette in an ashtray overflowing with butts molded into an ugly mess by clumps of chewing gum. He held the butt to his nostrils to dilute a pungent smell that permeated the room and stuck to his clothes, reminding him of unflushed toilets.

Father O'Bryan, as calm as a Monet landscape, said, "Nathan is convinced you stole those masters. He's asking that you hand them over to me." He stared over the rim of the shot glass and waited Danny out.

Patrice looked puzzled, her curious eyes shifting between Father O'Bryan and Danny.

Danny said, "Did you tell Nat my proposal?"

"I'm a man of my own word as well as God's." The priest pushed out his lips and formed a bittersweet smile, held the neck of the bourbon bottle like a chess player contemplating his next moves. "Nathan said he has no intention of ever making these songs public or recording again—even for Danny Manings. He wants me to have the masters in safekeeping for him when he gets back, the same way I already hold his music publishing in my name, to protect Nathan in future against scoundrels like those who ransacked his past."

"Gets back? Gets back from where? For how long?"

"I don't know. Nathan didn't tell me that part." The smile hung heavy on Father O'Bryan's avuncular face. "I did my best for you, Daniel, believing as I do in your quest, but his decision is set in concrete. He is determined that Nat Axelrod never returns to haunt Nathan Greene."

"Then why does he write his songs in the first place? Why does he record them?"

"Can you survive without breathing?"

Father O'Bryan blew out a thick sigh, took a healthy gulp direct from the bottle, wiped his lips with the back of his hand. "Granted, Nathan's is music the world would welcome, by a true genius who deserves to come out from a self-knit shroud of bitterness and denial." His gaze drifted. "When I came upon you at Ana Maria's, unexpected, uninvited, unannounced, I saw it as a sign. As Divine providence later, when you shared your thoughts and hopes about Nathan with me."

"And maybe cut yourself in for a share of the proceeds to help with your Mondays here at Duffy's Tavern?"

"Please. Be careful with your words, Daniel."

"I'm only looking for more truth, Pat."

"That's not the way to get it." The priest was scowling at him. "The Bible informs us, *Let God be true, but every man a liar.*"

"Do the liars include you?"

"I prefer cataloging what I do under *Invention.*"

"What's the truth?"

Father O'Bryan waved him off. "The difference between lying and telling the truth is not in what we say, but in what we hear. I told you of my desire to allow you his songs, but always to be, God willing, with Nathan's approval. Nathan chose otherwise. I respect that, as I fear you now must do as well."

"I want to see him, Pat. I want to meet with Nat. He has to listen to what I say."

"A man who doesn't half listen to himself most of the time? I don't think so, Daniel."

"Nathan hears me out. If I can't change his mind, he leaves with the masters."

Father O'Bryan snatched victory from the air with a clenched fist. "Hah! So, you do have them."

"Every man a liar, Pat."

The priest gave the table a victory slap. "The Bible also says, *Let us do evil, that good may come,*" he said.

His uproarious laughter was cut short by Al the bartender, who had rushed over to tell him, "Pat, Ana Maria Alfaro? The pretty one you come in here with sometimes?"

All three caught the edge of alarm in Al's voice.

The priest said, "What about Ana Maria?"

"Somebody just called, saying to tell you there's been a shooting or something at her place. Somebody dead. Maybe more."

Father O'Bryan gently eased Patrice from the booth and slid out after her, tugged at his cassock, hurried from the bar five paces ahead of Danny and Patrice, floorboards squawking under his heavy footsteps; moving with remarkable speed and grace for a man his size. He had U-turned on Cahuenga, heading south toward Melrose, by the time Danny got to his car. Two minutes later, Danny was following in his shadow, unaware of the dirty maroon-colored Honda trailing him by three or four car lengths.

Father O'Bryan banged on Ana Maria's door, shouting to be let in, while a dark-skinned neighbor with flaring cheekbones and nervous eyes twisted her kitchen apron and explained to Danny and Patrice how she had heard a gunshot, maybe two gunshots, and phoned for the priest, certain he would know what to do.

"It's Monday, so I know where to look for him," she said. At the sound of a lock and a latch falling aside, her head bobbed appreciatively. She fled as the priest pushed open the door and stepped into the apartment.

Danny told Patrice to stay put and followed him inside.

Father O'Bryan stopped abruptly. Danny narrowly missed banging into him. He angled around his generous back to see into the living room and laughed in wonderment. How many days had it been since Ana Maria had her Colt .38 pointed at him?

She stood like a marksman, the revolver aimed at the priest, who spread his arms wide against an invisible cross. She maneuvered her frantic eyes at him, then back to Father O'Bryan, and shouted something in Spanish. The priest answered back in Spanish, his voice more urgent than hers. To Danny he said in a whisper, "Keep behind me, Daniel. Out of the line."

"Don't be a hero, Pat. She looks like she's on something," he said, barely moving his lips. His anxiety climbed from his stomach to his throat and back down.

Father O'Bryan shrugged off Danny's hold on his sleeve and closed in on her, extending his hand as if expecting to receive the revolver.

"Basta!" she said, alternating her aim between Father O'Bryan and Danny.

Father O'Bryan glanced at him reassuringly and stopped short. He appeared to be trapped by something invisible to Danny, whose view was obscured by the sofa. "Dear Lord in Heaven." The priest crossed himself and dropped down on one knee.

Danny stepped into the room.

Ana Maria aimed the revolver at him. *"Basta!"*

Recklessly, he moved closer to see what Father O'Bryan saw.

He felt his knees give and clamped down hard onto the back of the sofa to steady himself. Took a deep breath and could not make it go away. He forced the air out his nose. Repeated the process two more times. Moved on Ana Maria, determined to take the gun away from her.

Ana Maria cocked the hammer.

Danny understood by the finality of her expression that she meant to shoot him, but kept advancing. Father O'Bryan called her name. Her eyes traveled to the sound. Danny covered the last few steps swiftly. He wrenched the gun from her grip by its barrel and locked an arm around her waist in a clumsy wrestling hold.

"Basta!" he said.

Ana Maria stopped struggling and dissolved in his arms.

"Don't be mad at me, *querido,*" she said. "Please don't be mad at me." Repeating herself like a broken 78, her voice scratched and cracking with emotion. She didn't appear to be pleading with him or with Father O'Bryan before she suddenly stopped, distracted by something across the room.

Danny followed her stare to the entryway, to Brian Malloy, menace written on his face, wielding a length of lead pipe, possibly a tire iron. "Now your turn's come, Manings, you God damned asshole son of a bitch," he said through clenched teeth, his jaw pulsating at the notion. "This time we finish what's been started."

Malloy hefted the pipe like he was at home plate and ready to take a slice. His voice was harsh and his words slurred enough to reveal he'd been drinking heavily. His laugh sandblasted the interior of his throat, quit when he took note of the .38 Danny held pressed against his thigh.

Danny's hand twitched. He thrust the weapon straight out.

A noise rumbled in Malloy's throat, growing to a roar as he lurched forward.

Without hesitation, Danny aimed for Malloy's face.

Before he could get off a shot, he felt the rain of spittle advancing ahead of Malloy's kamikaze scream, the lead pipe slamming down hard on his forearm. He thought he heard the bone crack under his own loud cry. The pain was immediate and immense. He lost his grip on the .38. It flew from his hand, landed a foot or two away from the lifeless woman on the floor. Her eyes were closed, but she seemed to be staring back at him like some Raggedy Ann at rest.

Danny braced himself. He shut out the room as Malloy raised the pipe to take a second swipe. It didn't come. He opened his eyes and saw Ana Maria grappling with Malloy, who was too large, too powerful and too drunk to feel her blows raining on his chest and face. He shook his head violently, to throw off the pain radiating from his arm. Danced around Malloy, bouncing from foot to foot, fending like a wrestler, looking for a point of attack.

Malloy shoved Ana Maria away by gripping both ends of the pipe and using it as a wedge between them. Danny caught her as she stumbled backward. The force of her weight pushed them to the floor, Ana Maria almost on top of him.

Malloy advanced, shouting profanities. He gripped the lead pipe with both hands. Raised it above his head, intent on making pulp of Danny's skull. Shouted, "What happens to anybody tries to steal my bitch of a woman from me."

Danny rolled away in time. The hardwood floor echoed with the sound of hollow thunder as the pipe connected. Danny rolled in the other direction, unintentionally braking against the dead woman, enough astride her to feel the warmth pressing through her body. Father O'Bryan was on one knee on her other side, administering last rites. He gave Danny a gentle push away.

Before Malloy could strike Danny, Ana Maria screamed and jumped for him, cursing him and beating on his back. Malloy mocked her and slapped her aside. Undaunted, she wrapped her arms and her legs around his body, trying to throw him off balance.

Malloy brought his elbow back hard and smashed Ana Maria's nose into her face, causing a geyser of blood. He did it a second time, and her left cheekbone made a splintering noise and sank out of sight. Her left eye hung like jelly on the lip of a jar. She relaxed her hold and fell to the floor, paralyzed with surprise. Malloy brought down the bat on her head, cracking it like a dry walnut.

Danny clambered to his feet. His arm felt useless. He lunged at Malloy, his arms chest high in front of him, horizontal to the floor. Malloy swung the pipe and caught him in the rib cage. There was a sound like the snap of a cigarette lighter. Danny made a howling noise. He dropped his arms and pressed his hands where the pipe had struck. Malloy made a backhanded swing and connected with Danny's neck. Danny charged him once more. He took a blow in the stomach and reeled backward into the dining room. He tripped over a chair and fell sprawling, pulled himself up and rushed Malloy. The pipe came within a fraction of connecting with his head.

Malloy was preparing to swing again when a gunshot exploded.

The bullet tore into Malloy's stomach and lifted him four or five inches off the floor. He made an abortive flight sideways, ended when he bounced face forward against the wall fronting the street and smacked into an inexpensive, ornately framed color lithograph of Jesus. Two more feet to the left and he would have crashed through the window to the sidewalk.

Malloy used the wall as a brace to push himself away, twisted around to look into the room, his face fractured by glass from the frame and bleeding freckles. He reached up for a bus strap with one hand, made a whimper of disappointment before he staggered forward and hit the ground face first.

Not more than thirty seconds had elapsed since his original charge at Danny.

Danny saw Father O'Bryan meditating over the .38 he had just used to kill Malloy.

He answered Danny's stare with a modest shrug of condolence and recited, "Answer a fool according to his folly." He transferred the weapon to his left hand and rose to his feet in a series of motions. He dropped his eyelids and his chins fell onto his chest. He made the sign of the cross and moved his lips in silent prayer.

Danny crossed to Ana Maria.

She was staring listlessly at the ceiling with her one good eye, whimpering and talking to herself, garbling the words that weren't choking her. Her complexion was bad and the coldness of her skin contradicted the tiny bubbles of sweat glistening on her forehead and upper lip. Blood trickled over a corner of her mouth and down her neck.

Danny leaned closer, hoping to hear her better.

He recognized the name *Nathan.*

Ana Maria reached for his face and kept her hand there, begging in a voice too low to be a whisper, "Don't be mad at me, okay?"

Danny looked anxiously at Father O'Bryan, who had squatted alongside Malloy to ponder the lifeless body painting a thick pool of blood on Ana Maria's clean floor. He pressed his lips to her ear. "Okay," Danny said, fearing if he said more she would know it was not Nat's voice.

Ana Maria forced a smile. "I love you, Nathan."

"I love you."

"All along I knew it, *querido.*" The wheeze in her chest started to rattle. "Always I heard the truth in your songs." She was unable to contain an ugly cough.

Father O'Bryan was beside her now, tearfully administering last rites.

Ana Maria let a sigh escape. Her mouth made a small turn upward. Her body gave a series of signals. Her hand slid off Danny's cheek and dropped onto her torso. Father O'Bryan was reciting: "Through this holy anointing and His most loving mercy, may the Lord assist you by the grace of the Holy Spirit, so that freed from your sins He may save you and in His goodness raise you up."

A police siren sounded in the distance.

The commotion had been reported.

Father O'Bryan broke his concentration to rush to the window and pull down the shade. He secured it by wrapping the pull ring around a painted nail in the sash. "We don't have much time," he said, already in motion. He carried the .38 to the dead woman by the sofa and worked her fingers around the handle, into a shooter's grip. "We'll leave it for the police to try and sort out . . . God forbid." He made the sign of the cross. "If God be for us, who can be against us?"

Patrice was struggling to stay on her feet by the entryway, using the wall for support, a trickle of blood sliding down the side of her face from her temple. Danny rushed over, engulfed her in his arms. He put a finger to her chin and moved her face up enough for him to reach her mouth with his own for hardly more than a hummingbird's kiss that sent a shock wave of relief through his system and lit a smile in her eyes.

Father O'Bryan urged them out the door and led them down the poorly lit hallway to the back stairs. They had turned the corner and were out of sight as the sound of cops and neighbors clattering to Ana Maria's door grew louder.

They managed on foot to the priest's church, arriving about forty minutes later, red-faced, ragged and unsettled by the specter of what they'd been through, Patrice the most shaken. Father O'Bryan asked to be excused briefly and left the vestry for the chapel, to light candles and pray for Ana Maria, Laurent and Brian Malloy; and, he confessed, insert some propaganda on his own behalf with Lord Jesus.

While Patrice stalked the four walls, Danny cleared sitting space more comfortable than the milk cartons they had been using by pushing aside a collection of packing cases. He settled next to her, held her close and saw for the first time that somewhere along the way she'd bitten her lip hard enough to draw blood. He painted the blood away with an index finger and kissed the open wound. That made her cry louder than the sobbing she'd been unable to control.

"It's my fault, my fault," she said, as if in litany to the dead. "Because of me, Danny. Because of me. Brian's dead because of me, and so is that poor woman."

"He's dead because of who he is and what he tried doing to us today, Patty."

"Brian was good to me. Why I loved him."

"Stop this. *Good* to you? You're talking about loving someone who never existed. Less than an hour ago Brian Malloy tried to kill you. He came close to succeeding, except probably for being in too much of a hurry to get at me."

Patrice put her hand to her temple, now covered by Band-Aids Father O'Bryan had pulled from a filing cabinet, and eased out a moan. "He would not have killed me, Danny. He loved me and I loved him. Not the way I love you, but I did. Should I deny it only because Brian is dead?"

"He beat you and raped you, murdered your unborn child, and you're defending him?"

Patrice jerked away from Danny. She moved across the room and settled against a crate tall enough to hold a refrigerator, arms folded tightly across her breasts. "You know why I kept going back to him?" she said. "I kept going back because, whenever I left, my loneliness became greater than my fear of Brian. You do it enough times, the pain and the violence get entwined in your mind with love. You make excuses—"

"Like you're doing now."

"You make excuses because you have nowhere else to go. Do you understand that? Can you?"

"You're with me now."

"Will you always be there, though? Will you, Lone Ranger?"

The best Danny could do was give her an answer without a guarantee. Patrice read him correctly. A corner of her mouth encroached on her cheek. "Brian was always there," she said, "and now he's gone."

"Let's hold off on this for now."

Patrice played her hands around her face like a washcloth and forced out a tension yawn. "Fine," she said, her voice as flat as her gaze. "I'm not running anywhere, *Kemo Sabe.*"

"I'd come find you if you did," he said.

Father O'Bryan stepped back into the vestry holding up an envelope.

"A letter I was expecting from Nathan," the priest said. "Delivered while I was away and in the keeping of Old Galindo Montalban. It gives me full power of attorney over all of Nathan's affairs. Everything, not only his songs. Do you know what that means?"

Danny studied the intent on Father O'Bryan's face. "You think it means you can legally come after the masters now."

"In accordance with Nathan's wishes."

"Without asking Nathan to meet with me."

"Not the way I'd wish it, but it is my obligation," Father O'Bryan said. He grimaced and shrugged his shoulders, but Danny couldn't miss the light of triumph in the priest's eyes as he stuffed the envelope in a cassock pocket and suggested, "We can now arrange for their orderly transfer, Daniel."

"I think not," Danny said. Father O'Bryan's eyebrows flinched. He threw Danny a questioning look. Danny said, "With your power of attorney, you'll grant me an exclusive on all Nat's songs and all rights to the master tapes."

"No can do, Daniel, and you know it."

"You can't, Pat, but you can and you will."

"Or?"

"Or I tell the police who really shot and killed Brian Malloy."

The priest studied him for the flaw. With a smile that claimed victory, he said, "Blame a poor put-upon parish priest and expect them to believe you over my own humble protestations, no evidence to the contrary? You're smarter than that, Daniel."

"Danny won't have to tell them," Patrice said. She moved to Danny's side and gripped his hands. "I will, Father."

Chapter 25

Rancho Musico resembled a cement block warehouse in depressing shades of brown and gray, but in fact was a state-of-the-art technological marvel without equal, where all the heavies came to record, sometimes even the heaviest of the heavies reduced to begging for studio time. The studio Rufus Hardaway cleared for Patrice looked large enough to hold the LA Phil and the Boston Pops, and he'd pulled in Swingin' Sammy Gold to produce her, Swingin' Sammy having produced Nat Axlerod in the old days and more Gold and Platinum albums than anyone currently working the mainstream. He was bald under his ten-gallon Stetson and wore the rest of his hair princess-in-the-tower style to just below the diamond-studded belt of his Bijan jeans.

Jimmy Slyde had settled in as engineer, over some early challenges from Mason Weems, who surrendered to Danny's insistence that he be rewarded for bootlegging Nat Axelrod's music out of the Nam on the cassette that brought them together and put them in business. There was a stronger reason than that, of course.

Slyde had worked the booth alongside Nat at the Nam.

He knew the new songs backward and forward, possibly better than Nat himself.

He'd proven it since the first prep sessions at Rancho Musico, enough to impress Rufus and have him talking about moving Slyde onto the board for Funky Miss Clunky, maybe even

Death Vader himself, if the Patrice Malloy sessions brought glory, Gold and Platinum to Shoe Records.

Those possibilities and either a natural high or the occasional snort kept Slyde's game major league as Nat's masters were digitized, then broken down and restripped; one track for each instrument, one for Nat's vocals, one for Patrice's vocals, one for the backup vocalists used to sweeten some of the songs; several tracks for the sampling, guitar licks and phrases from old Nat Axelrod albums taken to flesh out and enhance the new cuts.

So far, Nat's vocals were not being utilized, except as guide tracks for Patrice, spilling into her headphones on her vocal takes, especially five or six songs that seemed ideal for duets. Danny was as sold on the vocals as he was on the guitar work. Over the past ten years Nat's voice had taken on a greater depth and maturity. He was living his lyrics as never before, interpreting every word with the same mastery as Sinatra.

The sound on the masters was ragged.

The Nam, after all, was no Rancho Musico.

But the Rancho Musico magic would work as well with Nat's voice as with his guitar, stretched and molded by the computer wherever necessary.

The early taste Swingin' Sammy gave them astounded everyone after the first rough sample mixes were assembled, the levels averaged and the system punched into overdrive by Slyde. They were a revelation with Nat's vocals and a stone-cold out-of-the-park smash when Patrice chimed in from the recording floor on her solo or to make it a duet.

After the final fade, the sonic boom speakers gurgling with the sizzle of surface noise, Swingin' Sammy, tapping his custom alligator boots on the terra-cotta floor to the melody still running in his head, said, "People, I have frigging chills stretching from my ass to my armpits. Patrice Malloy is a frigging big-timer, no matter what, with Nat's songs and with her own. We take our best shots for the album and then the grooves take over, man."

A couple days into the sessions, a Friday, Patrice called from the studio floor, "Hello, remember me?"

Danny pressed the com button. "Swingin' Sammy and Slyde are adjusting some sound levels, Patty. Technical stuff. The last take was a gimme, but they want one more for protection."

"Fine with me," she said, and clamped the softball-sized earphones back on.

"She was popping all over the place on the last one," Slyde said to no one in particular. "No need for her to know that shit, though."

Joe Wunsch, stretched out on the lounger, legs crossed and eyes examining outer space, said, "Somebody maybe bring down the fucking lights. She does better when she got the fucking dark licking at her chops."

Swingin' Sammy nodded and adjusted the dimmer switch. The studio and the booth were swamped by a darkness broken only by board lights and the light on Patrice's music stand, which reflected onto her face like a key spot.

Her eyes were slits of intensity.

Her head bobbed to the click track in anticipation of her cue.

Nat's music track filled the booth with "Vegas on a Dime," an up-tempo tune that had everyone foot-tapping and head-bobbing. Swingin' Sammy had his own timepiece, a popping sound he made with his lips in synch with his boot.

"Another gimme," Slyde cooed into the com afterward. "Patty, you're my voice of choice, baby."

Patrice answered with a *baloney* wave.

There was more easy banter while Slyde and Swingin' Sammy changed reels and reset the board. Pee breaks. A Rancho Musico staffer with a face full of earrings and hair clusters the color of rejected rainbow replaced the coffee and tea urns and brought in fresh platters of fruit and assorted sandwiches, as well as an Egg McMuffin and a large sack of fries Joe had put on special order.

The next song was a simple melody that Nat had defined with an acoustic guitar, no other musical instrument, titled "Chalky's Song." The lyrics were a love poem from a father to a long-lost daughter that managed to choke up Danny every time he heard it.

Patrice's tears translated into a break in her voice that added an indefinable poignancy to "Chalky's Song." She sustained the sound and the mood through three takes. It was still there an hour later, when the studio went dark for the most complex of Nat's ballads, "Goodbye, Again."

"Goodbye, Again" was also a love song. Its haunting lyrics worked at counterpoint to a deceptive melody that defied categorization, disguising a longing and a loneliness that Danny caught at once, the first time he heard the song; as defiantly original and groundbreaking as the pick of the Beatles' litter, Brian Wilson's astonishing "Good Vibrations," and Don McLean's remarkable "American Pie"—straight on up to, through and beyond the gangsta rap revolution.

Danny had no trouble tracking Nat Axelrod's life inside "Goodbye, Again," but it was about far more than Nat Axelrod's life. "Goodbye, Again" was about life itself, as revealing as open-heart surgery.

Patrice wasn't satisfied after the first take. She waved at the booth and wondered into the mike, "You think I could try one more, Jimmy?"

Slyde said, "Everyone in here thinking you got it dead to rights already, Patty. Never no need to spend the tape."

"I think a phrase slipped past me in a majorly way, Jimmy,

and there's one other that could stand more shading."

Before Slyde could debate her opinion, someone said, "The lady is right, Jimmy."

"Say wha'?" Slyde said, wheeling around in his captain's chair. "Praise shit!" he said. "It's the main man."

Danny, Joe and Swingin' Sammy shifted their attention.

Slyde leaped to his feet, saluted deftly, and said, "How long you been lurking back there, my man?"

Nathan said, "Long enough, Jimmy." He was hanging immediately inside the door, by the service counter, peeling a banana. Father O'Bryan was beside him taking warmth from a tall cup of coffee.

A smile nicked the edges of Danny's mouth.

"Hello, Nat," he said.

"Hello, Danny."

"Long time no see."

"Long time."

"Far fucking out!" Joe announced to the world, shaking a victory fist.

Danny and Nat signaled they wanted time alone and moved from the booth to Rancho Musico's rec room, a museum of lavishly framed Platinum and Gold records. It was deserted, except for a few gaudily dressed people at the computerized pinball machines, two finishing a game of billiards and a couple gangsta types lingering at the microwave, handing off a joint while waiting for the popcorn to finish popping. They settled at a lonely table in the empty lounge area that afforded them relative privacy.

"I'm sorry about Ana Maria," Danny said.

"Yeah." Nat stared into his eyes, showing nothing. He turned away, focused on the wall-mounted TV across the room. It was turned to MTV, the sound too low to carry on top of the house system.

Danny said, "I met her before she was—I met her . . . She was quite lovely and . . . I went to her funeral Mass with—" He couldn't finish a thought.

"Yeah," Nat said, and shrugged.

"Father Pat says she was good for you."

"Better than I was for Ana Maria."

"Did you love her, Nat?"

"I think maybe. In my head. My heart's still somewhere else. There's a song on the tapes that explains it."

" 'Querido.' "

"Yeah."

"It's still Mae Jean Minter, isn't it?"

"Heidemann. Mae Jean Heidemann. Christ, that priest has a big mouth."

"You also knew the dead woman, the journalist?"

"About as well as you knew the son of a bitch who got what he deserved, your singer's husband. She tracked me down to do a story. She got killed first. What some writers won't do for a story."

"She called me, but we never connected."

"You could've told her all the sordid details if she got you to open up."

"I don't think so. Not my style, spilling guts."

"I never thought blackmail was your style, either, Danny. Would you have gone to the cops and ratted out Pat O'Bryan if he didn't green-light you on the tapes or if I was a no-show?"

Danny let him see he had no intention of answering a careless question that did not need to be asked.

Nat looked different, and not only because he was ten years older. The movie star nose he'd once been so proud of had been broken and hung slightly off center. His right cheek had a hollow spot and a permanent purplish bruise. His eyes seemed to measure life in shades of gray even when he forced a smile.

Age lines and other emblems of time were on Nat's face, along with a few small scars Danny didn't remember, except for the one hiding inside his right eyebrow, where Danny had accidentally caught him in a game of stickball, on a backward swing before Nat crouched into his catcher's position.

"Those were the days," he said, unaware he'd spoken out loud.

Nat flashed a glint of history, as if he understood where Danny's mind had visited. He said, "Sometimes I think I'd like to go back, but not that far."

"Maybe to the day I signed you at Decade?"

"Maybe the day you sat me down after you tried peddling our first tape and couldn't get past the shoeshine boys outside the record company parking lots." Danny cracked a smile. "I told you not to worry. I was certain it wouldn't take you any time at all to work your way up past the security guy at the main gate."

They laughed, Nat too much and too loud.

"We were really something, Nat."

"Street is what. When you're street, you learn fast how to survive anything, especially with an older kid like you taking me by the hand—"

The word stopped him.

Danny realized Nat had been sitting all this time with his hands buried in the pockets of his bomber jacket. Nat caught him staring. After a bolt of hesitation, he pulled them out and held them up for Danny to see.

His hands were a horror worse than Father O'Bryan's description. It gave reality to every image he had of the kid growing up, little Nattie Greene, and the man and rock-and-roll myth he became as Nat Axelrod.

Tears welled in Danny's eyes.

Nat shook his head and returned his hands to the pockets. "Save them for the next four-alarm, Danny. This fire was put out a long time ago."

"Is that why you shut me out back then, without explanation, when I couldn't get through to you anymore and finally learned from the authorities, from Ben Hubbard, that you'd done it to everyone? Your hands?" Nat looked at him with expressionless eyes. "Damn it, Nattie. Damn it to hell. Tell me. Close the book on the question."

"For my own personal reasons I shut down my old life, Danny. That included you. It was before this happened." He aimed his chin at one pocket, then the other. "In your case, there was a second reason."

"Do I get to hear it?"

Nat mustered the words. "You were going through your own shit then," he said. "Vickie, God rest her soul. Those fine boys and Dory disintegrating, taken from you." He strangled on a memory. "I got wind you fell back onto coke and some other shit, yet all the while you were strangling over my doctor and lawyer bills and you were out on your ass at Decade because of that backstabbing, bullshit son of a bitch Harry Drummond."

"Those were my choices."

"I had my own choices. I chose to make it possible for Danny Manings to put himself and his family in front of loyalty to a friend."

"We were like brothers. I could have handled both."

"Where? In your wildest snowstorm on the great rock candy mountain? I was trapped where I was, in the joint, Danny, but I could liberate you. Cut you slack so you could get your own house back in order. It appears to me like it worked out fine."

His expression appealed for understanding.

Danny said, "I had help along the way."

"I learned how to survive without it." He brought his hands to the table and began tapping out a tune, perhaps absentmindedly.

Danny forced a cough to clear his throat. "We did it together once before. The time's right for us to do it again. Work on the album with us." Nat's body drifted forward and back. He kept Danny locked in his vision, giving away nothing. "I won't beg, if that's what you're after, Nattie."

"That's not what I'm after."

Before he could say more, Rufus Hardaway swept into the rec room, trailed by a more casual Mason Weems, and screamed at the ceiling: "As I live and breathe, if it ain't Nat the Axe, my old classmate hisself from Indiana P.U."

"Hello, Rufus," Nat said.

Danny said, "You know each other?"

Nat said, "Hasn't Rufus mentioned that? Rufus is the man who stole my hands."

Danny turned to ice.

CHAPTER 26

"Don't y'all bother getting up," Rufus said. He pushed over a chair and joined Nathan and Danny at the table. "C'mon, Mason, you also in on this." Mason poured himself a cup of coffee and maneuvered a chair next to him.

Rufus said, "You got any bad in mind, Nat the Axe, tell me now, bro." He adjusted his bulk. His dark, menacing eyes defied the dance in his mellow voice and mouthful of piano keys.

There was a time years ago Nathan would have relished this confrontation, prepared for it, played out an old, recurring fantasy that got him through Rufus Hardaway's torment and torture, the ordeal of one hospital stay after another after Rufus and his goon platoon finished with him.

How many times?

Six?

Seven?

Until Chalky Ruggles told Rufus *Enough!* and threatened an all-out war.

Nathan lost the reality of pain before he lost count, but not the desire for revenge, until—

How many years later?

When the life Rufus took from him became as meaningless as a politician's promise, and a worse pain came from the mere act of surviving one day at a time.

"What went down between us is history, Rufus."

"Dig, Nat the Axe. Was expecting to hear them words from

you," Rufus said, nodding vigorously, adjusting the Nehru collar of his black silk caftan. "It were never about you and me, bro, only what goes down in the joint whenever any Mr. Thinker Man go in front a the system. Now, us in a prideful position to make beautiful music together, no one more surprised'n me how I come to be so major in this business like you onc't was."

"Still being the boss, Rufus."

"You don't abuse it, you don't lose it. Like allus before, I save my own abuse for the trim in *Hustler.*" He managed to glimmer a bigger smile. "Listen up," he said, chest puffed out with a need to continue bragging. "I come out a the joint this last time and seen how fast other brothers was making piles of green calling music what we used to call hanging out on a streetlamp. Got me talking to myself and figuring why shouldn't I pick up the beat? From dealing to rap just trading in one kind a shit for another, dig? A whole lot safer on these weary bones. Me and my homies, we done us some smart negotiating, and where I gots myself Thinker Mans who didn't see it my way—putty, putty—I lost them on the highway. You unnerstand?"

Nathan showed him he did.

Rufus winked.

"Danger Funk Records, it come like uncut treasure straight from the box, same as Mason here, who too legit for his own good, but I forgives him that all a the time. Only help me to look sweeter'n my mama's milk and some of it be rubbing off. The good life keep up like this, next thing you know I gonna be born again; find me my own cow what can drop some fine children; live happily ever after." He raised a power fist. "Amen, bro. Amen."

"Jesus, you can be a longwinded fuck sometimes," Mason Weems said. He finished blowing on his coffee, took a modest swallow and said, "Danny, did you have your nice little talk with your friend here?"

Gleaning Danny's reluctance to answer, Mason put the question to Nathan.

Nathan treated his turn like a nap.

Rufus caught on at once. "Don't tell me you still bein' that same old foolish Mr. Thinker Man like before, bro."

"A different Mr. Thinker Man, Rufus."

"Don't tell me there you go disrespecting me already. You tell Nat the Axe what going down with us, Danny?"

Danny said, "Nat understands everything. He would rather not take part in the sessions. I vote we respect his wishes and leave him off the album."

"You think that, you not this hot as a whore's cunt salesman Mason be telling me about," Rufus said, and made a light show of his anger.

Mason said, "Relax, Rufus." He found a half-finished Havana in a jacket pocket. Asked, "Mind if I smoke?" Lit up without waiting for answers. Announced, "You're outvoted, Danny."

Danny said, "If Nat doesn't want to do it, what kind of a performance would we get out of him? We're better off with just Patrice."

Mason threw a hand toward Danny and let two clouds of smoke drift upward from the corners of his mouth. "Nat, there's nothing personal in this. I've respected you as an artist, same as Rufus tells me he came to respect you while you were away."

Rufus said, "Bad as the damage ever got, he never onc't give them screws a name, for any time we come after him. Why there ain't no open book between us now . . . What that jive ass you give us times we come for you, bro?"

"Hob nit keyn moyre vendu host niy keyn ander breyre."

"Yeah, uh-huh, that *hob nit* shit."

"Don't be afraid when you have no other choice."

Mason said, "Danny made a valid point, Nat, but I want you to know something. You walk on us, we'll go with electronics for the work tracks on your masters and bring in a voice to plug the hole notes, so you're on the album whether you're on the album or not. You think about suing, the album will be history by the time the case is in front of a judge. Even if you win, any profits you stood to make—supposing the best accountant in the world could find them—would be going to pay off the lawyers."

Rufus said, "Also supposing you survives on the highway that long."

Danny said, "Rufus, God damn it. Any more talk like that and I'm out of here with Nat."

Nat smiled inwardly, seeing again the big kid who had never let the bullies get too close to little Nattie Greene. He flashed Danny an admiring look.

Mason said, "Tone it down, Rufus." He pushed his hair back over his ears, retrieved his cigar from the ashtray and parked it in a corner of his mouth, trying to play tough, a role that did not really appear to suit him. "So, what's it going to be, Nat?"

Nathan said, "I apologize. Danny mistakenly gave you the wrong impression." He pushed a smile at the three of them. "I'll be happy to work on the album."

Danny's expression accelerated from confused to swallowed relief. Mason breezed out a victory smoke signal. Rufus leaded back, his head askance, trying to read a con's truth into what he'd heard.

Nathan said, "There are a few terms and conditions."

Rufus said, "I done a few terms awreddy, bro, an' delighted at sharing the next one with you. Let's move on to them terms and conditions a yours."

"Maybe you and I can take a stroll, Rufus? The two of us?"

Rufus looked at him like he might be holding the playing cards and all four aces up his sleeve. "Counterclockwise, you like it, bro, like old times on the exercise yard, but you looking for a number to be owed you, maybe I gots a better one back atchoo—somethin' I been thinking 'bout this here girl Patrice."

It didn't take long, less than ten minutes, for them to come to terms on a spit shake, both swearing allegiance to the honor code of the joint that held an integrity missing in the free world.

"You trusts me then, bro?" Rufus said, softening his tough-as-nails manner.

"Distrust, Rufus, the second rule of survival."

"What's the first rule?"

"I don't know," Nathan said. "Nobody's ever trusted me with the first rule."

It was an easy laugh for both of them.

Nathan completed the last of his vocals with Patrice over the weekend. He audited and approved the playback from the booth and did some sequence shuffling of the album cuts with Swingin' Sammy and Jimmy Slyde.

Nothing of significance was left that needed his attention.

He had lived up to his end of the deal.

Now it would be Rufus Hardaway's turn to make good.

When Danny locked him in a congratulatory basketball embrace, he fought the urge to tell him what the look in Danny's eyes suggested he might already suspect:

Their reunion was over.

They would never see one another again.

Dr. Gautier seemed to sense as much for himself last week, but said nothing, when they met on the Long Beach dock and rode the Neptune Society boat to a quiet part of the ocean. The water was extraordinarily blue, silent as a beggar's wish and full of a perfume that lingered long after they had said a few words about Laurent before scattering her ashes over the calm surface while the sun sent echoes of heat rising to the clouds.

"She wouldn't want it, but she wasn't always so right, that girl," the doctor said, before he recited a prayer in Yiddish and repeated it in English for Nathan: *May he swallow up death forever and may Hashem, the God, wipe away tears from every face and remove the scorn of His people from throughout the world, for Hashem has spoken . . .*

"I would have kept her ashes at the cabin for company," Dr. Gautier said, "only I know how Lorraine loved the sea, maybe even more than she loved you, Nathan."

Nathan, with no answer that might satisfy the doctor, said, "It's only rock and roll, Dr. Gautier."

The doctor gripped the railing as the craft leaned into a turn for port, and reflected: "In time it might have been a symphony."

After docking, they went to the Anne Frank Home for a brief meeting with Rabbi Cohen, the home's executive director.

The rabbi dropped an elbow on the table and rested his bearded chin in the palm while he examined the cashier's check for thirty thousand dollars made out to cash and endorsed over to the home.

"For Sam and Bertha Mendelssohn," Nathan said.

"All praise to Hashem," the rabbi said.

"And maybe a little for Laurent Connart?" Nathan said.

The next day, Thursday, he stayed out of sight at the church service for Ana Maria, and skipped the caravan to Boyle Heights, where she was buried by members of her family in a dress he had bought for her on her birthday, a cassette of his song, "Querido," wrapped inside the lace handkerchief she'd coveted in her gloved hands.

He had wanted to go, but Father O'Bryan insisted it was dangerous. Someone might point him out to the police, who were searching for anything and anyone connected to the three deaths the media had labeled "The Love Connection Murders."

Mid-afternoon on Monday, an anxious Jimmy Slyde phoned the Church of the Blessed Bonaventure, where Nathan was staying in an area of the basement converted into a temporary bedroom. Father O'Bryan expressed puzzlement, telling Slyde he assumed Nathan, as usual, had been dropped off at Rancho Musico by Old Galindo.

He put Slyde on hold for several minutes, returned to report Old Galindo said he gave up waiting for Nathan after an hour. More curious than that, the priest said, checking just now, he'd discovered all of Nathan's belongings gone, as if Nathan had never been there in the first place.

He promised Slyde he'd call the minute he knew anything more.

Hanging up, he turned to Nathan, smiled and gave him a hearty double thumbs-up.

"So what's another lie among friends?" Father O'Bryan said.

Nathan said, "How about the truth?"

"And what's the truth, Nathan?"

Nathan's gaze circled the vestry before he decided. "Either what we make of it or a lie."

The priest looked into his wineglass. "Whatever it is, how is it you could keep longing after her, the girl responsible for causing you so much pain and misery in your life?"

Nathan shrugged. "Maybe Mae Jean had the answer for both of us."

Father O'Bryan emptied the glass. "God constantly warns us about the fortunes and follies of men who confuse the pot of gold for the rainbow."

"Where does it say that in the Bible, Pat?"

"Where I want it to."

Nathan paid him an appreciative smile and grunted away the notion. "After I'm gone, I'm counting on you for the truth. Anything else and I'll come back to haunt you."

"I'll miss you, you know? I'll pray for you, too."

Nathan stepped outside the church gripping the new suitcase

that was a goodbye gift from Father O'Bryan and the Blaupunkt *bandidos,* packed with the pillowcase holding his life, except for pieces he was leaving behind. Old Galindo was waiting for him in his late-model lowrider, the motor running. They drove to Union Station in the usual dullness of a Los Angeles Monday, the sun imprisoned by banks of wandering clouds.

Nathan exchanged farewells with Old Galindo and angled inside the terminal, admiring the magnificent arched windows and majestic bell tower of the building, whose stylish Rancho-Moderne architecture reminded him of a faded picture postcard, and tried to estimate the height of four skinny palm trees that guarded the central doors and danced casually in a calming breeze. He became part of the constant echo of several hundred people strolling to and from the Amtrak passenger loading docks, as well as the hollow shrieks and bouncing cries of youngsters lost in curious surroundings.

A panhandler in three layers of mismatched clothing stepped from nowhere, stretched his calloused hand and gave Nathan a stare he recognized and knew well. Nathan fished a twenty-dollar bill from his pocket, from his share of the last Blaupunkt *bandido* foray, and handed it over.

"God bless you," the panhandler said, in a voice colored by years of damage.

"That'll be the day," Nathan said.

* * * * *

Fifteen Months Later

* * * * *

Chapter 27

Nathan, calling himself Nat Greenberg now, fumbled with his third Bud of the evening at Rattlesnake Annie's bar on East Exchange in Fort Worth. He caught Bunchie the bartender, who looked like the pit bull sleeping on the floor alongside the cash register, spying on his hands again. He placed them on the counter to give the old geezer a better look and forced a grin urging him to turn up the volume on the TV.

Bunchie obliged the request, sank his eyes into the dishwater and pretended to be busy with a load of dirties as the Grammy Awards audience at the Shrine Auditorium in Los Angeles cheered the introduction of Patrice Malloy and the first notes of "Goodbye, Again," the fifth and final song nominated for Record of the Year honors.

Wearing a shimmering blue velvet strapless gown as elegant as her cascading hairdo, she entered with a certain majesty from the wings as the full orchestra launched into the melody. A few bars later, Neil Diamond joined her, substituting for the voice on the album that had carried the haunting duet to the top of the charts for twenty-two weeks. They won a standing ovation.

Patrice was back on stage minutes later, revealed as the year's Best Pop Vocalist—Female, for "Querido," another song from her debut album. She dedicated the Grammy to the memory of Ana Maria Alfaro on behalf of the composer, Nathan Greene, whose absence she explained away with the customary *Unable to be with us tonight,* as Babyface had done earlier revealing Nathan as Best Pop Vocal—Male winner for "Chalky's Song."

The honors came throughout the evening.

Patrice and Nathan tied as Best New Artists for their duet on "Goodbye, Again."

"Goodbye, Again" was honored as Song of the Year.

The engineering Grammy went to Jimmy Slyde, Swingin' Sammy Gold and Nathan Greene.

Nathan Greene was named for Best Album Arrangement, the Grammy accepted in his absence by the album's coproducer, Danny Manings.

Bono said something stuffed with Gaelic dignity, then made a game of opening the envelope and trying to decipher the Album of the Year winner. He deadpanned, "Fucking *'Goodbye, Again,'* " and struck a delectable grin.

In the audience, Danny's face disappeared between the lips of Patrice and Joe Wunsch. The gorilla arms that embraced him from behind belonged to Father O'Bryan, his teeth a mile long.

Patrice tripped over a cameraman dashing up the carpeted steps to the stage. Waved the new Grammy like it was her first, hid an eye behind its golden horn and set her mouth agape, as if viewing a kaleidoscope full of childhood dreams.

In the bar, a trucker making cheap grabs at the woman sharing his table told Nat and the other customers, "I had to run out and buy that damn album for my lady, or she was threatening to cut me off at the Little Big Horn."

Another customer pulled his nose out of a double rye long enough to insist, "You know what I think? I think maybe all them fucking awards shows is rigged."

Nat looked across to him. "Life is rigged," he said, and turned his attention back to the TV screen.

Patrice was halfway back to her seat, still acknowledging the applause, when Elton John and Aretha Franklin were revealed behind a majestic curtain laced with a snowfall of glittering bulbs. Elton was relaxed in a Disney cartoon costume and enough makeup for the entire *Folies Bergére* chorus at the Trop in Vegas and Aretha was having trouble with her cue cards as they hurried through the five nominations for Record of the Year, the final prize of the evening, but their duet on the winner's title was note perfect:

"Goodbye, Again!"

Patrice boogied on a dime, left a trail of congratulatory kisses heading back for the stage, joined by Danny, Joe, Mason Weems, Father O'Bryan, Jimmy Slyde, and Swingin' Sammy Gold, all in advanced stages of terminal exhilaration. Only Rufus Hardaway stuck to his seat in the VIP section, maintaining the illusion of no ties with Shoe Records.

While Patrice played cat's cradle with her eyes, Danny wore the victory like a brass band. Gripping his armload of Grammys, he used his free hand to point out the people cheering him by name and signaling with victory fists.

"It's good to be back," he said, and the audience roared—

Except for Harry Drummond.

A camera caught Drummond rising in his third-row aisle seat contorting his red-flushed faced, blue veins crackling at the temples as he brushed aside a few anxious ushers in ball gowns and tuxes and stormed out of the auditorium.

Danny took Patrice by the hand and appeared to search the farthest reaches of the Shrine, as if straining to locate some shadowy presence, the way children anticipate traveling dots on the horizon. His mouth moved with little twitches of anticipation.

Sorry, Danny, Nat said to himself. *Nathan Greene is as dead as Nat Axelrod now.*

Danny turned to the camera lens and seemed to be looking Nat squarely in the eyes, talking directly to him, telling him everything was all right with the world.

Nat shook his head. "It's only rock and roll, Danny. Only rock and roll."

Chapter 28

Two days after the Grammy Awards, a limo had Danny and Patrice at Indiana State Prison by noon. Twenty minutes later, they were in the visitors' area, wearing earphones and staring through the bulletproof plexi at Chalky Ruggles, a small, bent man with a feisty air.

"So, who are you people?" Chalky said, his distorted voice rotted by age and ill use. "I don't get much company these days."

Danny said, "Friends of Nathan Greene."

"Who the hell?"

"Nat Axelrod."

Chalky hesitated until the name got past the haze of memory and sank in. "A good kid passing through," he said, smiling as more history returned. "Thought too much and cranked out trouble, but standup all the way." More reflection. "Yeah, rock and roll. He wrote me music for a song."

" 'Chalky's Song.' "

"Yeah, right. 'Chalky's Song.' How you come to know that?"

Danny explained about the Grammy Awards and, on a quiet cue, Patrice lifted a statuette from her duffel bag and held it up for Chalky to see.

Chalky's eyebrows went up and he made a face that meant *Not bad looking.* "So what's the punch line?" he said.

Danny said, "When we were in the recording studio, Nat said, if he won this Grammy for 'Chalky's Song,' he wanted you to have it. Bring it to you and say it's for a number he owes you that's long past due."

"The guards will deliver it to you later," Patrice said.

Chalky's head inched left and right. "The kid don't owe me as much as I owe him," he said, studying Patrice's face. "What's your connection?"

"I'm a singer, too. I had some songs on the album with Nat." She dipped into the duffel, pulled out a *"Goodbye, Again" CD* and pressed it against the plexi. "This also is for you. Your song is on it, 'Chalky's Song,' and some others."

"Sure, great," Chalky said, and held up two thumbs. "Nice picture," he said, looking from the picture to Patrice several times. "Patrice, is it? Patrice Malloy?"

What appeared to be confusion covered his face, followed by what looked to be another direct hit on his memory. "I once know'd somebody name of Malloy," he said.

"It's not that uncommon a name."

Chalky turned his palms to the ceiling. "Whatever," he said. He pressed closer to the plexi. Stared hard at her.

Danny sensed tension building in Patrice. He grasped her hand.

With a wink, she let him know she was fine, turned back to Chalky with a glistening smile.

Chalky urged a grin onto his face. "She smiled like you, a little. Looked a little like you, this Malloy babe I knew." Patrice didn't know how to respond, so kept her smile intact. "Yeah," Chalky said, eyes running away, "not an uncommon name," and laughed as if he had just heard the best joke of his life. "You like it, Patrice? My song? 'Chalky's Song'?"

"I love it, Chalky. Your words are so absolutely beautiful. They remind me of lyrics by Irving Berlin. I mean that as a compliment."

Chalky checked his nails. "Irving's been my guy always."

Patrice looked at him curiously. "Nat told me you wrote your song for your daughter."

"Yeah." Awkward silence until, "Did he say nothing else to youse?"

"Only that you loved your daughter very much."

"Still do," Chalky said, full of melancholy. He ducked his head, scratched itches off his cheeks with a liver-stained hand.

"I never knew my own father," Patrice said.

"Uh-huh."

"But a lot of times, especially growing up, I thought about him. I wondered where he was and what he was like. Why he ever left me. Now I can add to that a wish, that once in his life my daddy thought enough about me to write a song like the song you wrote for your daughter."

Chalky coughed up phlegm, wiped it off on his blouse. After a moment, exploding with laughter, he said, "I see him, I'll tell him, Patrice."

The following Monday, in the wake of Harry Drummond's murder—the victim of what police were calling a random drive-by shooting—Father O'Bryan summoned Danny to his early-morning hangout in Hollywood, where the priest toasted his arrival and emptied the shot glass in a swallow before pushing a copy of *Billboard* across the table.

"Is it true what I just read here?" he said, his voice as steady as any functioning alcoholic. "You being offered Decade Records, the whole operation, and Joe Wunsch to run day-to-day?"

"Harry Drummond's old gig, but with more money and better perks; stock options; triple platinum parachute large enough to buy Bermuda."

"So new congratulations are in order."

Danny shook his head. "Save them, Pat. I'm sticking with

Shoe Records, same as Mason was always there for me. So is Joey."

Father O'Bryan seemed relieved. "And prospects of a rich merger or acquisition down the line? Maybe going public?"

"Whatever happens, Nathan's share will be safe and accounted for. Is that what you really want to know?"

"Never a doubt there, Daniel, either me or Nathan. The last time we spoke, he said so. He said he never felt better off in his life, protected by your brains and Rufus Hardaway's muscle." He inched up an eyebrow at the mention of Rufus and slapped the *Billboard,* which had the story of Drummond's death smeared across the front page.

"Was that Nathan speaking or—?" Danny pointed at the bottle.

Father O'Bryan mocked offense. "Have you ever known me to lie, Daniel?"

"Frequently. Like your unholy crap about having Nathan's power of attorney? In the event of Nathan's death, it turns out. Perhaps you forgot that Nathan was alive when you sat down with Mason and Rufus and worked out your deal?"

"Don't you know your Bible, Daniel? *With life comes death,* so I certainly was honoring the spirit of Nathan's letter. Besides, admit it, I satisfied Nathan."

"Like a bandit, and maybe yourself a little?"

Father O'Bryan dug into his travel satchel and handed over an envelope. His impish grin gave him the kind of face Hals would have hungered to paint three hundred years ago.

The letter was from Nathan, managed in an intense scrawl.

Dear Danny,

I told our reprobate priest to hold off giving this to you until the right time, so this must be it. First, congratulations. Second, thanks for everything, although I don't wish we could do it again, and this time there's no turning back.

By my reckoning, my share in Patrice's album and my music will cover for a long, long time everything already set in motion at my behest by Father O'Bryan. I'd like you to look after things now, the same way you were always so good at looking after me.

Continue sending checks on a regular basis to the Anne Frank Home for the Aging, care of Rabbi Cohen, to take care of a couple I once met named Bertha and Sam Mendelssohn. After they pass on, send the checks to Rabbi Cohen "In Memory of Laurent Connart," with a notation that the donor is Dr. Emil Gautier.

Everything else that makes sense goes to Father O'Bryan to pay off purchase of his church and maybe help get certain members of the congregation on their feet for good. Just figure I'm trying to make car radios safe for America's motorists, except Ana Maria Alfaro's family is always to be taken care of first.

One exception: If you ever need more money than you can muster for yourself or any member of your family, it comes out of my share. Understand? No questions asked.

This is no last will and testament or a power of attorney, Danny, although you can use it that way if you want. This is the power of friendship.

So, goodbye, again, and Sholom aleichem.

Nattie

"*Aleichem sholem,*" Danny said. "*Aleichem sholem,* Nathan. And unto you, peace."

Chapter 29

Nat finished his shift working sound in the concert showroom at Billy Bob's Texas in Fort Worth and within the hour was parking his Volks at the modest cottage in a blue-collar section of Irving, where he'd found Mae Jean almost a year and a half ago, looking as young, vibrant and beautiful as he remembered. In his eyes not a year older; not discolored or wasted away by the horrible cancer eating at her body, eroding her young life.

He dismissed the caregiver with thanks for staying the extra hours—Johnny Cash had gone overtime because of the demand for encores—admired the quilt she was crocheting and reminded her about medication to be picked up at the pharmacy on her way in tomorrow.

Dr. Heidemann was in the front parlor, half asleep, bound to his wheelchair and staring blindly at CNN. "Be with you in a minute, Doc, and get you ready for bed," Nat called to him. "Want to look in first on Wolfie Jr."

His beautiful boy, sleeping soundly, inched a shoulder when Nat kissed him gently on the cheek. "Guess what, Wolfie," he said, caressing the youngster's shoulder. "Guess what tomorrow is. Tomorrow is the day we visit Mommy at the cemetery." The boy shifted again. Nat adjusted his covers. "We'll bring more flowers and tell her the news about the prize you won at school. It will make Mommy very, very happy."

Later, lying awake in bed, Nat closed his eyes and visited his memory of the Indianapolis Speedway, how he stopped half a foot in front of her, heard his breath make a noise somewhere between a sigh and surrender.

She smiles back, revealing two perfect rows of white teeth; a smile to inspire miracles.

Pale green eyes glowing with secrets on an oval face set off by a cascade of light brown hair.

A model's body, long and lean, leggy, sending out hints of sensuality under a silk sheath dress.

She plays with her lips, rubbing them nervously over one another while he studies her face searching for words.

Finally, he says, "Wait for me."

She nods.

"You'll wait?"

She nods again.

"Tell me your name?"

"Mae Jean." Smiling that smile. "What's yours?"

ABOUT THE AUTHOR

Robert S. Levinson is the bestselling author of ten prior mystery-thriller novels. His short stories appear frequently in the *Ellery Queen* and *Alfred Hitchcock* mystery magazines. He is a Derringer Award winner of the Short Mystery Fiction Society, a Shamus award nominee of the Private Eye Writers of America, and regularly included in "year's best" anthologies. Bob served four years on Mystery Writers of America's (MWA) national board of directors. He wrote and produced two MWA annual Edgar Awards shows and two International Thriller Writers Thriller Awards shows. His work has been praised by Nelson DeMille, Clive Cussler, Joseph Wambaugh, Margaret Maron, David Morrell, Jeffery Deaver, William Link, Heather Graham, John Lescroart, Michael Palmer, James Rollins, Joseph Finder, Christopher Reich, and others. He resides in Los Angeles with his wife, Sandra, and Rosie, a loving Besenji Mix, who thinks she rescued them. Visit him at *www.robertslevinson.com.*